...several years in the corporate world she finally followed the advice of family and friends to 'give the writing a go, already'. She's oh-so-happy she did. When not at her keyboard she likes to spend time on the tennis court or golf course. Or immersed in a good read.

Melissa Senate has written many novels for Mills & Boon and other publishers, including her debut, *See Jane Date*, which was made into a TV movie. She also wrote seven books for Mills & Boon under the pen name Meg Maxwell. Her novels have been published in over twenty-five countries. Melissa lives on the coast of Maine with her teenage son; their rescue shepherd mix, Flash; and a lap cat named Cleo. For more information, please visit her website, melissasenate.com

Also by Nina Singh

Reunited with Her Italian Billionaire
Tempted by Her Island Millionaire
Christmas with Her Secret Prince
Captivated by the Millionaire

Also by Melissa Senate

The Baby Switch!
Detective Barelli's Legendary Triplets
Wyoming Christmas Surprise
To Keep Her Baby
A New Leash on Love
A Cowboy in the Kitchen
The Detective's 8 lb, 10 oz Surprise
The Cowboy's Big Family Tree
The Cook's Secret Ingredient
Charm School for Cowboys

Discover more at millsandboon.co.uk

SWEPT AWAY BY THE VENETIAN MILLIONAIRE

NINA SINGH

A PROMISE FOR THE TWINS

MELISSA SENATE

MILLS & BOON

First Published in Great Britain 2019
by Mills & Boon, an imprint of HarperCollinsPublishers,
1 London Bridge Street, London, SE1 9GF

Swept Away by the Venetian Millionaire © 2019 Nilay Nina Singh
A Promise for the Twins © 2019 Melissa Senate

ISBN: 978-0-263-27252-9

0719

MIX
Paper from
responsible sources
FSC C007454

FSC
www.fsc.org

This book is produced from independently certified FSC™ paper to ensure responsible forest management.

For more information visit: www.harpercollins.co.uk/green

Printed and bound in Spain
by CPI, Barcelona

SWEPT AWAY BY THE VENETIAN MILLIONAIRE

NINA SINGH

To my mom and dad,
who made possible my own many adventures.

CHAPTER ONE

IF ONLY SHE hadn't left her packing until the last minute.

Though the chore did give her something to do, didn't it? A task to take her mind off the catastrophic events of the past forty-eight hours. The time period in which she'd gone from being a happily engaged fiancée with a set, determined future to a woman betrayed.

Maya Talbot tossed the sandal she was about to pack across the room in utter disgust. It hit the wall with an unsatisfactory thud and left a dark smudge on matte beige paint. *Ha!* As if packing was her most pressing concern at the moment. No, there was a much more tragic issue she was dealing with right now: the fact that she'd suddenly found herself single, heartbroken and sorely disappointed. All as she was about to embark on the trip of a lifetime. A trip her hardworking grandmother had been generous and kind enough to gift her. A journey that had originally been meant for two. And now she'd be making that journey solo.

It was all too much. Maya plopped down on the bed and sobbed into her hands. *How could you, Matt? How could you do this to me?*

But perhaps the better question was, how long had he

been deceiving her? Exactly how many women had he betrayed her with?

A nagging voice in her head teased that, deep down inside, she had known. She had always suspected that things between herself and her fiancé were not quite right. She had to admit the trepidation she'd felt whenever the two of them began discussing wedding preparations. The utter lack of focus from Matt when she'd asked him to go over all the details. She'd put it all down to pre-wedding nervousness on her part and obtuse male disinterest on his. Clearly, she should have listened to her instincts.

This trip was one she'd often dreamed of being able to take. The fantastical trip she'd always referred to as her "bucket list" getaway.

All she'd ever wanted since taking that art history class as a university freshman was to be able to tour through Europe to witness the grand art in world-famous museums and to marvel at the majestic architecture within the most romantic cities in the world. It was all to begin with a stop in Venice. Followed by a trip by rail to Florence and Rome. Then on to Paris, with a final stop in the glorious metropolis of London.

Maya had talked about it so often with her grandmother. Through some miracle, Grandmama Fran had come across a charity auction being held in Martha's Vineyard where she lived. Bless her soul, the woman had dipped into her modest savings to bid on it for Maya as an early wedding gift. For a wedding that now would never take place.

Maya sucked in a deep breath. She couldn't do this. She couldn't go through with this trip; she had to have been kidding herself to even consider it. And there was not one other person she could think of to ask to accompany her. Working for her uncle's plumbing company as a contractor had left her with a severe shortage of female colleagues. And all her closest friends had gradually moved out of the Boston area over the years. Her cousins were quite busy with their own lives, as well—Lexie blessed recently with a newborn and Zelda immersed in a major project at work.

Unlike Maya, everyone around her seemed to be enjoying full, adventurous lives.

It was settled. Her mind was made up. She couldn't handle seeing all those glorious, romantic spots as a single woman. Not when the original plan had been so different. The only reason Maya hadn't canceled the trip immediately was because she couldn't bear to turn down the gift of a lifetime and have Grandmama's money go to such waste. It would have been bad enough for Matt's half of the trip to be a loss. Granted they would have shared hotel rooms. But all his meals, travel, and museum tickets had been paid for in advance.

But the more she thought about it, the less feasible the whole idea became. She just didn't have it in her. To traipse around Europe by herself, suddenly single and with a broken heart? No, she would stay here and try to pull her life back together. Beginning with somehow delivering the bad news of the broken engagement to Uncle Rex, Aunt Talley and her cousins.

Uncle Rex would be the toughest. He adored Matt and was going to be devastated. Not to mention the whole complication of Matt being the son of her uncle's business partner. The notion that she was letting her whole family down was hard to squelch.

The whole situation was one big mess.

She had to start with breaking the news to Grandmama. Maya owed it to her grandmother to explain exactly why she was essentially throwing away such a loving and generous gift.

Grandmama Fran would understand. She would have to. With shaky fingers, Maya reached for her cell phone on the bedroom night stand. This would be one call she'd never forget.

Her grandmother picked up right away. "Maya, dear. I was hoping to hear from you before you left. How nice of you to take time to call."

That was her grandmother. She was exactly the type of person to thank a grandchild for a simple phone call regarding a trip she herself had paid for. Maya swallowed yet another sob before trying to speak. "Hi there. I hope I didn't wake you."

"Nonsense. I'm much too excited to sleep." Her grandmother chuckled into her ear through the tiny speaker. "I know it's silly, but I'm as excited as if I were going myself. If only I was that mobile."

Maya found herself wishing more than anything that could be so. Having her grandmother accompany her to Europe would be the ultimate solution to this big, painful mess. But Grandmama's various health limitations made any kind of travel impossible.

"I shall just have to live vicariously through my favorite granddaughter," Grandmama added, sending a spear of hurt through Maya's chest.

Dammit. She had no reason to feel guilty. It wasn't as if she'd been the one to cause her breakup. What choice had she had? How could she continue with a man who'd so utterly betrayed her trust?

None of that would make this announcement to her

grandmother any easier, however. "Gran, I have something I need to tell you," she began with a shaky, soft voice.

"Oh, my. You sound quite serious. I hope you aren't about to thank me again, dear. You've already done so more than enough."

Every word Grandmama spoke was just making this endeavor more and more difficult. She should have prepared herself better, Maya thought.

Her grandmother continued without giving Maya a chance to respond. "I was so happy to do it for you, you know. You may think I'm joking, but you really are my favorite."

Maya couldn't help the smile that spread over her lips. Ever since she'd lost her parents, Gran had been one of the people to step into the sudden massive hole in her life where her family used to be. Sure, her uncle, aunt and cousins had all provided her with a substitute family, and she'd be forever grateful to them for that. But the bond she felt with Grandmama went far deeper than any other relationship in Maya's life. Gran had been as broken as Maya was over the tragic loss. The older woman's loving comfort had been the sole factor in pulling Maya out of the overwhelming grief and pain after the accident.

Maya wanted to crumble at the thought that she was about to deliver yet another, albeit much smaller, bolt of pain to the older woman.

"Thanks, Gran. I just…"

Grandmama jumped into the silence. "Are you sure you packed that red dress with the thin shoulder straps? You look so nice in that dress, dear."

This conversation was even more difficult than she'd thought it would be. Gran had actually been thinking of the wardrobe Maya would be taking. She really was living the trip vicariously through Maya.

"Oh, and it would go so well with those strappy sandals you wore the last time you came to visit. This is all so exciting, dear!"

Maya bit her lip as she faced reality: she didn't have it in her to disappoint her grandmother. Not after the woman had already endured so much in her life. She just couldn't bring herself to say the words. Grandmama was so happy on her behalf.

Somehow, some way, she would make herself go on this trip. For her grandmother's sake if not for her own. Besides, who knew? Wasn't one of Matt's complaints about her that she always played life too safe? That she always took the path of least resistance? Not that she had much concern any longer about what Matt thought. But maybe he'd been right about this one thing. Maybe she would take this as an opportunity to try to be different, more adventurous. Going on a solo trip through Europe would certainly be an adventure. Maya decided she would do it.

Though misery was certain to follow her at every stop.

In all his thirty-two years as a resident son of Venice, Vittorio Rameri had never actually seen anyone topple out of a gondola before. He supposed it happened, though it was quite rare. He'd just never witnessed it firsthand.

That appeared to be about to change. For the woman he was watching as he sat at an outdoor table at his favorite waterside café was clearly about to lose her balance completely. Vito had no doubt she was American. Everything, from the tiny clutch purse she carried to the sensible capri pants she wore, tagged her as a young professional from a large US city. Maybe New York. Or Los Angeles.

He thought about going over to help but at this distance there was no way he would make it in time. He was right; it took mere seconds. The gondolier reached for her but the poor man wasn't quick enough. With an inelegant gasp, she toppled over the side and landed with a sharp splash in the water.

Vittorio blinked his eyes against the bright sunshine. She had to be drunk, despite the relatively early hour of the afternoon. He'd seen his fair share of tipsy tourists, and certainly wasn't one to judge. He'd just never seen one actually drunk enough to fall out of a gondola before. She'd attracted a crowd of onlookers as she splashed and spluttered in the water. None of them seemed to be of much help, however. The gondolier wasn't having much luck pulling her out, either.

So much for a nice relaxing afternoon.

He didn't know what compelled him to leave his much-needed espresso and the unread newspaper in order to go over and assist the lady. Perhaps it was the look of utter despair on her face just before she tipped over. Her expression clearly stated that she'd been through quite enough already. And that this fall into the murky Venetian water might ultimately be the last straw.

When Vito reached the gondola, it took extreme effort from both himself and the gondolier to manage to hoist her out of the water and onto the wooden walkway where the gondola was docked. She came out cursing in English. He'd been right about the American guess. Being fluent, Vito understood every one of the curse words she muttered. Or slurred, to be more accurate. Yep, she was definitely drunk. She was also soaked to the skin.

"Are you hurt, miss?" he asked when she stopped swearing long enough to take a breath.

He got a good look at her then and a strange sensation shot through his chest. Her eyes were the color of the Venetian sky at sunset. Thick, dark hair now clung to her face and scalp. Her makeup had clearly not been the waterproof kind.

Yet it struck him that she still looked quite lovely despite her accident of seconds ago.

The gondolier stood next to them, pale and silent. Vito couldn't decide which one of them looked more shocked, the boatman or the American. For an insane moment, he had to bite back the urge to laugh. He barely managed to withhold a chuckle. How rude of him. Her state was no laughing matter, after all. For all he knew, she could be sporting some nasty injury. She still hadn't answered his question.

She shook the water off her face. "Thank you for your help, whoever you are." Turning back to the boatman, she said in a surprisingly steady and deadly serious tone, "I've changed my mind about the gondola ride, sir."

That did it. Vito couldn't hold it in any longer. A small chuckle escaped him before he could stop it. She whirled on him with such force, he thought she might topple over again.

"You think this is funny, do you?"

Her golden hazel eyes blazed bright with fury. Fury directed at him.

"I'm sorry, miss. I certainly did not mean to laugh at you."

She continued to glare at him, despite his apology. The gondolier had apparently heard enough. Without another word, he jumped back onto his vessel and began to pole away. All too hurriedly, Vito thought.

The man had essentially just left him alone with this wet, tipsy American woman.

A woman who looked very good in wet clothes that clung to her skin. Vito gave himself a mental shake. Where had that wayward thought come from?

"You didn't answer my question," he reminded her.

"What question?"

"Are you all right? You didn't hurt yourself or anything, did you?"

She rubbed a hand down her face. Vito watched as the anger suddenly seemed to just melt away from her. Replaced by something akin to total resignation. With a jolt of surprise, he realized that made him sad for some reason. He preferred her angry to defeated. As if it meant anything to him. He'd never laid eyes on the woman before.

"I'm okay," she answered. "Just embarrassed," she added, glancing to the crowd around them which hadn't fully dispersed yet.

He waved a hand in dismissal. "Don't give it a thought. People fall out of gondolas all the time in Venice," he lied.

She studied him up and down. Her eyes really were stunning. A rich amber color that shouldn't have worked at all with her dark olive skin tone. But somehow it served to lend her a rare and striking look that he couldn't help but feel drawn to, given his artist's instincts.

He couldn't seem to tear his gaze from her eyes. He tried to look away to avoid staring at her face too long, but failed.

"Why don't I believe you about that?" she wanted to

know. The slightest hint of a smile graced her full, pink rosebud lips.

"*Bene*. Perhaps because I've just made it up."

Her smile grew. "Nice try. You're quite the gentleman. First you come to my rescue from a certain and tragic watery death. And now you're trying to rescue my pride." She glanced down at the soaking-wet fabric of the red shirt she wore. It now clung to her like a second skin and accentuated her feminine curves.

What in the world had gotten into him? When was the last time he'd noticed a woman's curves? Certainly not in the last two or so years. Not since Marina's accident.

An awkwardly silent beat ensued before she stretched out her hand. "Thank you, Signor…?"

"Rameri. Vittorio Rameri," he supplied as he took her hand into his. Her skin felt surprisingly warm for someone who'd just taken a plunge in dirty water. "I'm often called Vito."

"Hello, Vito. I'm Maya Talbot. From the great Commonwealth of Massachusetts. And I wish we hadn't had this very mortifying meeting. Nothing personal," she added after a pause, wringing out the tail of her shirt.

Oh, but he was so very glad that they had met. Damned if he could put his finger on exactly why that was so. He only knew that today was the first time in a long while that he'd felt drawn to study the features of a woman. He wanted to examine further the way the sunlight brought out the golden specks of her eyes, how the dampness of her hair took it to a dark shade of ebony that framed her delicate chin.

He wanted to think of how it would feel to sculpt what he was seeing before him. An instant desire to squash the urge rose in his chest. In his soul, he knew he wasn't ready just yet. Not to handle clay.

"I suppose I better get going back to my hotel," she said as he continued to stare. If she noticed the way he was looking at her, she was too polite to mention it.

"Are you alone?"

Her shoulders fell. The question seemed to deflate her even more. He found himself intrigued. What exactly was her story?

She shrugged and looked away before answering. "I'm afraid so. It's just me. By myself. In one of the most romantic cities in the world. Go figure."

Now that was surprising. By the looks of her, Vito would guess she wasn't often lacking for male companionship. "I see."

She dabbed a wet, trembling finger against his chest. "It wasn't supposed to be this way," she supplied. Vito guessed it had to be the alcohol that had her talking so freely to the stranger who'd just pulled her out of the canal. "I was supposed to be here with my fiancé," she continued.

"Uh-huh."

"But the…what do you call it? *Bastardo?* Yes, that's it. He was a *bastardo.* I learned that word from the hotel housekeeper who brought a complimentary bottle of valpolicella to my room earlier." She smiled at him.

Well, that explained the early drinking. Maya Talbot was a jilted bride. Or almost bride, as the case might be. But had she had the whole bottle? Still, he felt a twinge of admiration at the fact that she'd decided to come solo on a trip that had obviously been planned to include a romantic partner.

She twirled her fingers at him. "Well. Ta-ta. I should be going."

Vito reached for her arm before she could take a step. *"Un momento."* He couldn't just let her walk away. The woman was in no condition to be by herself in an unfamiliar city.

She blinked at him in surprise. "Yes?"

"Do you actually know where you're going?"

She blinked yet again before looking off into the distance to her left. Scratching her forehead, she turned to look the opposite way. It was blatantly clear she had no idea where she was. Let alone where she was going. "Well, I'm sure I can figure it out."

Vito weighed his options. Leaving her to her own devices was out of the question under the circumstances. For all he knew, she might actually trip and fall into the water again. He could offer to buy her a cappuccino at the café; clearly she could use the caffeine. But she was soaked to the skin. He doubted she'd be comfortable for long sitting in a wooden chair as wet fabric clung to her skin. Not to mention the attention the sight of her would attract from passersby. He could always load her into a *vaporetto* and send her on her way, but the likelihood that she'd get seasick was all too real.

Based on some past benders he'd been on himself, he figured the thing she needed the most was just to be able to lie down until the effects of the alcohol passed.

"Perhaps I can be of help."

Her eyebrows lifted over those dazzling amber eyes. "How?"

"My place is just over the bridge." He pointed in that direction. "We can go get you dried off and cleaned up."

She narrowed her gaze on him, suspicion clouding

her features immediately. Not that he could blame her. She didn't know him from the street vendor selling gelato a few feet away.

"You expect me to accompany you, a man I've never laid eyes on before, to your apartment? Thanks, but no thanks."

He should have explained better. Fluency only got a person so far, it appeared.

Shaking his head, he tried to explain. "*Scusa*. First of all, it's not an apartment. I own an art studio near Le Mercerie. A public studio. Open for business. There's a comfortable sitting area complete with a sofa for browsing patrons. I might even have some dry clothing for you."

She looked him up and down. "I doubt we're the same size."

"I meant ladies' clothing."

Relief and understanding washed over her features. "Your wife's clothing, you mean."

Vito cringed inwardly at the word. Even after all this time, he hadn't quite adjusted to the new reality that he no longer had a wife. And he never would again.

He shook his head. "I don't have a wife. But my models have been known to leave things behind." Not that any kind of model had graced his space in the past several months.

"Your models? What kind of studio are we talking about exactly? Are you a photographer? Or some kind of artist?"

That was one way to put it, Vito supposed. Though, truth be told, he hadn't been any kind of artist in quite a while.

CHAPTER TWO

SHE'D CLEARLY BEEN dining on cotton. Maya tried to swallow past the dry ash that seemed to be coating her mouth and tongue. All she managed was a squeaky croak.

Water. She was in desperate need of water.

Maya forced her lids open and winced at the pain behind her eyes once she did. For heaven's sake. She hadn't even had the whole bottle. Just went to prove what a lightweight she was. After all, wasn't that a point that Matt had continually made? How often had he told her that she needed to let loose a little? To not be so constrained and proper all the time.

Maybe if she had done so every once in a while, her tolerance level would be a little higher.

Well, if he could only see her now. Sprawled out on a couch in what appeared to be the back room of an Italian art studio that she'd followed a stranger to. She could hear soft Italian voices from somewhere in the building. Two male voices and one female. Maya didn't understand a thing that was being said. She heard the sound of a door open, then close.

Maya struggled to sit up. She wore a soft cotton tunic of some sort. She vaguely remembered stepping behind a curtain to take off her clingy wet capri pants and tank top, nearly toppling over in the process.

But she also remembered other things. Gentle, sympathetic chestnut-brown eyes. Wavy hair so dark it had reminded her of the moonless New England sky. A set of strong arms steadying her on her feet after helping to lift her out of the water. Who was he, exactly?

She really had no idea of the identity of the man who'd brought her here.

A gasp escaped her chest. How utterly mortifying. She'd left herself at the total mercy of a complete stranger. A stranger in a foreign city where she didn't know a soul. No one would even know to come looking for her if this handsome artist man turned out to be a cold-blooded psycho killer.

Maya bit back a groan. Definitely one of the dumber things she'd done. But it wasn't as if she'd followed the man back to his private residence. Technically, she was in a public place of business. There'd even been browsers in here when they'd arrived after her drunken mishap with the gondola. Sure. Like that kind of reasoning would pass muster with Uncle Rex if he ever got word of any of this.

Uncle Rex. She hadn't technically lied to him and the rest of her family. She'd just bought herself some time, inadvertently doing the same for Matt. She'd concocted a vague tale about Matt running into some kind of emergency at work that would delay his travel and that he would join her in Europe as soon as he could. Just a small fib in order to postpone the nastiness that was certain to follow once she announced the demise of her engagement to the man her family considered to be the catch of the decade. Little did they know.

Little had *she* known.

Sudden tears stung the back of her eyes, exacerbating the pounding pain in her head. Fire burned behind her throat. All her earthly possessions for a drop of water.

The universe answered her prayers.

"May I come in?" she heard a masculine voice ask from the doorway. "I heard rustling. Figured you must be awake? *Sì?*"

"That might be one word to describe it."

Her rescuer walked in carrying a tray of assorted plates and dishes as well as a steaming carafe. But the only thing Maya could focus on was the glass pitcher of icy water with wedges of lemon floating on top.

"How do you feel?" he asked as he set his load down on the marble table between them.

How could she possibly answer that? So many apt descriptions came to mind. Embarrassed. Ill. Thirsty. Out of her element.

And to dig deeper, she was utterly confused as to what her future held now. A boring dead-end job. Her most significant relationship in complete shambles. Nothing to look forward to. She forced the thoughts away and focused her eyes on the man standing before her.

Maya had to suck in a breath. Now that her gaze had cleared, she realized her memory of their initial encounter had not done the man justice. He was breathtakingly handsome. Tall and dark, with broad shoulders and richly tanned skin. He wore dark pleated dress pants with a pressed collared shirt the color of the Cape sky at dawn. He looked like he'd just stepped out of a print ad for expensive men's cologne.

She pulled on the collar of her smock. Dear heavens,

in contrast to this stellar specimen of a man, she must look like a walking demolition site.

Without waiting for her answer, he lifted the jug of water and began pouring into a clear glass with yet another lemon wedge at the bottom. So the man had mind-reading skills in addition to killer good looks. Either that or she looked as parched as she felt.

She took the water gratefully with a shaky hand as she spoke. "I feel like I might have drunk too much on an empty stomach and then fallen into a river in front of a crowd of strangers."

He gave a playful shrug as she took a massive swallow of water. The ice-cold liquid felt heavenly as it poured over her thick tongue and down her dry throat.

"Hey, these things happen," he said, giving her a playful wink.

Maya wouldn't have thought she had it in her to laugh.

Vito Rameri. See, she couldn't have been too far out of it earlier by the canal if she remembered his name. Though it would be hard to forget the sole person who'd helped her out of a situation like that. An artist and a gentleman. Even the gondolier had taken off at the first opportunity. Vito was the only one who'd stayed to make sure she was okay. Which begged the question: Had she even so much as thanked him yet?

She cleared her throat. "I don't know how to thank you, Signor Rameri."

He cut her off before she could continue. "Please. Call me Vito. Signor Rameri is my father."

"Okay. Vito, then. I'm not sure what would have happened if you hadn't come along." She studied her fingers. "I don't know how to pay back your kindness. I vow to find a way."

He waved a hand in dismissal. "Nonsense. Anyone would have done the same. We Venetians take care of the visitors to our city."

"Well, you shouldn't have had to take care of this tourist. Please believe me when I say that my behavior today was quite uncharacteristic. This isn't how I normally behave. I'm not even much of a drinker."

"Clearly."

Between his accent and the absurdity of this conversation, Maya couldn't tell if he was being sarcastic. If so, he had every right.

"I didn't think I'd had that much. Only I hadn't eaten anything since arriving yesterday and I guess I don't know my tolerance too well." Or lack thereof.

"Alcohol on an empty stomach can certainly catch up with someone who's not used to it."

She nodded. "Exactly. And I should have known better. It's just that I'm dealing with an unexpected…disappointment."

"Ah, right. The *bastardo*."

She'd forgotten about that tidbit in their conversation. "Yes, that would be Matt. My fia—" she caught herself. "My former fiancé. As of about three days ago." Though it seemed like she'd been dealing with the loss and betrayal for far longer.

Maya didn't think she could feel any lower. Between having to explain herself to this handsome Italian and the feeling of complete and utter rejection, her loser status was quite confirmed. And did the Italian have to be quite so good-looking? Why couldn't she have been rescued by a balding, older, grandfatherly type? Would that have been too much to ask? Instead, her savior had

had to come in the form of a dark and charming Adonis clad in Armani.

Yet another way she'd failed at life. Another indication that she didn't fit in with the accomplished, overachieving family she'd been taken in by after losing her parents. Both her cousins had ideal careers and relationships. Her aunt was a revered professor at one of Boston's top universities. Her uncle a respected and successful business owner. And here she was, unable to enjoy a dream trip she couldn't have even afforded on her own without the assistance of her grandmother.

"Why don't you tell me about it? While you eat. You mentioned you haven't eaten since yesterday. It's just criminal to go without nourishment that long in a city with such gourmet cuisine."

Her stomach growled in response to his words. She studied the food-laden tray he'd set down earlier. An elaborate antipasto plate with olives, several varieties of cheese and small glass bowls of various dipping oils. A crusty loaf of Italian bread looked like it had just been pulled out of the oven. Maya's mouth watered despite herself. And bless the man, she could smell the rich aroma of strong Italian espresso wafting from the silver pitcher. In spite of the queasy roiling in her stomach, she really was quite famished.

"You shouldn't have gone to all this trouble."

"No trouble. I just stepped into the trattoria next door. I do it all the time." He motioned to the food. "Go on. Eat. The bread won't stay warm much longer."

Maya ducked her head. As much as she wanted to indulge in the mouthwatering array of goodies before her, she felt like a helpless child who had to be taken care of. It was enough that he'd pulled her out of the water then given her a safe place to sober up. He certainly didn't need to be waiting on her, as well.

Not that the child comparison wasn't an adequate description. What she ought to do was to find her clothes, determine exactly where she was and make her way back to her hotel room overlooking the piazza. Then she should sit there and contemplate all the ways her life had gone so horribly astray.

Still, Vito had been so kind to get a meal set up for her. It would be rude to turn it down. "Only if you'll join me."

"I never turn down an offer to share a meal with a beautiful woman."

Wow. He really was a charmer.

"It will give us a chance to talk," Vito added, pulling up a chair to the marble table between them. "I get the feeling you could use a…how do you say…an ear lender?"

That tickled a smile out of her. "Close enough." She shook her head. "But I couldn't do that. I've already taken up so much of your time and graciousness."

He released a long sigh, one heavy with a meaning she couldn't guess at. Lifting the carafe, he poured steaming espresso into both their cups.

"Trust me. At the moment, I have more than enough time."

Why exactly did he care? Vito really had no business wanting to know more about the sad American beauty currently sitting in his back-room office. But he found himself genuinely curious.

She called to him. Unlike anyone he could remember. Even Marina. A stab of guilt tore through his chest. Would he ever be able to think of her without the guilt eating away at him? Would her memory ever cease to tear him to shreds inside?

Across from him, Maya sat sipping her espresso. The way she seemed to savor each taste made him want to capture the expression on her face. His fingers actually tingled with the desire to find his sketch book yet again. Twice so far this afternoon, when he hadn't created anything in months. He couldn't remember the last time he'd felt that longing. No. Actually, he could. He could trace it back to the day his world had turned tragically upside down. And he had no one but himself to blame for any of it.

He realized she was speaking.

"I wonder if I should have even come."

"You were in no condition to go back to your hotel."

She bit down on her bottom lip. "I mean I shouldn't have come to Venice. I should have stayed home. In Boston."

"One should never regret visiting Venice."

She swallowed the piece of bread she'd bitten into. "Look how much trouble I've been. And it's only day two," she said on a miserable-sounding groan.

"Then we must assume it's only going to get better from here."

She grunted a laugh. The sound held no amusement. "It couldn't get much lower, could it?"

"Come now. Things could have been much worse."

Her eyebrows lifted. "How do you figure that?"

"Well, you could have been hurt during your fall. You haven't broken anything. By tomorrow, all of this will be forgotten. After all, I didn't see anyone with a phone out, filming or snapping photos."

The blood rushed from her face as she clapped a hand

to her mouth. "Oh, my God. Are you sure? That would be all I need. To have all this posted somewhere online for everyone to witness."

"Including the *bastardo*?"

"Yes! Even him!"

Interesting phrasing on her part. Something tightened in his chest at the look of horror on her face. This former fiancé of hers had done quite a number on her. Despite his betrayal, she desperately cared still what he thought of her. The man clearly hadn't deserved the affections of such a lady. "Relax," he reassured her. "I was watching the scene as it unfolded. No one had any type of recording device."

Relief flooded her face. Then, to his surprise, she let out a small chuckle. "I'm guessing it was quite a sight to behold."

Vito bit down on his tongue to keep from laughing himself. She noticed his struggle. "It's all right. Go ahead and laugh. I won't take it personally."

He clasped his chest in mock offense. "I would never laugh at a lady in such a manner."

"I wouldn't blame you if you did. I'm sure I looked quite ridiculous as I lost my footing and splashed into the water."

"On the contrary, it was quite a graceful fall. Perhaps the most elegant instance of a lady tripping I've ever had the opportunity to witness."

"Somehow I doubt it. I'm certain it wasn't my most ladylike moment."

"I think being too ladylike is overrated, myself."

Her lips tightened. "So I've been told."

Indeed, he'd been right. The fiancé had left a mark on her psyche that would last for a long while. Vito felt a sudden intense dislike for a faceless man he wouldn't know if they crossed paths on the nearest bridge.

"I think you should forget everything this man ever told you," he ventured, though he knew he was perilously close to crossing a line. After all, he'd barely met the woman. For all he knew, her ex-fiancé was the love of her life. A loss she might never get over. Something he couldn't quite put his finger on told him that wasn't the case. Still, the tightness in his chest intensified. How silly of him.

"I'll have to give that a try." Her words were utterly unconvincing. She'd be licking her wounds for some time.

He wished he could find the right words to say, words that might reassure her, persuade her that this Matt wasn't worth the love she'd wasted on him. Even given what little he knew of the situation, he had no doubt the man had been given a gift and had been too selfish to cherish it.

As if that wasn't the most hypocritical thought, coming from someone like him, of all people.

"I wish there was a way I could be of help, *cara*," he said, dropping the endearment without thinking. Her surprised intake of breath told him she was familiar with the word.

"You've done more than enough."

"Yet here you are. Miserable and alone on a trip that was clearly meant to be a romantic getaway."

She slumped where she sat. "It was supposed to be so much more than that."

"Oh?"

"My grandmother won this trip for me at a charity auction. To raise money for a substance abuse shelter on Martha's Vineyard. She spent a good chunk of her retirement savings on my behalf."

And she felt guilty about that. His artist's eye could almost see it manifested. The guilt practically sat like a heavy, tangible weight on her shoulders. "Sounds like a deserving and noble cause."

"It was. She wanted the trip to be an early wedding present. A pre-honeymoon. Because she knew how much I've always wanted to see the historic art of the European continent. Matt would have never agreed to come if we'd had to pay for it ourselves. He's more a tropical island type of traveler."

"I see."

"It was such a generous gesture on her part. She'd tell me about all the marvelous trips she and my grandfather used to take. She wanted me to be able to experience something like it firsthand."

"Well, all I have to say is—better solo than never. Does that make sense as an American idiom?"

The pensive look on her face gave him the answer to that question. "I know what you mean," she assured him. "Nevertheless. I never should have attempted it alone. I've come to the conclusion that I'm going to cut this trip short. And stay in my room in the meantime. It was foolish of me to think I could enjoy this after everything that happened back in Boston. I've been kidding myself."

Vito couldn't help his next move. Reaching across the table, he took her trembling hand into his own. "I would be completely remiss as a Venetian if I allowed that to happen, *cara*. You mustn't leave. Not just yet."

"How can I let you leave this majestic city so soon? And without the opportunity to fully explore it?" Vito Rameri wanted to know.

A jolt of awareness flashed between them as he took

her hand in his. For a moment Maya couldn't get her mouth to work. Electricity seemed to sparkle along her skin, originating at the exact spot where he touched her.

Once she managed to get her brain to focus, Maya wanted to answer him with a few questions of her own, albeit rhetorical ones. Questions like: How could she go on acting the happy tourist when her whole reality had just crumpled? How could she pretend all the activities she'd been so looking forward to as part of a couple would be anything less than awkward for her now?

Slowly she pulled her hand out of his gentle grip. She was clearly overcompensating for Matt's rejection. Looking for validation from a stranger. Sure, that stranger happened to be achingly handsome. Straight out of a romance novel. But she'd be remiss to start reading things into small gestures.

It was no wonder she was overreacting to the man before her. He was simply being kind. Worse, he'd probably taken pity on her. How pathetic that she thought there was some kind of mysterious current between them.

"I don't know," she began. "Day two didn't go so well."

"It's not over yet, however."

She supposed he had a point. And she could have done worse than meeting this charming, charismatic man. Though she would have preferred a much different set of circumstances leading to said meeting.

She watched as he poured more coffee into both their cups. What if they'd met under different circumstances? What if somehow she'd made this journey years ago as a single woman? Or perhaps with a bunch of girlfriends? She imagined wandering into his studio purely by coincidence, simply to admire a local artist's work. What might such a different introduction have led to? Would they have hit it off? She wasn't the type of woman to typically attract a man like the one she sat eating with right now. But maybe, just maybe, he would have seen something in her.

Who was she kidding? Vito Rameri probably wouldn't have given her a second glance under normal circumstances. It took literally falling into a canal for someone like her to be noticed by the likes of him.

She wasn't the striking, alluring type. In fact, it had taken her by surprise two years ago when the outgoing, successful, not to mention strikingly handsome son of her uncle's business partner had first asked her out. She'd almost been too stunned to accept his invitation to a leisurely pasta lunch in Boston's North End. To her further shock, Matt seemed to have genuinely enjoyed her company that afternoon. So much so that he'd asked her out again before their lunch was even over.

Maya had hoped she might have finally found the man who would help her create the kind of future she so desperately craved. A future with a family of her own. Not one she'd been thrust into after tragedy had left her orphaned and alone. One she actually felt she belonged in and fit into.

But she had to admit that, deep down, she'd sensed something wasn't right about the whole thing. Even on that first lunch date, the vibe between her and Matt had seemed forced. Rather than giving her the future she so desperately wanted, she'd known somehow Matt was going to let her down. Or vice versa.

Maya had ignored the warning bells that seemed to go off every step of the way. Those bells had morphed into all-out ringing alarms when Matt proposed. In many

ways, he was too much for her. Too outgoing, too talk-
ative, too *everything*. They'd both known and done their
best to pretend not to. She'd also ignored her suspicions
that she'd been nothing more to Matt than a convenient
way to present himself as a settled and serious career
professional rather than the philandering party man he
really was. Again, she'd foolishly brushed it all aside.

She looked up to find Vito studying her. "You appear
to have drifted off thousands of miles. Back to Boston,
perhaps?"

Maya gave a shake of her head. "I'm sorry. Just thinking about some things, is all."

"I saw." He leaned back, inhaled. "Did anyone tell you
that you have the most transparent face?"

"I don't understand."

"It's almost as if your features completely alter as your
thoughts do. It's difficult to explain."

As far as lines went, that was a new one. If Vito was
trying to come on to her, this was the most unusual way
she'd ever heard.

"No. I can honestly say that no one has ever told me
that before."

"It's true. Someone who creates art for a living can
see it clearly."

Yeah, that was definitely not any kind of flirtation on
his part. "Well, I think you may be the first real artist
I've met. No one's actually commented on my face that
I can recall."

She saw his hand move ever so slightly before he
curled his fingers into his palm. For an insane moment,
she thought he might have been about to touch her. She
imagined him trailing a finger along her jawline, cupping her cheek in his palm. A shiver ran down her spine.

The effect of his gaze was hypnotic. He wasn't so much looking at her as discovering, exploring her features. The air around them suddenly grew thick. In that moment, Maya had the strangest notion that she somehow knew this man. Had known him forever. She'd seen him in her dreams, heard his voice in her imaginings.

Or maybe she'd actually hit her head on the side of the gondola while toppling over the side.

"I have a confession to make," he stated. His tone as he spoke the words took her breath away. "I'm afraid you may not like it."

CHAPTER THREE

MAYA COULDN'T QUITE decide if she liked it or not. It was hard to believe what she was looking at. Was that really her depicted on the easel Vito had led her to?

He'd sketched her as she slept. At least, she thought it was her. For the woman portrayed on the canvas in charcoal appeared to be another version of herself.

"You're not saying anything, *cara*." Vito spoke softly behind her as she stood staring at the easel.

"I'm not really sure what to say."

"I will destroy it if you wish. We can pretend it never existed." The stiff quality of his tone told her clearly it would pain him to do so.

But was that what she wanted? Part of her felt flattered, proud that she'd provided any kind of inspiration to an artist of his caliber. Because he was clearly talented, given what she was looking at.

Another part, however, felt more than a little uneasy, as if her privacy had been breached when she hadn't even been aware.

She cleared her throat. "No. Don't do that. I just—I just need a moment to decide how I feel."

"That sounds fair."

"I've never been drawn by anyone before. I can't even really tell if it's indeed me."

"It is most definitely a sketch of you. Why do you not see it, I wonder?"

She scrounged for the words to explain. Maybe the alcohol was still addling her mind, but it was tough to summon them. "I don't know exactly. It's just that this woman on the paper…she seems much more…at peace with herself and her life. Confident in the decisions she's made." How he'd portrayed all that in one quick sketch was truly magical. She found herself in awe of his talent.

"This is my profession. As an artist, I capture what I see."

Maya trailed a finger along the edge of the paper. "And this is truly how you saw me as I slept?"

"It is how I see you," Vito answered with no hesitation.

Though it was flattering, she knew she couldn't read too much into his depiction of her. The man had laid eyes on her mere hours before. He had no idea who she really was. He didn't know any of the decisions she'd made that had led her to where she was right now—alone and licking her wounds. If Vito knew all that, he'd have drawn her much differently. Of that she had no doubt.

"If I may ask, what compelled you?"

"To put your likeness down on paper, you mean?"

Maya nodded. Surely he had better things to do, could have easily found a better subject. She had no doubt she was merely an inconvenience; the poor man had felt compelled to assist her as no one else seemed willing to. So she had no idea what his motivations may have been. She was far from muse-like.

So she was surprised with his answer. "You're one

of those rare people whose inner strength can be seen clearly on the outside. It's a very uncommon quality."

Maya had to laugh at that. She couldn't have heard him right. In fact, none of this seemed real. Maybe she was still asleep on his sofa, having an alcohol- or concussion-fueled dream. Or perhaps she should go even farther back than that. Maybe she really had managed to injure herself during the fall from the gondola. And she was actually lying in an Italian hospital somewhere in the midst of a deep coma.

Dream or coma, Vito didn't return her laugh. "I see you find that amusing."

"Only because it's quite ridiculous. You obviously see something that isn't there."

"Or something you refuse to see yourself. Because you've let someone else convince you what's real."

Ouch. Served her right for confiding in a stranger. This random man she hadn't even known existed a day ago knew all too well about her humiliation. Maya felt her cheeks flame with embarrassment. Why had she ever left her hotel room? In fact, why had she ever left Boston?

The question made her cringe inside. She had to admit there was a very simple reason. She'd told herself that she hadn't wanted to let her Grandmama down, but the truth was that she hadn't been able to face her family after what Matt had done. She couldn't handle the thought of standing in front of the four most perfect people she knew to let them know that she'd failed. Even though none of it was her fault. Matt had been the one to throw away their relationship. She didn't want to admit that she hadn't been enough for him.

So she'd fled. And it had been a mistake to do so.

Because now some stranger was trying to psychoanalyze her. Irritation skittered along her skin. He may have helped her out of a sticky situation, but he had no right to try and read her or judge her in any way. She was beginning to wonder if she was some type of magnet for overbearing men all over the world.

"Don't pretend to know me," she bit out. "You really have no idea who I am."

"Maybe I know more than you think."

"Or maybe you're simply a heavy-handed alpha male who's much too quick to make blanket judgments about people he's just met," she snapped without thinking.

Vito chuckled. That made her irritation turn to anger. Now he was laughing at her.

"And why is that amusing to you?" she demanded to know.

"Because you're so clearly proving my point."

That was it, she'd had enough. She had no idea if there was some kind of language barrier that was fueling this agitating conversation. But she wasn't willing to participate in it any longer.

"Destroy the sketch or don't. I don't care. But I think I should be going. If you would get me my clothing, please."

Vito studied her face before silently and slowly nodding. "Of course. If you're sure you feel well enough."

"I feel fine. And I'll find a way to repay your hospitality. I'm in Venice for a few more days." Only now that she'd said the words, she realized exactly what a difficult feat that would be. Now that the fog was slowly lifting in her brain, she distinctly remembered her phone and clutch purse falling into the water right before she'd gone over herself.

Which led to another embarrassing predicament. She

had no idea how to get back to her hotel on foot. And she had no cash fare for any kind of boat ride.

She was at Vito Rameri's mercy yet again.

The atmosphere around them had definitely grown awkward. Vito knew he had only himself to blame. Obviously he'd learned nothing from all his mistakes of the past.

Maya was right. He was heavy-handed. And hopelessly incapable of sensitivity to others' feelings. He should never have shown Maya the sketch. Better yet, he should never have drawn it in the first place.

But when he'd come down to check on her, she'd seemed so serene and peaceful on his office couch. The way her arm was draped casually over a plush cushion. The afternoon sun sending shadows along her skin. She really had looked like something out of a classic Renaissance painting. The woman had just been pulled out of the murky summer Venetian water and she'd looked none the worse for wear.

Though he was a sculptor by trade, most of his creations originated with a sketch on paper. Vito had taken one look at the tangled mass of hair framing her angular, patrician face and he'd felt once again that familiar yet so elusive tingling in his fingers. A feeling he hadn't experienced in more than three years. Not since the accident.

He hadn't been able to bring himself to ignore it. A decision he regretted now, given the way the *signorina* was glaring at him. He had no right to use her to grasp at a sudden and unexpected reprieve from the artistic block he'd been grappling with for the past three years. She was merely an unsuspecting passerby.

"I apologize, Maya. I should have known better than to draw you without your knowledge." In fact, he'd never done such a thing before. Never had he sculpted or sketched a human subject who wasn't aware he was doing so.

What had gotten into him?

He could venture a guess. Something about this woman was bringing forth an awareness he didn't want to acknowledge or examine. It made no sense.

Was it her sorrow he was drawn to? That had to be why. He felt bad for her. She was clearly hurting and lonely when she should have been enjoying one of the most beautiful destinations in the world.

She didn't look ready to accept his apology. In fact, she looked like she might be even angrier at him.

"You think I'm upset that you drew me?"

He could only shrug. If not that, then why?

"Never mind," she bit out. "I guess it's not important. Please tell me where my clothes are. And then I'll be on my way."

"Of course. I'll bring everything out. It should all be dry by now." It was downright silly of him, how disappointed he felt about her leaving. Or about how likely it was that he would never see her again.

"Thank you." She seemed to hesitate, looking up at the ceiling. "Also, can you tell me how to get to my hotel?" she asked after a long sigh.

"The easiest way would be by boat. You can catch one by the bridge across the walk."

"I'll have to walk. I lost my bag in the fall. Along with all my money, credit cards and cell phone." Her lips trembled as she spoke the words. She was clearly nearing her breaking point. There was no way he was going to leave her to her own devices under the circumstances. Particularly as he'd been the one to cause her latest upset.

"I can't let you walk back by yourself. It's already getting dark. You don't even know your way."

"I can manage. You've done more than enough."

She was certainly a stubborn one. But what did she expect him to do? Let her walk out into the night without a cent on her and no idea where she was headed?

How would he ever live with himself if his actions were even slightly responsible for the injury of yet another female? It was hard enough to live with himself as it was.

"Let me at least arrange a boat ride for you. A water taxi can get you right to your destination without any stops along the way." He held a hand up before she could argue. "I insist. I'll call while you get dressed."

Vito watched the internal battle as it played out in her eyes. Her pride versus common sense. He breathed a sigh of relief when she finally answered. It appeared common sense had won out.

"Fine. If you insist. And I'm only doing this for your peace of mind."

Vito bit down on the amusement that bubbled up within his chest. To make it sound as if his arranging her transportation was a favor she was doing for him instead of the other way around. She really had no idea how magnificent she was. If she only knew.

And if only things were different between them, he mused. If only this charming, enigmatic woman who seemed to have reawakened his senses wasn't about to walk out of his life for good.

As quickly as she'd fallen into it.

She couldn't stop thinking about him.

Maya rolled over onto her stomach and adjusted the pillow under her head for at least the hundredth time since she'd crawled into her hotel room bed. She'd been certain she'd fall asleep within seconds after the harrowing day she'd had. And she definitely needed the rest. There'd be a long day ahead of her as she made the calls to replace her bank cards. She had no idea what to do about her cell phone.

But none of that had any bearing on why slumber was so stubbornly eluding her. It was because of him. Every time she closed her eyes, she saw a dark, enigmatic face with charcoal-black hair framing expressive, sad eyes.

She couldn't begin to explain it. Here she was, jilted by her fiancé, newly single after losing the man she'd hoped to spend the rest of her life with. But she'd barely given Matt a thought since she left Vito's studio. What exactly did that say about her? Or about the marriage she'd been about to enter into?

Vito said he saw strength in her. He'd challenged her when she questioned it. In response, she'd snapped at him and stormed out with barely a thank-you for all his efforts to help her. Now that she thought about it all, it hadn't been her proudest moment.

Maya sighed in resignation and slowly sat up in bed. It was no use. She wasn't going to get any sleep no matter how hard she tried.

In any case, she needed to update the folks back home about the loss of her phone and credit cards. Hopefully, the correspondence wouldn't lead to further questions about Matt. With no small amount of resignation, Maya propped open her laptop and logged into the hotel Wi-Fi network. After summarizing the essentials in a group email to her family and letting them know they'd only be able to contact her via email for a few days, she fired off a quick message to her bank explaining the loss of her credit cards. Then she called up the browser to do a quick check on various US news sites.

An email alert popped up immediately on her screen before she'd had so much as a chance to click on the appropriate icon. Her aunt. Maya should have known. The woman was constantly connected, mostly because she was constantly working. No real surprise there.

You lost your most essential belongings on the second day?

She'd included a laughing emoji but Maya had no doubt the response held a heavy dose of derision. Her aunt and cousins would never have been careless enough to let such a thing happen to them. Maya was the only one who had her head in the clouds. She no doubt owed it to her mother's genes. The woman had been a true free spirit, constantly in pursuit of one artistic endeavor or another. Her father had indulged his wife's less-than-stable career choices. Her aunt, uncle and cousins were much more practical. Bad enough they'd been burdened with the awkward and shy newly orphaned preteen. They'd been good to her; they really had. Still, she'd never felt the sense that she'd actually really fit in.

Maya typed out a quick response.

It's an amusing story. Will tell you all about it sometime.

She hadn't had a chance to hit Send before her aunt sent another message.

I'm sure Matt can bring a replacement phone and funds once he arrives. Honestly, Maya. How would you manage without him? When are you expecting him, anyway? We can't seem to get a hold of him.

Hah! She'd just bet Matt wasn't making himself available to her family these days. And Maya would have to discover quickly just how she'd manage without Matt by her side. To think, all these years she'd tried so hard to avoid letting her aunt and uncle down. Not to mention her two cousins. And now she was going to have to disappoint them about a broken engagement.

Maya wanted to slam the laptop shut and launch it across the room. As much as she hated to lie to her aunt yet again, her shattered relationship wasn't the type of news one delivered via email from half a world away. The only thing to do was to ignore her aunt's question for the time being. Though Maya knew the older woman wouldn't let her get away with it for long.

Clicking back to the news sites, Maya worked to distract herself from all the jumbled thoughts scrambling through her brain. No wonder she was suffering from insomnia.

But that endeavor proved futile, as well. After a quick check on the Sox, her mind wandered back to the afternoon. More specifically, her thoughts returned to the man she'd spent it with. An image of the picture he'd sketched flashed through her mind. The idea that she might never see it again sent a surprising surge of sadness through her. She should have asked to keep it. As a way to remember all of this. A way to remember him.

But the whole notion was silly. It had been a simple impromptu lunch with a man she'd probably never lay eyes on again. Even if she did manage to somehow run into him before leaving Venice, they were from two different continents. Given the way she couldn't stop thinking about him tonight, she wouldn't need anything physical to provide memories of Vito Rameri.

Who was he, exactly? Any kind of artist prominent enough to have a studio in Venice had to be fairly successful. The flashing cursor on the search engine's query bar was practically winking at her, daring her to do something to find out. Without giving herself a chance to think, she pulled the laptop close once more and typed in his name with the word "art."

Now who was the one disrespecting someone else's privacy?

But what she was about to do wasn't really intrusive at all, she reassured herself. Technically, Vito was a public figure. He probably even had a large commercial presence online. She just wanted to see some of his professional works. To find out how prominent he was as an artist.

The answer to that was abundantly clear within seconds as her search returned pages and pages of results. To call Vito successful was a woeful understatement. Turned out that his creations were some of the most sought-after artworks in the world. His clay sculptures were in particularly high demand throughout the European continent.

Maya physically thwacked her forehead hard enough that the skin actually stung along her hairline. She'd petulantly thrown a tantrum because a world-class sculptor had taken the time to render her likeness on paper. He must have thought her beyond childish. He probably also saw her as a completely ignorant fool. How many women would have been honored to be where she'd been?

Maya cursed under her breath and scrolled through several more pages. One article detailed the last renowned sculpture Vito had completed. The piece had sold for six figures at auction.

But something didn't add up. That article was dated years ago. About three and a half years, to be more specific. Nothing was mentioned after that. As far as she could find from this search, Vito's artwork hadn't been covered for the last three years or so.

The bottom of the screen prompted another link: *Rameri accident*. Something made her hesitate a split second before she moved her fingers to click on it. When she finally did, she had to suck in a deep breath. The headlines that appeared were vastly different from the write-ups about his art. The more Maya read, the more her heart slowly bruised for the man she'd spent the afternoon with. The sadness behind his eyes was justified, it turned out. Far from being the carefree, internationally renowned artist she would have pegged him for, Vito Rameri had a sorrowful past.

The pages she read now only told of heartbreak and tragedy.

CHAPTER FOUR

THIS WASN'T GOING to be the easiest conversation. Maya slowly walked toward Vito's studio, trying to summon the courage to say what she had to say. Best to just get it over with.

Yesterday the afternoon had been sunny and bright. Thank goodness for that, as she'd spent a considerable part of the day soaking wet. By contrast, that day's weather was overcast and gray. She hoped it wasn't any kind of indicator of the reception she was about to get.

But she had to talk to Vito. She didn't want his last impression of her to be one of a stubborn hothead storming out his door after he'd been nothing but kind and helpful to her.

When she reached the studio, she took a deep, fortifying breath before stepping inside. The man who stood up from behind the counter to greet her wasn't Vito.

"Buongiorno, signorina." He was tall and tan, with a wide smile and bright brown eyes. Upon closer inspection, Maya noted clear similarities between the two men. She wondered if they were related.

"I'm Leo Rameri," he said with a friendly grin, confirming her suspicions. Same last name. My, the good looks clearly ran in the family. "How may I help you?"

"I was hoping to find—" But he didn't let her finish.

"A readily available piece? I'm sorry. Vito has no inventory at the moment. I'd be happy to speak with you about a potential commission." His lips suddenly grew tight before he continued. "Though, I have to be up front and tell you that he may or may not accept the project."

He thought she was here as a potential patron. She didn't get a chance to clarify the reason behind her visit before the door opened behind her. Maya didn't need to turn around to know who'd just arrived. It was him. She could sense Vito's presence.

"Maya? Is that you?"

Maya took a deep breath before turning to face him. If possible, he somehow looked even more handsome today. He was dressed much more casually in a soft white cotton shirt and khaki pants, and his hair wasn't quite as casual. He'd combed it back off his face, lending him a rakish quality.

"You two know each other?" Leo asked from behind her.

They both answered at the same time, talking over each other. Leo came to stand between them, giving them curious looks.

"We met yesterday," Vito supplied.

"Vito was kind enough to help me out of a rather precarious situation. It's why I'm here. I realized that I should come back and thank him properly."

"That isn't necessary," Vito said in a firm, steady voice, his eyes fixed on hers.

Leo spoke before she could respond. "Wait a minute. You look quite familiar. Have you and I met before, as well?"

Maya was finding it hard to focus on whatever Leo

was saying. She couldn't tear her eyes or her focus from Vito. He seemed surprised to see her. The only question was, was it a pleasant surprise or an unwelcome one?

"I don't see how you would have," Vito answered for her.

Leo rubbed his chin as he contemplated her. "Are you certain? Your face is quite familiar."

Maya made herself form an answer. "Unless you've been to Boston and we somehow coincidentally ran into each other, I can't imagine that we might have met at some point, Signor Rameri."

"Call me Leo. I'm Vito's cousin." He'd barely gotten the last word out when he suddenly clapped his hands in front of his chest. "It's you! That's how I know you. You're the young lady in Vito's sketch."

She could have sworn she heard Vito groan. "I think Maya might prefer if I destroyed the sketch, Leo. Or if it had never existed."

Leo whipped his head around to glare at his cousin. "What? How can you even think such a thing?"

Vito shrugged as he walked in and set down the parcels he was carrying. He motioned with his chin in Maya's direction. "The lady is unhappy with it."

She cleared her throat. "Now, that isn't exactly what I said. And that's part of the reason I'm here."

Both men gave her curious glances, then waited expectantly for her to clarify.

Maya should have better prepared herself for what she was going to say. Having Leo here didn't exactly help matters. It would have been difficult enough to try and talk to Vito without an audience. But she couldn't be rude enough to ask the man to leave his own cousin's showroom, now could she?

She cleared her throat. "I just wanted to come back and tell you that I feel badly for the way I left here yesterday. I should have been more gracious, especially considering your kindness and hospitality."

Looking at Vito's face became disconcerting as she spoke the words. So she glanced to where Leo stood staring at her. His mouth had formed a small O of surprise. Clearly, Vito hadn't told the other man about all that had transpired during her afternoon with him.

"And I shouldn't have taken the liberties I did," Vito responded. "We shall call dual *mea culpa*, then, Signorina Maya. And leave it at that."

Leo's mouth fell further agape. Based on his expression, he was clearly drawing some rather scandalous conclusions about what had happened between them.

"That sounds fair enough," she replied, trying to insert a lightheartedness into her tone. As if this conversation wasn't awkward in the least. "And please don't destroy the sketch." She wasn't brave enough to ask for it. It was a professional work, after all. Lord knew, she wouldn't be able to pay what an artist of his caliber was worth. "In fact, I wish I could take a picture of it to show the folks back home. But as you know, my phone fell into the bottom of the canal right before I did."

Leo suddenly held a hand up to stop her. "Wait. Wait a minute, *per favore*. Did I hear correctly that you fell into the water?"

She nodded. "That's right. Vito pulled me out."

"He did?"

"Mmm-hmm. Then he brought me back here to help me get cleaned up."

"I see." To Maya's confusion, Leo held a hand out to her. She hesitantly took it for lack of anything else to do. "You'll be joining us for lunch, Signorina Maya. My cousin has just brought back some mouthwatering pancetta and homemade pasta. I'm sure there'll be plenty for all three of us."

"Oh...uh... I'm not sure if—"

Vito interjected. "I'm sure the lady is too busy to drop her whole itinerary simply to dally around with us."

Leo wasn't having it. "I insist," Leo declared as he led her toward the back room where she'd collapsed on the sofa to sober up less than twenty-four hours ago. "I'm anxious to hear all about this fall of yours and exactly how my gallant cousin came to your rescue. Surprisingly, he's failed to mention any of it to me."

Maya found herself at a loss for words. She really hadn't seen this coming. But she had to think of something, some way to get out of this lunch invitation. Because if Leo wasn't aware of the murderous glare Vito was casting at him, she certainly hadn't missed it.

Vito Rameri clearly did not want her here.

If they'd been alone, Vito would not have hesitated to give his cousin a good, hard smack. In fact, he was planning all the ways he would deliver it as soon as he got the opportunity. The man was too nosy for his own good. He could give Nonna a run for her money when it came to busybody meddling.

It was bad enough that Maya had shown up here in the first place. She had no idea how hard Vito had been working to forget she even existed. How desperately he'd tried to put those few short hours they'd spent together in his rearview mirror so that he could continue moving forward with the steady existence he'd worked so hard to create for himself since losing Marina. He'd been foolish to mistake a fleeting bout of artistic inspiration for anything more. Her sorrow had called to him that day as he'd sat watching her from the café. There was nothing more to it than that.

But now he'd have to somehow endure a meal where she sat across from him, where he'd be required to look at her expressive face and notice again her flawless bone structure and features. After he'd tried so hard all these hours to forget.

"So, tell me about this fall you suffered, *bella*," Leo said as they sat. Vito focused on pulling out the food and serving plates. The steaming aroma of fresh pasta and fine Italian Parmigiano-Reggiano wafted through the air as he did so. Normally the enticing scents would be enough to make his mouth water. But today all he could focus on was the delicate flowery scent of lilac and rose from whatever perfume she was wearing. A heady mixture that seemed to be fogging his brain.

Maya ducked her head before answering. "If you don't mind, I'd rather not discuss it. It wasn't one of my finest moments."

Vito wanted to tell her she had nothing to be embarrassed about. But he could only guess what type of conversation that might lead to. He decided it was better to not say anything at all. Just get through this unexpected meal as best he could.

"Understandable," Leo assured her. "I'm just glad you're all right. And that my cousin here was able to help."

He had to change the subject. "The sketch is yours if you want it," Vito said, handing her a plate of hot pasta.

She seemed taken aback; her hand shook as she took

the food. "But I couldn't do that. After all, it's an original Rameri."

So she'd done some checking up on him. Her knowledge of his exact identity was new, he had no doubt. She'd had no clue who he was yesterday.

"That may be, but it belongs to you more than me. It's only right that you should have it."

"But why would you do such a thing?"

He shrugged. "You weren't a paid model, more of an inspiration."

She gasped. Now why had he gone and said that? It opened up a whole new slew of avenues she probably wanted to examine. And he had absolutely no desire to do any such thing.

Vito felt off, out of his element around this woman. It didn't help matters that his cousin sat watching the two of them interact as if he were a scientist observing a lab experiment. Yeah, Leo definitely had a nice hard whack coming his way as soon as Maya left.

"That's more than generous. I would never have been able to afford any kind of original art under normal circumstances."

"It's only a sketch," Vito repeated.

"Nevertheless. It is indeed quite a generous gesture," Leo said, giving him a questioning glance and causing Vito's anger with him to spike even higher.

He ignored his cousin. "Don't mention it. I'll have my assistant prep and package it to be shipped to your Boston address. Be sure to give it to me before you leave."

She nodded slowly. "Thank you, Vito. Again."

Several moments of silence passed. Leo was the only one even pretending to eat. Vito couldn't seem to summon the appetite that had had his stomach loudly grumbling only an hour earlier. Maya was simply pushing her pasta around on her plate.

Leo was the one who finally spoke. "So, tell me, Maya. What are your plans for today? Will you be visiting some of our many historic sights?"

"Well, first I'll have to pick up an Italian burner phone. But yes. I'm scheduled for a sightseeing tour of St. Mark's Cathedral and the Doge's Palace. An exclusive guided tour for two. Only now the guide will have to settle for one." She wrangled a clearly forced smile that was just a bit too wide.

"Maya finds herself in the unexpected position of traveling alone." Vito answered the questioning look his cousin threw his way.

"Well, that won't do at all. We'll have to find you a tour companion."

Maya chuckled. "Oh, I don't mind," she said. Vito had to wonder if her statement was something of a fib. She sat ramrod straight, throwing out the words as if daring someone to argue with her. "Though I came very close to asking the housekeeping worker who came in this morning. But she mentioned it was her sister's birthday and she had plans. But I really don't have any kind of issue going by myself." She swallowed some water. "None at all." Again, the words were uttered with just a bit too much vehemence.

Vito had no doubt she was putting on a brave front. Yet again, a stab of anger at the faceless man who'd so callously abandoned her seared through him.

"Perhaps Vito might be able to—"

Vito suddenly stood before the other man could finish his sentence. He knew exactly where Leo was headed and had no intention of letting him go there.

"I should go back up front. It won't do to have a patron stop by and find the counter empty."

The look Leo gave him relayed his thoughts just as well as spoken words could have. As if any real buyers had bothered to stop by the studio in over two years. There had been nothing available to sell.

He gave Maya a slight bow. "Please, stay and enjoy your meal, Maya. My cousin will show you out once you finish."

Leo's voice followed behind him. "Must you leave so soon?"

Vito didn't bother to respond out loud to the query. But the answer to his cousin's question was a resounding yes. Vito did have to leave. Because otherwise he might be tempted to do something he had no business even considering: he might foolishly offer to accompany Maya Talbot on her tour of Venice.

CHAPTER FIVE

Turned out Vito would be the one getting smacked. As he watched Maya step out the door less than twenty minutes later, he felt his cousin's open palm swat him across the back of his shoulder.

Vito had to clench every muscle in his body to resist the urge to hit him back. For, if he did, he would deliver a much harder blow than the playful one he'd received. And then things might very well escalate.

When was the last time he and Leo had actually indulged in a physical row? They'd had to have been teenagers. Nonna would throttle both of them if she ever got word they were fighting as adults.

Still, he had to wonder if the risk would be worth it.

He slowly turned to face the other man. "And what was that for, cousin?" he asked, with all the calm and steadiness he could muster.

"For being downright rude just now. To an American tourist, no less. One who was here as a guest at your studio."

"Through your invitation, let's not forget."

"That simply proves my point."

Vito sighed in dismissal and turned back to the newspaper article he'd been trying to read for the past several minutes. "You have no point. You're just a meddlesome pest who doesn't know how to mind his own business."

Leo wasn't taking the bait. "You're family. That makes you my business."

"Not when it comes to volunteering me to play baby-sitter to some lonely tourist."

"She's only here in Venice for a few days. What would be the harm in accompanying her?"

"If you're that worried about her lack of company on this trip, you should have gone with her yourself."

His cousin gave a sardonic laugh. "And try to explain to Lynetta why I'm spending the day with an unattached American tourist? *Dio mio.*" He physically shuddered at that possibility.

Leo came to stand right in front of Vito, casting his shadow on the article he was pretending to read. "Do you seriously think we're not going to talk about this?"

"About what?"

"About the fact that you haven't so much as picked up a pencil in several months let alone handled any clay. Up until a day ago, that is. When you sketched that young woman."

"So?"

Leo blinked. "So your sudden inspiration appears to have everything to do with the lady you just let walk out of here."

"She fell asleep in the back room. I simply felt a desire to capture her features. It isn't the grand breakthrough you're making it appear to be."

"Isn't it?"

"Not to me."

"That's mind-boggling. You come here every day simply to remind yourself of the life you used to lead, the

passion you used to have. Someone may have finally re-
vived that passion in some small way and you don't find
it significant at all."

Vito slammed his hand down on the counter. "It's a
simple sketch, Leo. Stop trying to turn it into some type
of milestone. I'll know when or even if I'll be ready to
create again. Trust me, this isn't the time."

"Not if you don't let it be. It's been three years, Vito.
Surely that's enough time to at least consider moving
forward."

"Family or not, I wish you'd remember what is and is
not your place to try and lecture me about, Leo."

Leo's lips tightened as his eyes clouded with disappointment. "And I wish you'd remember that you were
not the one who drove Marina's car over the rock cliff that
day." With those words, Leo walked to the exit and shut
the glass door none too softly behind him.

Vito bit out a curse. Leo was being downright bel-
ligerent. What business was it of his if Maya would be
touring the basilica and palazzo on her own?

*An exclusive guided tour for two. Only now the guide
will have to settle for one.* Her words replayed in his
mind.

And what kind of guide would she have, he wondered.
No doubt a distracted University of Venice design student
who simply wanted the extra cash and was willing the day
to be over soon. A random guide wouldn't be able to help
Maya fully appreciate the historic art and architecture of
the cathedral. He'd no doubt go on and on about lines and
angles and historical facts that anyone could look up online or in a textbook. Such a shame and a waste of time
for everyone involved.

There was also something else he didn't want to think

about. After the soulless tour, she'd be eating dinner by herself.

Vito gave his head a brisk shake. What did it matter to him? Again, it was absolutely no concern of his. He'd spent enough mental energy on Maya Talbot as it was. He already had too little to spare.

After buying an inexpensive phone, she was down to her last few euros. Thank heavens she'd left an emergency stash in her hotel room before she'd ventured out the other day. Her bank was in the process of delivering new credit and debit cards; she could only hope they arrived at her Venice hotel before she moved on to the next destination.

Now that she'd pulled herself together and had some time to think, she'd decided to continue with her European tour. The conversation with Vito and his cousin earlier in the studio had unexpectedly settled it for her. She might be alone, but she was going to try hard not to be lonely. After all, hadn't she decided back in Boston that part of her new attitude about life was to be more carefree? To worry less and do more?

Her fall had simply been a mishap, a bump in the road.

Maya cursed once again her monumental decision to drink so much wine before her first-ever gondola ride. But if it hadn't been for that decision, she would never have met Vito. Her heart gave a little tug in her chest as she thought of him. No doubt she'd seen the last of the man. A man she would never forget. Maya would have to chalk their meeting up to just one more memorable experience on this trip. A teaser of what her life might have been like if she'd been born under a different sky.

Though, in some ways, maybe it would have been

better if she'd never met him at all. It was so much easier to not actually know what one was missing in life. Maya sighed and slipped her newly acquired cell phone into her dress pocket, her thoughts still centered on the enigmatic, handsome artist who was sure to haunt her dreams for years to come.

So she thought she was imagining it when she looked up to find him approaching her from the other side of the walkway. She shut her eyes and gave a shake of her head before she looked again, just to be sure.

Yep, it was definitely him. And he was definitely approaching her.

"Vito?"

"*Buongiorno.* I was hoping I would catch you. Luckily this is the only cell phone store within a mile of the square."

"But why?"

He shrugged. "Most likely because there isn't enough of a demand to warrant any other retailers." The hint of a smile at the corners of his mouth told her he'd deliberately misunderstood her question.

"If only more tourists dropped theirs in the water as I did."

"Yes, indeed," he answered with a small chuckle before turning serious once more. "It occurred to me after you left that you never did leave your address in Boston."

"My address?"

"Yes. So that I could have my assistant mail you the sketch."

Realization suddenly dawned on her. How foolish could she be? To think she'd even considered for a moment that he might have followed her because he wanted to speak to her again, to see her again. Although…he could have called the hotel for the information later.

Nonsense. Maya shook off that thought. The simplest explanation was often the right one. Vito only wanted her address so that he could mail her the sketch, just as he'd explained. She shouldn't try to find other motives simply because she wished for them.

"Here." He handed her his cell phone. "You can type in the information on my contacts list."

She did as he asked and handed his mobile back to him. Her fingers brushed over his, ever so slightly, and the same current she'd felt yesterday traveled down her spine and through her limbs. Whatever effect this man had on her, it was enough to make her tremble inside.

She quickly pulled her hand away, fast enough that Vito seemed on the verge of dropping his phone before being able to fully grasp it. Great. All she needed was to be responsible for yet another damaged mobile.

"Care to walk with me to the piazza?" Maya blurted out without thinking. What was the harm? She really wouldn't mind his company for a few more moments. Bad enough she'd be spending the rest of the day essentially alone.

Vito shifted from one foot to the other. He wasn't saying he would. Maya's heart sank down to her toes. She shouldn't have asked him, should never have risked it. Now he had to find a way to turn her down. So his next words surprised her yet again.

"It would be an honor and a pleasure to walk with you on such a beautiful afternoon, *cara*."

He was beginning to think he might have lost his mind. Vito had had no idea when he left his showroom to go and find her that he'd be spending yet more time with her. But there it was. Clearly, both her own question and Vito's response to it had surprised Maya, judging from the bemused expression she currently wore.

Except maybe part of him had known that his jaunt to the mobile store was simply a way to see her again.

There'd been no real need to venture out to find her. He certainly could have called her hotel later, asked about her address and wished her well with the rest of her travels. And the rest of her life, for that matter.

For some reason, he'd felt compelled to come and find her.

"I'd like that," she said with a smile. "I'd like that very much."

"Excellent."

He should have turned her down, told her he had things to do. So why hadn't he done just that? Damned if he could explain it to himself. Part of him blamed that busybody, meddling cousin of his. Leo had planted the seed, after all. Whatever the reason, it was too late to pull back now. Rather than dwell any further on his motivations, he offered Maya the crook of his arm. "Shall we?"

She took it with zero hesitation, her touch sending warmth up to his shoulder blades and down along his back. He was completely unprepared for such a reaction to a simple touch on his arm.

He didn't like it. Not one bit.

It was one thing to notice her physical qualities and want to capture them, given the artist in him. But this physical reaction was something else altogether.

Vito had to wonder exactly what he might have just gotten himself into.

* * *

It was ridiculous to be this excited. Maya made a point of reassuring herself that her overblown reaction to having Vito join her this afternoon was born of pure relief. After all, who would want to go sightseeing in one of the most beautiful destinations Europe had to offer all by herself? She certainly hadn't been looking forward to doing so. Thanks to Vito, her afternoon just became much more interesting.

"You are to start at the piazza? Correct?" Vito asked her.

"Yes, I'm to meet my tour guide there. Though I have a few moments to spare." She glanced at her sensible watch. She had a much more extravagant one at home, with a gold band and jewel-encrusted face. But she'd never wear that one again. It had been a birthday gift from Matt. She gave herself a mental kick. She refused to think about him today. Or for the remainder of this trip, for that matter.

"Excellent. That will give us some time to enjoy the square."

A crowd was already gathered in the piazza when they reached St. Mark's. The line outside the basilica snaked back and forth. Dozens of gondolas and various other watercrafts dotted the canal ways.

"This is the busiest I've seen it since I got here," Maya commented.

"Pretty common for a Friday afternoon. Good thing you booked a tour," Vito remarked. "It's the only way to bypass the lines."

"I have my grandmother to thank. This really was the ideal wedding gift." Too bad the wedding in question would never happen.

"Your grandmother must think very highly of you."

Maya couldn't help the smile that formed on her lips. "She says I'm her favorite. Though I'm not sure how true that is. I think she simply feels a particular kinship with me."

"Oh? Why is that?"

"Because we both lost so much when my parents passed. She lost a cherished son. My father. And I lost my entire family."

"You're an only child?"

She nodded. "Yes. Though I grew up with two cousins. They're more like sisters, really. My aunt and uncle took me in after the accident. They raised me. I was fortunate that they stepped up."

"But you never stopped missing your parents."

A lump of sorrow lodged in her throat. She had to swallow past it before she could answer. "No. I think about them every day. And how much I miss them."

Vito stopped walking as he turned to face her. "Grief is a rather unforgiving monster," he replied. His voice had taken on a distant, pensive tone. His eyes darkened with emotion. And pain. Maya had no doubt he was speaking from firsthand experience.

She and Vito walked farther into the center of the square. A toddler squealed by them, laughing as he chased a pigeon then ran after another. His mother followed close behind with a genuine yet exasperated laugh of her own. The child nearly careened into a young, well-dressed couple sharing a chocolate gelato cone.

"You've lost someone, haven't you, Vito?"

He seemed focused on a point off in the distance. "I hope you don't mind my asking," she added when he didn't answer right away.

He gave a shake of his head before turning his gaze

back to her. "No, it's all right. I'm just not used to being asked about it. This is a rather small city. Everyone already knows the story. It doesn't come up often."

Maya got the distinct impression that was most likely because he clearly discouraged it. Vito didn't seem like the type of man who took comfort from confiding in others. No, he appeared much too private for that. Too stoic. But something compelled her to press on. "Do you want to tell me?"

Pain and anguish were etched in his face.

"My wife. I lost my wife about three years ago."

The words confirmed what she'd read online. He was a widower. Vito Rameri had lost the woman he loved. And, by the looks of him as he spoke, he still grieved for her deeply.

She should not have pursued the subject. A virtual curtain seemed to close behind his eyes. The warmth and camaraderie they'd shared on their walk over had suddenly dissipated. She wasn't surprised when he quickly changed the subject as they approached the appropriate line for entry.

"Be sure to note the influences of other eras in the artwork," he reminded her.

"I'll try."

He gave her a small bow when they came to a stop at the place she was to meet her guide. "Enjoy your tour, *bella mia*."

With that, Vito turned and walked away. Without so much as a goodbye.

Vito didn't know how long he stood there, watching her from a distance. He tried to tell himself he was simply being conscientious, making sure she was met by her tour guide. He couldn't help noticing, however, that aside from an elderly man reading a newspaper and Vito himself, she was the only one in the entire square without a companion. And she looked nervous, shifting from one foot to the other. Despite her words at the studio earlier, Maya was clearly feeling awkward and out of place standing there alone.

But what business was it of his, really?

Vito told himself he should turn away, walk back to his studio and not give Maya Talbot another thought. The fact that he was even wavering over doing so was absolutely Leo's fault. That meddlesome cousin of his was the only reason Vito was even entertaining the notion currently nagging at him.

Leo's words echoed in his head. *She's only here in Venice for a few days. What would be the harm in accompanying her?*

On the surface, it appeared such an innocuous question. Perhaps there was no need to dig too far into it. Maya didn't know a soul in Venice. They'd met by accident and had gotten to know each other somewhat. Maybe they were even on their way to becoming friends. Truly, a genuine friend would try and help another out of an awkward and uncomfortable situation.

That's all this was, he assured himself. He made his way back to where she stood before he could give it much more thought.

She jumped when he tapped her on the shoulder.

The smile that greeted him when she turned around nearly knocked him off his feet. Maybe this hadn't been such a great idea. "Vito? You're back!"

He didn't often lie, but it seemed to be the best course of action at the moment. For the sake of her pride. "Leo just called me from the studio. It appears I've had a sudden cancellation of a previously planned appointment," he fibbed. "I find myself free for the afternoon."

Her eyes grew wide with shock. And pleasure. "You do?"

He nodded. "Since I'm already here, I wonder if I may take advantage of your extra tour ticket. That is, if I won't be intruding," he added quickly.

The smile she gave him was as bright as a sunny Venetian morning. "Why let a perfectly good tour ticket go to waste?"

He offered her his elbow. "Why indeed?"

CHAPTER SIX

IT NEVER CEASED to amaze him, the sheer wonder and awe on the face of someone entering the Basilica San Marco for the first time. Maya was no exception. Her jaw had been agape since they'd stepped through the arched doors. Her reaction could best be described as that of a small child experiencing her first amusement park ride.

But it was his own reaction that came as a bit of a surprise. Vito felt pleasure warm through his chest at the sight of her as she took in the majestic beauty surrounding them.

He'd been right about the tour guide. A disheveled and distracted university architecture student, barely out of his teen years. He'd introduced himself as Angelo. Now, as they entered the ancient church, the glances the young man kept throwing in Vito's direction were a clue that the student recognized who he was. Vito appeared to be making him nervous.

Vito wished for some type of miracle that might somehow have the whole cathedral cleared except for Maya and himself—including their distracted guide.

"It's breathtaking," Maya uttered, her voice barely above a whisper. But he managed to hear her. She was taking it all in with an appreciation so often lacking in foreign tourists. Not many of them appreciated the sheer genius of the artwork on the domed ceiling. The religious symbolism so craftily on display was lost on most.

Not on Maya. She could see clearly what a master work of art this whole building was. And she appreciated it.

Their tour guide was explaining the influence of Byzantine architecture on the cathedral and the religious importance of the mosaics. He then launched into the history of the artwork and when it was completed, what previous works the art had been influenced by. Maya politely nodded at his words without tearing her eyes away from the walls and the dome overhead.

Angelo continued to dart glances his way as he spoke. Vito wanted to tell the young man to relax. No doubt he was wondering why Vito Rameri, of all people, would be participating in a guided tour of San Marco.

If he only knew.

Maya sighed. "The pictures I've seen in various books can't compare to the reality of this place."

"Pictures can't do justice to a true masterpiece."

"No. They can't. I knew the mosaics were mostly done in gold but I couldn't have imagined the sheer luminescence of the effect."

Angelo interrupted them with a none-too-subtle clearing of his throat. "Should we continue on toward the apse?"

Vito motioned for him to lead the way and placed a hand on Maya's elbow.

Despite his own prompt, Angelo didn't move. He stood staring at the two of them, his gaze dropping to where Vito held Maya by the arm.

Great. Depending on who this young man's mentoring professor was, this little outing might very well fuel a fresh new round of talk among Vito's acquaintances. Vito wasn't sure he could deal with a gossip storm again. The last one had nearly destroyed him. He let go of Maya and dropped his hand to his side, clenching it in anger and frustration.

Angelo blinked and lifted his chin, as if summoning the courage to speak. Vito could guess what was coming and sought in vain for a way to head him off at the pass.

This was the reason he preferred to stay home.

"Scusa, per favore," Angelo began. "Are you not Signor Rameri?"

Vito merely nodded, hoping against all hope that the young man would just drop the matter once it was confirmed.

No such luck. Angelo thrust his hand in Vito's direction and spoke in Italian. "It is an honor to meet you, sir."

Vito had no choice but to shake the other man's hand. "Thank you for your kindness," he responded, reverting to English for Maya's sake. This was her day, after all. He had no desire whatsoever to make any part of it be about him. Angelo would just have to understand that.

For her part, Maya was giving them both a curious look.

"Do you two know each other?" she asked.

Angelo chuckled nervously. "Anyone studying art in Italy, or most anywhere else in the world for that matter, knows of Signor Rameri."

Maya turned to give him a look, one eyebrow raised. "Of course. How silly of me."

"If we could continue," Vito prompted.

"I would not have expected to be giving you a tour when I signed on for this job," Angelo said, obviously taking the hint that speaking English was the polite thing to do.

"Life is full of surprises." Some of those surprises were bigger than others, Vito thought. Some surprises came in the form of a vicious sucker punch and turned a once-content life full of purpose into a shattered mess.

"I knew I was right," Angelo continued.

"Right about what?" Vito asked, despite the trepidation warning him to just ignore the statement.

"About all the incorrect rumors. I argued to everyone who would listen that you were not, in fact, retiring."

Vito wanted to tell him it was none of his business. The only person his career concerned was Vito himself. Bad enough his cousin was a thorn in his side on the subject. Like he'd told Leo earlier, he would go back to work in the studio when he was good and ready.

"Retiring?" Maya asked.

"Why else would you be here if not for creative inspiration?" Angelo looked quite smug about his reasoning skills. He had no clue just how completely off his theory was.

"Rumors are the devil's playthings," Vito declared with a finality he hoped would compel everyone to just drop the topic.

But Angelo had still more to say. "No one can blame you for taking a sabbatical given everything that happened. I knew it was just a matter of time before you came back."

Vito cursed under his breath. This was why he kept to himself, why he didn't socialize or attend functions. His past always came up as a topic of conversation. One he had no interest in accommodating.

He should have known better.

* * *

Maya knew she wasn't imagining the tension coursing through Vito as their tour guide went on and on in a flat monotone voice. The stiffness in Vito's shoulders and neck was sure to cause one monster of a headache if he didn't let it loose fairly soon. She also hadn't missed the way he'd tried in vain to shut down Angelo's reference to his work or supposed retirement.

Whatever the exact story was, between her internet search the other night and all of Angelo's ramblings, she'd been able to surmise that Vito hadn't produced anything in a considerable length of time.

It had to have something to do with his wife.

To top it off, their tour guide hadn't been the only one to recognize Vito as they'd toured the basilica. Maya had caught more than one person doing a double take as they walked by. One young woman who'd been sketching in the apse looked on the verge of approaching him. Vito must have noticed her intent, as well, for he quickly walked in the other direction even as Angelo was still in the middle of a comment about a particular mosaic right above where they stood.

Now that the cathedral part of the tour was over, Vito seemed anxious to be out of there. She was feeling a bit claustrophobic herself. The crowds had multiplied since they'd arrived. At one point she'd found herself jostled badly enough that Vito had to reach over and steady her. She decided to ignore the little flip her stomach did as he placed his hands around her waist to keep her from careening into another church visitor.

"Shall we make our way over to the Doge's Palace, then?" Angelo asked once they'd stepped outside to stand by the lion statue. "Follow me."

He made a move in that direction but Vito held a hand up to stop him. "That won't be necessary."

Angelo blinked. "I beg your pardon?"

Maya's heart fell. Vito was cutting the tour short. He'd had enough. Though she shouldn't be surprised. He had definitely not enjoyed the tour. She'd have had to be oblivious and blind to not notice his discomfort.

"You won't need to accompany us," Vito added.

Wait a minute. It was one thing to be done with touring with her but it was something else entirely to send her guide away. This was part of her package trip. She began to protest but Vito interrupted her. "I can take it from here. We appreciate your time." He reached into his back pocket and pulled out a leather wallet.

The young man seemed taken aback but recovered quickly once he saw the wad of bills he was being offered. Maya waited until he was out of earshot before turning to Vito.

"May I ask why you just did that?"

He bowed his head slightly. "I apologize. I should have asked you first."

"But you didn't." She wasn't exactly miffed about that fact, but she would have appreciated being consulted on the decision.

"I can catch up to him and bring him back, if you'd like." Even as he made the offer, Vito's expression made it clear how distasteful he found that prospect.

"I'd just like to know why."

"A structured tour is so flat, so boring. You have access to the internet at home back in Boston, do you not?"

"Of course."

"And you are able to read books on history or art?"

She began to see his point. "Angelo wasn't telling us

anything that can't readily be found in an art history textbook."

"Precisely."

"And I suppose you can make the rest of the tour more stimulating?"

He clapped a hand to his chest in mock offense. "You wound me. I think I can manage a bit better than a distracted, uninterested graduate student."

Did that mean that he was interested? In showing her around? In spending more time with her? Was there even the slightest chance that he'd sent Angelo away because he wanted to be alone with her?

She shook off the fanciful thoughts. Of course not; she was just foolishly searching for ways to mend her shattered pride after being duped by her fiancé.

Speaking of which, it came as a bit of a revelation that she hadn't thought of Matt in all this time. She should probably be missing him more, wishing that he was here with her. But he hadn't so much as crossed her mind.

That fact spoke volumes about her choice of a potential life partner. Then again, maybe it had more to do with the man smiling at her right now outside the cathedral.

Vito Rameri was definitely the sort to help a girl forget about other men.

"Well, let's go see if you can put your money where your mouth is, Signor Rameri."

He quirked an eyebrow at her. "Another American idiom."

Maya just laughed in response.

Moments later, they entered the historic museum that was once the residence of the Doge di Venezia. The artwork was no less breathtaking here than what she'd seen at the basilica. The entire palace was one monumental masterpiece with elaborate paintings on the ceilings and walls. Her senses were in overdrive; she couldn't decide where to look first. It was as if history had actually come to life around her.

She could sense Vito staring her way. How lucky was she to be able to visit these places with him by her side? A true native son who knew exactly how to appreciate the beauty and history that surrounded them.

Right. As if that was the only reason she was so thrilled that he was here with her.

"Well, what can you tell me about these paintings?" she asked him.

"Ah, *cara*. Don't you get it? It's about what you can tell me about them."

Maya turned to him in question. "I don't understand?"

"Tell me what you see." He reached for her then, and she could swear the blood stopped pounding in her heart. He touched a gentle finger to her temple. "What do you see in here?" Then his hand dropped to her collarbone, then lower to the area of her heart. "And in here?"

"Come, let's walk along the Grand Canal side," Vito said close to two hours later when they were back outside.

The tour of the palace had taken longer than she would have thought. But Maya would have spent days and days in there if given the opportunity. The visual magnificence of the venue was beyond anything she'd seen before. Now, as they stood back, Maya was still in the process of absorbing all the wonders she'd observed in both the basilica and palazzo.

"There's something else you need to see," Vito informed her.

Moments later they were standing atop a bridge

around the corner looking up at yet another bridge—
the arched structure that connected the Doge's Palace
with another building—the *Prigioni Nuove*, the prison.
Maya recognized it immediately. "The Bridge of Sighs."

"Another stunning work of Venetian architecture,"
Vito supplied.

That was one doozy of an understatement. The detail
in the architecture alone was a sight to behold.

"The windows are so small. Why did they even bother
with them?"

"Those poor prisoners from centuries ago had to have
one last view of the city before they were doomed to in-
carceration."

"Yes. But it seems terribly unfair that the last view
of Venice those poor ancient prisoners saw before being
sent to their cells had to be through those small holes."

Vito rubbed his chin. "What else do you see? Look
closely, beyond the basic structure."

Maya studied the bridge, squinting to make out the
details. It was magnificent. But she wasn't sure what exactly she was supposed to be looking at. Then it struck
her. Several ornamental carvings in the surface. "Are
those faces?"

"Good eye."

That wasn't the first time he'd said that to her. Each
time had sent a childish surge of pleasure through her
chest straight to her toes. It had to mean something, didn't
it? If a professional artist of Vito's caliber complimented
you on your observational skills?

"They're meant to ward off evil spirits. And to guard
the bridge as well as the two buildings it connects."

"As far as the prison goes, were the faces meant to
keep evil in or keep it out?"

"That's the question, now, isn't it? I'm sure the poor souls passing through it on their way to their foul new residence contemplated that very thing."

Maya felt an involuntary shiver down her spine. Both the bridge and the jail must harbor the ghosts of angry and despondent souls who'd been sentenced to a term of misery.

Vito noticed her reaction. "Come now. Don't focus so much on the sadness of it."

"Hard to help it."

"Ah, but it isn't all doom and gloom. There's a romantic story linked to the bridge, as well."

"There is?" In all her readings regarding Venice, she didn't recall anything romantic associated with the famous bridge which led to dark and solitary prison cells.

"Certainly."

She would have to hear this to believe it. "Please, do tell."

Vito crossed his arms and leaned over the railing of the bridge they stood on. "There's a local legend that says under a precise set of circumstances, a couple that kisses under the Bridge of Sighs is destined for a lifetime of love and happiness."

Maya raised her eyebrows at him in question. She was definitely intrigued. "What are these circumstances?"

"That's the difficult part. The chances of all the variables falling into place are highly unlikely. Yet I hear it does happen."

"Oh?"

"See, if a couple can get it right, they can look forward to a bright and fruitful future together full of love and affection. That is, if they manage to time it so that they're under the bridge right at sunset just as the bells of San Marco ring out. If so, they will be granted eternal love and a lifetime of bliss."

"You're right. That's a lot of pieces that need to fall into place."

He nodded. "Adding to the uncertainty is the fact that St. Mark's bells don't even ring every hour. Still, couples do try."

As luck would have it, they watched as a gondola slowly glided under the bridge at that very moment. The two couples on board embraced and each shared a loving kiss.

"They've obviously heard of the legend," Vito remarked.

"Obviously."

"I don't hear any bells, though. Plus, it's not quite sunset."

Maya wasn't sure any of that mattered. Both couples looked like they were having the time of their lives.

Would she ever have that? she wondered. She realized now that she had never had it with Matt. Not for the first time since arriving in Italy, she couldn't help but wonder if Matt hadn't, in fact, done her a huge favor. Maya had no doubt he would have betrayed her after they'd gotten married. Once a cheater…and all that. Better that she find out and deal with it now, before she took his name. Or became a parent with him. She didn't know if she would have had the strength to leave him once she became his wife. Or the mother of his children.

Her gaze traveled to the man standing next to her. It was hard not to compare him with Matt. On the surface, they both seemed to exude confidence. But when it came to substance, she had to acknowledge that Matt didn't have much of the genuine quality. She didn't know all that much about Vito but he seemed successful on his own terms. Whereas Matt had made never made a secret of the fact that he'd used his father's connections and clout as a businessman to get to where he was in life. Matt actually regarded that with pride. He liked presenting himself as the deserving son of a prominent and wealthy Brahmin family. Upon inspection now, she could see the image he wanted to create must have included a doting spouse.

In contrast, Vito seemed very much self-made. Everything he'd achieved, he would have had to do on his own. Professional artists couldn't rely on family connections. They either had the talent or they didn't.

Vito seemed deep in thought, as well. Deep creases lined his face; his lips had drawn tight. Maya had no doubt he was thinking of his late spouse. She had to wonder what she might have been like, what type of woman was able to attract the attention of someone like Vito Rameri. She must have been quite something.

Maya might have lost the future she'd planned. A development that had brought her to her knees several days ago, but one that she was gradually but surely recovering from.

Vito, on the other hand, had lost the love of his life.

Vito didn't know how long they'd stood there in silence, simply watching the steady flow of gondolas drifting under the Bridge of Sighs. In a scene that could have been straight out of a stormy painting, all too suddenly, the sky grew several shades darker. Clouds that Vito could have sworn weren't there mere seconds before suddenly burst open and released a torrent of heavy rain.

What the…? Nowhere in the forecast had there been

any prediction of rain, let alone the downpour they currently found themselves in.

The shrieks of fellow visitors filled the air around them as they ran to find shelter. Maya was reacting differently, though—she was laughing hysterically, in a manner the Americans would call "cracking up."

"What exactly is so funny?" he asked with an answering smile of his own, once they'd run off their perch and reached the large umbrella of a flower vendor nearby.

"Oh, I'm just wondering why it is that the fates have decreed that I need to get soaked to the skin every couple of days in Venice. And that you're certain to be around to witness the spectacle for some reason."

He returned her laughter with a chuckle of his own. "You know, the very thought had just occurred to me, as well."

"*Scusa*, flowers for the beautiful young lady?" the vendor was asking.

Vito didn't hesitate. He motioned to a wrapped bouquet of budding pink roses. A purchase was the least he could do; they were taking advantage of the man's shelter, after all.

Something told him he might have bought Maya flowers in any case.

Maya didn't say anything as he handed them to her. But her cheeks flushed a shade of pink not unlike the roses she currently sniffed.

"They're beautiful. Thanks, Vito," she said with a pleased smile, ducking her head shyly.

He hadn't forgotten the last time he'd bought flowers for a woman. How could he?

That particular flower purchase hadn't been quite as pleasant as this one. The day seemed a lifetime ago. But he replayed it clearly in his mind. He and Marina had had yet another heated exchange in a long line of chaotic and dramatic arguments—like so many that had plagued their marriage toward the end. Marina had snatched the bouquet out of his hands and thrown it in the bin.

Her voice, shaking with anger and disgust, resonated in his brain. *Do you think such a futile gesture would make up for the way you've been ignoring me for all these weeks?*

Vito pushed the memories away. What good was it to dwell on them now? He'd have plenty of time later, when he was alone. When he was sitting at his round wooden table in the apartment he occupied above the art studio, staring off into space and contemplating all the ways things had gone so horribly wrong in his life.

His gaze fell to where Maya stood admiring her roses. Her thick curls had escaped the sensible ponytail she'd shown up with this morning. Her eyes were bright, sparkling with merriment. Perhaps it was the artist in him but Vito could swear there was a visible aura around her. An aura full of light and laughter. He had to acknowledge that she'd brought both light and laughter back into his existence these past few days. A lightheartedness he didn't think he'd experience again.

Too bad it was all so temporary.

"I guess I should make my way back to the hotel," Maya said, interrupting his thoughts.

He couldn't let her walk or take a boat, as soaked as she was. "My studio is much closer, *cara*. Let's go get you dried off. Once again."

He didn't give her a chance to argue. He simply took advantage of the lull in the rain to take her by the hand and lead her back to his place.

* * *

"I'm having a profound sense of déjà vu." Maya wiped the wetness from her face after they arrived back at Vito's studio. "Only this time I'm much more sober."

So why did she feel so light-headed? Slightly dizzy? The afternoon had grown considerably darker. Shadows fell over Vito's features, the overall effect lending his face a mysterious, brooding quality that sent a small tremor down her back.

Vito handed her a large rag that he pulled out of a wooden cabinet against the wall. Maya took it gratefully and started to dry off.

"I can offer you refreshment of a more warming variety, if you're interested. You look like you might be chilled," he added with a playful wink.

She motioned to her wet clothes and did a little mini swirl. "You think so, huh?"

He shrugged. "Just a guess."

"I'm definitely interested in anything that may warm me up. What did you have in mind?"

He pointed to the ceiling. "I have an espresso maker in my apartment upstairs."

Was that an invitation? If so, was she prepared to take him up on it? His next question put her in the exact position of having to make that decision.

"You're welcome to come up there, of course," Vito offered. "Or I'd be happy to bring a cup down here when it's ready."

He was leaving the ball completely in her court. So what was she going to do? She didn't relish the idea of sitting down here in the darkened studio by herself. And she'd already spent an afternoon alone with him the previous day. Despite having just met him, Maya felt an unwavering sense that she could trust this man. Enough to be alone in his apartment with him.

"I'd love to help you make the espressos upstairs, Vito."

She didn't realize he'd been holding his breath until she watched the drop of his shoulders as he released it. What exactly did that mean? Probably nothing. There she went, trying to read into things again.

"Just one thing first?" she asked.

"What's that?"

She tugged at the collar of her damp dress. "Do you have any more of those smocks I might be able to borrow?"

Vito watched as Maya sat in the middle of his small, cozy kitchen, sipping on her espresso as if the cup had been sent to her straight from heaven. Her curls had all completely escaped at this point; the elastic in her hair had either fallen out or it was lost somewhere in her tresses for all he knew. Her cheeks had gone from a rosy pink to a deeper, more reddish color. The smock he'd given her hung like a shapeless curtain over her frame.

Still, he found her to be achingly beautiful. How the woman managed to look so attractive after getting caught in a rainstorm and while wearing a painter's smock was truly beyond him.

Whatever her appeal, it behooved him to ignore it. She'd be gone from Italy and out of his life in a few short days. Not that it would matter one iota if her stay here had been a permanent one. Vito wasn't at a point in his life where he could entertain any type of attraction to a woman. Permanent or otherwise. He had to pull his life back together. He had too much baggage, too much to figure out about himself and how he'd let the woman he'd married down so tragically.

Not to mention, Maya was pulling together the pieces of her own broken heart. The last thing she needed complicating her reality right now was a short and meaningless fling.

Vito sucked in a breath at the direction his thoughts had suddenly taken. A fling shouldn't have even crossed his mind. What was wrong with him? Was he desperate for female companionship?

He had to get a grip.

"I think the chill has finally left my skin. Thank you for letting me dry out, Vito. Once again. I'll have quite a repayment to make if you ever find yourself in Boston."

"If I'm ever there, I will take you up on that," Vito replied, simply out of politeness. He had no desire or inclination to travel outside of Europe at this stage of his life. If only he'd been able to temper some of his wanderlust before Marina had grown so fed up with his absences. Both his physical and mental ones. He'd not only withdrawn from her physically, he'd done so emotionally, as well. His only excuse was that he'd needed solitude and distance in order to create his art.

He made himself push away the useless thoughts.

"So, what's on the agenda for tomorrow?" he asked to try and change the subject before Maya could pursue any kind of questioning about the possibility of him going to the States.

She clasped her hands together in front of her chest. "It's quite exciting. I'm to visit a glass blower's shop. Followed by some shopping near the Rialto Bridge."

"Sounds like quite a day. And how about the evening?"

The excitement immediately drained out of her. Her eyes suddenly darted to the ground while a frown creased her lips. She fought valiantly to replace it with a smile, but the effect only served to lend a tight, forced set to her mouth. "Oh. That's to be another very exciting excursion." Despite her words, her tone was flat and rather empty.

Vito lifted an eyebrow in question. He could guess the reason for her poor attempt to hide her disappointment. The evening no doubt held another romantic activity meant for two. "What's the plan?"

Maya swallowed and nodded with enthusiasm. Too much enthusiasm, in fact. "Something I wouldn't miss for all the gold on the planet."

He'd guessed right. Whatever had been on her agenda, it was meant for a couple to enjoy together. He found himself reaching for her over the round glass coffee table between them, and taking her small, delicate hand in his. How could her fiancé have let this woman go?

"Tell me, *cara*. What is this exciting excursion you have planned?"

"One of the highlights of the trip," she repeated. "A sunset dinner cruise along the Grand Canal. Complete with champagne and authentic Italian gourmet cuisine. It was one of the activities that most thrilled me when I first found out about the itinerary."

Vito gave her hand a small squeeze. "Your fiancé is a fool of a man," he bit out, with more vehemence than he'd intended.

Maya sucked her bottom lip. "Thank you for saying that. Fool or not, there's no way I'm going to miss out on such an experience myself. Matt has no idea what he's missing. I thought I might ask around at the hotel to see if there'd be any takers for the extra voucher. You know, just so it doesn't go to waste. Not that I mind going alone." It was another clear instance of the lady doth protest too much. Vito kept that thought to himself.

"You have your heart set on this outing, I can tell."

She gave a small shrug. "Yeah, I do." He wasn't imagining the sudden sheen of wetness in her eyes. Vito didn't want to examine too closely the feeling that came over him at the sight. Pure anger and outrage on her behalf. "Not quite what I initially imagined it would be like, being alone and all. But still, an experience of a lifetime." Her lips trembled slightly as she forced a smile.

"I'm sorry, *bella*," Vito said softly, then wanted to kick himself. Maya was not the type to appreciate any kind of pity directed toward her.

Her next words confirmed that suspicion. "Oh, don't say that! I know how lucky I am to have this chance, regardless of the circumstances. How many people can say they've dined aboard a glamorous ship while sailing the Venetian waters? I refuse to let anything mar the experience for me."

She really was one of the most extraordinary people he'd ever met. Not many other women would approach the prospect of an evening alone aboard a romantic dinner cruise with such fervor and enthusiasm.

On the surface, Maya seemed upbeat. But Vito could see what was below the outer shell. It was all clearly yet another act on her part. It was breaking her inside that she'd be experiencing such an activity by herself. Just like the tour earlier.

She leaned over and crooked a finger at him to come closer. "I have a confession," she said in a conspiratorial tone and followed it with a wink.

"What's that?"

"See, I made a bit of a resolution before I left Boston."

That had his curiosity piqued. "What kind of resolution?"

"I decided that I was done taking the safest route, the path of least resistance."

He blinked in question. "And what does that have to do with a dinner aboard a boat?"

"Don't you see? It would be so easy to just skip the whole thing. And sit in my hotel room, instead. The Maya Talbot of a few weeks ago would be quick to tell you that option is the one that made the most sense. But I'm done with easy. And I'm done with being sensible. Even if it means I'm the sole diner at one of those candlelit tables meant for two."

He couldn't be certain who she was trying to convince. Vito or herself.

"Does this resolution allow for partners, *cara*?"

She leaned back in surprise. "What do you mean?"

What, indeed, was he suggesting? Where was he going with this, exactly?

Damned if he knew. He just knew he couldn't stand the disappointment clouding her eyes despite her words of resolution and newfound bold spirit.

"I wonder if you might be up for having a partner along for this next adventure."

Maya finally looked up. She was staring at him wide-eyed. "Vito, I don't want to make a fool of myself by jumping to any conclusions here. Could I ask you to just come out and tell me what you're getting at?"

He gave her a small smile. "Well, *cara*, it's just that it occurs to me that it's been quite a long while since I've enjoyed a nice, relaxing dinner while admiring all of Venice's beauty from a boat on the water."

CHAPTER SEVEN

SHE'D BEEN HALF afraid he wouldn't show up. As much as she'd enjoyed the shopping expedition and her time at the glass blower's studio, Maya had been unable to tear her mind from the anticipation of the evening to come.

But he was here. And, dear heavens, was he handsome. Dressed in a finely cut tuxedo and polished leather shoes, Vito Rameri had every woman he passed along the walkway nearly swooning. Or perhaps that was just Maya projecting her own reaction onto others.

She watched now as he approached her while she waited to board the ship that would serve as their restaurant. He had his hair in the same combed-back style he'd had the other day. He hadn't shaved fully and now sported a subtle goatee.

She might as well have been watching one of her daydreams play out.

Who would have thought Maya would be thanking her lucky stars for falling into these very same waters that day Vito had pulled her out. He stopped short when he reached her side. He smelled of spicy sandalwood with a hint of some type of mint. Maya resisted the urge to lean toward him and inhale deeply of the alluring masculine scent.

"Bellissima," he said when he approached her, looking her up and down.

"Grazie," she replied with a small curtsy. "You're not looking too shabby, either, Signor Rameri."

He held out his arm to her. "Shall we?"

Moments later, they were watching the dazzling lights of Venice from the deck of an authentic galleon.

Maya wanted to pinch herself. Was this all really happening? How had she ended up in such a stunning setting with this charismatic, charming and devilishly handsome man as her companion?

"This view is unlike anything I could have imagined. It's enchanting," she said, her voice sounding as breathless as she felt.

"Sì. It most certainly is."

Her heart fluttered when she realized he was staring at her profile as he spoke the words.

If only she were able to flick a magic wand and make this dream part of a permanent reality somehow. But this was a fantasy, a once-in-a-lifetime magical evening. Even if, by some miracle, they lived on the same continent, Vito was a man battling demons. The vibes he gave off made it clear he wanted to deal with those demons by himself.

A waiter appeared beside them. He carried a tray with two full wine glasses of ruby-red wine. "Valpolicella."

They both lifted their glasses, then Vito tipped his toward hers in a toast. "To elegant evenings with newly acquired friends."

Maya felt a squiggle of disappointment in her center. If she'd harbored any illusions that any of this was romantic for him, that last word was a cold dose of reality.

She would choose to ignore his choice of words. Nothing was going to ruin the thrill of this evening for her.

If she had to pretend for a couple of hours that this was a real date with her real boyfriend then what would be the harm in that? It would be her secret. Vito didn't need to know.

She tapped the rim of her glass to his and took a small sip. A burst of rich, fruity flavor exploded in her mouth. "Oh, wow. That's really good."

She took another sip, a little too hastily, and some of the wine splashed out of her glass. She managed to avoid getting any on her dress, but a splash of it landed on the side of her cheek.

Vito chuckled and pulled the satin handkerchief from his tuxedo pocket. "Here." He dabbed the soft cloth on her skin, his face inches from hers. His touch suddenly turned to a gentle caress along her jaw.

"Vito?"

She knew she'd been the one to move first. But Vito didn't hesitate to respond. In the next instant, she felt his firm lips against hers as his other hand moved around her and down to the small of her back. His tongue moved over hers, the sensation sending shock waves through every cell in her body. He tasted of wine and mint. His heat suffused through the surface of her skin. Never had a kiss turned her insides to molten lava or had the effect on her that she felt right now.

It ended much too soon.

A sudden jostling of the boat pulled Maya out of his grasp and back to her senses. For a moment neither one of them spoke or moved.

Something shifted in the vicinity of her heart. It all suddenly made so much sense. Having Vito's lips on hers had set her nerve endings on fire. Had she ever felt such a jolt to her insides when Matt had kissed her? She didn't have to think hard to come up with the answer. With Matt, there had never been fire. Or any kind of electricity. She'd been fooling herself. She had to admit, once and for all, that the attraction to Matt had been more about finding a place for herself. In her defense, she really hadn't known. Not until now, when she finally had something to compare it to. Now that she'd met Vito.

Dear heavens. What had she gotten herself into? Maya struggled for some composure. She would take this experience with Vito for what it was. A magical, enchanted evening that had opened her eyes to what true passion really could be. As temporary as it was.

Vito stuck the handkerchief into his pants pocket and turned back to look out toward the city.

"Tell me, is the wine as good as the bottle you enjoyed in your hotel room the day of your uncompleted gondola ride?"

Maya ducked her head, trying to recover some semblance of control. "I have to be honest and say that I don't really remember. I didn't really bother to try and savor the taste of that wine. The point was just to drink it fast enough to flush away the harsh memories."

"Well, then we'll make sure you get to enjoy every drop of the wine you'll be served tonight."

"I will. And I'll make sure to enjoy it slowly," she said, reaching for some kind of normal conversation though she was still shaking inside, from the effect of his kiss as well as all the realizations that had come with it.

He nodded with a smile. "Quite slowly."

They watched silently as they drifted out farther into the lagoon. The palazzo and cathedral they'd toured just yesterday were both lit up majestically against the Venetian skyline.

"It's not difficult to see how a city such as this inspires such unforgettable art," Maya commented. The view before her would compel most people to try and capture it in some type of permanent way.

Vito turned so that he was facing her profile; she couldn't bring herself to look away from the city lights. "You really are quite visual, do you realize that?"

"So you mentioned. You said more than once during our St. Mark's and palazzo tour that I had 'a good eye.' To quote you directly."

"So I did. It happens to be the truth."

"Well, I'm going to take it as a compliment." She tipped her head in a slight bow. "Thank you, my good sir."

"You're quite welcome. And it's most definitely a compliment. Too many people sleepwalk through life without appreciating or so much as noticing the beauty that surrounds them. You are clearly not one of those people."

"I'm glad you think so." Though it didn't really do anything for her, did it? This talent she had that Vito seemed to want to point out. She was stuck at a dead-end job with her personal life in shambles. She would have much preferred a talent for recognizing lying, cheating scoundrels before accepting their marriage proposals. She still hadn't told anyone back home about her broken engagement. That thought gave her pause. She wasn't hurt anymore so much as angry with Matt. How dare he put her in the position of having to disappoint her beloved family? She'd worked so hard all her life to avoid doing so. Yet another realization that she wasn't hurt so much as she was angry.

"You're scowling," Vito commented.

Maya groaned inwardly. She refused to let Matt intrude on any more of this fantasy night. Her feelings for him were growing duller by the minute. As if he were some kind of distant memory of a past mistake she'd never be foolish enough to make again. Not now that she'd met Vito. She flashed him a wide smile. "Not anymore."

The moon appeared from behind a cloud and silver light fell over the surface of the water.

"So, tell me what you do back in Boston, *cara*. It occurs to me we never discussed how you spend your days."

Maya wanted to ask Vito to take back the question. She could still taste him on her lips. That's what she wanted to focus on right now. And the chance that he might kiss her again before the night was over. She didn't want to think about her ordinary, mundane, daily routine. This was supposed to be her fantasy, after all.

A fantasy which didn't involve her boring cubicle behind the front counter of her uncle's plumbing business.

"Tell me, *cara*." Vito prompted. "What do you do for a living? We can start there." Vito realized he was genuinely curious about her. His first impression of her as a jilted bride-to-be had gradually worn off and now he could see the dynamic and fascinating woman she truly was.

He wanted to know more.

"Let's see if you can guess what the answer to that may be."

"Ah, I am being challenged, I see."

"Let's see how well you do."

Vito rubbed his chin, not that he hadn't speculated about what career she might be in. "Hmm. Well, I recall reading in an article that Boston is quite the location for movie shoots. I believe several recent blockbusters were filmed there. Are you maybe involved in the film industry?"

Maya gave him a thumbs-down with her free hand and shook her head. "Try again."

"All right. I also know that several well-known international ad agencies have satellite offices in Boston. Do you work for one of them? Designing ad campaigns, perhaps?"

She gave him a smile that could only be described as sad. "I'm afraid it's not as exciting as any of that," she told him. "In fact, it isn't terribly exciting at all." Then added under her breath, "What an understatement that is." She must have thought he didn't hear her.

Maya took another small sip of her wine, deep in thought. Then she released a long, resounding sigh. "I do the numbers for a business my uncle runs. A plumbing business. I keep the books for him."

Her response took him by surprise. She didn't seem the type for an office job. Frankly, she didn't appear as if she could sit still long enough. But then, what did he know? How often would he have to remind himself that they'd literally just met a couple of days ago?

"If you don't mind me saying, *cara*, I can tell by the look on your face that you quite hate it."

"You are quite the observant one."

"So then why do you do it?"

Maya appeared to be weighing her answer. But before she spoke, the waiter appeared once more to announce they were to be seated for dinner. They followed him off deck to an intricately set table with a tall lit candle as the centerpiece. Vito heard Maya's gasp of pleasure as she took her chair.

He'd felt torn when he offered to accompany her. Her disappointment as she'd talked about having to miss this cruise had sent a mixed bag of emotions churning around in his chest. He didn't need to complicate things by spending any more time with her. But watching her earlier as they'd stood on deck sipping wine, and given her delighted reaction when they reached their table, he had no doubt coming here with her had been right.

It felt right.

Now that they were in the better-lit dining room, he indulged himself in studying her. She wore a simple red satin dress. But it looked far from simple on her. The delicate material hugged her feminine curves and accentuated her figure. The bright color did wonders for her olive skin tone and chestnut hair, which she wore in some type of complicated up-do that made him want nothing more than to take it down and run his fingers through her thick curls.

"I know I keep saying this, but this is all so spectacular."

So are you, was the immediate thought that came to his mind. Vito bit his tongue before he could say the words out loud. He'd learned long ago that empty compliments could sometimes do more harm than good.

One waiter set a large wooden salad bowl in the center of the table while yet another placed the first pasta course in front of each of them.

"I can't believe the sheer number of calories I'm consuming on this trip," Maya remarked. "I'll have to walk for miles each day to even come close to covering it. For the sake of my hips," she said with a small chuckle.

"You have nothing to worry about, *cara*. Not as far as your hips go—or anything else, for that matter."

Now why had he gone and said that? He'd just warned himself to keep such comments in check. Maya's cheeks reddened to a color that almost matched the hue of her dress. Luckily, the sommelier appeared just then to pour them more wine.

Once they were alone, Vito figured he'd better get their conversation flowing again. To get past the awkwardness of his previous comment.

"So, you never did tell me why you stay in a position which makes you so unhappy."

Maya released a deep sigh. "I studied finance to help my uncle."

"With his business."

She nodded. "That's right. He had a bookkeeper who swindled him. By the time the crimes were discovered, the man was nowhere to be found. He'd finagled the books and embezzled a staggering amount of money."

"I see."

"For years after that, my uncle didn't trust anyone else to do his bookkeeping. He tried to do it himself. On top of maintaining the business. The extra responsibility really took a toll on him. He worked nonstop."

"So you saw to it that he had a bookkeeper he could trust."

"That's right. I knew he could use someone he didn't have to worry about stealing from him to help lighten his load."

Vito leaned over the table. "It was commendable of you to assist him in that way."

She lifted one elegant shoulder. "My uncle's done a lot for me. His whole family has. They took me in when they didn't have to. After I lost my parents."

"Isn't that what family does?"

She bit her lip. "Maybe. They could have let me disappear into the US foster care system. Some relatives would have done just that."

"So you felt obligated to become his employee."

Maya stilled in the process of lifting her fork. "What? No, I didn't do it out of a sense of obligation."

Her words surprised him. Did she not see it? "I'm sorry if I've made any kind of assumption."

"I did it out of love. And respect. My uncle stepped up when he didn't have to. He made sure I had a roof over my head and food on my plate."

"He sounds like an honorable man."

"He is. My aunt and my cousins, too. They gave me a family when they didn't have to."

Something about her history still wasn't falling into place. Vito couldn't explain it. There was a piece missing. He couldn't quite put his finger on it.

It occurred to him just as their main course arrived.

"It surprises me that you studied finance in the first place. Regardless of the motivations," he stated once the servers had left their table.

"Why do you say that?"

"It's not a subject that I would think matches your personality. Or your interests. You clearly felt compelled to do it for the sake of your family."

She quirked an eyebrow at him. "And you can tell all that after a simple sightseeing tour with me?"

Referring to a visit to two of Europe's most historic examples of architecture and classic art as a "simple sightseeing tour" was a bit belittling. She was getting defensive. Not the direction he'd intended the conversation to take at all. He simply wanted to know more about her. He wanted to discover all that he could so that he could form a strong basis for memories once she left Venice and walked out of his life for good. He wanted to know what made her tick.

He remained silent, waiting for her to continue.

"Not all of us have what it takes to become world-renowned artists, Vito. Being able to appreciate beauty and someone else's talent doesn't mean one has any of her own. Some of us just need to find a way to make a living and provide for ourselves."

Ah, no doubt she'd been told she didn't have said talent. Most likely by the family who took her in. Or perhaps some overbearing professor whose own failings clouded his judgment. Maybe both theories were true.

"Clearly you don't have to worry about earning a daily living," she added. "That would make you the exception to most of the planet's population."

He tilted his head in acquiescence. "I've been lucky enough to have chosen well how to invest what I earned from my commissions. Both in real estate and the financial markets."

"Most people aren't quite that lucky, Vito."

"I don't mean to overstep, *cara*. I'm simply curious about you."

She sighed. "You're right. I'm sorry. It's just… I did contemplate studying a more creative subject. I particularly liked an introductory art history class I took. I remember poring over the textbook. Particularly the pages on the European Renaissance. Showed it to Grandmama. I think that's when she first realized how much I'd love to see all the magnificent art in Europe."

He'd been right in his assumption. And judging by the longing look on Maya's face as she discussed the class from her student days, she still thought about her choice often.

"What happened?"

She gave a small shrug. "Nothing. That was the last of it. More sensible minds prevailed. The university didn't have a terribly large art department. And I didn't see enough of a future in such a field of study to do anything else about it."

What a shame. Maya seemed to have missed her true calling in life and appeared to have ignored a genuine passion in order to appease more "sensible" minds. And to pay back some sort of debt she felt she owed. To the very people who should have loved her without condition. He knew nothing of her family, but something told him she'd taken on the burden solely on her own volition.

She picked up her fork again with a sudden shake of her head. "That's enough about me. What about you?"

Vito suspected her desire to shift the conversation toward him was less about her curiosity and more of an attempt to change the subject. Maya was clearly uncomfortable discussing her missed opportunities.

He could relate.

"What would you like to know?" Hard to believe he was opening himself up to her questions. But turnabout was fair play, wasn't it? He'd opened this Pandora's box and didn't have the right to shut it when it was her turn.

"Tell me about your family. Leo seems quite charming."

Despite the lighthearted innocence of her words, Vito felt a sudden spear of dislike for his cousin. So Maya found him charming.

"He charmed one of the most beautiful women in Italy into marrying him. Lynetta is too good for him by half."

She smiled at his answer. "Despite your words, I can tell by your voice that you two are close. Your tone holds true affection."

And she'd called him observant.

"What about your parents?"

"They've retired and live in Sweden. I see them once or twice a year."

"Who else?"

Vito couldn't help the smile that creased his lips. "Then there's Nonna."

"Your grandmother?"

He nodded. "Yes. On our paternal side. Leo and I don't see eye to eye on much. But we both agree she's a force of nature." A sudden wish that Maya would be able to meet his grandmother surprised him. He had no doubt the two would get along fabulously. "We're heading out to see her tomorrow, as a matter of fact. A two-day birthday celebration as she turns eighty-five. Though you'd never guess. She's as active and sprightly as a twenty-year-old."

"You're lucky to have such a close family."

Did that mean she didn't feel particularly close to the family who'd adopted her? In her brief discussion of them earlier, she'd mainly referred to her relatives with a sense of gratitude. That had to be a terrible burden to bear as one was growing up.

"Close can often mean meddling and just plain annoying."

"He says again with yet another smile," she quipped, smiling herself. "Meddling and annoying would be worth it, to have such loving people who care for you." The longing in her voice tugged at his chest.

Vito started to reach for her hand across the table but he was interrupted by another server carrying yet more steaming bowls of pasta. Just as well, he thought, leaning back in his chair.

The less he touched Maya Talbot, the better for his well-being.

* * *

"I know I'll never forget this night, Vito," Maya stated by way of conversation an hour after they'd finished their dinner. They were back up on deck. The galleon was on its way back to its port in Venice. She wanted to thank him for accompanying her. But the words didn't seem adequate. Besides, how many times could she thank the man for coming to her rescue in one way or another?

And she could no longer try to ignore the awareness that he evoked within her. The way he'd looked at her during dinner had made her insides quiver. Now, standing next to him in the moonlight in the crisp Venetian air had her senses in overdrive. His closeness sent a shiver down her spine.

Vito mistook her visible shudder for a chill. Without a word, he shrugged off his jacket and draped it over her shoulders. Maya snuggled into the fabric. It smelled of him, that heady mix of sandalwood, mint and man that had been tickling her nose all evening. The scent that had made it difficult to resist the urge to lean into him and inhale of it deeply.

"I'm glad you enjoyed yourself, *cara*."

Cara. She liked it when he used the Italian endearment for her. It would be one of the many things she would miss about him once this fairy-tale evening was over.

For it *was* nearly over.

In fact, her time in Venice and with Vito was coming to an end. The thought that she'd be on her way on the rest of her tour sent a deep sadness through her heart. How was the rest of her trip supposed to compare to what she'd experienced here in this magical city?

For that matter, how was she to return to her bland,

boring reality in a couple of weeks when she arrived back in Boston?

"There's a term the Americans use…" Vito disrupted her thoughts. "I believe it's something along the lines of I'll give you a penny if you tell me what you're thinking."

Maya chuckled. "Close enough, Signor Rameri. I was just thinking of the past few days. And how spectacular they've been."

Hopefully, Vito hadn't caught the small hitch in her voice, the one that came from the knowledge that the end of this magic was near. In many ways, she almost wished she'd never set foot in Venice. Though she'd cherish this time spent with Vito for the rest of her days, her heart would break every time she thought of what she'd had for just a few short days in his company.

To think, all these months she'd thought she'd been in love. It was clear now, she'd simply been going through the motions.

Vito leaned over and pointed toward the city skyline. "Look at how stunning the cathedral is at night, the way it's lit up. Every structure around it serves simply as a backdrop to its splendor."

Hard as she tried, Maya couldn't really focus on the beauty that sat before her in the distance. Vito's shoulder brushed against hers.

She cleared her throat and grasped at some semblance of an appropriate response.

"Our visit to St. Mark's seems so long ago." Despite the truth of her statement, she remembered every detail of the previous afternoon. Including the questions that had been nagging at her. She took a chance on voicing one of those questions. What was there to lose at this stage of the game?

"Our tour guide that day, Angelo…" She paused, summoning some courage at the way Vito stiffened next to her at the mention of the young man. Still, she continued. "He seemed to know a lot about your career."

"I'm an artist in residence in the city. It isn't particularly noteworthy that an art student has heard of me." He shrugged but the gesture didn't quite catch the aura of nonchalance Maya was certain he was trying to project.

There was more to her question, more that she was trying to get at. He had to know it. "Angelo also had some very interesting theories about you. Your potential retirement, in particular."

Vito dropped his head to look down at the water below. "He was just speculating. People around here tend to do that about my career. It's quite irritating."

Maya ignored the insinuation that her own questioning was irritating him, as well. "Was he right?"

"About my retirement?"

Maya nodded, recalling the young man's words. "It seems that he was the only one of his peers who thought you were just in a temporary lull."

"I suppose that makes him right. It's true that I'm having a bit of a dry spell, that's all. I have no intention of rushing past it, however. Nothing is pulling at me enough to make my way back to my workroom."

She could have dropped the matter at that point; his explanation was reasonable enough. On the surface. But in for a penny, in for a pound. "Does your dry spell have anything to do with losing your wife?"

His noticeable cringe made her want to somehow yank the words back into her mouth, to find a way to undo uttering them. She had no right to pick at the scab of his wound this way.

He must miss her terribly; the pain emanating from him made that abundantly clear. If there was a way to somehow take that pain away, to ease his anguish, Maya would have happily provided it.

But she couldn't bring his love back. Nothing could.

"It's been over three years since her accident," Vito said. His voice was surprisingly flat, as if he were spouting some meaningless statistic.

"It takes more than three years to lessen such pain."

He nodded slowly, his gaze still focused on the bright lights of the approaching city.

"Indeed it does. Particularly when the pain is so intricately intertwined with guilt for one's role in causing said pain."

"It's natural to feel some responsibility after a tragedy—"

He cut her off before she could continue. "Oh, but I do bear the responsibility. It's so much more than just a feeling on my part."

Maya's mouth went dry at the implication of his words. Vito made it sound as if he'd had a direct hand in his wife's accident. His hands clenched into tight fists over the railing. "I don't understand."

"It isn't terribly complicated," he answered, his voice rasping and thick. "See, if she hadn't married me, Marina would still be alive and well."

CHAPTER EIGHT

EVEN AFTER THEY'D docked and disembarked, Maya still hadn't quite found her voice. She'd been afraid to say anything after Vito made his stunning declaration. So she'd stayed silent, giving him the time and opportunity to clarify or explain.

So far, he hadn't.

Nor did he seem inclined to do so, Maya noticed, as he helped her step off the boat and onto the wooden boardwalk.

This was all wrong. It was their last night together; their time spent in each other's company couldn't be ending on such a mysterious and loaded note. Maya placed a gentle hand on his arm as they approached the center of the square. Even under the current circumstance, the heat of his skin under his silk shirt caused a warm sensation to travel up her arm. Maya still wore his tuxedo jacket.

"Vito, I'd really like to talk."

He rubbed a hand down his face. "About what I said on the boat regarding my wife's accident."

She nodded, but they didn't get a chance to continue the conversation. A female voice suddenly called through the night air.

"Vito!"

Maya turned to see a tall, statuesque woman in a flowing white lace spring dress approaching the two of them, her arms outstretched and a wide smile gracing her strikingly pretty face. Hard on her heels was Leo. For his part, Vito's cousin seemed quite surprised to see them.

Vito's quiet groan wasn't low enough that she didn't hear it. He was far from thrilled to see these two.

The other couple reached them seconds later. The lady threw her arms around Vito's neck and he returned her embrace with one of his own. There was no hint of flirtation or attraction. Simply genuine affection.

This had to be Leo's wife.

"What a surprise to see you here, cousin." Leo spoke in English. "And with Maya by your side." He eyed the two of them up and down.

"A bit dressed up, aren't you?"

Lynetta didn't let them answer. "This must be the lovely American lady Leo's been telling me about." She jabbed her husband playfully in the ribs. "You didn't mention how pretty she was."

Coming from someone who looked the way she did, that was quite the compliment.

"Very glad to meet you," Maya said, extending her hand. But Lynetta ignored it. Instead, she threw her arms around Maya's shoulders and planted a kiss on each cheek.

"I'm so happy we ran into you before you left our beautiful city." Lynetta's accent, though subtle, lent another layer of charisma to her ample charm.

She crooked her hand through Maya's arm. "Come, let's walk a bit."

Maya cast a hesitant glance in Vito's direction. His cousin still had his full attention. They were discussing something in Italian. Leo was quite animated. She could have sworn she heard her name thrown about at least twice.

Lynetta led them farther toward the square. By the time the men had caught up to them, Maya had heard all about the couple's two toddler sons and how she and her husband had managed to sneak out for a quick drink thanks to the teenager who babysat for them occasionally.

"We can't make it too late a night, however," Lynetta now added. "We are traveling early tomorrow to Verona. To celebrate Vito and Leo's grandmother's birthday."

"Yes, Vito mentioned that earlier this evening. Please wish your grandmother a happy eighty-fifth. I hope she has a lovely time with her family."

"What have you got planned for tomorrow, dear?" Lynetta asked. "Any excursions through our beautiful city?"

Maya shook her head. "It happens to be a free day. Nothing on the agenda. I think I'll take the time to just relax in my hotel room. Or maybe do a walking tour."

Lynetta blinked at her. "By yourself?"

Maya had to laugh at her tone. She sounded as if Maya would be walking across that prisoners' bridge by the palazzo on her way to a cell rather than strolling through the beautiful streets of Venice.

"I'm sure I'll find plenty to do."

The other woman stopped pacing. "Tell me, Maya. Do you have plans to visit Verona?"

Maya shook her head. "It isn't one of the destinations on this trip. From here, I'm off to Florence. Then Rome."

Lynetta clasped her hands in front of her chest. "That settles it, then. You must come with us."

Maya sensed more than heard Vito's sharp intake of breath behind them. "Lynetta!"

The other woman whirled to face him, bit something out in Italian. Then added in English, "And don't you dare take that tone of voice with me. It was rude of you not to invite her yourself."

Maya held out a hand to interject. "Please. I don't want to intrude where I don't belong."

It was her turn to face Lynetta's harsh glare. "Are you turning down my invitation? To an old lady's birthday gathering?"

Maya found she couldn't find the words to reply. The way Lynetta posed the question, she sounded like Maya was committing a dire faux pas by declining. Never mind that Vito stood slack-jawed, watching this unexpected development unfold without saying a thing. If he'd wanted her at his grandmother's birthday, he would have invited her himself.

Not that she'd even wanted the invitation. Had she?

Maya felt a flush of embarrassment and confusion creep up on her cheeks. The whole situation had somehow gotten out of hand. It didn't help matters that Leo was chuckling softly as he watched the three of them.

"But I couldn't possibly intrude that way," Maya repeated, stumbling over the words. "I'm sure the travel has all been prearranged and everyone's tickets already purchased."

Lynetta's glare softened. "Don't be silly, dear. It's not an intrusion. Nonna would love to have you there. She loves America and would quite enjoy an American visitor. As for as any type of ticket, we'll be traveling on Vito's private aircraft."

So much for any kind of practical excuse. Vito suddenly stepped in front of her.

"Please excuse my cousin-in-law's domineering attitude, Maya. She can't help herself."

From behind him, Lynetta gave Vito a firm swat on his upper arm. He ignored her. "Additionally, I would love it if you'd accompany the three of us, along with my two nephews, to Nonna's birthday celebration in Verona."

Maya wasn't going to delude herself. Vito clearly felt obliged to extend the invitation. He must have felt like he had no choice after what Lynetta had started. Maya knew his motives for offering the invite had nothing to do with wanting to spend time with her. Lynetta had simply forced his hand.

So why was she so tempted to accept it?

"Well, it's settled, then," his meddlesome cousin-in-law stated with finality before Maya had even had a chance to respond. "Let's celebrate with some gelato in the square, shall we?" Lynetta continued. "Vito, as usual, you'll be buying."

He let the two women walk ahead once more but stopped Leo before he could move. "What the hell has your wife just done?"

Leo actually laughed. Why was Vito surprised? Why had he even expected some hint of sympathy from the other man?

"Why, I believe she's just done you a favor. And now you can thank her with some chocolate gelato."

Vito tilted his head back and took a deep breath to calm down. "Is that really how you see this disastrous development?"

Leo squinted at him. "Why not? You're actually out with her right now. You two have clearly just enjoyed some kind of date. Taking her to Nonna's would simply be an extension, wouldn't it?"

"We weren't on any kind of date, Leo."

Leo eyed Vito's pressed tuxedo pants and the white silk shirt he wore adorned with gold cufflinks. "You could have fooled me."

"She had reservations on a galleon dinner cruise. She was clearly not relishing the thought of attending it alone. I didn't want her to have to miss out on the joy of something like that because of her worthless ex-fiancé's actions."

Leo studied him a beat. "And?"

"And that's the only reason we were out together."

"Right. So you asked her out on a date. You just lucked out that it was already paid for. Got it."

That was it. Vito gave up. Why was he even trying? He followed Leo to where the women stood ordering gelatos.

Vito understood that both Lynetta and Leo had good intentions. They wanted him to move on with his life. They wanted for him what they themselves had: a strong union, beautiful children, a happy homelife. For an insane moment, he let himself indulge in just such a fantasy as he watched Maya walking ahead of him. He pictured the two of them putting a couple of rambunctious toddlers to sleep then slipping out to spend some alone time together.

Then he made himself shake the images away. Things like family and a home full of children simply weren't in the cards for him. Marina had told him repeatedly that he didn't have the capability to fully love someone. That he was too consumed with his art, his craft. To the detriment of everything else that was important. He'd denied it right up until the point when he'd proven her right.

When he reached her side, Maya gave him a hesitant look. If things had been awkward between them before, they were downright uncomfortable now.

Maybe she would find a way to wriggle out of the invitation to visit Nonna. It wasn't like she'd have to face Lynetta if she blew them all off. Once she left Venice, she'd never see either of his cousins again.

He wasn't the slightest bit surprised that the notion of her bailing on them sent a bolt of disappointment through his chest.

"Maya mentioned you two had already had tiramisu," Lynette informed them. "So we only got the two cones. We can all share."

Right. Somehow he was supposed to watch Maya lick an ice cream cone then share that same cone with her. His body tightened in response to the image.

"She's…uh…something else," Maya said on a near whisper, handing him the cone.

"It's all yours. And, yes, my cousin's wife is certainly one of a kind."

"Great. Even more calories." He had to look away when she took the first lick. How the hell was he supposed to spend a whole day with her in Verona?

"There'll be more tomorrow. There's never a shortage of food at Nonna's place, even under normal circumstances. Let alone any kind of celebratory event like a birthday."

Maya swallowed the bit of gelato. "So it's real, then? I'll be going to Verona with you."

"That's totally up to you, *cara*. You might have to deal with Lynetta's displeasure, however, if you back out."

She gave an exaggerated shudder. "Why does that prospect frighten me so?" She glanced to where the other couple stood taking turns with their own cone. "They both care deeply for you."

"I suppose that would be one way to describe their heavy-handedness."

Maya looked down toward her toes. "Listen, Vito. I know Lynetta sort of finagled this whole invitation. I will find a way to back out of it and face her wrath if I have to."

"Is that what you want?"

"I guess I'm asking what it is that you want."

Now that was essentially the question, wasn't it? The question he hadn't been able to make himself face. Until now. She was due to leave Venice at the end of the week. After that, he might never lay eyes on her again. The thought was increasingly causing him an unwelcome sensation of pain he didn't want to acknowledge. So he decided to tell her the truth.

"I want very much for you to come with me and my family to Verona, *cara*. I'd be honored if you would join us."

What had she gotten herself into?

Maya plopped down fully clothed on the bed as soon as she'd shut her hotel room door behind her. Vito had walked her over to the lobby, then he had bid her a hasty good-night, stressing that they both needed to rest before the big day tomorrow.

She'd expected to be knee-deep in tissues right now, and wondering about what might have been after having bid a final goodbye to Vito. Instead, she was wondering what she should wear tomorrow and how much she should pack. What exactly did one wear to an Italian grandmother's eighty-fifth birthday?

If someone had told her three days ago she'd be pondering that question, she would have pegged them as delusional. She wasn't sure how to feel about this new development. On the one hand, she was thrilled to be able to spend more time with Vito; the moments spent in his company had been some of the most fun-filled of her days so far. On the other hand, she wasn't sure if her heart could handle it. The longer their goodbye was delayed, the harder it was going to be on her emotions.

She was falling for him. Any outside observer would say she was no doubt rebounding, that it had been way too short a time since meeting Vito to have developed any kind of real feelings for him.

They'd be wrong. She knew the truth. As did her heart.

Meeting Vito had made her realize that she hadn't been in love with Matt so much as she had loved the idea of being in love. The idea of having a husband. A future and a family. One she could finally call her own. Not one she'd been forced into.

Now, in contrast, she could tell that she and Matt had never been right for each other. And they never would be.

Her tablet dinged across the room signaling a text. It was her cousin Zelda.

Maya. If you get this text please check your email. Can't get a hold of you.

Maya cringed at the message. She'd been woefully negligent in letting her family know her whereabouts after the loss of her phone. The truth was, she'd been putting off telling them the truth about Matt. A truth she couldn't put off any longer, however.

With a resigned sigh, she walked over and powered up the tablet then tapped the mail icon.

Sure enough, a slew of new messages sat in her inbox. Most of them from Zelda.

Why haven't you called or emailed? We're all worried about you. Matt still in Boston. Says we should ask you for answers. What's going on?!?!

Her other emails were essentially different versions of the same message. Maya tapped the Reply button and began to type on the screen keyboard.

Zelda, sorry to have worried you and everyone else. The truth is I haven't been completely honest with you. Things aren't exactly going well between Matt and me right now. It's why I traveled here alone for the time being.

She'd barely hit the Send button when Zelda's response popped up on her screen.

I knew it! What did he do? I'll strangle him. Better yet, I'll tell Dad. He'll do worse. You better call me, Maya Papaya. As soon as you can. I mean it!

Maya felt her eyes well up, touched by Zelda's immediate and automatic loyalty in response to her announcement. She and her cousins had had their share of differences and arguments; they'd grown up as sisters, after all. And sisters tended to argue.

But deep down, she knew they would both battle the

devil himself for her if they had to. Same with her aunt and uncle.

Despite their loyalty and all their love throughout the years, Maya had never quite been able to feel a sense of true belonging. It was nothing overt that her family did to make her feel that way, it was more in the subtle nuances of family dynamics.

That feeling was probably the reason she'd been too hasty in trying to form a family of her own. Committing to a man who was so blatantly wrong for her.

Maya began replying to Zelda's latest email.

No need for strangulation. Matt and I not right for each other. Please don't say anything to Grandmama. She gave so much so that I could enjoy this trip.

Zelda's second response came as quickly as the first.

I won't say anything to Grandmama Fran. Double pinkie swear. But I can tell there are things you're not telling me. Spill!

Maya had to smile at the reference to the sworn declarations they'd made as children, hooking their little fingers to seal any and all deals. She began to type.

I'll call as soon as I can. I promise. Damaged my phone and still trying to work out use of Italian burner. No need to worry. All is well. Just figuring things out right now. Talk soon. Xoxo

With that, she powered down the tablet and stuck it inside her carry-on bag. As much as she loved Zelda and the rest of her family, she didn't have it in her to continue communicating with anyone right now. Not even via dueling emails.

She felt utterly and completely spent after the day of roller-coaster emotions she'd just spent with Vito. No doubt spending a full day with him tomorrow would prove just as perplexing. Plus, the rest of his family would be there to observe and note every move she made. Would she be able to hide her growing feelings for one of their own?

But there was a bigger question that needed to be addressed. How in the world was she supposed to handle those feelings once this fairy tale inevitably ended?

"You did what?" Vito couldn't believe the nonsense Leo was spouting. They'd just disembarked from the jet at Villafranca Airport and were in the process of entering the spacious van that would take them to the Rameri family estate in Verona. And Leo had waited all this time, through about an hour of travel, to mention that he'd told their *nonna* a colossal lie.

"She would have jumped to the conclusion anyway," he explained now, not even slightly contrite for what he'd done. "You know how she is."

Vito had pulled his cousin to the side as Maya and Lynetta handed their luggage to the waiting driver and wrangled the two toddlers into their car seats in the back of the vehicle.

"Did it even occur to you that this might embarrass Maya?"

Leo gave a careless shrug. "I think she'll go along with it. She seems like a flexible sort."

"But what were you thinking, Leo?" Vito demanded

to know. "Why would you tell Nonna that I've asked Maya to marry me?"

Leo placed a hand on Vito's shoulder. "She's worried about you. She thinks you've been wallowing in your grief too long." Leo paused then to give him a pointed look. Clearly, he thought the same way Nonna did on that particular topic. Finally, he continued. "When I called to tell her you'd be bringing a guest, she automatically jumped to the most hopeful conclusion. I didn't have the heart to correct her. She's not getting any younger, you know. It's just a small fib to make an old woman happy for a few days. On her birthday."

"So we're supposed to act like a newly engaged couple around her, is that what you're suggesting?"

"I think you can pull it off. You were doing a pretty good job of it when Lynetta and I came upon the two of you at San Marco."

Vito wasn't going to justify that with any kind of response.

"And what about afterward? When she calls to check on me in a few days and I have no fiancée to speak of? When the woman in question has traveled to a different country?"

Leo gave his shoulder a squeeze. "Then she will have had a few days of hopefulness, won't she?"

"All based on a lie."

"Is it?"

Vito had to give his head a shake. "What do you mean? Of course it's a lie to say that Maya and I are engaged."

His cousin waved his hand in dismissal, as if Vito was missing the point entirely. "Yes, yes. We both know you're not really engaged."

"So that would be a lie. You have lied to Nonna."

"I told her a small fib. And there's something you're not considering."

"What would that be? Please enlighten me, dear cousin."

"Maya doesn't have to be thousands of miles away in a few days. You can simply ask her not to leave."

Leo didn't give him a chance to respond before turning to join the women in the car, leaving Vito to watch his retreating back.

Had his cousin always been so invested in Vito's personal life? What was possessing him to behave so intrusively lately?

His gaze was drawn to where Maya sat in the car. He would have to find a way to explain to her what Leo had done and the resulting chaos that might ensue as a result. Heaven help him find the words to do so. Now she was playing some kind of peek-a-boo game with his older nephew, who was buckled into his seat. The child was squealing with laughter at her antics.

It appeared Maya Talbot had some kind of effect on all manner of Rameri males.

Vito was exceptionally quiet during the ride from the airport. Maya slid another glance in his direction where he sat next to her in the third row of the passenger van. The children had finally calmed enough to settle down and one of them looked on the verge of falling asleep.

By contrast, Vito looked about as far from relaxed as one about to attend a grand party should be.

Was he having second thoughts about having her here? She ought to have thought this through. His invitation had ultimately seemed sincere enough but she couldn't pretend he hadn't been pushed into it by his cousin's wife. He'd probably considered it overnight and regretted asking her. This was to be a family affair, after all. She certainly wasn't family. She was barely more than an acquaintance.

But his reaction to her last night had said otherwise. Her mind drifted to the kiss they'd shared during their cruise. It seemed a lifetime ago. But she hadn't forgotten the way the touch of his lips against hers had made her insides quiver like gelatin.

As much as she hated to admit it, given what it might say about her decision-making abilities, she couldn't recall Matt's kisses having as dramatic an effect on her. And she'd been ready to marry him.

Was she making a different version of the same mistake? Because something clearly wasn't right, judging by Vito's scowl.

Either one of her cousins would be skeptical if she tried to tell them that she was falling for a man she'd met days ago. They'd tell her she was rebounding, that she couldn't see clearly from the hurt. Her aunt and uncle would agree. Perhaps she'd moved too fast. Maybe the kiss on the ship meant nothing to Vito. She might have read too much into it. It obviously wouldn't be the first time she'd misread a man or his intentions.

The questions rambled around in her brain. Questions she could only guess the answers to. She'd never been in a situation like this before. Then again, she'd never met a man like Vito before.

He was charming and enigmatic, without doubt. But his sadness practically resonated in the air around him.

She shouldn't be foolish enough to think she could

possibly be the one who might be able to take that sadness away, not even temporarily.

Vito spent most of the ride from Verona airport to the villa trying to decide how he might explain to Maya what Leo had done. They were less than a mile from the mansion and he still hadn't quite figured it out.

Well, he had to think of something. He couldn't let her be ambushed without a clue when she first met Nonna. He could guess pretty well what Nonna's reaction would be when they were introduced. She'd probably hug the younger woman within an inch of her life. Then she'd start referring to Maya as her future granddaughter to anyone within earshot. Maya had to be prepared for all of it.

In any case, right now she looked like she was ready to be out of the car. The road was full of curves and bends, the driver not exactly the smoothest operator he'd been driven by. Judging by the greenish hue of her complexion at the moment and the way she kept clasping her hand right below her breastbone, he figured she might have had enough of the car ride.

He turned to her. "Would you mind if we walked the rest of the way? I'd love to show you the vineyards."

Maya seemed to be taken by surprise but she soon nodded and began to gather her sweater around her. In Italian, Vito instructed the driver to stop so that the two of them could get out.

"Please let Nonna know we will be there shortly. Tell her we wanted to get some air after a long morning of travel and that I wanted show Maya the countryside." He addressed Lynetta with the request, his annoyance with Leo still too close to the surface.

"*Sì*, Vito."

Maya turned to him after the vehicle dropped them off and drove away. "Was my car sickness that obvious?"

"It was. But there's another reason I wanted us to walk together for a bit."

"There is?"

He took her gently by the elbow and they started to stroll on the grassy verge by the side of the road. "I'm afraid there's something you need to know before we greet my grandmother. You may not like it."

Hadn't he said those exact words to her that first day at his studio?

"Wow. That sounds pretty serious," she commented.

There really was no easy way to break it to her. Better to just blurt it out. He inhaled deeply. "See, the thing is, my grandmother is under the impression there's more between us then there really is."

She blinked at him. "I beg your pardon? I don't quite understand."

Vito rubbed a weary hand down his face. How had he found himself in such a messy predicament? It was as if he had no idea what direction his life was headed in at any given moment.

Without giving himself too much time to think, he gave Maya the basic rundown of what Leo had done and why. She appeared a bit shell-shocked once he was done. *Welcome to the club*, he wanted to tell her.

They'd reached the sprawling vines that abutted the estate gardens. The aromatic scent of grapes permeated the air. Vito reached for a ripe bunch and held it out to her. She still hadn't said a word about what he'd just told her.

Maya took the fruit from him and popped one of the

grapes into her mouth. She seemed to savor the taste as she chewed and swallowed. A sudden unwanted desire to feed her one himself made his palm itch. His gaze fell to her mouth. He could still taste those lips of hers on his own, feel their lush fullness. Vito had to remind himself to focus on the matter at hand.

"So, am I supposed to act as if you and I are betrothed?" she asked.

"I know it's ridiculous. You have to believe I had nothing to do with it."

"Oh, I have no doubt you had nothing to do with any of it, Vito."

He could have sworn her tone held a hint of disappointment when she spoke the words. Which made zero sense. He had to have imagined it.

"I'm not sure how I feel about deceiving an unsuspecting grandmother, to be honest."

"This is the type of untruth that's meant solely to give her some pleasure on a milestone day." Truth be told, he hadn't exactly been looking forward to spending the entire time fielding questions about whether he was ready to move on with his life. Not to mention hearing about all the eligible young granddaughters of her friends that Nonna always wanted him to meet. At the least, it would be a refreshing change to spend some time at his estate with the entire family and not have to duck unwelcome suggestions about all the women his family wanted to introduce him to. Of course, this way he and Maya would have to find ways to answer all sorts of questions about how they'd met and fallen in love.

Surprisingly, he didn't think that would take much effort. They could even stick mostly to the truth.

Still, he had to make sure Maya was completely certain that she was up for what he was proposing. "It's only for the afternoon. I understand if you want no part of it." Heaven knew he couldn't blame her for that. "I'll work something out if you're not comfortable."

"It's okay. I'll do it."

Vito released the breath he didn't realize he'd been holding. "You will?"

She slowly pulled another grape off the bunch she held and ate it before she answered. "Sure. Why not? It's your grandmother's birthday, after all. And I find myself attending without a gift. This one small fib seems harmless enough. If it will make her happy on such a momentous day, then I'm happy to do it."

"Grazie, mia bella," Vito said, planting a small peck of a kiss on her cheek. When he straightened, he couldn't help where his thoughts drifted. For one insane moment, he wished with all his heart that the pretense wasn't even necessary. That it might all somehow be real.

CHAPTER NINE

WHAT HAD SHE just agreed to? To think, when he'd asked her to walk with him, she'd initially thought it was because he wanted to spend time alone with her before the chaos began. As if.

Still, Maya hadn't quite been prepared for what he'd just announced. In fact, she was woefully unprepared for this whole day. How was she supposed to spend the entire time by Vito's side, ignoring the way he affected her? How would she clamp down on the arousal he fanned deep within her core? Now there was the added complication of having to pretend they were lovers.

Not that she hadn't imagined just such a thing. Though, in her imaginings, there hadn't been a need for pretense.

"I suppose we ought to get some sort of basic story in order. At the least, we should be consistent about what we tell everyone. Lynetta and Leo will have to play along, of course."

"It's probably wise to stick as close to the truth as possible."

"I would agree."

"We could tell them I fell when I first saw you. Quite literally. And you fell in a much more poetic, figurative sense." See, she could be good at this. Not bad for an off-the-cuff suggestion.

Vito chuckled beside her. "I like it, *cara*. Though maybe we should be sparse with the details."

"Like how tipsy I was?"

"More that you had just freed yourself of one fiancé."

What an apt description. She hadn't known it at the time, but Matt had, in fact, freed her. From a mistake that would have followed her for a lifetime. She had to wonder if Matt had simply seen the inevitable: that they both deserved more out of life than what they'd been settling for. She might actually owe Matt a thank-you if one were to truly examine it. That thought would have had her quaking in shock a few short days ago.

"Yes, let's definitely omit that little tidbit," she said as they walked farther along. Once they crested the hill, the house came into full view.

Maya had to do a double take. She wasn't sure what she'd been expecting, but it was certainly a bit more modest than this three-story structure with Ionic columns surrounded by rolling hills.

"That's your grandmother's house?"

"Yes. More accurately, it's the family estate. Leo and Lynetta come here often with the boys. As do I. It's a short enough trip from Venice."

"It's quite the mansion."

"Do you like it?"

What was there not to like? "It looks like something out of a painting. A sprawling house and the lush greenery as the backdrop."

Vito placed both hands on his hips and studied the house in the distance. "Huh, I guess you're right."

She gave him a playful shove on the arm. "You're toy-ing with me. Of course you must have seen it yourself. Accomplished artist that you are."

He shrugged. "I guess I just always viewed it more as home."

Once they drew closer, Maya could see the festive decorations. The house looked every bit ready for a birthday bash. Decorative balloons adorned the windows. Colorful streamers had been wrapped around the columns. Lively music could be heard coming from somewhere within.

Without warning, a large mound of fur came flying at them from the direction of the house.

"Romeo!" Vito shouted, then he roared with laughter as the ball of fur reached him and jumped up. He spoke affectionately in Italian as he gave the dog a thorough petting.

"This is Romeo," he told her. "He's a very good *mimmo*."

Maya leaned down to greet the dog. He responded with a wet lick on her cheek.

"He likes you," Vito declared. "Juliet should be around here somewhere."

Maya straightened. "You have two dogs that are named Romeo and Juliet?"

He gave her a playful smile. "We are in Verona, after all."

Of course. That made sense.

"There's a surprise twist," Vito added in a mock whisper, cupping his hand against his mouth as he spoke.

"What's that?"

"They're both boys."

"Hmm. That is surprising, indeed. I did not see that coming."

Vito nodded solemnly, rousing a gurgle of laughter from her. "When you meet Juliet, please do not inform him that he is the namesake of one of fiction's most notable heroines."

"Why not?" Maya asked. "For all you know, he might find it an honor."

Vito rubbed his chin, contemplating this possibility. "Huh. Never thought of it that way."

She winked at him and popped another one of the luscious grapes into her mouth from the bunch she still carried. It exploded in her mouth, a mini ball of flavor.

Vito's expression suddenly hardened and turned serious as he watched her. His eyes grew dark. *Heaven help me.* She thought she read desire in their depths.

He stepped toward her, his hand reaching for her face. Maya's breath caught in her chest as he rubbed his thumb over her bottom lip.

"Not all of the juice from your last grape made it into your mouth, *cara.*" His voice was thick and raw.

Maya turned her face into his palm. Tremors ran over the surface of her skin. The slightest touch from this man had the most dramatic effect on her. She longed for more; she wanted him to kiss her once again. Without thinking, she tilted her chin up, ran her hand along his forearm.

"Mia bella," Vito whispered, so close now that the heat of his breath danced over her cheek. Then she lost any sense of focus whatsoever as his lips touched hers.

A sudden commotion from behind her had her startled and stepping out his grasp. Maya turned to find a rotund older woman emerging from the house then heading in their direction. She had to be Vito's grandmother.

Of course, Maya thought as the older woman approached them with her arms outstretched and a wide grin on her face. Vito must have known his Nonna was watching this whole time.

Their kiss had been nothing more than a show for her sake.

CHAPTER TEN

"I BROUGHT YOU a plate."

Maya looked up to find Lynetta standing before her where she sat on one of the porch rocking chairs. The last hour had gone by in a dizzying haze. She'd been introduced to so many people, and Nonna had kept finding her to affectionately pat her on the cheek at regular intervals. So far, the charade was going off without a hitch. But Maya found herself exhausted and in need of a break.

"I hope I'm not intruding on a private moment," Lynetta added. Maya reached up to help her with her load. In addition to a large tray piled with food, she was carrying two bottles of iced tea. Maya relieved her of the beverages; the tray looked much too precariously balanced to attempt to take it.

"No. You're not. I just needed a quiet moment. You Rameris are a boisterous lot."

Lynetta sat down on the matching rocking chair next to her and placed the tray on the little table between them.

"This was very nice of you," she told Lynetta, enjoying a long swallow of the iced tea. She hadn't realized how dry her throat had become after holding so many language-challenged conversations.

And now that she was presented with a loaded antipasto tray, her stomach reminded her with a low growl that she was hungry, as well.

"You're welcome. Though you might not be thanking me once dinner is served and you're already full," Lynetta answered with a smile. "It's never a good idea to munch before Nonna's big dinners. But the side table full of artisan cheese, cured meat and pickled olives looked too good to ignore."

"So I see. Did you happen to leave anything on the table for the rest of them?"

Lynetta bit into a crusty piece of bread and Maya followed suit. The morsel tasted fresh out of the oven and practically melted in her mouth.

"Trust me, there's more than enough for every man, woman and child here."

"As well as some aptly named canines?" Maya jokingly asked.

"Yes, them too," Lynetta replied.

"Nothing like massive quantities of Italian food to ensure everyone's happiness."

Lynetta's expression suddenly turned much more serious as she stared at the rows of vines in the distance. "Actually, this is the happiest we've seen Vito in quite some time. The last few years, when we've all gathered for one reason or another, he just appeared to be going through the motions. As if he couldn't wait to get the day over with and return to the dark depths of his studio."

Maya's heart tugged at that depiction. From what Lynetta was saying, Vito hadn't even found comfort and joy surrounded by so many of his loved ones.

"I'm so sorry to hear that. He deserves much more in his life."

Lynetta nodded in agreement. "He certainly does.

That's why we're all very happy that he seems to be turning the tide somewhat. Leo swears the change started right when he met you."

Maya's pulse quickened at the implication. "I'm not sure what to say to that, Lynetta," she responded honestly. "Only that Vito maybe needed a temporary diversion in the form of a distracted, clumsy American tourist. One who is set to leave Venice in a few days."

The other woman turned to her with one elegantly shaped dark eyebrow lifted. "You appear to be much more than a mere diversion, Maya."

Maya suddenly found it hard to swallow the small cube of provolone she'd popped into her mouth. What Lynetta thought she saw between Maya and Vito wasn't necessarily real.

She found herself admitting out loud the concern she'd been harboring all this time and had been too chicken to address. "I think the temporary nature of my presence might be what's drawing him, Lynetta." She hated the needy quality that dripped from her voice as she spoke the words, though she felt a profound sense of relief at being able to finally share her fear with an interested party. She took a deep breath and made herself continue. "I think the fact that I'll be leaving in a few days and out of his life after that makes me a safe bet as a distraction." Maya bit back the sob that had lodged itself in the back of her throat.

"Is that what you really think?"

"He hasn't mentioned anything about staying in touch afterward. Aside from promising to mail out the sketch he drew of me that first day, he makes no indication that we'll be in touch at all."

"Have you mentioned doing so?"

Maya looked down at her toes. "I don't want to push a man who isn't ready. Not with what little I can offer."

Lynetta didn't tear her gaze from the rolling hills in the distance. "I see," she offered simply.

Maya felt compelled to continue. It felt good to be able to get this off her chest, to talk to someone who seemed to care about Vito. And who might have a care or two about the new American she'd just met, as well. "He's been through a lot. I know he needs time to grieve. And to heal."

"I don't disagree." Lynetta kicked off her sandals and slowly rocked her chair. "But at some point, he needs to start."

At Maya's silence, the other woman continued. "Until you came along, he hadn't showed any signs of beginning that process."

A bud of pleasure blossomed in her chest at Lynetta's words. It was quickly followed by a profound sense of sadness. Even if everything Lynetta said was the absolute truth, it hardly made a difference. She and Vito had separate lives thousands of miles away from each other.

No matter what was happening between them, they would always be worlds apart.

"Vito takes too much of the blame upon himself," Lynetta stated several moments later after a contemplative silence had settled between the two women. Her comment didn't take Maya by surprise at all. Not after what Vito had said during their time on the galleon. The sounds of laughter and music could be heard echoing from the house behind them. An occasional child's shriek and the bark of a dog punctuated the background noise.

"He alluded as much to me," Maya answered. "But

then he seemed uninterested in talking about it further. I didn't want to push."

"Vito never wants to talk about the accident. Not that I can blame him. I do blame him for trying to take full responsibility for it, however. It's dreadfully unfair."

"Is there a reason he does so?"

"He believes there is. Has he told you much about Marina?"

Maya shook her head and took another sip of her drink. "Nothing, really. He must have loved her very much."

"Mmm-hmm. They were both very much in love." She paused briefly. "In the beginning."

The pause was not lost on Maya. "Did something happen?"

"Yes. And no."

Well, that certainly clears it up, Maya thought sarcastically. She waited for Lynetta to elaborate.

"Marina was an…interesting type of woman. So passionate about everything. Sometimes her passion was too much for one man to deal with. Even a man as capable and as willing as Vito."

Maya was trying desperately not to take the things Lynetta was telling her to heart. It was difficult to sit there and listen to someone talk about Vito's love and life with a different woman. A woman he clearly still pined for.

"When they first met, Vito created some beautiful sculptures. Even more noteworthy than what he'd done before. His career was already on its way. But suddenly it took off. She truly inspired him."

So, he'd lost his muse as well as his wife. Was it any wonder he was having trouble moving on? Not that it was any kind of competition, especially considering the poor woman had passed in such a tragic manner. But if it were, how could Maya possibly compete with someone who'd shared Vito's bed *and* provided him with creative impetus?

Lynetta continued. "But Vito is a true creative. He was constantly growing. Constantly expanding the scope of his work. Eventually, Marina became less of a factor in his creations. That's when the trouble began."

"Trouble?"

It hadn't occurred to Maya that Vito and his wife had been anything less than blissfully happy. Why else would he be so hard on himself about losing her? She didn't know the details and couldn't bring herself to ask him. But she'd assumed that he was plagued with guilt about not being able to protect the woman he loved.

"He never spoke to us about any of it. He would never have betrayed her privacy that way." Lynetta stopped her rocking. "But we witnessed enough of the arguments firsthand. And the way she lashed out after each one."

"She…lashed out?"

"Oh, yes. In phenomenally dramatic fashion. Sometimes in public. Several times in front of Vito's family and friends."

Maya didn't want to think about what that would have done to a man like Vito. He seemed so private, so proud. Having witnesses to the failings of his marriage must have been a terribly difficult burden. No one should be subjected to such a public display of their relationship troubles.

Maya shuddered at the prospect. She dreaded the moment when she had to finally confide to her family about her breakup with Matt. Bad enough that she would have to tell them about it. She didn't want to think about how it would feel to have had them witness it firsthand.

"Nothing Vito did was enough," Lynetta went on. "Marina wanted his complete attention. When she didn't get it…"

Lynetta didn't finish her sentence. Suddenly, she performed the sign of the cross and closed her eyes tightly. Maya could hear the quick prayer she uttered in Italian.

"Forgive me for speaking ill of the deceased," Lynetta said, opening her eyes again. "I just felt you should know the basic facts about Vito's past. It's only fair to you, given how close you and Vito have become in such a short time."

The questions rambled through Maya's brain. What had led to Marina's fatal accident? Why exactly did Vito think he was directly to blame for it?

Would he ever trust her enough to confide in her about any of it?

Lynetta stood then, lifted the tray of half-eaten food and walked to the front door. "I should go check on the boys. Excuse me."

But Maya had so many other questions; Lynetta couldn't just leave after all she'd revealed. "Lynetta, wait. Please, I'd just like to know—"

But the other woman didn't let her finish. "I'm sorry. I really am. But I've said more than enough. The rest he will have to tell you himself."

"There you are."

Maya wasn't sure how long she'd sat there after Lynetta left. When Vito found her, she was still deep in thought and dusk had settled across the horizon.

"I was just admiring the view."

"If you think that view is special, wait until you see what's in store next." He held out a hand to her. "Come on. Let's go."

"Where are we going?"

He'd already taken her wrist and pulled her up. They walked to the side of the house and down the porch steps. Parked around the corner were three golf carts.

"You still haven't told me where we're going," she reminded Vito as he led her to one of the carts and had her climb in. Leo and Lynetta noisily burst through the side door and commandeered the cart behind them. They were followed by two other couples she'd been introduced to upon arrival though she couldn't quite recall any names. Soon they were driving past the house and into the fields.

"Am I the only one who doesn't know what's going on?"

"You'll see, *cara*. I think you'll like it."

Maya studied his profile as he drove. His hair ruffled in the wind as he picked up speed. A deep smile creased his lips. He had his shirtsleeves rolled up and the top buttons of his shirt undone. The man could carry off any look, like a male magazine cover model. He was just as strikingly handsome dressed in a casual shirt and khakis as he had been in a tailored tuxedo.

She recalled Lynetta's words. In all fairness to Marina, she could see how a man like him would elicit strong and passionate emotions from the woman he loved. But what Lynetta had described sounded toxic.

Maya didn't get a chance to further explore that thought. When they cleared a large hill, she got a glimpse of what all the activity was about. In front of them sat three large hot air balloons.

Maya couldn't hold back her shriek of delight. "Oh, my!"

"Surprised?"

"Thrilled!"

A bolt of excitement shot down her spine. Vito came to a stop about a yard away from the balloons. Seconds later, Leo parked next to them.

Maya jumped out of the cart and took in the sight of the towering, colorful balloons. She'd never been in one before. To have her first ride happen in Italy was almost too good to be true. To think, in a few short moments, she'd be gliding through the air over some of Europe's most majestic sights.

And Vito would be by her side.

She couldn't help it. The excitement was too much. She turned and threw her arms around his neck. His reaction was immediate. His hands gripped her waist and he pulled her closer. Then he dropped a small kiss on her lips.

"I like knowing I've pleased you," he whispered against her ear, his breath hot against her cheek.

Good thing he was holding on to her. Her knees almost buckled.

"Let's go, you two." Leo's voice sounded from behind them. "You can do all your embracing after we ride." Lynetta was hard on her husband's heels. She seemed at least as excited as Maya.

"Shall we go, then?" Vito asked but made no move to release her.

Maya reluctantly pulled herself out of Vito's arms. He kept his hand at the small of her back as he led her to the balloon in the middle. The pilot greeted them with a wide smile and helped her in.

Within moments, they'd lifted off. The breath left

her lungs as they rose higher and higher. The thrill of it was exhilarating. She realized she was laughing out loud with delight.

Once they reached altitude, Vito came to stand behind her. He wrapped his arms around her middle, her back snug up against his chest.

"I don't have the words to describe what I'm feeling right now," she said over the noise of the burner that heated the air inside the balloon. To think, she'd almost spent the day back at her hotel, wallowing alone and missing Vito with all her being.

A small voice nagged at the back of her mind that Leo had been the one to initiate her presence here. Not Vito. She pushed the thought aside. All that mattered was that she was here. With Vito holding her as she enjoyed the experience of a lifetime.

In the distance, they could see the river Adige meandering through the city and out into the countryside.

"Turns out it's the perfect evening for it, *sì*?"

"*Sì*, Vito. Everything about this day is perfect."

He responded with another soft kiss, this one to the side of her cheek. Maya reveled in the sensation of having him so close to her, the way his lips touched her skin. The thrill of being up this high combined with the effect Vito had on her was wreaking havoc on her senses.

"I'm not sure what we would have done if you'd been afraid of heights, *cara*."

She laughed in his arms. "Are you kidding? Do you know the number of times I visit the top of the Prudential building in any given year? My uncle does a lot of work in high-rise buildings."

"That's good, I wouldn't have been able to bear leaving you behind."

"You'd have gone without me?" she asked, teasing him. "Never."

Again, Maya made herself ignore the fact that his original intention had been to be here without her. To experience this ride by himself while she sat alone in a lonely hotel room in Venice. She swatted away the useless, wayward thought like an annoying pest. Right now, all she wanted to do was enjoy herself and take all this in.

The buildings and bridges throughout the city made for quite the view below them in the distance. Grand churches and stone buildings lined the river. The weather was cooperating beautifully. Not a cloud could be seen in the early evening sky.

Maya knew the image before her would be seared into her memory for all time. "I know I've said this often on this trip, but I really do feel as if I'm living inside a large painting at this moment. Like I've somehow stepped into a magnificent work of art that has just happened to miraculously come to life."

She tilted her head slightly to look up at him. "Why don't you paint it?"

He rested his chin atop her shoulder. "I'm a sculptor, *cara*. That sketch I drew of you is the closest I've come to creating a painting. Painting is not my craft."

She shrugged. "So, don't do it for your craft." She snuggled tighter against his length and continued to enjoy the view. As well as the feel of Vito's heat against her back. "Do it for fun. Because doing so calls to you."

Vito didn't respond to her suggestion. He just pulled her tighter against him.

Vito tried to imagine how much different this day would have been without Maya by his side. Rather than thoroughly enjoying it, as he had, he'd have been counting down the minutes until it was over. He might have even skipped out on the hot air balloon ride altogether.

So what did that mean about the reality of his days after she left?

He wasn't sure if he was ready for the answer. He watched her now as she exited the balloon in front of him. Her skin was flushed, the fabric of her summer dress clinging to all her glorious curves.

Pure temptation.

They'd landed moments ago and were waiting for their ride back to the villa. Vito wasn't sure where they'd landed exactly; he didn't recognize the spot.

The pilot spoke into his phone and informed them that their transportation would arrive shortly. Then the man went to work on his balloon.

It appeared Vito and Maya would have some time to themselves. The other balloons had drifted in different directions throughout the flight.

"Come. Let's sit while we wait." He led her to a tall, lush tree and helped her sit at its base. Then he joined her. Without a word or any kind of preamble, he gathered her into his arms and partly on his lap, with his back up against the tree trunk. She didn't argue or resist.

When had this happened? This ease and familiar level of comfort he felt with her. She belonged here, in his arms. They both seemed to know it.

"I can't wait to tell Zelda and Lexie about my hot air balloon adventure."

He nuzzled his face into the soft texture of her hair; she smelled of roses and fresh fruit. And outdoor Italian air.

"What else will you tell them about, *cara*?" he asked.

She shifted closer into him. Vito cursed internally. His body was reacting to her closeness in ways that weren't exactly convenient at the moment.

"Well, I would tell them I met a hot, charming Italian who swept me off my feet, but I doubt they'd believe me."

"Why not?"

"Because it's too much like a fairy tale I might have dreamed up. Almost as if you're too good to be true. They would no doubt think I've made up an imaginary man in order to make them jealous."

"They'll just have to travel to Italy. To see for themselves."

"Or you could travel to the States."

Vito trailed his knuckles down the soft, smooth skin of her arm.

"Would you consider that, Vito? Traveling to the States?"

Given that the question was a hypothetical one, he wasn't quite sure how to answer. He could lie and tell her that he'd consider it.

No, he wouldn't consider traveling to North America. Not even at the bidding of the desirable woman he held in his arms. For it would be a waste of her time. He had nothing to offer her. No more of himself to give. Vito wouldn't lie to her. He couldn't pretend he was fit to be any kind of man that a woman like Maya deserved.

So he decided on the truth. "I have no plans to travel to America in the future, *cara*. I'm content to stay here where I am."

Maya sat up and shifted to her knees, facing him directly. "Are you, though, Vito? Are you actually content, like you say?"

He felt himself bristle in surprise. Where was this coming from?

"Please, tell me honestly," she continued, her voice pleading. "Lynetta and I were speaking earlier and—"

But he'd heard enough. He stood without giving her a chance to continue. Judging by the direction of her questions, he could guess what she and his cousin-in-law had been speaking of. His failed marriage. And the tragedy that had ensued after it had come crashing down around him.

Neither of them had the right.

"You and Lynetta were talking about me? About my marriage?"

She blinked up at him. "Clearly that bothers you. Why?"

Why? She needed to ask? Wasn't it obvious? He wasn't some torrid subject to be hashed over by one of his relatives and a woman he'd just met and would most likely never see again once the week ended.

He ignored the question. If she didn't know the answer, he didn't have it in him to explain.

He'd been a fool. He'd let himself get careless when it came to Maya. He should have heeded the warning cries that had tried to stop him from walking her to the piazza that day. He should never have accompanied her on the tour. And he certainly shouldn't have had dinner with her that night on the cruise.

He'd let himself indulge in a fantasy because he knew it was all so temporary. He'd allowed himself to forget that he had no business caring about the loneliness of a jilted American as she pursued her newfound goal of being more adventurous. He shouldn't have cared whether she felt awkward and alone at dinner by herself on an intimate cruise meant for two. None of that should have moved him in any way. He'd let his guard down and it had only opened up old wounds he'd fought much too hard and waited way too long to heal. He should have known better.

"I hear the truck approaching. Our ride will be here any minute," he said, without meeting her gaze. He lowered his hand to help her up. She stood without taking it.

What had she said?

Maya sat staring at the moving scenery outside the window of the SUV that was driving them back to Vito's villa. Vito sat unmoving in the seat next to her. Neither of them had spoken a word to the other after being picked up.

She couldn't decide if she was hurt or angry. Both. Now that she thought about it, she could say she felt both. Vito had been beyond offended that Lynetta had spoken to her about him. Clearly, he didn't feel Maya warranted any knowledge of his past.

Not even after the days they'd spent together. Not even after the way he'd held her and caressed her during the balloon ride.

And not even after the way he'd kissed her the night of the dinner cruise.

Her breath hitched in her throat when she recalled the indignation and anger in his eyes while they'd been waiting. He might as well have come out and told her that Vito Rameri was none of her business. That he was no concern of hers.

He was right, of course. She'd been foolish to ever think otherwise and should have known better. Unbelievably, this felt worse than Matt's betrayal, which made no sense whatsoever. She'd been ready to marry him, for heaven's sake.

Despite the magic of the past few hours, she suddenly wished she hadn't come to Verona with him. Because now she had to mingle with all these people, all these strangers she didn't know, and she had to pretend everything was right with her. That she was a woman in love.

Laughable, really. Considering how she now realized that the man seated next to her was little more than a stranger.

CHAPTER ELEVEN

HER RACING PULSE hadn't slowed any by the time their car pulled up beside the wide wraparound porch she'd left only a couple of hours ago.

Vito's grandmother stepped out the front door to wave them in. "You're finally back," she declared in a thick Italian accent that served to make her even more endearing. "Come. Dinner is served. Eat."

The elderly lady seemed so happy to see them. As upset as she was, Maya didn't want her sour mood to mar the day whatsoever for anyone else. Particularly not the matriarch that they'd all gathered here to celebrate. Maya resolved to make sure no one enjoyed this day any less due to her presence.

That included Vito.

She waited until his grandmother went back in and laid her hand on his forearm. "Wait."

The look he gave her was loaded with impatience. "What is it?"

Maya took a steadying breath. He wasn't making this apology any easier. Nevertheless, she started giving him one. "I'm sorry if I've overstepped. Lynetta and I were chatting and the subject shifted, not surprisingly, to you. You're the reason I'm here, after all."

"I don't like being the subject of speculation."

"I understand that. I'll be sure to MYOB from now on."

"MYOB?"

"It's an acronym we Americans use. It stands for Mind Your Own Business."

He was about to respond when his *nonna* stepped back onto the porch. "What are you people still doing out here? Your lasagna is getting cold." She added something in Italian with a wave of her hand in Vito's direction.

He took Maya by the elbow. "Come on. We better go in. We can discuss this later. You don't want to keep an Italian grandmother waiting when food has been served."

She followed him silently back into the house though she wanted to ask what was left to discuss. He'd gotten angry and she'd apologized. Episode over.

Everything was now over.

Lynetta had told her that for Maya to find out anything more about him, Vito would have to tell her himself. Clearly, that wouldn't be happening. If she was disappointed or hurt by that fact, she had only herself to blame.

When they made it inside, everyone was already seated around the table and had started serving. One of the toddlers seemed to be wearing marinara sauce all over his face. Numerous Rameris motioned for them to come in and sit.

"What took you so long, cousin?" Leo wanted to know. "Wanted to be alone for a while?"

Vito gave him a look that would have flattened most men where they sat. Leo just laughed in response. Lynetta glanced in Maya's direction, an eyebrow raised in question. Maya gave her a small shrug.

Conversation roared around them, most of it in Italian. Maya took a small bite of the gigantic piece of lasagna that had been set on a plate before her. The smell of garlic and spices tickled her nose. As delicious as it was, and as hungry as she was, she couldn't fully focus on the feast. Vito sat in the chair right next to her, throwing loaded sideways looks at her.

It didn't help that with so many people seated at the table, their legs kept brushing. Each time she felt the contact, she remembered how it had felt to be held in his arms. How his lips had felt on her. Something she was not likely to feel again.

Suddenly, Nonna slapped her palm against the table where she sat at the very end. It wasn't a hard smack but it was loud enough that it got everyone's attention.

"English, everyone," she ordered once all eyes were on her. "Let's not be rude to our American guest."

Maya had never necessarily been shy, but it was a little daunting to have everyone's focus suddenly lasered in on her where she sat. "Oh, that's all right. Please don't inconvenience yourselves. I don't need to understand everything that's being said."

Nonna shook her head. "Nonsense, dear. Of course you do. You're one of us." She clapped her hands in front of her chest. "Vito will have to teach you the language soon, however. Not everyone you'll have at your wedding will be fluent. Tell us what plans you two have made already."

Maya's jaw dropped. Sure, she'd agreed to the pretense of a false engagement. But she hadn't actually expected to be speaking about any kind of wedding. And she certainly hadn't been expecting to do so in front of close to two dozen people.

Her mouth went dry as she tried to come up with

something to say. She suddenly felt Vito's hand on hers; he gave it a reassuring press.

He cleared his throat, sat upright. "Nonna, there's something I need to tell you."

Oh, no. Not like this. Maya willed him to read her mind. His intention was clear. He was going to come clean. Probably to try and spare her from this tortuous situation. She couldn't let him do that. It would ruin everyone's dinner. Not to mention the scrutiny Vito would have to deal with afterward. She gave his knee a gentle squeeze below the table and shot him a subtle wink. Her silent plea somehow worked. Vito got the hint and sat back in his chair. He gave her a small nod.

"This is all still pretty new, Signora Rameri—"

The older woman interrupted her. "I told you to call me Nonna, dear."

Maya cleared her throat. "Yes… Nonna…what I mean to say is, we're still getting used to being together."

None of that was a lie.

Vito cleared his throat. "That's right. I haven't even got around to getting a ring."

Again, not quite a lie.

"I'm afraid our newfound relationship has caught us both somewhat by surprise," Vito added. He may have been addressing the whole table, but Maya noticed he didn't take his eyes off her as he spoke the words.

It was hours later by the time the dishes had been cleared, rich cannoli had been served for dessert and everyone was getting ready to retire. Vito had given her a small peck on the cheek in view of his grandmother and bid her good-night. Lynetta then showed her to a guest room.

Maya uttered a silent prayer of thanks that no one

had had the bright idea to try and put her and Vito in the same quarters. Spending the night alone with him in bed would be more than her emotions could handle right now. She didn't trust herself not to ask for what she so badly wanted.

He was determined to hold back from her, didn't want to share any part of himself. But she couldn't be certain that she wouldn't settle for what she could get if she found herself alone with the man.

She'd just finished brushing her teeth and had slipped on her nightdress when a knock sounded on the door. It had to be Nonna making the rounds to wish her guests good-night. Maya walked over to the door and flung it open, ready to thank the woman for all her hospitality.

She came up short as the words died on her lips. Vito stood in the doorway, an arm casually braced against the wooden frame. When he saw her, his eyes grew dark and traveled down the length of her body.

Maya resisted the urge to cross her arms in front of her chest. Her nightgown was a strappy silk number that she hadn't thought was particularly sexy. But the way Vito stared at her now had her wondering.

"Vito?"

"Sì, cara. Sorry to disturb you."

"I…uh…was just getting ready for bed."

"I must say I like the way you slumber."

He didn't look so bad himself. He'd undone yet another button on his shirt, revealing a V of golden tan. His hair had grown more disheveled after the long day they'd had. A wayward curl rested over his forehead, lending him the look of a man with mischief on his mind.

For all she knew, that was an accurate description. Then she remembered the way they'd left things between them. How cross he'd been. Simply because she and Ly-netta had discussed his marriage. Clearly, it was a sacred subject as far as he was concerned.

So why was he here at her door right now?

"Do you have a minute, *cara*? There's something I'd like to show you. It shouldn't take long."

"Uh, sure. I just want to grab something decent to wear."

He said something under his breath. Maya could have sworn he said, "That's too bad."

He was waiting patiently outside her door when Maya returned after grabbing the light cotton sweater she'd packed.

"What is it that I'm to see?"

He motioned for her to follow. He led her down the hall to another doorway. But it wasn't a different room they stepped into. Maya found herself outside on a high balcony overlooking the vineyards and rolling hills. She realized right away what Vito wanted to show her. It wasn't the land.

"Oh, my," was all she could muster. The sky above was the color of deep blue velvet. Stars dotted the darkness and sparkled like the finest diamonds.

Another stunning visual she was not likely to soon forget. Why had she not visited Italy before this? Maybe she might have met Vito if she had. Maybe they would have had a chance to get to know each other before he was married. Before they'd become two people who were so wrong for each other. Before it was all too late for the two of them.

"You should see it during a meteor shower."

If only she could. Maya ignored the sorrow that filled her heart at the thought that she'd never be able to do such a thing. She'd probably never set foot on this balcony again after tonight.

"Can we stay here awhile?" she asked, any hint of tiredness suddenly evaporating.

"Of course." He motioned to the outdoor patio love seat behind them. "Make yourself comfortable."

Maya did so and tucked her legs beneath her on the comfortable cushion. Vito joined her and draped his arm over the back of the couch. A comfortable silence followed, both of them focused on the dazzling view above. She couldn't guess how long they sat there, simply gazing up at the night sky, before Vito finally spoke.

"You handled yourself admirably at dinner. Consider me impressed."

"I didn't want your grandmother's birthday ruined."

"No one but Leo would be to blame if that had happened."

She couldn't argue with him there. Whatever the other man's motivations had been, Leo had to know the truth was bound to come out sooner or later. Not that she'd be around to witness the fallout.

What would Vito tell Nonna the next time he visited with no fiancée in tow? Would he confess it had all been a ruse? Maybe he'd make up a story about their unexpected and terribly sad breakup.

Again, she wouldn't be around so it really was none of her concern. But she couldn't help but want to know. Maybe he'd call her in Boston. They could have a chat about it over the phone. Like casual long-distance friends who kept in touch once in a while.

She had to bite back a sob.

Vito interrupted her speculations with his next comment. "I'd like to apologize for the way I reacted after the balloon ride today. When I learned about the conversation you had with Lynetta."

She hadn't seen that coming. "Why did it bother you so much, Vito? That we'd discussed you."

His profile made for a stark silhouette in the darkness. He exhaled deeply before he answered. "Because it most likely meant you discussed my marriage. My marriage is not something I like people to dwell on."

She'd guessed correctly on that score. "Fair enough." She would let the matter drop. Despite her burning curiosity, she would respect his wishes.

To her surprise, Vito was the one who continued with the topic.

He bent over and leaned both elbows on his knees. "My wife was a woman with strong emotions. I thought I was up for the challenges that came with such a characteristic. I was wrong. I didn't handle it very well."

She reached for him, rubbed a hand over his shoulder in comfort. "You can tell me, Vito. Only as much as you like."

He was silent so long that Maya thought he wasn't going to do any such thing. His voice was strained and gravelly when he finally did speak. "Marina was used to being the center of attention. When we first met, I was happy to give her all of mine. I even based some of my creations on inspiration she provided. But that didn't last. It couldn't."

That wasn't a burden that a healthy relationship could survive, Maya thought. But she remained silent, letting Vito get all that he wanted to off his chest.

"As you can guess, things went sour quickly. I convinced myself none of it was my fault. I told myself I couldn't be expected to be all that she wanted, that she needed. I had my career. My name recognition and accolades of my artwork were growing throughout the world. The more in demand my work became, the more miserable Marina grew. She complained I never had time for her. That we never did things together. Even accused me once of being unfaithful."

He sighed before continuing. "She started giving me ultimatums. But I was too busy to pay attention. The perfect cliché of the distracted artist too engrossed in his work to realize what was happening right under his nose."

"What happened?"

"Marina was growing more and more resentful. Depressed. She said she'd make me sorry for tossing her aside like a useless doll. For the life of me, I didn't think she'd take things that far."

No wonder the man behaved like he carried the weight of the world on his shoulders.

"The more she threatened, the less I listened. I thought she meant she was getting ready to leave me." Vito rubbed his eyes. She couldn't be sure in the dark, but she thought she saw his hand shaking. "I'm ashamed to say that didn't bother me as much as it should have. I felt maybe a divorce wouldn't be such a bad idea, given how bad things had become."

"But that wasn't what she meant, was it?"

"That's just it, *cara*. I don't know for certain. I'll never know what she meant."

"I don't understand."

"She stormed out one afternoon, said she was heading to visit her parents on the Amalfi Coast. I didn't hear from her for a whole week." He sucked in a deep breath. "And I never bothered to call and check on her."

"Oh, Vito." Maya felt the sting of tears in her eyes; the anguish pouring from Vito was nearly tangible.

"I got a phone call late one night that she'd lost control of her car while driving along the cliffs in Sorrento. I hadn't so much as spoken to her in days."

Maya wanted desperately to comfort him, to find a way to console him. But she knew there weren't any words to address what he was going through and the guilt he still dealt with even after more than three years.

Nothing she could say would make a difference. Not only did Vito have to contend with his wife's death, it appeared he would always question whether or not it had indeed been an accident.

And if he had indirectly been the cause of it all.

CHAPTER TWELVE

"You didn't have to walk me back to the hotel," Maya said softly as they reached the entrance.

Vito had spent most of the trip back from Verona trying to determine exactly what he would say to her once they reached Venice. He found himself still at a loss for words now that they'd arrived. He reached over to tug a wayward strand of hair that had fallen over Maya's cheek before he answered. "What kind of gentleman would I be if I left you to see yourself home?"

"I'm not sure how to answer that." She bit her bottom lip and shifted from one foot to the other. There was something on her mind. Something she was debating whether or not to voice out loud. "I'm also not sure if I should invite you upstairs."

There it was. He'd been wondering how this particular goodbye would play out. "Would you like to?"

"Me wanting to do something doesn't always mean it's a good idea."

"If you were ready to do so, it wouldn't be such an agonizing decision." He wouldn't push her. The decision was hers and hers alone to make. He knew she only had one more day in Venice. Then she was off to Florence. And making her way farther out of his life. One step at a time.

A weight settled in the area of his chest at that thought. But he knew it was for the best. She needed to move on with her life. Her days in his city were nothing more than a fun getaway for her. A nice little vacation that happened to come at a time of a major upheaval in her life. No doubt the hurt she was nursing from the scoundrel who'd betrayed her was clouding her judgment. She hadn't even had time to really process the breakup. Now that her visit to Venice was ending, Vito needed to give her the time to do just that. He had no choice but to watch her walk away. They'd both known whatever they'd enjoyed together was to be finite.

"I know I've said it before, but your ex-fiancé is a fool, *cara*."

She blinked up at him, a wealth of emotion behind her eyes. "You can't say things like that, Vito. Not when you're standing here trying to figure out a way to say goodbye to me. Forever."

"That's not what I'm doing."

"Isn't it?" She blew out a deep breath and looked away, off to the side.

"You still have one more day in Venice, do you not?"

She nodded slowly.

"You know where to find me, *cara*. Come by the studio tomorrow if you'd like." He hadn't known he was going to say the words until they'd actually left his mouth. But he found he simply wasn't ready to have it all end so suddenly. Not when she had a few more hours. He would take any of that time she was willing to give him. But it had to be her choice, and hers alone. "It will be your decision whether this is to be our goodbye or not."

She didn't answer before she turned and entered the lobby.

* * *

She should spend the day packing and finally catching up on her missed emails and texts. Then she should indulge in one last walking tour around this beautiful city. After all, Maya didn't know when, or even if, she'd ever be back. Despite spending some of the most momentous days of her life here.

What she absolutely should not do was take Vito up on his offer to see him once more.

Maya walked over to the small bathroom in her hotel suite and turned the shower on. As the steaming hot water washed over her, she decided that she'd made the right decision. A clean break would be easiest. Better to just rip off the bandage. Only sometimes ripping said bandage off too quickly resulted in losing a bit of skin. Sometimes it resulted in a wound that left a lasting scar.

By the time she'd toweled off, Maya knew she'd been fooling herself. Who was she kidding? Of course she was going to go see him. There was no way they could leave things between them as it all stood now. Her mind might be trying to tell her one thing, but her heart had other plans.

In the end, her heart won out. She found herself pushing through the door of Vito's studio an hour later.

He immediately stood up from behind the marble counter. "You came, *cara*. I wasn't sure that you would."

Well, she hadn't been, either. Right up until she'd found herself at his door. "I actually turned around twice to go back."

Looking at him now, she was so very glad she'd trudged on. He looked like he hadn't slept a wink since leaving her side. Dark circles framed his eyes and his hair looked as if he'd been ramming his fingers through it all night.

Was it possible he'd been thinking of her as often as she'd thought of him?

"What made you change your mind?" he wanted to know.

"Which time?"

Vito chuckled and stepped closer. She could smell that distinctive scent of his that had somehow grown familiar in such a short time. He trailed a finger along her jawline up to her temple. The simple touch sent a fiery surge of longing through her center.

How could she have thought she'd been in love with Matt? She'd been so naive.

"We'll have to find a way to celebrate your final day in Venice," Vito said softly, leaning in so close, she thought he might kiss her. He didn't.

He took her by the hand. "I want to show you something."

Maya followed him to the back room where she'd fallen asleep just a few days ago. He led her to the easel in the center of the room.

A painting. It was in its earliest stages. But she could see clearly what he intended it to be: the view of the Verona countryside from high above. The view they'd watched together in the hot air balloon. The way he'd captured the images, the sunlight as it fell on the countryside, the sheer detail—it was nothing less than breathtaking.

"Oh, Vito. It's lovely," she murmured, though the word fell far short.

"You're the reason it exists. I was up all night working on it."

"I don't know what to say."

"Don't say anything, *cara*. But to tell you the truth, as much as I enjoyed painting what I have so far, I'd like to put this project aside. For now, anyway."

"You would? But why?"

"There's something else I'd like to begin painting. Some*one*, to be more specific."

"There is?"

"Yes. You. If you'll allow it, I'd like to paint a portrait of you."

Maya bit back her cry of surprise. This was not how she'd expected their final day together to begin. She'd tossed and turned all night; images of Vito and the time they'd shared haunted her dreams if she so much as closed her eyes. It looked like he'd been thinking of her, too. Only in an entirely different way.

She wasn't sure quite what to make of that.

"You want to paint me?"

He nodded. *"Sì."*

"Like one of your French girls?" It was a bad joke, and one he didn't seem to get.

"I beg your pardon? What French girls?"

"You know, from the movie?"

Vito continued staring at her with a blank look.

"You have to know it. It was a huge blockbuster. In fact, there's a famous Italian actor who stars in it."

He shook his head. "I don't watch too many movies."

"Never mind."

"So what do you say, *cara*? Are you ready to be my subject?"

Maya thought once more about how differently this day was playing out than anything she could have imagined. The man before her seemed to have entered her life only to throw one curveball at her after another. But, like it or not, she had to admit she'd found that part of his charm.

"What do you want me to do?"

Twenty minutes later, Maya found herself perched atop a high stool in Vito's back room.

Even though he stood several feet away and wasn't so much as touching her, it had to be one of the most intimate experiences she'd ever had with a man. Maya may have been fully clothed, but the way Vito had tousled her hair, the way he'd arranged her flowing skirt to cover only halfway down her thighs and the way he'd pulled her blouse off her shoulder made her feel as if he'd stopped for some reason in the process of undressing his lover. And that's how she felt. As if she were waiting for her lover.

Vito worked silently, the only sound in the room the steady ticking of the clock hanging on the opposite wall.

After what seemed like an eternity had passed, just when she thought she couldn't hold the pose a second longer, he set down his brush on the easel's holding tray.

"We can stop for now. I think I have enough detail to continue on without you having to model."

Maya sighed with relief and kneaded out the kinks in her various muscles. Who knew so many parts of the body could go stiff and tight all at once? When she felt some of the circulation returning to her limbs, she slowly stood and walked over to where Vito was still stroking a brush over the surface of the canvas.

"What do you think?" he asked her when she'd reached his side.

Maya did a double take when she saw what he'd created. She hardly recognized the woman on the canvas.

It took a moment to form the words. "I'm in awe, Vito. What you've created here…"

It was so much more nuanced than the initial sketch he'd drawn of her that first day. Layers of depth that captured her likeness in a way that made her want to become more like the woman he must view her as to be able to paint this portrait.

Maya wasn't sure how to put what she was feeling into words. "This woman you've drawn, she seems so sure of herself. The way she holds her head, the upward tilt of her chin. The steadiness in her eyes. These are all qualities you see in me?"

"Yes," Vito answered simply. "I think the better question is, how do you not see all that in yourself?"

Maya hadn't answered his question. She hadn't spoken much at all since she'd taken a look at his work. By contrast, whenever he'd created anything with Marina in mind, his wife had made all sorts of suggestions and comments. Marina had had no shortage of opinions on his work, whether she'd inspired the piece or not.

But Maya still wasn't saying much. She simply stood staring at the easel, openmouthed. He had to acknowledge the potential blow to his artistic pride if she actually disliked the painting.

"Is something the matter, *cara*?"

Maya nodded slowly, still silent. In fact, her silence was about to drive him crazy.

"What is it, *bella*?"

"I have a confession to make." She finally spoke, though in barely more than a whisper. "I've been thinking about the way you kissed me the night of the dinner cruise. And how much I'd like you to kiss me again."

Vito couldn't stop himself; he was human, after all. He pulled her toward him and indulged himself the way he'd so badly wanted to since he first laid eyes on her.

But this wasn't the short, light kiss they'd shared the night she was referring to. Vito unleashed all the desire and passion he'd been feeling for her.

She tasted of strawberries and sweet cream. She felt like redemption.

When they finally managed to pull apart, he almost couldn't bear the separation. Her lips were swollen from his kiss, her eyes cloudy with desire. He reached for her again as she spoke.

"I have another confession."

"Yes, *cara*?"

"I'd like more than a kiss, Vito. Much more."

A ball of fire rocketed through his entire body. There was no way he could deny her. Or himself. Though he knew this was oh, so wrong of him. What he was doing was beyond selfish. Perhaps the most selfish thing he'd ever done. Warning bells rang in his head about taking the next step.

He ignored them and lifted Maya in his arms. She felt right in his embrace. Like she belonged there. She belonged with him. He leaned down to give her another long lingering kiss that stole the breath from them both.

Then he carried her upstairs.

Maya didn't have to open her eyes to know that Vito had left the bed. She'd felt his absence, the loss of the warmth of his body next to hers. Her muscles felt languid, spent. In a very good way. She longed to reach for him again, to have him touch and caress her the way he had most of the afternoon.

Where had he gone?

Forcing herself to sit up, she grabbed the sleeveless shirt he'd been wearing when she'd walked in. Her cheeks flushed when she remembered how she'd practically torn it off him earlier. The way his taut skin had felt under her fingers when she'd finally rid him of it. Throwing the shirt on now, she walked out of the bedroom into the kitchen area.

She found Vito at the stove, tossing some pasta into a pot of boiling water. He was shirtless, wearing only a loose pair of gray sweats that shouldn't have been appealing in the least, but somehow made her fingers itch to touch him.

She wasn't going to fight the urge.

"I thought you might be hungry. I certainly am." He didn't turn around as he said the words. Maya walked up behind him and wound her arms around his waist. His spine straightened ever so slightly; the muscles of his stomach and back stiffened under her touch.

Maybe it was simply her imagination. But a nagging voice began sounding in her brain. Then it turned into a loud, ringing alarm. Something was off. Maya released her arms and stepped back.

"I don't have much to offer for food," he threw over his shoulder. "Just some packaged pasta. But there's homemade marinara sauce that Nonna sent back with me after my visit."

Me. My.

Vito may not have even been aware, but he was using singular terms. Nonna had presented that jar of sauce to both of them when they'd left her home.

It was as if he was mentally erasing her presence in his conversation. Maya's pulse was racing by the time the pasta was done and they were sitting across from each other at the small circular table.

Suddenly, she didn't have much of an appetite.

Vito began piercing the pasta with his fork, so far avoiding all eye contact. Maya knew she wasn't imagining things. She didn't think she could take it if Vito regretted what had just happened between them.

Only one way to find out.

She waited for him to swallow his latest bite. "We need to talk about what just happened between us, Vito."

He didn't bother to stop eating. "I'm not so sure that we do."

"How can you say that?"

"The fact of the matter is that you'll be gone after tomorrow, *cara.* Anything we say to each other will only be empty words. In a few days, we'll be both be back to our normal lives."

He sounded so casual, so nonchalant. Maya wanted to literally cover her ears. But she had to try and get through to him. Or she'd never forgive herself. "I'll be in Europe until the end of the month, Vito. That's a good amount of time."

"To do what?"

What kind of a question was that? She blinked up at him. Was he being deliberately obtuse? "To spend more time together. To try and figure out what we might mean to each other."

"I told you. I have no intention of traveling."

"Not even with me?"

He shook his head. "I'm afraid not."

Each word landed like a sharp spear into her heart. Maya pushed past the hurt and forced her mouth to move.

"So that's it, then? And will it be so easy for you to forget all about me after tomorrow?"

"That's not what I said."

"What are you saying, exactly?"

He shrugged. "That I have nothing to give. Nothing to offer."

"That's not true. It's simply the excuse you use to avoid taking any risks."

"But it is the truth, *cara*. I'm not capable of falling in love." He sighed. "I just don't have it in me."

"And what if I've already fallen in love with you, Vito? What then?" Maya blurted out the words. She had no reason to hide the truth of it now; there was nothing left to lose, after all.

The blood visibly drained from his face. Pushing his plate away, he leaned back in his chair. "I'm sorry, Maya. I can only tell you to try and get past what you think you feel for me. Move ahead with your life as if I don't exist."

A brick settled in her throat. She had to fight to get the words out. "How can you ask me to do that? Do you really think I can?"

He remained silent, and it was answer enough.

"So that's it, then?" she threw out, not bothering to suppress her hurt and anger at his infuriating nonchalance. All the while she was shattering inside. "You've made your decision. And you're basing it all on your grief."

Something visibly shifted behind his eyes. A hardness appeared in his gaze that had her flinching. But she met his stare dead-on. She wasn't about to back down now.

"What is that supposed to mean, exactly?" he asked, his tone gritty and tight.

"I think you know."

"Please indulge me and explain." His voice held a very clear warning. Maya decided she would ignore it.

"I mean that you're so invested in grieving for the past that you refuse to see what the future may hold."

Vito didn't so much as blink. "I see you've decided you can analyze me. Please, tell me more."

She knew he was goading her, that she shouldn't take the bait. But she couldn't seem to help herself. Suddenly, she had too much at stake to stop. She'd never forgive herself if she didn't lay it all on the line. For this man, she had to. "You don't want to move on, Vito. You want to live in the past and examine then reexamine your role in the tragedy that you've had to endure. You don't want to move past it. Because it's easier to dwell on it. Because you're scared."

Vito finally moved. He leaned ever so slightly over the table toward her. "I see. And what about you, *cara*?"

"What about me?"

"What makes you think you've moved on from your past?"

What in the world could he be talking about? He had to see she no longer had any kind of feelings for the man she'd been engaged to. He had to see all her feelings were laser focused on one man and one man alone. "I don't know what you're talking about. After the afternoon we just shared in your bed, you have to know I've moved past my engagement to another man."

He actually laughed at her. A harsh, mocking sound that echoed off his kitchen ceiling and made her want to shrink away from the noise. "Don't insult my intelligence. I knew it the first time I kissed you on that galleon. I mean the way you've held yourself back your whole life in order to please others."

Her mouth went dry. He had no business speaking of such things. He didn't know her life at all. "Others?"

"Your adoptive family."

"What about them?"

"You've spent your life making sure they never regretted taking you in. From your choice of study in college to your career choice to the man you committed yourself to."

"That's not true. I didn't—" But the words died on her lips. The arguments she wanted to make completely escaped her. It was too hard to think, given the hardness and utter derision in Vito's expression.

"It's exactly what you did," Vito spat out. "You've spent your life making sure you fit in with your adoptive family, molded yourself into what you thought they wanted. Determined to make yourself worthy of their love and acceptance. And you dare accuse me of living for the past."

A cry of anguish tore from her throat before she could stop it. There was nothing more to say, no way she could respond to all the things he'd just said to her. So, he saw her as nothing more than a weakling who'd spent her life trying to appease others. He had no idea. He had no right to make such judgments about her.

She'd been made a fool of. Again by a man. Only this time her heart would never recover.

Maya pushed away from the table on shaky legs. She had to leave before she did something stupid like weep or grovel. She couldn't let him see her do either.

The sooner she got out of there, the sooner she could break down.

CHAPTER THIRTEEN

By the time she checked into her hotel in Florence and went up to her room, close to forty-eight hours later, Maya felt as if an entire lifetime had passed since she'd left Vito's studio. She had a voucher for a late lunch in the hotel restaurant but couldn't summon the will to eat alone yet again. Though it was something she needed to get used to. She'd be spending the rest of this journey by herself.

He could have come with her. Instead, he'd chosen to watch her walk out of his life.

Dropping her bags in the middle of the floor, she willed herself not to cry again. This felt wrong. Totally wrong. A stunning view of the Florence skyline sat before her through her hotel window. She couldn't enjoy it. Instead, she yanked the curtains closed and leaned her forehead against the wall.

This felt worse than the first morning she'd arrived in Venice, alone and heartbroken over a man she'd thought she'd been in love with.

How mistaken she'd been.

Now that she found herself really and truly in love with Vito Rameri, Maya realized how empty her feelings toward Matt had been in comparison. Matt had never made her insides quiver; he'd never sent desire pulsing through her whole body with a simple smile. He'd never made her want to weep with abandon at the thought that she might never see him again.

Only one man had ever made her feel that way.

And he'd asked her to leave.

The sob she'd been trying to hold in finally escaped. Vito was right. She had to admit it to herself. She'd spent her whole life making sure she never let her immediate family down. Even her decision to get engaged had been made with thoughts of how it would impact her aunt, uncle and cousins.

Maya grabbed the silly burner phone. Calling up the keypad she dialed a familiar Boston number.

But the call didn't connect. Instead, a robotic voice came over the speaker telling her something in Italian. Maya tossed the phone aside and dropped down onto the bed, staring at the ceiling in the dark.

She had no idea what to do next. Her cell phone was useless, she was alone in a strange city and her heart was shattered. What was supposed to have been the trip of a lifetime had turned into nothing more than a source of anguish.

She had no one to blame but herself.

Maya allowed herself a good hour to wallow in sadness and self-pity. Then she sat up and grabbed the hotel phone. Pressing the button for the front desk, she waited.

A friendly female voice answered after the second ring. "*Buongiorno*, Signorina Talbot. How can I assist you?"

"I'd like to make an international call, please."

Zelda's familiar voice came on the line after a series of long beeps.

"Maya Papaya!"

The use of the silly nickname her cousins had tagged her with years ago pulled a smile from Maya's lips. "Hey, Zeezee."

"About time you called. Good timing, too. Lexie is here with the baby."

Longing pulled at Maya's heart. She'd missed them. All of them. Her aunt, uncle, Zelda and Lexie.

She missed the tiny little infant she considered her nephew more than a little cousin. A deep feeling of homesickness rushed through her core, surprising her with its sudden intensity.

"Here, I'll put you on speaker. Say hey to Lexie. And to little Owen."

"Hey, Lex. Hello, little O-man."

"Hi, cuz. We miss you."

"You can't hear it, but he's cooing at you, Maya." The image made her smile even more.

"So, tell us. How is Italy treating you? Were you unable to call until now 'cause you were busy with a hot Roman lover?" Lexie asked, her voice teasing.

Maya bit down on her lip to keep from crying out loud. "Oh…um…"

Zelda immediately read into her response. Or lack thereof.

"Maya? Tell us what's wrong. Is this about Matt? He keeps calling here, you know. Asking how to get a hold of you."

She couldn't bring herself to spare a single thought for Matt right now. He simply wasn't worth it. "No. It's not about Matt." The last word came out with a strained hiccup.

"Sweetie, please talk to me." The genuine concern

and affection she heard in Zelda's voice served to finally break the last string of control Maya had been holding on to.

On a shaky breath, she began to tell her cousins the whole complicated story, the words rushing out of her like an overflowing river delta. Beginning with her discovery of Matt's dalliances with a colleague at work and ending with how she'd fallen for a handsome and charming Italian artist who'd turned around and shattered her heart after she'd so willingly and completely given it to him.

When she'd finished, a long silence ensued. For a millisecond, Maya thought maybe the connection had dropped. But then both her cousins started speaking at once. It was impossible to make out the words, though she heard "bastard" thrown about more than once, with a few other choice expressions that would have made Aunt Talley glare in disapproval.

Debatable exactly which man they were referring to.

Finally, the line went silent again.

"Listen to me, Maya." It was Zelda's voice. "Just come home. Come back to Boston."

Maya sniffed and wiped her cheek with the back of her arm. "But Grandmama paid—"

"Grandmama will understand," her cousin assured her. "She cares more about you than some silly trip she paid for."

Maya couldn't argue with that. When Gran knew all she was dealing with, the woman would waste no time gathering Maya into her arms and consoling her with gallons of tea and mountains of chocolate cake.

"Yes," Lexie added, her voice firm. "Come back here, Maya. As soon as you can."

"Just come home," Zelda repeated. "Come back and let us all take care of you. We'll help you get through this."

Maya couldn't hold back any longer. At the risk of further upsetting her dear cousins, she finally let all the sobs and tears loose. They were right. She had no business traveling through Italy by herself any longer.

She needed to be back in Boston. She needed her family.

Vito's gaze, as well as his focus, kept drifting away from the folded newspaper he had sitting on the table at the outdoor café he frequented. The same café where he'd first laid eyes on Maya Talbot, right before she toppled out of a gondola and fell into his life.

His eye kept wandering to the same spot where he'd first noticed her, as if somehow time might turn back and he'd see her there once more.

She'd said she'd fallen in love with him. And he'd responded by crushing her heart and her spirit.

Vito would have to find a way to live with that knowledge. He'd have to deal with the fact that he'd been a selfish bastard who should never have let things get that far between them. But his callousness had come through yet again.

A shadow suddenly fell over his line of sight. "I thought I'd find you here, cousin."

Leo pulled over a chair from an adjacent table and sat down across from him. Normally, Vito might have groaned with annoyance at the interruption of his solitude by his boisterous, noisy cousin. Today he found he could use the company. Still, he couldn't resist a sarcastic retort. "Please, have a seat, Leo. I'd love it if you'd join me."

Leo reached over and took a sip of Vito's espresso without asking. "You appear to be more mopey than usual. I take it you missed your opportunity to retain something special in your life."

"What's that supposed to mean?"

"You let Maya leave, didn't you? Yesterday was her last day in Venice, yes?"

"Yes. To both questions. And I don't want to talk about it."

Leo signaled to the waiter who gave him a nod. Both men were regulars who didn't need to actually place their drink order.

"Of course you don't want to talk about it. You'd rather not hear me tell you what a fool you can be."

"I presume you're going to tell me anyway. In detail."

Leo rubbed his eyes with the palm of his hand. "Vittorio. Believe me when I say I wish I didn't have to."

"Then don't. I told you, I don't want to discuss Maya. She's gone and will not be returning. The conversation will be moot. Don't waste your breath and my time."

"Fine. Let's talk about you, then."

This time, Vito didn't bother to suppress his groan. Leo ignored it and continued. "How long are you going to beat yourself up about an event that may or may not have happened? An event you weren't the cause of, regardless of how often you try to convince yourself otherwise."

Vito had half a mind to leave the table. But he had no doubt Leo would simply follow him. If they hadn't been out in public, things could very well have turned physical. Vito was all too tempted to head in just such a direction—between the stunt Leo had pulled with the fake engagement at Nonna's and the way he was pressing Vito right now.

He clenched his fist on the table. "I will beat myself up for as long as it takes to come to terms with all that has happened."

"Is that really what you think you're doing? Coming to terms with what happened?"

"Yes, that's exactly what I think," Vito said with finality, hoping against hope that Leo might get the hint and finally drop the subject.

He should have known better.

"Really? Because from where I'm standing, it looks like you're using the past as a reason to hide from the future."

Vito flinched in his seat. The other man's words were nearly identical to the ones Maya had thrown at him. "You go too far, Leo."

But his cousin wasn't ready to back down. He leaned closer over the table between them, bracing his elbows on the glass surface. "You forget I was the one who first saw you after you got that tragic phone call, Vito. I saw the self-loathing you punished yourself with when you had no reason to do so."

The reminder of that night served to temper Vito's anger with Leo. He didn't know what he'd have done if his cousin hadn't shown up to console him moments after Vito had received the news.

"What would you have me do, Leo?"

"Stop punishing yourself," Leo immediately answered.

Vito started to argue. But what would be the point? Leo couldn't understand. Leo had never let his wife down on such an unforgivable level. Lynetta had never felt unloved or ignored. Unlike Vito, his cousin hadn't failed so devastatingly as a spouse.

"Your stubbornness is draining you of all your passion. And all of your will," Leo continued. "You haven't created anything in three years. It's destroying you from inside out to be so dormant. It has to be."

He was wrong about the creating part, Vito mused, thinking of the painting currently sitting on his easel. A painting he'd covered with a drop cloth, unable to bear looking at it now that its subject was gone. Though now he was at a loss as to what to do with it. He died a little inside every time he walked by it. But neither could he bear to throw it away.

"It's not a switch I can flip on and off, Leo."

"Of course not. But you have to have seen over this last week that you can gradually move past your grief. The way you were with Maya reminded me of the man you used to be. Before…" Leo leaned back, not completing his sentence.

He didn't need to. But the man Leo was referring to was gone. Vito had long ago buried him deep within his soul. "I'm not meant for relationships, Leo," he tried to explain. "I learned that the hard way. I can't risk so much again with another woman who might end up paying too steep a price for having loved me."

"Everyone pays a price for love, cousin. You are no exception."

"Nevertheless, I can't give a woman like Maya what she needs. She deserves stability, steadiness. A full commitment from a man to love and cherish her without limits or conditions. I know for a fact that I'm not capable of being that man."

He thought of the way he'd lashed out at her that last

day. The look of sheer hurt on her face when his dagger-like words had found their intended targets. What he'd done that day only proved his point: he was unworthy of the love someone like Maya had to give. And incapable of providing all that she deserved.

He slammed his paper down on the table in disgust. This whole conversation was so terribly pointless. "What difference does it make in any case? She's gone. She'll be in Florence by now, then off to the rest of her adventures through Europe."

Leo frowned. "Florence is less than a day's travel." Then he glanced at his watch. "And it's still fairly early."

Vito slowly shook his head. "No. I'm afraid it's too late, Leo. I said some things I can't take back. I doubt very much that she'll forgive me for them." Vito cringed when he thought again of how he'd hurt her in order to ultimately spare her.

"Don't decide that for her, cousin," Leo said. "And it's never too late."

"I'm afraid you're too late, sir. You've just missed Signorina Talbot."

Vito cursed out loud so viciously, the poor young woman at the Grand Hotel Firenze took a startled step back.

He muttered a clipped apology before turning away. Maya was gone. This time for good. She must have altered her plans and left Florence several days early.

Before she returned to Boston, Vito had no way of locating where she was.

He had no choice but to turn around and go back to Venice. Alone.

CHAPTER FOURTEEN

HER AUNT WAS waiting for her at the luggage turnstile at Logan International Airport when Maya deplaned after leaving Florence half a day earlier. A wealth of emotion immediately had tears pooling in Maya's eyes when she saw her. Maya swiped at them before they could fall. She had to resist the urge to run into the older woman's arms and make a spectacle of herself in front of all her fellow travelers.

"Aunt Talley, what are you doing here? I had a car service arranged."

Her aunt gave her a warm smile. "I canceled it, dear. You know you could have asked any one of us to drive you home. Why did you arrange for a car and driver?"

"I didn't want to be a burden."

Her aunt took her by the elbow and walked her to some of the more isolated seats in the arrivals area. "Maybe it's time we had a little talk about that."

"About what?"

"This notion you have that you might be a burden in any way, shape or form to any of us."

Uh-oh. Maya could guess where this was coming from. In her anguish and sorrow when she'd spoken with her cousins over the phone from Florence, she'd over-shared all that Vito had said to her. Clearly, word of it all had gotten to her aunt.

As annoyed as she was at her cousins for spilling the proverbial beans, Maya had to concede they'd only had her best interests at heart. She must have sounded like a mess during that call for Zelda and Lexie to have called in the big heavy. As much as Maya loved and respected her uncle, Aunt Talley was the true guiding force behind the Talbot family.

"I was just upset the other day, Aunt Talley," Maya began as they sat down. "I shouldn't have said all that to Zelda and Lexie. I wish they hadn't burdened you with any of it."

Her aunt sighed. "There you go again. Using that word."

"Oops."

"But is it true?"

Maya started to deny it. But Vito's harsh words echoed in her head. How could she deny that she'd taken up an area of study that she otherwise might not have if her uncle hadn't needed help with his business? Or that she might have pursued a different career with a bigger company after graduation considering how heavily she'd been recruited? Or even whether she would have started dating Matt if her uncle hadn't been so fond of him?

The truth was, she didn't really know anymore how to answer her aunt's question. In so many ways that she hadn't even acknowledged to herself, she supposed she had considered herself something of an unwanted burden upon the family that had taken her in. Subconsciously, she'd been trying most of her life to make sure they never felt that way about her.

"I don't know," she finally answered truthfully. Then

she wanted to kick herself at the expression of utter distress on her aunt's face at her response.

"Oh, Maya." Her aunt gently cupped her chin in her hands. "My dear, sweet girl. I will never forgive myself for not reassuring you often and vehemently that you were always a loved and cherished child. Even before your parents were gone, your uncle and I loved you from the moment you were born."

This time, there was no stopping the tears. Maya bit her lip to avoid making a spectacle of herself.

"Forgive me, my dear," her aunt continued, "for not knowing that you might have felt that way for even one minute."

"Please don't say that," Maya pleaded. "I should have known better. I should have come to you."

Aunt Talley gathered her in her arms and held her tight. "Well, allow me to clear the air right now. Uncle Rex and I are both beyond impressed with and fiercely proud of the woman you've become. And we would feel that way no matter what you chose to do with your life. Because we love you, sweetheart. I'm sorry if we didn't say that to you often enough."

Maya couldn't help herself; she leaned into her aunt's embrace and accepted all the love and comfort the woman offered.

It may have been years in the making, but Maya finally felt a warm sense of acceptance and belonging that she'd only been denying herself for far too long.

And she knew she had Vito to thank for it.

Maya jumped in her seat at the booth as Lexie slammed a plastic-coated drinks menu on the table in front of her.

"Pick something to order, already," her cousin directed. "We're on our second round."

Maya made a show of opening the menu and pretending to peruse it. What she wanted to drink wasn't available at the popular, trendy Mexican spot that had just opened in Southie. She didn't need to look at it to know that this place didn't carry a rich, fruity Valpolicella like the one she'd been poured the night Vito had kissed her for the first time.

"Hey, come on now." Lexie settled into the seat next to her and nudged her shoulder. "It's been two weeks, Maya Papaya. Try and have some fun tonight."

"I'll try," Maya lied. She was being so unfair and beyond what could be described as a party pooper. This was supposed to be Lexie's first real girls' night out after having the baby and she didn't want to cast a cloud of gloom over her cousin's first outing as a new mom.

"You're still thinking about him, aren't you?"

Maya could only nod. "I'm sorry, Lexie. I should have just stayed home and not risked raining on everyone's good time."

Lexie wagged her finger at her. "We wouldn't have let you. You've been doing enough staying at home since you got back. You go from work to home with a visit to the museum in between. We would have dragged you out if we had to."

Maya leaned her head against her cousin's shoulder. As much as she wanted to, she just couldn't get into the party mood. More than one flirtatious man had tried to approach the table with the four laughing and drinking women. None of those men had even come close to evoking a spark of attraction. She couldn't help but compare them to a dark-haired, charming Italian who'd stolen her heart only to crush it. Each guy had fallen way short in comparison.

"I take it you haven't heard from your man yet?" Lexie wanted to know.

It struck Maya as more than a little funny. She'd been engaged to Matt for close to two years. But every time one of her cousins referred to "her man," they meant the one she'd known for less than two weeks in Italy. A man neither of them had even met.

Not that the term was accurate. "He isn't my man, Lexie. And, no, I haven't heard from him. He hasn't called or emailed. The sketch was delivered but his assistant's name was listed as the sender."

"What about you?" Lexie asked.

"What about me?"

Lexie performed an exaggerated eye roll at the question. "Why haven't you called him?"

Maya straightened in her seat. Calling Vito was out of the question. She'd said what she needed him to know the day he'd sent her away.

"Because he made his feelings very clear," she answered. "I bared my soul and told him I'd fallen in love with him. And do you know what he said?" Maya asked despite the fact that Lexie knew full well the answer to that question. Both of her poor cousins had been made to listen to the whole sordid story almost daily since Maya had landed back at Logan.

Still, Lexie played along. "What did he say?"

"He said that I needed to get past whatever it was I was feeling for him."

"And then what?"

Maya blinked at the query. This was a new line of questioning. Usually Lexie and Zelda simply let her vent and unload everything. Apparently, they'd decided a new approach was in order. "What do you mean?"

"Did you tell him that you didn't want to get past it?"

"Why would I do that?" Maya asked. "What would be the point?"

Lexie shrugged and took a sip of her non-alcoholic beer. "I dunno. I do know you've told us that he's afraid to take a risk, that he was stuck in the past and that's why he let you leave."

"And?"

Lexie reached for her hand over the table and gave it a tight squeeze. "You don't appear to have taken any kind of risk yourself."

"Back again, miss?" The pleasant, smiling young woman on the other side of the window handed her the entrance ticket Maya had just paid for.

Maya returned her smile. "What can I say? I really like the exhibits."

Passing through the turnstile, she walked through the lobby of the Museum of Fine Arts in Boston. Maya had spent every lunch hour here for the past two weeks. She'd splurged on a year-long membership soon after she'd returned to work. Maybe she was being silly, but being here made her feel closer to Vito somehow.

Never mind that he was an ocean away and had probably already forgotten she existed. Well, she would find a way to move on, as well. She had to, didn't she? These museum visits weren't all completely frivolous, either. Maya had made it a point to check MOFA's website online for openings she might qualify for. She didn't mind starting at a lower position and working her way up. Not that she planned on leaving Uncle Rex's employ all at once. He still needed her. But she needed to make a career change and would do it gradually to eliminate any whiplash effect.

Maya hadn't mentioned the potential job switch to anyone. Not even Grandmama.

She wouldn't do that until she had a few more details solidified. Plus, it didn't help that the person she most wanted to talk to about it was thousands of miles away. Oh, and she couldn't forget that he'd made it more than clear that he didn't really care what her plans for the future held.

Maya had been nothing more than a fling.

Shaking off thoughts of her fateful Venetian trip, she walked over to her favorite gallery, the one featuring Italian paintings. Each time she looked at the masterpieces on the wall, she noticed another detail or learned something new. Each afternoon spent here was never like the one before.

Plus, if she closed her eyes and tried hard enough, she could almost pretend she was back in Italy admiring the paintings on the walls of the palazzo. And that Vito was by her side.

Her imagination had to be functioning particularly well today, because she could swear she heard his voice behind her.

"I find the still life with fruit paintings particularly compelling, don't you, *cara*?"

Maya didn't dare turn around. Her wishful mind was merely playing tricks on her. She refused to be fooled. No one was behind her. In fact, she was the only person in the hall of this particular gallery.

But the voice somehow continued. "Of course, this one has the added feature of dead birds in the picture.

What do you suppose Ruoppolo intended when he included them?"

Maya whirled around so fast her head spun for the briefest second. Then she almost lost her balance completely. For there in front of her, through some miracle, stood Vittorio Rameri. In the flesh. As devilishly handsome as she remembered.

He flashed her a heart-stopping smile.

"Buongiorno, mia vita."

It took several moments before she could get her mouth to work. Her peripheral vision grew dark; the only thing in her focus was the man standing before her. "Vito? Is it really you?"

He spread his arms out, his grin growing wider. "None other."

"But how? What are you doing here?"

"I stopped by the shop first. Talbot's Expert Plumbing. Your uncle told me where I could find you."

Okay. "No, I mean, what are you doing here? In Boston?"

"Ah, see, that question might take a bit of explaining."

"Perhaps you could give me the overall gist."

"Nothing felt right after you left, *cara*. The city I loved suddenly became empty, much smaller all of a sudden once you were gone. Lonelier." He paused to run a finger down her cheek and along her jaw. Her skin warmed wherever he touched it. "Then there was the painting I'd begun of you."

"What about it?"

"I wanted badly to finish work on it, because it reminded me of you. But I couldn't bear to uncover it. Because it reminded me of you."

He stopped speaking and blew out a frustrated breath. "I'm not explaining at all well, am I?"

"No, no. You're doing fine. Don't stop, please."

Vito chuckled then stepped closer to where she still stood dumbfounded and unable to move so much as a muscle. "I'll do better, *cara*," he said on a soft whisper. "I'll show you."

As he took her in his arms Maya thought for certain none of this could be real. That she was, indeed, going mad. But then Vito took her lips with his and she couldn't think at all.

When they finally parted, Vito drew her even tighter against him, nuzzling his chin against her hair. Then spoke softly on a whisper in her ear in Italian. Maya didn't need a translator to understand his words.

"Ti amo." I love you.

EPILOGUE

"I DON'T KNOW about this, Vito. Last time I attempted getting into one of these things it didn't go so well." Although she *had* ended up meeting Vito as a result.

Still, Maya wasn't so sure a gondola ride was the best way to celebrate the one-year anniversary of the day they'd first met. Vito was trying to be romantic, but all she could focus on was making sure not to reenact the scene where she'd fallen into the water.

"The difference this time is that I'm by your side, *cara*. I won't let you fall."

That wasn't the only difference. "Also, I'm quite sober this time around," she reminded him with a laugh.

Vito hopped into the boat first then helpfully lifted her in. "See? That went pretty smoothly."

"Thank goodness."

She sat next to Vito on the padded seat and let him pull her into his arms. Slowly, the gondolier began navigating them through the Venice canals.

"Why was it so important that we do this today, anyhow?" Maya asked, though now that the initial boarding was over, she found herself thoroughly enjoying the outing. The splendor of Venetian architecture still took her breath away.

"You need to get used to gondola rides if you're going to be living in Venice part-time."

"I suppose that's fair. After all, you've had to get used to Boston rush-hour traffic."

"Hardly the same."

Maya nestled closer against his length as they approached the waters by St. Mark's and the palazzo. The setting sun had turned the sky above to a striking shade of gold. Moments later, they were heading under the Bridge of Sighs.

"Do you remember the legend I told you about this bridge all those months ago?" Vito asked her.

"I do, as a matter of fact. The legend says that a couple on a gondola as it sails under the Bridge of Sighs will share eternal happiness if they happen to share a kiss just as the bells of St. Mark's Cathedral are ringing."

"Very romantic, *si*?"

"Yes, it is," Maya agreed. "I also remember discussing that it was statistically almost impossible. Too many random variables."

Vito sighed. "I suppose you're right." He sounded so disappointed that Maya couldn't restrain her laughter. "That doesn't mean we shouldn't try, however," she suggested, not that she needed an excuse to kiss this man.

"Of course, we should. Also, we can create our own little legendary story."

Maya turned in his arms to look at Vito's expression. His mischievous smile and the teasing in his voice told her he was definitely up to something.

"What did you have in mind?"

To her delighted surprise, Vito reached into his pocket and pulled out a small velvet box. Maya's breath left her lungs as he flipped it open to reveal a sparkling square-cut diamond set in a band of pink gold.

"Oh, Vito. It's beautiful."

"Amore mio," he began, "would you do me the honor of becoming my wife?"

She felt the sting of happy tears in her eyes as he slipped the ring on her finger then turned her hand and kissed her palm affectionately.

"Yes! I'd be honored to marry you," Maya managed to blurt out through all the emotion pounding through her heart. Their gondolier turned to give them a whistled cheer.

Vito lifted her chin and brought her face close to his. His lips settled over her own for a long lingering kiss, one that made her blood burn through her veins. Just as she heard the bells of St. Mark's Cathedral ringing through the air.

* * * * *

A PROMISE
FOR THE TWINS

MELISSA SENATE

For Max, with love.

Chapter One

Nick Garroway had three items on his to-do list for this warm and breezy July morning, and the sooner he dealt with the complicated first two, the sooner he'd get to the third—the prize.

One: check on a woman named Brooke Timber. Make sure she was all right/see if she needed anything. He had no idea if Brooke was still pregnant or had given birth. He'd soon find out.

Two: visit his father whether the man liked it or not, despite the fact that Nick's brother would probably punch him in the face if he stepped foot in the family home.

Three: buy a ranch far, far away from Wedlock Creek. He envisioned a couple thousand acres, a white farmhouse with a weathered barn, a few dogs from the local humane society running around, a horse, a hundred head of cattle to start, maybe some sheep. Definitely chickens.

Nick parked his Jeep in the public lot by the Wedlock Creek town square and got out, stretching his legs. It had been a long drive from Texas, and he'd started well before the crack of dawn. With his aviator sunglasses on and his brown Stetson pulled down low, he headed toward Main Street. He wondered if Dee's Diner was still around. He hoped so. He could use a big plate of scrambled eggs, bacon, and Dee's really good hash browns with peppers and onions. And lots of coffee. An entire urn wouldn't be enough to deal with the second item on his list.

He glanced up the street, which was bustling already at just before 8:00 a.m. with folks heading to work, into the coffee shop, the bakery, a line of little kids in Wedlock Creek Day Camp T-shirts turning into the gated entrance to the park just a few feet away, and lots of dog walkers.

He was glad to see Dee's Diner still there, at the end of Main Street, with a swanky new sign depicting a cowgirl roping a plate of pancakes atop the door. Small towns were all about mom-and-pop businesses, and Dee's must be doing well. He headed in, taking off the shades and hat and hoping no one would recognize him and make small talk. Nick wasn't in the mood.

And who'd recognize him anyway? He hadn't been back in Wedlock Creek in almost five years, since his brother had let him know he hadn't been welcome that Thanksgiving and should spend the holiday from now on in Afghanistan "since he preferred military life and combat over his family." His father hadn't said otherwise, so Nick had stopped bothering to come home on leave or between tours.

His brother's scowling face came to mind. Good

God. The thought of dealing with Brandon Garroway today almost made him lose his appetite. But Nick was starting a new life, and the only way to actually get going on a new one was to square away the old one. Nick needed to square away things with his dad.

He pulled open the door to Dee's Diner and took in the delicious aromas of pancakes, French toast and bacon. And coffee. His appetite was saved.

Nick was greeted a warm hello, led to a small booth by a waitress with a coffeepot in her hand and, within five minutes, his order was before him, along with today's *Wedlock Creek Gazette*.

The home fries were as good as he remembered. As he ate, he flipped through the newspaper, full of town happenings and local sports, ads and classifieds. He already had three solid leads on ranches a few hours or so from Wedlock Creek, but figured he'd check out any listings the *Gazette* might have. He scanned them—all too close to town. He did want to live in Wyoming— his roots were here—but a few hours' distance between him and the Garroways sounded about right.

Nick forked a bite of eggs and bacon and was about to close the paper when a name in a boxed ad taking half the page caught his eye.

Nanny Wanted

Experienced, caring, tenderhearted nanny sought for relatively easy three-month-old twins. Monday–Friday, 9–1. Hours negotiable. If interested, call/text Brooke Timber: (307) 555-1022

So, she'd had the twins. Nick didn't know anything about Brooke Timber other than that she was very pretty—he'd seen a photo—had long brown hair, enormous pale brown eyes and a dimple in her left cheek, and that someone he owed a big favor to, the ultimate favor, had "done her wrong" and wanted to rectify that. Between having two reasons to come home to Wedlock Creek—making good on a promise to a fallen soldier and dealing with his dad—here he was.

He finished his mug of coffee and was grateful when the waitress appeared with a fresh pot and refilled. He tore out the ad so he'd have Brooke Timber's telephone number. He'd already googled her address and had that memorized. She lived over on Oak Lane, which was within walking distance from here, a couple houses off Main Street.

He stared at the words *relatively easy* in the ad. That had to be a good sign that Brooke was okay, that she was fine and he could cross her off his to-do list after a quick visit to her home. A couple of guys in his unit had been fathers, and one talked a lot about his very colicky baby but had always said he'd give anything to be with the screamer rather than thousands of miles away.

Once upon a time, Nick would have said he didn't know anything about that. Or babies at all. But now the stirring of a memory socked him in the gut, a little face with big dark eyes and shiny black wisps of curls, fifteen pounds at most in his arms, and he closed his eyes against it, downing half the mug of coffee to keep the face at bay.

Take care of business, he told himself. *Check on Brooke Timber, talk to your dad and then you'll be*

*home free to buy a ranch. The land and hard work will
make you forget anything you need to.*

The waitress glanced at him with her coffeepot lifted,
and he nodded and smiled. Oh yeah, bring on the third
cup. He'd need it.

Waiting in a long line at Java Jane's coffee shop,
single-mother Brooke Timber hoped her three-month-
old twins wouldn't get too fidgety and start screeching
before she could order a large iced coffee. She glanced
at the huge sign on the wall, the menu handwritten in
colored chalk. Small, plain iced coffee: $1.95. What she
really wanted was a large iced mocha with whipped
cream, but that was $5.45. And forget the cherry Danish
in the display case. She could bake something at home
for free—if she could find the fifteen minutes to stand
still at her counter with flour and eggs.

Money was tight. Time was tight. Brooke's nerve
endings were tight.

"Ga ba!" Mikey gurgled from his stroller, waving his
little chew toy, which he promptly threw on the floor
with a big smile.

Brooke scooped up the sticky orange toy and shoved
it in her stroller bag. Yes, fine, things weren't easy.
She'd known that would be the case. A single mother
with baby twins, no family, trying to run a business—
Brooke was a wedding planner—with four competitors
in town? Her bank accounts, both personal and business, were dwindling. She could not, it turned out, "do
it all"—at once.

"Ba ba!" Morgan gurgled at his brother and threw
his own chew toy on the ground.

Brooke's heart melted at Morgan's thrilled, gummy grin and snatched up the toy; those happy faces of her boys never failed to ground her. Yes, she was stretched to the limit. But look at what she had. These two little dumplings: heathy, adorable babies. Before they were born, Brooke didn't have a relative left in the world. Now she had two precious children. Life was good. A challenge, but good.

"Didja hear the news?" the barista was saying to the woman in front of her. Brooke was next in line and could not wait to be sipping her iced coffee, back out in the gorgeous sunshine. She planned to take Mikey and Morgan to the park, spread out a blanket, and she and the twins could watch their favorite nature show: two squirrels chasing each other up and down a particular tree with huge green leaves. Then she'd take them home for their nap and develop a plan to bring in more business. Of course, she'd lost out on potential clients, even when she'd had a part-time nanny— single motherhood made things that much harder on a new parent—so she had no idea how she thought she'd bring in new business with *no* childcare. The good news was that her industry—weddings—was *big* business in Wedlock Creek.

Despite being a small Wyoming town, Wedlock Creek was famous for its century-old wedding chapel, which came with a beautiful legend: couples who married there would be blessed with multiples. Some scoffed at the legend but there were multiples—twins, triplets, quadruplets and even two sets of quintuplets—all over town, so there had to be something to the legend, or just something in the water.

Weddings, particularly at the chapel for those who wanted many babies at once, were the name of the game here. There were *five* wedding planners in town, including two newbies who didn't scare Brooke the way the two other established ones did. But none of her competition was trying to keep their beloved late grandmother's twenty-seven-year-old business, Dream Weddings, going. Brooke *was*. And she couldn't let her grandmother down. No husband, no nanny and very busy little twins aside.

"The Satler sisters are engaged!" the barista exclaimed, handing the woman in front of Brooke her change. "Isn't that incredible?"

Brooke's ears perked right up. The Satler triplets had gotten engaged?

When the woman moved to the pick-up area, Brooke rushed herself and the stroller to the counter.

"Did you just say the Satler triplets got engaged last night?" Brooke asked the barista. "All *three* of them?"

"Yup, it's true!" the barista said. "And I hear they want a triple ceremony and a lavish reception."

Brooke's eyes widened, her mind whirling. A triple wedding. She would estimate the guest list at five hundred. Maybe 550.

"Isn't that wonderful?" the barista cooed. "All three engaged on the same night, at the same time, in different locations. The boyfriends planned the whole thing. So sweet and romantic!"

"*So* romantic!" Brooke agreed, turning the stroller around and heading for the door. Forget the iced coffee that she could also make for free at home. She had a triple wedding to secure! She rushed the two blocks back to her house, with her mind hard at work.

"Ba ga ba!" Mikey gurgled as Brooke pushed the stroller up the walkway to her front door.

She paused and bit her lip. The boys would miss the squirrels. They loved watching those furry critters chase each other. "I promise to take you to see Lenny and Squiggy later," she told them, opening the front door and wheeling the stroller through.

The names she'd given the squirrels were a necessary reminder of her grandmother, who used to laugh her head off while binge-watching episodes of her favorite old show, *Laverne & Shirley*. Lenny and Squiggy were two goofballs, just like the squirrels. And for her grandmother's legacy, Brooke would focus right now on Dream Weddings.

She took the twins from their stroller, and with one in each arm, headed into the Dream Weddings office, off the hallway. Her grandmother had turned a first-floor bedroom into an office and installed a door to the outside, with a porch, a hand-painted white wooden sign hanging from ornate iron scrolls, and lush satin white drapery in the bay window that was reminiscent of a gorgeous wedding gown.

With the twins in their baby swings beside the desk, she sat and turned on her laptop and created a Dream Weddings possibilities file for her prospective triplet clients. She talked through her ideas to Mikey and Morgan, two sets of big blue-green-hazel eyes hanging on her every word. Mikey got fussy, but a brisk walk around the office, with a back rub and extra-animated talk of pretty flowers and the best bands in the county, calmed him right down.

Forty minutes later, she finished her proposal, forcing herself to wait until the acceptable-to-call hour of 9:00 a.m., and then she phoned Suzannah Satler, the one triplet she knew from the knitting class she'd taken right before the twins were born. Brooke offered congratulations and her services as owner of Dream Weddings, "a full-service wedding planning company, right here in Wedlock Creek." Because of that knitting class and how open and chatty Suzannah had been, Brooke knew quite a bit about the Satler triplets—that they loved country music, the color hot pink and all things glam. Brooke was able to excite Suzannah over the phone in one carefully crafted sentence.

The Satler sisters were due at Dream Weddings at 10:00 a.m. to discuss. Yes, yes, yes!

"I'm back!" she trilled to Morgan and Mikey, waving her hands in the air like a lunatic. Or just like a very excited wedding planner who *had to* sign the Satler sisters.

She plucked the twins from their swings, put them in their baby seats and carried them upstairs. She changed their diapers, then settled them against her on the glider chair for a made-up story about their favorite squirrels. Their little eyes drooping, Brooke carefully transferred each back into his baby seat, praying they wouldn't wake up.

Yes, success! With an eye on the time, she brought the carriers into her bedroom, set them on the floor and opened her closet door. Thank heavens she'd showered this morning. At 4:50 a.m., she'd taken a fast, hot shower, with the baby monitor on the sink, since the twins woke at five o'clock and, if she wanted to shower in peace, she had to do it very, very early. She looked through her closet, nodding at her elegant white pantsuit. Very Satler sisters. She took off her T-shirt and shorts and put on the pretty outfit, adding a watercolor-patterned silk scarf and three-inch peep-toe red fabric heels, which were also very Satler sisters. A quick application of pressed powder, mascara, and lipstick, ponytail off and hair fluffed, a dab of Chanel No. 19, and voilà—the harried single mother turned into the sign-with-me businesswoman. She stared at herself in the mirror, almost amazed at the transformation.

Carrying a baby seat in each hand, she headed back downstairs, on heels she wasn't used to anymore, and went into her office. She gently placed the baby seats under the big ornate desk; its backing completely obscured them from view of the sofa, where her clients would sit.

Also under the desk was a complete stash of baby paraphernalia: diapers, bottles, pacifiers, chew toys, burp cloths and an extra set of pajamas. A single mother without childcare for the time being had to be at the ready.

Brooke had timed the appointment for the twins' usual midmorning naptime, and if things went her way, she would have forty-five minutes to an hour and a half of blessed silence to conduct business with the Satler sisters. Her former nanny, a wonderful, patient saint of a woman, had had to take four to five weeks off to help her daughter, the new mother of twin babies herself. That was two weeks ago. Brooke had had interview after interview with prospective nannies, but for one reason or another, none was right for the job.

One applicant had reeked of marijuana. Another said she couldn't stand the sound of crying, but "that's what binkies were for, right?" A very loud talker insisted that Morgan and Mikey should be separated in the home to ensure independence from each other starting at the most tender of ages. And then there was the one great prospect, who burst into tears during the interview because she was having fertility issues and ran out the door.

I can do this, Brooke chanted to herself in her head. The lack of childcare had presented problems during the past couple of weeks, but Brooke had managed to bring in one client—a small New Year's Eve wedding, at the stroke of midnight. She'd signed that bride earlier this week, with the twins napping under her desk, and her new client none the wiser. Three other prospective clients had slipped through her fingers because of the lack of childcare, but her babies came first. They always would.

For you guys and for gram, she thought, *I'm going to secure the Satler sisters' business.* A triple wedding, particularly Satler style, would mean being back in the black instead of the scary red she was in now. It would mean saving her grandmother's business. The Kardashian-esque Satlers were very popular in town, and signing them would have new brides beating down her door.

She heard a car pull up into the driveway and three doors slam, then the chatter of voices as the Satler sisters approached the Dream Weddings entrance. Brooke got up to open the door and welcome them. Last thing she needed was for the doorbell to wake the twins.

"Congratulations!" Brooke said, giving each triplet a quick hug.

"We're so excited!" Samantha Satler said as the women sat down on the sofa. "Of course we want the ceremony at the Wedlock Creek Chapel, and Suze said you mentioned the Wellington Hotel's grand ballroom—that is *exactly* where we want to have the reception!"

Ha! She knew it. The tall, slender, blonde Satlers, who each wore a different-colored pastel leather cowboy hat, super-skinny jeans, and high-heeled hot-pink perforated cowboy boots, liked bling. Their engagement rings, matching big square diamonds, twinkled on their fingers.

Brooke launched into her plans, giving each sister a handout bullet-pointing their Dream Weddings possibilities for their triple wedding. From the knitting class, she knew the triplets worshipped Carrie Underwood and never missed an area concert, so she'd listed ten fabulous country bands with Carrie-esque female vocalists. A mix of local small businesses and companies in the nearby big town of Brewer, for everything from flowers—the sisters loved white roses—to catering—all three were gluten free, which was another tidbit she'd learned from Beginning Knitting—and Brooke's most trusted printing shops, for exquisite shades of barely-pink invitations and the most delicate velum.

"It's like you're in our heads!" Samantha Sattler trilled. "This is amazing!"

Suzannah Sattler flipped through the handout. "I agree! Okay, so can we talk about the Wellington Hotel's grand ballroom and what we envision for tables and—"

"WAAH! WAAH-WAAH!"

Oh foo. Brooke bit her lip and felt her cheeks flame. She forced a smile. "Excuse me. Just one moment," she said to the sisters, and then she bent under the desk to give Mikey's seat a gentle rock. "There, there," she whispered to Mikey, who was screeching bloody murder. Morgan, miraculously, was still fast asleep.

"Omigod," Shelley said. "Do you have a *baby* under your desk?"

Brooke's cheeks now burned. She quickly told them about her nanny—or lack thereof—situation. She caught the triplets sliding each other uncomfortable glances.

And then it happened.

The worst possible thing, at the worst possible moment.

The unmistakable smell of…baby poop filled the air.

"Ugh, gross!" Samantha said, pinching her nose closed.

Suzannah's face crinkled in disgust and she waved the air in front of her. "Oh God, I think I'm making it worse."

"We're having lunch with our soon-to-be mothers-in-law in an hour and now we'll smell like baby dung!" Shelley muttered.

Brooke stood and pulled out the baby seat, unlatched Mikey and held him in her arms. He screamed, making little fists. "I'll just change him and we can get right back to discussing your dream wedding," Brooke said, trying to keep the pleading out of her voice. She grabbed a diaper and the pack of wipes from her stash under the desk and hoisted Mikey up. "I'll be right back—"

She was about to flee into the restroom when a man she'd never seen before—tall, dark and crazy hot—opened the door to Dream Weddings and walked inside. He was holding her ad from the *Gazette*. Dear Lord, was he here to apply for the job as her nanny? This guy? He reminded her physically of every actor who'd ever played Superman. Down to the piercing blue eyes.

The Satler triplets, who'd been about to run out, stopped and stared at him. Newly engaged or not, a gorgeous specimen of man was a gorgeous specimen of man.

But then Mikey let out a high-pitched shriek that could shatter a window. Shelley slammed her hands over her ears. A wail came from under the desk. Now Morgan was crying too.

First an explosive poop diaper. Then an applicant—an incredibly sexy one—for the nanny job, walking right into one of the most important meetings of her career. Now two babies screaming bloody murder.

She could kiss the lavish triplet wedding at the Wellington adieu.

The stranger looked at Brooke, then at the baby in her arms and glanced toward the desk, where more wailing could be heard, if not seen. Suddenly, Morgan stopped crying, though she was sure it would be short-lived. He eyed the frowning triplets edging toward the door. "Looks like you have your hands full," he said to Brooke, setting the nanny-wanted ad on the credenza. "Allow me. I'm pretty good with babies."

He stepped toward her, arms extended as if to take her child, and Brooke stepped back, shielding Mikey from him.

"Listen, bucko, I don't know you," she said.

God, he really did have the most gorgeous blue eyes with long dark lashes. The slightest of five-o'clock shadows graced his strong jawline.

Shelley Satler was staring at him. "Hey, aren't you Nick Garroway?" she asked him. "You were a year ahead of us in high school. You played football and baseball, if I remember correctly."

"You do," he said with a smile. "And of course I remember you three. The lovely and smart Satler triplets. Copresidents of your class. One of you—maybe *all* of you, at various points—used to babysit my younger brother. It's very nice to see you again."

The triplets beamed and swooned and chatted with this Nick Garroway about old times.

So, he wasn't an axe murderer. Or baby-napper. The Satlers were four years older than Brooke, so Nick was out of high school by the time Brooke would have been a freshman. She would have had a serious crush on him if she'd known him back then.

He stepped closer again. "May I?" he said, reaching for Mikey. "If you direct me to a changing area, I'll take care of this ASAP and you can continue your meeting."

Uh, I guess? How weird was this? She handed him the diaper, the wipes, and her precious baby son, and pointed toward the restroom, where she had a changing station set up. "Where I can see your every move," she whispered to him, and he nodded as he took Mikey inside, keeping the door half open. The Satlers couldn't see into the bathroom from where they stood—thank heavens—but they could all hear him humming a lullaby. Brahms's.

"Well, Brooke, looks like you found your new nanny," Shelley said with a grin. "And just in time."

"You mean her new *manny*," Samantha corrected,

with a wiggle of her eyebrows. "Male plus nanny equals manny."

"A *hot* manny," Suzannah put in. She grinned at Brooke, tipping her lemon-yellow leather cowboy hat at her. "Brooke, you seriously impress! Listen, why don't you write up a comprehensive plan for our wedding, with all the new info we discussed here today, and we'll go over it, but we're 99 percent going to hire you and Dream Weddings for our big day."

Thank you, universe.

And thank you, Hot Manny.

The man himself emerged from the restroom, with Mikey smiling and grabbing Nick's chiseled jawline. "Now this little dude smells like snips and snails and puppy dog tails and everything else good that little boys are made of."

Brooke stared at him, speechless. Where on earth had he come from? Was he even *from* earth?

Each Satler sister winked at Brooke, made a little fuss over Mikey, said goodbye to Nick with one last admiring glance at him and then left.

"The job is yours," Brooke said to him as she pointed at the ad. "Can you start immediately? I guess you already have."

The Hot Manny tilted his head and stared at her. "Oh, I'm not here about the job."

Chapter Two

"I'm confused," Brooke said, reaching for the baby in Nick's arms.

He almost didn't want to let the little guy go. He liked how the sturdy small weight felt in his arms, against his chest. He'd been surprised by that back in Afghanistan—how satisfying, how gratifying it was to hold a tiny baby. How hard it was to hand the baby over.

Some things just sneaked up on a former US Army combat soldier unexpectedly. Like how raw he felt about his reason for being here. The sooner he gave back Mikey, the sooner he'd have to explain why he'd come. He had no idea how that conversation was going to go.

"You're *not* here to apply for the nanny position?" she asked, taking the baby and giving Mikey a kiss on his cheek. Mikey gurgled and then immediately spit up on the jacket of Brooke's white pantsuit. It had to take courage to wear something like that with baby twins.

She barely seemed to notice. She reached under the desk, grabbed a burp cloth, dabbed the drool, tossed the cloth on her shoulder, and then put Mikey in his swing and transferred the twin beside him. With both babies occupied and playing with chew toys attached to the swing, she turned her attention back to him.

Those driftwood-brown eyes of hers had stopped him in his tracks when he'd seen that one photo of her on Will Parker's phone. Intelligent and assessing. And tired now. He could see the dark shadows and the pull of exhaustion. He'd known she was pretty. But the instant wham of connection he'd felt when he'd first laid eyes on her in person was anything but expected.

"No," he said. "I was on my way to see you and happened to notice the ad for a nanny in the *Gazette*. I ripped it out so I'd have your phone number if you weren't at home."

But she had been at home. Fortified with caffeine from the diner, he'd pulled up in front of her house, taking note of the well-kept small white Cape Cod with black shutters and a red door, the lawn tended to, two black-and-white cats snoozing on a padded swing, two cars in the driveway—one a brand-new Range Rover that must have cost a mint. He now realized the Range Rover probably belonged to the Satlers. The second car was a decade-old Honda. He'd breathed a sigh of relief that Brooke Timber was clearly doing fine and that he could be on his way to dealing with number two on his list. But then he'd heard the sound of babies wailing and high-pitched shrieks from adults, and that hadn't sounded too okay, so he'd followed the noise to the side door, a business entrance, and marched in.

Brooke hadn't looked fine at all, not in the slightest. He'd sprung into action, as was his wont, and somehow the four women in the room had managed to mistake him for a nanny.

At six foot two, 185 pounds, with a small tattoo of "purple mountain majesties" on his left bicep and size-thirteen black work boots, he wouldn't have thought anyone would confuse him with an applicant for a baby-sitting job—*Gazette* ad in hand or not.

"Ah! So you must be a prospective client," Brooke said. "When's the big day?"

Client? Big day? What was she talking about? Then he remembered the Satler triplets with their huge rock engagement rings and the shingle outside her side door. Brooke was a wedding planner.

"Good God, no," he said with a shake of his head. Now he was taken for a groom? "I'm not the marrying kind."

She raised an eyebrow. "Everyone is the marrying kind. My clients have been all sorts. Last year, a search-and-rescue worker fell in love with a man who lived off the grid, in the mountains, without electricity or running water. She got him to upgrade to a real cabin with the basics and even Wi-Fi, but they're way out in the woods, eating only what they forage themselves."

He smiled. "I'm surprised that a woman who'd live in a cabin in the woods with a mountain man would even hire a wedding planner."

"I know, but the groom scoffed at everything she suggested, and only when his bride threatened to run back to civilization did he agree to let her handle the wedding her way, with him *in mind*. Her job was so demanding that she had no time or interest in figuring it all out, so she hired me. I planned a small, quiet ceremony on the bank of the Wedlock Creek river, with the mountain as a backdrop. The 'caterer' was a fisherman, who made an amazing clambake. The 'band' was a fiddler. But guess who put on a rented tuxedo to make his bride happy? Yup."

"Well, I'll be," he said on a laugh. "I guess you never know. That may be the only thing I do know for sure."

She laughed too, and for a moment he couldn't take his eyes off her. She had silky, straight brown hair past her shoulders, a dimple in her left cheek and, though he was usually drawn to more casual women, he liked the fancy outfit and little scarf at her neck and the pointy, polished high heels. Maybe because she gave the appearance of having it all together. And whether or not she did was the reason he was here.

"So, what *can* I do for you, Nick Garroway?"

Brooke looked happy and peaceful at the moment, and he didn't want to spoil it. But she was staring at him with those big brown eyes. Waiting for an explanation.

"I'm newly medically retired from the army," he said. "For the past month, I've been recuperating from a foot injury at a base in Texas, after eleven years as a combat soldier in Afghanistan."

"Thank you for your service," she said, her voice turning hesitant and her entire body stiffening. "And you came to see me because…"

He could tell she was bracing herself. "Will Parker was in my unit."

She glanced at the babies in their swings, her shoulders slumping. Then she lifted her chin and let out a breath.

Her cell phone rang in the silence of the room.

"I'll let voice mail get it," she said, then dropped down in her desk chair as if her legs had been about to give out on her.

The phone stopped ringing, but before he could say a word, the annoying ringtone started up again. He could tell she needed a breather—but from *him* and what else he had to say. "Take the call, Brooke. I'll keep an eye on the twins."

"Really?" she asked. "Even though you're not here about the job?"

He nodded. "Go ahead. Might as well while I'm here."

She snatched the phone as if it were a lifeline. "Brooke Timber of Dream Weddings speaking. How may I help you?"

He kneeled down in front of the baby swings to make funny faces at the twins, but he was distracted by Brooke—how hard she was listening, how tired she looked, how rigid her shoulders were now, probably from his news about being here because he knew Will.

The twins' father.

"Absolutely, Francesca," she said into the phone. "The salmon is out, the sole almondine is in. I'll make it happen."

Brooke put down the phone. "One of my clients wants to switch her menu. Someone told her that salmon was dated and that she should go with the hipper sole."

He smiled, but a call like that would push him off the edge. Salmon was dated? Sole was hip? *What?* "Bride's wish is your command?"

"Pretty much. Unless they're dead wrong and I need to do reality checks. But if sole almondine will make Francesca Perry happy? Done."

"You're like a wedding genie," he said.

She gave him a bittersweet smile. "Well, my grandmother named this business Dream Weddings when she opened up shop in this very room, twenty-seven years ago. I promised her in the hospice last year that I'd run the business just as she had, with everything she taught me. My job is to make brides' dreams come true for their big day. And no dream is silly or wrong or too small or too big. That's what Gram always said."

A wistful expression filled her eyes, and he could see how much she missed her grandmother. He knew from Will Parker that Brooke was all alone in the world—no parents, no other family. Couldn't be easy raising twins under those circumstances. *And* running a business, to boot.

Family businesses, family ties. He also full well knew the grip those could have. He'd let go. But not everyone could or would, was willing, or wanted to. Brooke spoke of her grandmother with love and reverence and seemed to truly like her job, so it was clear her family ties weren't like the rope he'd had to cut with a sharp knife.

"Well," she said. "Why don't we talk in the house. It's close to lunchtime for Morgan and Mikey."

He looked at Brooke in her fancy outfit, with two babies to feed, no nanny and work to do, given the project she had in front of her to secure the Satlers' weddings. And then he heard Will Parker's voice in his head, usually so light and full of devilish mischief, asking something of Nick with regret and sorrow in his tone.

He could certainly be of help while he was here, re-laying Will's message.

"May I?" he asked, ready to scoop up Morgan. The little guy wore orange-and-white-striped footsie paja-mas. He—and Mikey—both looked a lot like Brooke, but he could see hints of Will.

"Sure, thanks," she said, picking up Mikey.

The beautiful baby boy in his arms reached up and poked his cheek. He smiled. "Hi. I'm Nick."

Morgan drooled in response.

Brooke laughed and pulled a burp cloth off her shoul-der. "Here. I made the rookie mistake of not having this close enough earlier."

He took the burp cloth and gave the little lips a dab, then put the cloth on his shoulder, but that felt remark-ably stupid, so he just held on to it.

He followed her through an arched doorway, into a living room with a baby play area off to the side. A big carton with one side open was against the wall, with a picture of a white bookcase on the front, a set of in-structions and a toolbox next to it.

"Haven't gotten around to putting it together yet?" he asked.

She sighed. "I keep meaning to. It's for the twins' nursery. But then it's time to feed them or put them down for their nap, or the phone rings or a client comes over. This morning I got the twins out for the gorgeous summer morning air and a Java Jane's run, fully intend-ing to come home and at least start the bookcase, but then the Satler sisters got engaged and securing them as clients became everything."

He nodded. "Well, sounds like you did just that."

"Thanks to you. If you hadn't walked through the door and reminded them of high school before changing Mikey while singing a lullaby, they would have run screaming out of my office, straight to my competition."

"Well, then I've already fulfilled some of my promise," he said.

She tilted her head. "Promise? What do you mean?" The moment the words were out, she slightly shook her head as if she didn't really want to know and kept her gaze off him, so he stayed quiet.

She put Mikey in the baby seat on the kitchen table, and he did the same with Morgan beside him. She made up two bottles, and he couldn't help but notice the sink was full of dishes, despite the dishwasher right next to it. A basket of laundry—whether clean or dirty, he wasn't sure—was beside one of the chairs. Clearly Brooke needed help—the nanny she'd advertised for so that she could operate her business and take care of the everyday stuff.

Yup, she wasn't waiting for his answer, which made him think she wasn't ready to hear what he had to say. She went into the living room and put the two bottles on the coffee table, then came back into the kitchen and picked up Morgan. He picked up Mikey and followed her, settling next to her on the couch.

He watched the way she laid Morgan slightly upright, giving the baby the bottle. He did the same with Mikey, then was about to answer her question. About the promise.

"Have multiples yourself?" she asked before he could. "Is that why you're so good with Morgan and Mikey?"

He almost laughed. "Kids? *Me?* No. Not the marrying kind, not the dad kind. I got some unexpected baby-care experience overseas. Long story." And one he wasn't interested in talking about. The less he thought about what he'd been through in Afghanistan, the better.

"Well, it's nice to have someone else to help so they can both eat at the same time," she said. "I had a wonderful nanny the first two months, but she had to leave town to help her own daughter. I guess I've been so focused on taking care of the twins that I've neglected everything else. I'm sure you noticed the state of the kitchen."

"You're busy and on your own," he said. "A single mother, raising baby twins alone, running a business— something has to be put off, and it sure as hell should be the dishes."

She laughed. "Right? I agree." The smile faded fast and she slid a glance his way.

He tilted the bottle up as Mikey drank it down, then inwardly sighed. This was not going to be easy.

"So, about the promise you made," she said. She closed her eyes for a second as if bracing herself again, then opened them, keeping her attention on the baby in her arms.

He cleared his throat. "Will asked me to check on you and to pass along a message."

She stared at him hard. "He asked you to check on me? Why? It's been nearly a year since he sent me a Dear Jane email, so I'm surprised he cares one iota about me—or the twins."

"Will was killed six weeks ago," he said as gently as he could. But there was no gentle way to say such a thing.

He lowered his head out of respect for the fallen soldier, and to give Brooke some privacy with her emotions.

"I didn't know," she whispered. "What happened?"

"IED—improvised explosive device. I might have been killed if he hadn't thrown himself on top of me. He took the brunt of it."

"Oh God." She shook her head.

"Will and I had never been close or even friends, really. But we were from the same hometown, and that connected us. Maybe that was why he saved my life. Or maybe he'd always had that in him and I didn't know it."

"That he could be a hero?" she asked, tears in her eyes.

He nodded. "Will liked to make jokes, pull pranks. Never all that serious about anything. And then he saved my life. Can't get more serious than throwing yourself on another soldier to protect him."

They were quiet for a moment, and she nodded.

"Will was fading," he finally continued, "but I could see he wanted to tell me something. He said there was a woman from Wedlock Creek, a beautiful, kind, good person named Brooke Timber, who he did wrong. Ghosted her when she told him she was pregnant with twins, then sent an email that he wasn't cut out for fatherhood and they'd all be better off without him."

Her lips tightened. "That's almost verbatim. All two lines of the email."

He glanced at her for a moment. She was waiting for him to continue. "Then Will said, 'Garroway, will you check on her when you get home? Make sure she's all right? See if she needs anything?' And I assured him I would. The last thing he said was, 'Tell her I'm sorry.

She deserved better.'" He winced, remembering the look on Parker's face. The regret.

She smoothed her hand over Morgan's wispy dark hair. "Your daddy was a hero," she whispered to the baby. "And he sent a guardian angel to check on us. That's not nothing."

The backs of his eyes stung, and he blinked hard.

"Well, message delivered," she said, slashing a hand under each eye and standing up. "As you can see, we're okay. Everything is okay."

"Waaah!" Morgan started crying, the little face crumpling and turning red.

She closed her eyes and took a breath, then opened them. "I need to burp and change Morgan. Thank you for coming, Nick. You can put Mikey in his swing in the kitchen and let yourself out," she added before rushing from the room with Morgan.

Was she crying? Just emotional? Needing to be alone and get control of herself?

You can let yourself out... He could, indeed. Mission accomplished, right?

But there was no way he was leaving. Because Brooke wasn't all right. And he'd promised the soldier who'd saved his life that he'd make sure she was.

He looked down at the baby in his arms, the blue-green-hazel eyes staring up at him so trustingly.

Nick didn't always get it right, but he wasn't about to get this wrong.

Chapter Three

Brooke got a hold of herself in the bathroom, cuddling Morgan against her. After her five-night stand with Will Parker last year, she'd vowed never to be stupid about a man again. And for a minute there, all she'd wanted was to fling herself into Nick's arms and let him hold her. He was so tall and muscular and kind, and connected to her past and present in a way that had stolen her breath. What she would give for a long hug where she could let someone else be the strong one for just a minute.

No, no, no, she cautioned herself now, staring at her reflection in the mirror as she held her son. Been there, done that—and wouldn't be so dumb again. Last year, grieving for her grandmother and overwhelmed by running Dream Weddings on her own, she'd given into a tall, sexy blond soldier, whose easy smile, soulful eyes and outstretched hand let her believe all kind of foolish things.

Will had been in between tours and had a week to himself in his hometown. They'd met while she'd been walking Paco, a Great Dane she'd been dogsitting, on Main Street. Will, sauntering down the sidewalk, had fussed over the majestic dog, and just like that, she'd had a date the next afternoon. He'd invited her to the rodeo, and after three dates in three days, they were in bed the rest of the week. They'd connected over both losing their parents, over loving Mexican food and margaritas, over their love of the rugged Wyoming countryside and fresh, open air. He'd listened to her talk about growing Dream Weddings and had said, looking seriously and meaningfully into her eyes, that maybe someday soon she'd have a dream wedding of her own.

They'd had the most amazing five days and nights together, and then he'd had to return overseas. There were a few emails that first month, and then he barely responded to hers. When she'd discovered she was pregnant nine weeks after their time together, she'd emailed him the news, having no idea how he'd react. But she hadn't expected him to act like she—and their twins— didn't exist. He'd washed his hands of her, and that was that.

She'd known immediately that Will Parker was about fun and games, but those real moments they'd shared, the connection, had tricked her into letting her guard down. She'd never felt so alone after losing her grandmother, and Will had made her feel part of something, a duo. She'd had no idea how badly she wanted to belong to someone, and for someone to belong to her. But the idea of ever falling for another man had gone right out the window.

Morgan and Mikey were her family. Will had given her the twins. For that she was grateful.

And he'd saved Nick Garroway's life. She would tell her children that their father had died a hero. For that she was also grateful.

And now her precious baby boy was downstairs with someone who was practically a stranger! Where the hell was her judgment? She rushed out of the bathroom, telling herself to breathe.

He's not a stranger, she reminded herself. *The Satlers know him. He came here to fulfill a promise to your babies' father. He can change a diaper and sing a lullaby at the same time. Mikey is fine.*

Was *she* fine, though? She'd been barely able to drag her eyes off Nick Garroway every time they were in the same room together.

She went into the kitchen and stopped in her tracks. Mikey was happy in his baby seat on the table, playing with his chewy attachments. Beside him, on the chair, was the clean laundry she'd neglected for three days, folded and stacked. And Nick Garroway was loading the dishwasher and telling Mikey a story about a lost raccoon named Rocky.

"Everyone was looking for Rocky," Nick was saying. "But no one could find him, Mikey. Guess where he was?" He waited a beat, looking over at the baby. "Yup, you got it. Fast asleep under a pile of leaves!"

She smiled and put Morgan in the seat next to Mikey. "He loads dishwashers. He tells stories. He folds laundry. He changes diapers. He makes good on promises."

He's too good-looking and too helpful. Do not lean into him. He came here for a reason and now he'll be leaving.

Good thing too. Brooke hadn't thought she'd be attracted—even on a purely physical level—to another man for a long time, after the way Will had treated her. And here she was, clearly still very red-blooded. Add in all of Nick's other attributes, and that made him truly dangerous.

He turned and flashed her a smile. "You okay?"

Brooke nodded. "Just needed a minute. You didn't have to do all this," she said. "I'm sure I'll find a nanny soon. I have a lead on a trustworthy possibility, but she's in college and I'd have to work around her hours."

He put a glass in the dishwasher and turned to her. "I've been doing some thinking while I've been rinsing bowls and stacking plates. Remember when I said I wasn't here about the job?"

She nodded, wondering where he was headed with this.

"I might not have come for the job," he said. "But I'm taking it."

She stared at him. He looked dead serious. *"What?"*

"What what? You heard the Satlers. I'm the hot manny."

She laughed. She couldn't help it. She honestly didn't think she'd be able to laugh for at least a few months after the conversation she and Nick had had in the living room fifteen minutes ago.

He *was* hot. Insanely so. She watched him scrape a plate clean and rinse it before putting it in the dishwasher. She looked at the folded baby clothes. She looked at Mikey, so happy in the swing, which meant he'd been burped just right. A half hour ago, she'd been ready to promise him the moon if he'd take the job. But that was before she knew why he'd even sought her out. And why he wanted the job. Heavy stuff. And she'd had enough heavy to last her a few years.

Her phone rang again.

"Could be another bride, Brooke. And with your manny on the job, you might as well as be working."

"We'll finish this conversation in two seconds," she said.

She grabbed her phone. A new client! Yes! The woman envisioned a small and intimate ceremony for family and close friends, at a local wellness retreat a friend owned. Very fast turn-around in a couple of weeks, but only thirty to forty people, tops. *Possible*, Brooke thought, her mind whirling. They made arrangements to meet tomorrow, at 6:00 p.m., for dinner at the woman's fiancé's house. If the Satler triplets were a definite, adding this client for July would mean she could take off the first couple of weeks of August, which were always slow for Dream Weddings, and just be with her twins.

Which would mean needing Nick Garroway as her nanny—manny—until her regular nanny returned. Leanna could take some time off herself and start mid-August. Win-win for everyone.

A temporary manny. A necessary temporary manny.

"Well, I've consulted with myself," Brooke said as she put the phone on the table. "The job is yours. I'll only need help until August first. Then I'll take some time off, and Leanna, my regular nanny, will be ready to come back to work for me."

He nodded. "Sounds good. Oh—and I know your ad

called for hours of nine to one during the week, but I'll make you a deal. I'll be your around-the-clock nanny, as needed—for room and board."

She swallowed. "You mean live here?"

"Temporarily. I'd rather not stay with my family. And I never liked hotels much. Besides, this way, you can work when you need to, not be boxed into someone else's hours."

Even a part-time nanny was very expensive—more than she could afford—but Brooke had always been grateful that necessity would make her limit her work so that she could spend real time with her babies. Now she'd have as-needed care for the twins without spending a penny.

Once again she wondered where Nick Garroway had come from. He was like a miracle—and everything Brooke needed right now.

"I think I'm getting the better deal," she said. "But my grandmother always said not to look a gift horse in the mouth." Especially when that gift horse was clearly a workhorse.

"Good. You get what you need and I make good on that promise. Works for both of us."

She glanced at him. He might be gorgeous and sexy, and too capable with a diaper and a stack of dirty dishes, but he *wasn't* her fantasy in the flesh; he was here because he'd promised her babies' father he'd make sure she and the twins were all right. Will had saved his life; now Nick was doing what he could to save hers. She had to stop thinking of him as a man— somehow, despite how attracted she was to him on a few different levels. He was her nanny, her manny.

But what was sexier than a man saying, "Take a break, I'll handle it. Take that call, I've got the kids. Go rest, I'll load the dishwasher and fold the laundry"?

Nothing was sexier. Which meant Brooke would have to be on guard 24/7.

Because her brain had caught up with her: the hot manny was moving into her house.

Every now and then over the past two hours, Nick would find himself doing something *so* strange, such as dividing a can of Seafood Surprise cat food between the two black-and-white cats rubbing against his leg, and he'd glance up and wonder where the hell he was and what had happened to his life. One minute he was going through his to-do list, checking on Brooke Timber. The next he was a live-in manny—at his own insistence. Caring for very small humans and cats, and making sure one particular woman was A-OK.

What?

He spooned out an equal portion for each cat in their mouse-decorated porcelain bowls, and they attacked it with gusto. After making sure their water bowl was full enough, he washed his hands—cat food kind of stank— and dried them with a little towel with dancing teacups on it. Again: *Where am I? Who am I?*

He found himself a bit surprised at how much he'd actually enjoyed all the stuff he'd taken care of around the house, such as folding the laundry—the tiny pajamas and burp cloths and soft sheets decorated with little dinosaurs. Fixing the storm door that had annoyingly squeaked. Tidying the nursery by putting away storybooks left on the table beside the glider and cleaning up sprinkles of cornstarch on the changing pad. He even liked when those two black-and-white cats jumped on the couch, beside him, and sniffed him, then sat down next to him, grooming their faces.

Nick had been one thing his entire adult life: a soldier. But this? Changing babies' diapers and telling them stories and giving them bottles and rubbing their backs when they cried? Feeding cats? This was something else entirely, and his work in this house was strangely satisfying. He had no clue why this would be the case. Playing house wasn't his thing and he had no interest in making a future of it. So, why did he feel so comfortable here when he should feel the polar opposite?

Maybe it had something to do with how coming home to Wedlock Creek had made him uneasy, unsure how the transition to civilian life would go. He'd been unsettled about the idea of seeing his father and his brother, and once again of having to leave town to start a new life elsewhere. But here in the Timber household, as this manny, of all things, he was in strange, uncharted territory, but with a defined mission for a set amount of time. The new job kept him completely distracted from those other thoughts. Being here was like a balm.

His life at the moment was as if an alien from another planet had plunked him in the least likely existence and said, "This will be weird, but you belong here right now."

That was how he felt. Like he belonged here. But still—and wasn't there always a *but* or a *still*? Something was throwing him. Brooke herself. She drew him in ways he wasn't even clear on. A sexual pull, yes, but it was more than that. When she talked, he understood her, understood the context, understood what she wasn't saying, read her expressions and knew what to say.

When had that ever happened—let alone so instantly? Never. Nick had had rare opportunities for relationships, but he'd always felt the women he dated had spoken a language he didn't understand. It was different with Brooke. And he barely knew her. He didn't know her at all, actually. He'd have to be careful not to get overly involved emotionally.

Just remember you're here on a final mission and you'll be fine, he assured himself. In fact that *was* probably why he felt so comfortable here in the first place. This was a mission, and he knew how to handle those. But all missions came to an end and then a soldier moved on. As a civilian, it would be his job to move on to what came next. His ranch. Waiting for him in sun-drenched, lazy August.

And now, officially the Timber manny for two hours, Nick was on a roll. Brooke had worked on the Satler triplets' file, then taken the nap he'd insisted on, a long, hot shower, eaten the grilled cheese and bacon he'd made for her, and sighed with happy relief when she realized he'd dabbed sunscreen on Morgan and Mikey's faces, arms, and legs, packed their stroller bag and settled them inside the double stroller. Brooke had mentioned something about taking the twins to the park to see their favorite squirrels in an oak tree.

Now she stood by the front door, one hand on the stroller, the other reaching into the tote bag and pulling out her keys. "Oh, I guess I don't need to lock up. You'll do that. Or…" she said, but trailed off.

Or did you want to join us? He had no idea why he could read her so well. She seemed to be both anxious to get the hell away from him and wondering if she should invite him on the outing.

Getting away from him seemed to be winning. He could see it in her eyes, in the way she held herself, which was the opposite of relaxed.

"Here's an idea," he said, wanting to give her the easy out. "I need to go to see my dad, let him know I'm back in town. Then how about we meet here in a couple of hours, and we can sit down and discuss your needs."

"My needs?" she repeated.

"While I'm here, I want to make your life easier. Caring for the twins, helping around the house. Whatever you need, Brooke."

She tilted her head just slightly. "You really want to make good on that promise, don't you." Not a question.

"Of course I do. Will saved my life. I owe him everything."

She took in a breath and nodded. "Well, I guess we're ready to go. Oh, you'll be needing this," she said, pulling a key off the horseshoe keychain and handing it to him. "Front door."

The key felt strange in his palm.

She gave him an awkward smile and then hurried the stroller out the door. Man, it felt weird watching her wheel the twins out of her own house while he waved goodbye on the porch as if he lived here. Which he supposed he did, for the time being. He hooked the keychain onto his own keychain and put it back in his pocket, his gaze on Brooke pushing the stroller up Oak Lane. She turned her head back to him, he held up a hand, and she waved, then crossed the street and disappeared down Main.

Part of him wanted to go after her. Which was nuts. She was a grown woman and had been caring for the twins for the past three months. She could surely handle a trip to watch squirrels on a tree without him hovering. He recognized what he was feeling: responsibility. Well, that and a soft spot for Brooke and those very cute little people.

That made sense to him. It was why he was here, after all.

For a minute he was so overtaken by all these crazy new notions, that he just stood there. But when he noticed a woman two houses down, across the street, staring at him on her porch, he went inside. He'd forgotten what a small town Wedlock Creek was. Neighbors were friendly—but nosy.

"Well, Snowball," he said to the cat with the white smudge on her nose as she rubbed against his leg. "Wish me luck. I'm off to see my dad. Think he's speaking to me?"

Snowball didn't respond, but her sister, Smudge, who had a gray smudge on her black face, stared up at him with her big green eyes.

"Yeah, we'll see," he said, giving each cat a scratch on the back.

He headed for the door and pulled out his keychain, marveling at Brooke's key, which was right next to the gold key to the house he'd grown up in, the one he wasn't welcome in anymore. Once, he'd almost taken it off and chucked it, but he'd been unable to do that. He shook his head and grabbed the fob for his Jeep, trying to forget the other two keys entirely for the moment.

After almost five years, Nick expected the Garroway house to look different, and it did, but he couldn't put his finger on why. Same white Colonial with green shutters and a black door, stone path from the driveway to the three granite steps. But something was different. There were two cars in the driveway, neither of which he recognized. His dad had company? Maybe his brother was over.

And maybe Nick should come back another time.

Or maybe the company part was good. Jeb Garroway had his Kentucky bourbon every night, at 5:45 p.m., and Nick had timed his arrival for 6:05 p.m. and a slightly less uptight version of his father. If he had people over, his dad would be civil.

He glanced at the cars, wondering if one was his brother Brandon's. He hoped not. Nick wished the two of them could fix what was broken between them, but despite being just four years apart in age, the two were never able to get past shouting at each other in person and telling the other to screw off in emails.

Nick rang the bell, then shoved his hands in his pockets. He waited, hearing the footsteps. He probably should have called first, so his father could brace himself, prepare himself. Now he'd open the door and find the black sheep of the family standing there.

The door opened. Jeb Garroway looked as surprised as Nick expected—and he looked good too. Healthier, somehow. His father was tall like Nick, but except for the height and same blue eyes, Nick, like his brother, looked more like their late mother.

"I'm medically retired from the army. Foot injury," Nick blurted out instead of saying hello like a regular son might, a son who felt welcome. "I'm planning to buy a ranch somewhere in the state. Just wanted you to know I was back and what my plans were."

"Foot okay?" his dad asked, looking his son over. Jeb was guarded—Nick could see that—but there was concern in the man's eyes, in his expression. Huh. That was unexpected—and a good sign that maybe the two of them could finally work toward putting their disagreements to rest. The rift between them always felt like a boot pressing on Nick's chest, no matter how he tried not to think of home, of family.

"Almost good as new. I was at a rehab in Texas for the past month. They fixed me up."

His dad nodded. "Well, it's good to see you."

Another good sign. A shock, really.

"You too, Dad." And it was. No matter their differences, Jeb Garroway was his father and he'd always love him, always respect him.

"Why don't you come in, Nick? Have a drink?"

"Sure," he said, surprised this was going so well. He hadn't seen his dad in so long, and the last communication, via email, had been terse. He might not have been welcome at the family house, but he'd always shot off holiday and birthday greetings in emails to his dad, despite being sure they were deleted immediately.

Nick's crime? Twelve years ago, he hadn't gone into the family business. Paper. Garroway Paper. Copy paper, stationery, construction paper, card stock. When

Nick and his brother were young, his father would take them out for hikes through the woods and tell them which trees made which types of paper. Jeb had been making it all up, that the big bur oaks were where the poster board they used for school projects came from. That their report cards were from lodgepole pines. The scrap paper they jotted down grocery lists and reminders on: spruce. Back then Nick had thought the world of paper, and Garroway Paper in particular, was everything. But as he'd gotten older, become a teenager, and developed his own interests and goals, paper had become…paper, something he didn't think much about. Like most people. His father—and brother—to whom paper could be discussed every night over dinner and was, thought Nick was disrespectful. And when he chose the military instead of a business degree and working at Garroway Paper, they both hit the roof.

Even at fourteen years old, his brother, Brandon, had been a mini Jeb Garroway, shaking his finger at Nick for turning his back on family.

Nick could have handled that. But his "betrayal of the family" turned in a direction he didn't see coming, and there was no way to argue, no words to even form. The lump in his chest had blocked all of that.

His brother had blamed him for their mother—frail from cancer treatment—taking a turn for the worse not long after he announced he'd enlisted. Neither had spoken to him at the funeral, which had been between boot camp ending and his deployment.

"You broke her heart!" his brother, who was then just a scrawny teenager, had screamed at him. "Turned your back on the family and tradition! Shame on you."

His father had just hung his head in sorrow and said nothing.

How do you defend yourself against a brokenhearted fourteen-year-old whom you love? You don't. In emails and letters to your brother, you try to explain why you enlisted, but you get back one-line replies, all the same: "go to hell!"

For those first few years, Nick hadn't always been able to come home for holidays, but when it had been possible, he'd showed up, despite the harrowing silences, the seething anger on his brother's face until Brandon had exploded and said that Nick wasn't welcome anymore.

Now here he was, about to walk inside for the first time since then.

He followed his dad and immediately noticed a difference in the place. He'd only been here three or four times over the past twelve years, but he'd always felt the chill, the starkness, the lack of life. His father had loved his mother deeply and mourned her loss, and the curtains had always been drawn, the rooms dark, the flower arrangements his mother had liked in every room no more. Now the house was infused with light. He couldn't put his finger on what else was different, but the living room was…warmer. A huge flowering plant was by the sliding doors to the patio. A bouquet of white roses graced the mantel.

And his dad did look kind of happy instead of his usual serious glumness. And definitely healthier too. Jeb had developed a belly after his wife had passed, but now was fit, with his back straight like a soldier's. That was certainly new. Jeb Garroway had always been something of a hunched-over type, hunched over the books, spreadsheets, his desktop. Suddenly his dad looked athletic. And his thick salt-and-pepper hair was freshly cut instead of its usual bushy, overgrown mop.

Nick had a feeling his dad had a lady in his life. Only thing that would explain such a transformation.

He watched Jeb pour them each two fingers of his favorite bourbon, and Nick thanked him as he handed him a glass.

"A toast," his father said, holding up his glass.

"To?" Nick asked.

"Two things. The first—you're back home, where you belong, so we have a chance for a new start."

Nick almost choked. Who was this man and what had he done with Jeb Garroway? Back where he belonged? New start? A warmth spread inside him as if he'd already swigged his bourbon.

Though…he wasn't quite sure what his dad meant about *belonged*, if Jeb thought Nick would be finally going into the paper business or not. But a new start? He'd take that.

"A new start sounds good, Dad," Nick said, holding up his own glass.

"And the second thing. I'm getting married."

Nick grinned, both at being right about his dad having romance in his life and the big news. "Dad, that's great. Who is she?"

Jeb's blue eyes lit up. "A wonderful woman named Cathy Wylie. She's exactly my age, beautiful, and she cares about paper."

Nick smiled. "She does, huh. Is she in the business?"

"No. She's a yoga instructor. She's teaching me to

elongate my muscles and to breathe." Jeb Garroway took in a deep breath, then let it out in a slow whoosh, complete with arm movements. "We met in line at Java Jane's. She heard me order my usual three shots of espresso with four sugars, and lectured me for a solid minute about the glycemic index. I was like, the *gly-what-ic what-now*? But she was so beautiful, I stood there and listened."

Nick laughed and took a sip of his drink. His father was standing here, talking to Nick, sharing his life, his happiness, his world. Nick hadn't been a part of his dad's universe for so long. Too long. Now things would be different.

"She had me try some crazy green-tea thing," his dad continued. "I didn't like it one bit—in fact I thought it was awful, but I didn't tell her that. Prettiest green eyes you've ever seen. And nothing flusters her. She calls it being grounded and level with the four elements. According to Cathy, paper is rooted in one of the four elements—earth—and a vital part of human communication."

This Cathy Wylie sounded heaven-sent. The woman cared about and respected paper! "I'm very happy for you, Dad. I hope I get to meet her."

"Well, of course you will," Jeb said. "We're having dinner here tomorrow night. Your brother will be joining us. I'd like you to be there."

Nick wasn't so sure *Brandon* would like Nick to be there. He didn't respond, but he had a feeling his expression and the slight nod let his dad know it was a possibility. Given the big changes in his dad's life, maybe the same was happening for his brother and the guy had moved on from his anger at Nick. For all Nick knew, Brandon was ready to shake on a fresh start too. *I sure hope so.*

They sipped their bourbons and then Nick noticed a small brown-and-white dog with long, furry, floppy ears running around outside in the big fenced yard, chasing a squirrel to a tree, which brought to mind Brooke and the twins. He wondered if they were watching those squirrels she'd mentioned. "Who's that?"

"Ah, that's Fritz. He's a cocker spaniel. Wonderful little guy." With absolute joy on his face, his dad watched the dog zipping through the yard, sniffing away, his ears flopping.

Thank you, Cathy Wylie, Nick thought, his guard lowering just a bit—and man, did even that tiny bit feel good. *You've turned my dad around in a great way—that's for sure.*

Jeb's smile faded. "Your mom always wanted a dog and I always said they were too much work, too much trouble. But that was wrong. Dogs are good companions and they're fun to watch. They need people and we need dogs."

Nick heard the catch in his father's voice. He put a hand on his father's shoulder, and they just stood there for a moment, watching Fritz stare up at the squirrel, which was safe on a high, leafy branch.

They might not be talking about the past, but maybe they didn't have to. Maybe they could just let bygones be bygones and start new, like his dad said he wanted. That would be just fine with Nick.

A door opened and shut, and Nick turned to see

his brother glaring at him as he came in the room and headed for the bar.

"Well, well, look who's back," Brandon said. "The prodigal son."

Brandon hadn't changed at all in the five years since Nick had seen him last. His brother had always run five miles a day and worked out four times a week, and he was as fit as ever, his dark hair corporate cut, his suit and shiny black shoes pristine. Nick couldn't see that scrawny, sobbing fourteen-year-old anymore in this guy. Maybe that was a good thing.

"I don't think four tours of duty as a combat soldier for the US Army makes for the prodigal anything," Nick said, leveling a stare at his brother.

Brandon poured himself a bourbon and took a sip of his drink, then continued the glare at Nick. "You had a duty to your family and to the family's bottom line, not to mention future generations of Garroways. But we didn't matter, did we." It was stated, not asked.

Let it go, he told himself. Dad did, and Brandon would too.

"And poor Mom, God rest her soul—" Brandon began.

There it was. There it always was.

"Brandon, that's enough," their father snapped. "Nick's home for good and we're celebrating that. I've invited him to dinner tomorrow night."

He caught the flash of anger in his brother's eyes, then something like...sadness before the anger was back. But for a second Nick did see that fourteen-year-old boy, shaking and screaming, devastated over the loss of their mother. Needing someone to blame, an outlet for his anger. Nick had been able to take it, to bear the heart-wrenching brunt, but there'd been a cost beyond losing his family. He knew that then and he knew it now. When the most important people in your life made you dispensable, you learned to deal with it however you had to.

Nick finished his drink and set down the glass. "Congratulations, Dad. I need to get going, but maybe I'll see you tomorrow night. I need to check my schedule."

"What schedule?" Brandon scoffed. "Give me a break."

Check your temper, Nick reminded himself. "I've taken a temporary job. I need to check with my boss."

"If you worked for Garroway Paper," Brandon said, "You wouldn't have to check with the boss. You'd *be* the boss. Well, co-boss."

He ignored Brandon and turned to his dad, putting a hand on his shoulder. "I'll let you know, Dad. And... thank you." With that, he headed to the door, needing to put some space between himself and his antagonistic brother.

Given Brandon's attitude, Nick had no idea if he'd show up tomorrow night for dinner. If he could, Nick would drive straight out of Wedlock Creek and put this town behind him again.

But he couldn't. He'd made a commitment—to Brooke and to Will Parker—so he was here till August, which meant he'd have to deal with Brandon whether he liked it or not. He definitely did not like it. But he'd learned in the army—and at the base rehab—that the only way forward was to actually embrace the hardship in order to come out ahead. He'd have to deal with his brother head-on.

Suddenly all he wanted was to be at Brooke's house, surrounded by her and those cute babies and the black-and-white cats. Strange as it was there, and as strange as his job title sounded to his own ears, being at Brooke's had somehow become his haven.

Chapter Four

Brooke could tell that something was bothering Nick, something that *wasn't* bothering him before he went to see his dad. The two of them were sitting at the kitchen table, eating the amazing chili and corn bread Nick had made. Of course the man cooked. She barely knew Nick Garroway, but she would not be exaggerating by calling him a domestic god. He didn't look the part; he looked more like he should be on a horse or out patrolling the streets. But he sure *was* the part.

I have a manny, she thought, smiling to herself. *Oh, that's my manny*, she imagined herself saying if someone asked who the hunk holding her twins was. *Meet my manny*. She almost laughed out loud at how crazy it sounded to her own ears.

Well, Nick Garroway might be the twins' new

manny, but she loved bath time and readying the babies for bed with fresh pajamas and stories, so she'd insisted on taking care of that, and he'd unexpectedly made them dinner. To come downstairs to the aroma of chili almost made her think she'd dreamed this whole arrangement. When was the last time someone had cooked for her? He'd even set out the cloth napkins. She'd forgotten she actually had those.

"Everything go okay at your dad's?" she'd dared to ask, not sure if she was prying.

He pushed his chili around on the plate. "Yes and no." She almost lost her appetite as he explained how his father and brother thought he'd betrayed them by enlisting in the army instead of working toward a business degree and joining Garroway Paper, and how his brother had explicitly blamed him for making his frail mother sicker. How his relationship with his father and brother had never recovered from that. "But now he's engaged to a yoga teacher who appreciates the origin of paper, and I guess happiness and her more zen qualities rubbed off on him, because he practically welcomed me home with open arms. He even invited me to dinner tomorrow night."

Her mouth dropped open and she felt her eyes going wide. "Wait a minute. My prospective new client is a yoga instructor. She invited me to dinner tomorrow night, at her fiancé's house, to meet the two of them and discuss plans." She grabbed her phone and checked her calendar for the note she'd made. "Is your father's address 249 Applewood Road?"

He smiled but seemed hardly surprised. That was life

in a small town. "Guess you'll be seeing where I grew up. Oh, and you'll meet my brother, who hates me."

"*Hates* you? That's a pretty strong word."

Nick nodded, his blue eyes narrowing. "Trust me. He does. Over a decade later, he still blames me for my mother's death."

You'd never know it from Nick's expression, but somehow she could tell that he was deeply affected by it and had been all those years. She wondered if he blamed himself too. She sure hoped not.

He dug into his chili and barely looked up, so she sensed he wanted to change the conversation, that maybe he'd decided he'd said too much. She took a piece of his delicious corn bread and lathered it with butter. Pure comfort.

"Feel free to make corn bread every single day," she said. "It's so good."

He smiled. "Army cook's recipe. I begged for it. I've never been much of a cook, but I had to know how to make Doogie's chili and corn bread. You'll soon see that my chef skills are limited to about five basic dishes."

"Eating home-cooked food that I don't have to make when I can't afford to get takeout?" she said. "Sounds very good to me."

He eyed her, then took a piece of corn bread himself. "Dream Weddings isn't doing well?"

Brooke frowned, her appetite disappearing for good. "Well, it's not what it was when my grandmother was here. She *was* Dream Weddings. Everyone knew Aggie Timber and she knew everyone. My gram was very warm and friendly, a real schmoozer, the type who'd talk to the person behind her and in front of her in line at the grocery store. I'm on the quieter side and kind of shy. I don't have her larger-than-life personality."

"Do you need that to plan someone's dream wedding, though?"

"No. But sometimes I wish I were more like her. One of my competitors is. She's raking in a lot of new engagements. And weddings are a big tourist draw here in Wedlock Creek, as I'm sure you know."

"Because of the chapel, right? Some legend about multiples?"

She nodded, picturing the beautiful century-old white chapel in the center of town. "According to the legend, those who marry at the chapel will have multiples in some way, shape or form, whether through luck, science, marriage or happenstance."

He nodded. "Not sure I believe in the legend, but we definitely have a lot of multiples in Wedlock Creek. Including your two."

"And I didn't even get married in the chapel. Or at all," she added. She hadn't figured on getting pregnant at twenty-five and turning twenty-six as a single mother. But as her gram always said, *Expect the unexpected.* It was Aggie Timber's motto for running her business. *You plan an outdoor wedding and the big day arrives, raining cats and dogs. What's the plan B? Always have a plan B and you're fine.*

In Brooke's case, a plan B for how to raise twins without a husband, or any family at all, was to *make* family: good friends, good neighbors, good nanny. But Brooke's two closest friends had moved out of town before her grandmother had died, and her neighbors were busy with their own lives and their own children. So what was left was a good nanny. And right now, thanks to Nick, she had that.

"Have you planned a lot of weddings at the chapel?" he asked.

"It's split half and half. Some couples want nothing to do with multiple babies at once. Some hope for quadruplets." She smiled. "Anyway, I like believing in legends and magic and fate and all that, so I'm a sucker for the legend. Something is definitely in the water in Wedlock Creek. We have more multiples here than just about anywhere. So brides from far away who believe in the legend hire wedding planners in town. I've had clients from all over the country."

"Well, I have no doubt my dad's fiancé will sign with you instead of your chattier competition. I hear you have an in with the son of the groom." He grinned, and for a moment she lost herself in the way his entire handsome face lit up. But then his expression darkened, as if remembering that being the son of the groom came with its own problems.

"I just realized something, Nick. The dinner with your dad and Cathy is work for me, so I'll need my manny to watch the twins. But my manny needs to be at the dinner too."

"Let's bring them. Babies have a way of calming people down."

"Or enraging them with their cries and poop explosions. You witnessed that firsthand."

He laughed and ate the last of his chili. "That's a good point. I'll ask my dad. He loves babies, so I'm sure it's no problem."

The doorbell rang, and Brooke headed over to answer

it just as a cry came from upstairs. She waited a heart-beat to see if Mikey would self-soothe back to sleep. But the cry came louder. Then louder.

The doorbell likely hadn't woken up Mikey, but Brooke was struck by the notion that she could actually answer the door, because Nick was heading up the steps to check on the screecher. By the time Brooke pulled open the door, the crying stopped, which meant Nick had Mikey in his arms and was sitting with him in the glider.

On the doorstep were two of her nosiest neighbors, one from across street and one from two houses down on that side, standing there with strange smiles and peering past her.

"Evening, Brooke," said Amy Landon. The middle-aged redhead gazed past Brooke's shoulder as if expecting a naked man to be standing there. "We heard you have a new male nanny—a *live-in*—so we thought we'd come say hi and meet him so we know who's coming and going from your house."

Her gram used to call Amy their own personal Mrs. Kravitz—a real busybody.

"Someone said he looks like he's part of a motor-cycle gang," Erica Jarello added, also peering past her.

Brooke almost smiled at that one. She was more likely to envision Nick on a horse, working cattle, but she could see him in a black leather jacket, revving a Harley. Oh yes, she could.

"Nick," she called behind her. "Some neighbors would love to meet you."

He came down the stairs with Mikey, bright-eyed and holding a little finger puppet, propped up in his arms.

"Hello," he said with a smile to the women. "I'm Nick Garroway. You know Mikey, of course."

Brooke watched both women stare up at him, practically licking their lips. The man was unusually attractive—she'd attest to that. Tall and lean and muscular in those low-slung dark jeans and a blue T-shirt.

Amy feigned interest in the baby for a second before dashing her eyes back up to Nick. "That little sweetie—of course, we do," she said, then introduced herself and Erica before Brooke could even get a word in. Both their hands lingered in Nick's for the handshake. "We live just across the street."

"It's very nice to meet you both." A high-pitched shriek came from upstairs. "Ah, that's Morgan, who just discovered he's alone in the nursery," Nick said. "I'd better go check on the little guy."

Brooke would swear both women literally swooned. Of course, it would be all over town the minute she closed the door behind them that Brooke Timber had a male nanny. Tongues would begin wagging about whether or not they were "involved." Fine, let them talk. Brooke, meanwhile, would enjoy her home-cooked chili and corn bread, and the novelty of watching someone with rippled muscles changing diapers and playing peekaboo with her children. If the neighbors would begin wondering if something was going on between them, Brooke herself would enjoy thinking about that very subject too. She might not be remotely interested in anything to do with romance—men said one thing and then did another—but fantasizing about kissing Nick? No harm there. It wasn't like she'd ever *do* it. Look But Don't Touch was a motto for a reason.

Amy and Erica peered behind Brooke again, clearly hoping for something juicy to see or hear to spread around the neighborhood, but there was no sign of the manny. They smiled at Brooke, and Amy said, "Well, that's sure a change from the usual!" and then the two women finally turned and left.

Nick came back downstairs, this time with Morgan in his arms. "Mikey's eyes drooped halfway up the stairs. He's asleep again. This one?" he said, hoisting up Morgan. "He got lonely up there by himself and asked me for a story, so I'll tell him one about the time a lizard tried to steal my lunch and then put him back down."

"Oh, he asked for a story, did he?" Brooke said with a smile.

"I can read him. Mikey too. For example, just before, Mikey made it clear he wanted a back rub, so I gave him one before laying him down and wham—asleep."

"*How* are you so good with them?" Brooke asked in wonder.

He shrugged. "Probably because I'm just passing through. Novelty makes everything easy and fun. Doesn't it." Statement, not a question.

Damn straight it did. Will Parker's good-looking face appeared in her mind. She'd been a novelty to him and he'd made her feel like she was everything. But he'd just been passing through too.

Nick might as well have dumped a bucket of cold water on her head. Then again, that was a good thing. She needed to keep being reminded that he wasn't her fantasy come to life. He wasn't the man of her dreams. The man of her dreams wasn't just passing through. And anyway, there *was* no man of her dreams, because she didn't believe in any of that anymore. People did one thing and said another. Said one thing and did another. She could only trust herself. Once burned so badly, a million times shy.

And with her life, there was no room for anything but what was already there: her children and her business.

"About the neighbors," Nick said, gesturing toward the door. "Is my living here going to be a problem for you?"

"Tongues wagging?" Brooke asked. "Let them. I'm used to being the focus of gossip. I went from being single, quiet Brooke to suddenly being visibly pregnant and, boy, did that spark a lot of gossip. I actually overheard one of the neighbors who was at the door, talking about me in Java Jane's one day, wondering who the father was and if he'd abandoned me." She shook her head. "I wanted to poke my head around the column blocking me from view and say, 'Why, yes he did, Amy.'" All that old hurt and embarrassment—more at her own stupidity for falling for all that nonsense Will had sputtered—came over her, and she crossed her arms over her chest.

"Happens to the best of us," he said.

She eyed him. "Including you?"

"Including me—for the craziest reasons that often have nothing to do with us. Know what I mean?"

She shrugged. "That it's not always personal? If that's what you mean, sorry but it's baloney. It's always personal. I wasn't this or that enough."

"To one particular guy, at one particular time," he said. "In the space-and-time continuum, Brooke, you're *everything*."

"The space-and-time what?" She laughed. "I have no idea what you mean and totally do at the same time."

"I'm just saying that *everyone* gets hurt. Victoria's Secret supermodels. The Pope. Little kids. No one is immune, no matter how gorgeous or how good or innocent. And it very often has nothing to do with you and everything to do with someone else. No immunity."

"Including you," she said with a bit of a prompt in her tone, hoping he'd elaborate on his own love troubles.

But he didn't. Rats. She wanted to know the juicy details. Plus she wondered who his type was, what kind of woman could win his heart.

"Yeah," was all he said, then did a one-handed peek-aboo with Morgan. "I see you," he said in a singsong way to the baby, who gurgled happily at him.

I want to know more about you, she thought. *I want to know everything about you.*

But she didn't want to pry. If he wanted to talk about his ex, he would. She certainly didn't want to talk about hers.

"I think this little one is ready for bed again," he said. "There's another big yawn. Tell you what, Brooke. Let's me settle him back in his crib and then I'll take care of the kitchen."

"I'll put him back," she said, reaching for him. "I know I need a nanny for when I'm working, but I'm certainly not working right now." She cuddled Morgan in her arms, kissing his baby-shampoo-scented hair. "Giving them their baths, putting on their pj's, snuggling them as I read a story in the nursery, then laying their sleepy little bodies in their cribs. Every night, when I do that and then just watch their eyes start to close, I feel like I have everything."

She sighed inwardly. There she went again, saying too much, making herself look…needy. She didn't want to come across that way.

"Well, you do have everything," he said.

That made her wonder. He'd said he wasn't the marrying kind. Or the father kind. And yet, because she had Morgan and Mikey, this sweet little family of three, he considered that *everything*. There was a contradiction there. Or maybe just ambivalence.

It doesn't matter, she reminded herself. *You're not looking for holes in his story about who he is.* And was there anything worse than ambivalence?

"So, you go put Morgan back to sleep, and I'll straighten up in the kitchen. Then we'll meet in the living room and talk about my schedule and what you'd like me to handle, and you can give me the grand tour of the house."

Part of her was glad to escape him again—he listened too intently, looked at her too closely, inferred too well. The other part never wanted to be more than a foot away from him.

Fifteen minutes later—Morgan needed a story and a little rocking to fall back asleep—Brooke came downstairs to find the dishwasher going and the kitchen spotless. In the living room was a pitcher of iced tea that he must have made and a plate of the mixed cookies she'd picked up yesterday, unable to resist anything from the Solero Sisters bakery. The man was amazing. Every woman should have one of him.

"Army taught you all this?" she asked in complete

wonder. "Making a kitchen spotless? Whipping up iced tea with lemon wedges?" she asked. Or had a previous live-in love? An ex-wife? An ex-girlfriend? She doubted he'd been married before. But he'd hinted at an ex. She was *so* curious.

"Not so much how to clean a kitchen counter or load a dishwasher," he said, "but to take care of business. Do what needs doing, the right way and efficiently, and it's done. A little initiative is all it takes to learn how to do something—and correctly."

Did he have any idea what an aphrodisiac this kind of talk was to her? Someone she could trust to take care of stuff? Without her even asking? "It sure is nice to have you around, Nick Garroway."

He smiled—that big, sexy smile that made her knees wobble. "I'm glad one person in this town feels that way."

She reached out and touched his shoulder, which was hard, muscular and broad, and he looked at her for a moment. Uh oh. She quickly pulled her hand away. He was attracted to her; she could tell. And if it wasn't obvious, now he knew she was attracted to him too. Dammit. She needed that to be a secret. From him.

"About that work schedule," she said, clearing her throat and moving into the living room, trying to be all business.

But he poured her a glass of iced tea and nudged the cookie plate toward her, and she felt so taken care of that again she just wanted to run with it and lay her head against his chest, feel his arms around her. Just for a few moments, even. Ever since her grandmother had passed away, and then she had found out she was pregnant, she'd had to tell herself that everything was going to be okay. In Nick's company, she *believed* it.

She took a sip of the iced tea, so refreshing and perfectly sweet and lemony. He sat just a foot away from her on the sofa, angled toward her, and again she was struck by the urge to lay her head in his lap and have him stroke her hair. Or to kiss him hard on the lips. She sat back, so aware of him. Brooke was five foot seven, so not exactly petite, but Nick towered over her.

To distract herself from him, she started talking about the ideal schedule for her, and of course he said that whatever worked for her worked for him, since his whole point in taking the job was to be of help to her. They decided on a similar schedule that her former nanny had. He'd do overnight wake-ups so that she wouldn't be bleary-eyed during the day while working on weddings and dealing with bridezillas—her New Year's Eve–client was one of those. She'd care for the twins from 5:00 a.m. to 9:00 a.m., for breakfast and playtime, and then he'd take over from 9:00 a.m. to 1:00 p.m., including on Saturdays, which was always a busy workday, and again between 5:00 p.m. and 6:00 p.m., when for some reason her brides tended to panic most. Sunday would be a complete day off for him—unless she needed him to watch the babies because of a crazed client or wedding emergency. In fact, he'd added, he would be on call all day, all night.

"I'm here for you," he said—quite seriously.

What was that famous question by Sigmund Freud? What did women want? Brooke Timber wanted someone there for her. Someone in her corner, someone who had her back. Someone she could count on. Trust. Until August, that someone was Nick Garroway.

"And I mean it," he added. "Let's say you get a call that the caterer can't switch the hip sole for the dull salmon and you have to find a new caterer the night before the wedding. Text me and *poof*—" he snapped his fingers "—I'm in the nursery. That simple."

He had no idea how much that made her want to lean over and kiss him. Full on the lips.

He was becoming way too indispensable—in every possible area of her life. But Nick *would* only be here for another couple of weeks. She had to remember that.

"I appreciate that. Very much," she said. "Thank you."

"My pleasure," he said.

Because she could barely handle being so close to him on the couch, she took him on a tour of the small house. The cozy living room, the sunny kitchen and the Dream Weddings office made up the first floor. Three bedrooms on the second floor—the nursery, her room and the guest room, which was his bedroom. She peered in to see his big green duffel bag on the bed. Tonight he'd be in that bed.

There was no way she'd get any sleep knowing that. Even if she didn't have to get up to take care of her own children.

Just after midnight Nick heard a cry and got out of his very comfortable bed in the guest room in Brooke's house. He hadn't been sleeping anyway. He'd been thinking about Brooke. All about her.

He kept seeing her face—all her different expressions. Concentration, curiosity, frustration, surprise, contentment. Contentment was usually when she was holding one of her babies. And when she discovered he'd taken care of something she hadn't yet gotten to— changing a lightbulb, scooping the litter box, replenishing the diaper stack in the nursery from the huge bag in the garage. Putting together that bookcase for the nursery. He'd just walked around the house while she'd been working earlier tonight, checked things out and he'd done what needed to be done, whether or not it was baby related. The way he saw it, taking care of the babies meant taking care of their home too. And their mom—their beautiful, sexy mom.

He headed out of his room just as Brooke was coming out of hers. She wore yoga pants, with a long T-shirt and furry slippers, and her hair was in a high ponytail.

"I've got this," he said, wagging a finger at her. "It's my job."

She smiled and slapped a palm to her forehead. "I heard Morgan cry and just popped out of bed without thinking. I forgot I had help."

Morgan let out another shriek, and they smiled at each other and both headed into the nursery.

"I know I could be getting back into bed and blissfully going to back to sleep," she said, "but I guess it's just instinct to want to make sure he's okay. Tired as I always am, I like cuddling the twins in this chair, rocking them back to sleep. I always want them to know everything will be okay."

"I get it. You're looking out for them, and I'm looking out for you."

She smiled. "Is that why I was saved from scooping cat poop earlier?"

He nodded. "If you're not doing those kinds of chores, you're freed up to spend quality time with Morgan and Mikey."

"Yup, I thought it before and now I'll say it aloud— everyone needs one of you."

As she crossed in front of the window, where a sliver of moonlight shone through, she was silhouetted and he was struck—again—by how beautiful she was. He had a sudden yearning to touch her, feel her hair, her face, her lips.

None of the above was why he was here, though, so he tried to focus on the baby fussing. But once they had reached the crib, Morgan had stopped crying; perhaps the voices had lulled him back to sleep. They crept back out of the room and stood in the dim lighting of the hallway.

He had to prolong this. Anything to keep her from turning and disappearing into her bedroom. He wanted to talk to her, look at her, drink her in.

He was surprised by how much too. After Elena and the way she'd blindsided him, he thought he was done with women, done with it all. Now here he was, unable to take his eyes off Brooke, the pull of her too strong.

Then again, he had thought another baby couldn't possibly grip his heartstrings and yank, and the Timber twins were doing just that.

"Well, good night again," she said.

Well, hell. He was about to suggest making some hot chocolate—with marshmallows. Or maybe a game of backgammon, not that he remembered how to play, but he'd seen a set on the coffee table. Or they could watch an old movie.

Except Brooke had to work tomorrow and so did he. If he had to get up a few times a night with the twins, he'd better sleep when he had the chance or he'd be no good to anyone.

Rats. "From now on," he said, "burrow right back under the covers if you hear one of the twins in the middle of the night. I've got it."

"I'll try." She glanced up at him, shaking her head with a smile. "Are you even real?"

"Here," he said, taking her hand and putting it on his cheek. "Real?"

He hadn't meant to do that.

She held his gaze, and parts of him he'd suppressed for months came back to life.

Then suddenly they were kissing and he wasn't even sure who leaned closer to whose lips first. Her hands were on his back, his shoulders and then his hair as they deepened the kiss, and his were inching under her long T-shirt, higher and higher until he felt bare skin. He felt her shudder and he drew her closer.

"Waaah! Waah-waah!"

Noooo. He never wanted this—warmth and magic and sensation—to end.

"Waah-waah!"

"That's Mikey this time," she whispered against his ear. "And a good thing too, because this is crazy." She stepped back and crossed her arms over her chest. "We can't do this, Nick. I can't do this. For many reasons."

And he could probably list them right here. She'd been hurt pretty badly by Parker—that went without saying. Her trust level was probably at an all-time low. Plus she had enough on her plate without adding a love affair with her live-in manny to the mix. Her *temporary* live-in manny.

Plus he'd said it himself. He wasn't a family guy. She was a family woman, a package deal. So he'd better keep his lips and hands and mind off her.

And anyway, tomorrow night they'd be having dinner at his dad's house. With his brother running his mouth. Nick had no doubt he'd need all his focus on getting through the meal without making a fist.

He headed back to his room, one of the black-and-white cats—Smudge, he thought—padding up the stairs and stopping in front of his doorway. The cat stared at him with narrowed green eyes, as if shaking his furry head at him. *Hands off the woman*, he was pretty sure Smudge was telling him, but then the cat went into his room and jumped on the bed, making himself comfortable. A few seconds later, Snowball joined him.

If he had to be honest, he was glad for the company. Nick had become something of a loner over the years—lately in particular—but he didn't like being alone. Not at all.

We can't do this, Nick. I can't do this, for many reasons...

Listen to the cat. No more touching Brooke—no matter how badly he wanted or needed to.

Chapter Five

As if she could sleep after that. Brooke did close her eyes; every moment was committed to memory. The way his lips felt, his hands on her, the pure desire she'd felt. If Mikey hadn't cried, she might have taken his hand and led him to her bedroom, and that would have been a huge mistake. Not in the immediate short-term maybe; in fact, despite *everything*, sleeping with a man who looked like Nick Garroway struck her as exactly what she needed, the way a double espresso or two glasses of wine or a big slice of chocolate cake could have an immediate impact.

But in the morning—the awkwardness. The weird thing they'd have to do to get back to a professional relationship. Even if—and it was a big even *if*—Brooke was willing to let herself fall for another man, she was under no illusions that Nick was going to fall magically in love and become a family man just because he had the moves.

Put him out of your mind, she told herself. *You're wide awake, so you might as well get some work done.* She grabbed her laptop and opened up the Satler file. Soon she had pages filled of options, graphics of how they would complement one another, such as table settings and centerpieces, wedding gowns and bridal party dresses, caterers, bakers, and three individual wedding cakes that worked together yet fit each sister in a particular way. And of course, how each bride could feel it was *her* day, rather than *their* day, in a triple extravaganza. She'd give it a polish in the morning, then email the Satlers, pretty confident they'd hire her.

Her email icon lit up, and Brooke clicked it. Her New Year's Eve–bride, Francesca, was obsessing over what to do at midnight.

Should we have the ceremony start at midnight, or should the minister time the "I now pronounce you husband and wife" at midnight? Or should just the kiss come at midnight? Thoughts?

Francesca ended the email with a stressed-face emoticon.

If Brooke knew her more-than-slightly neurotic client, Francesca, and she did, she had a very strong hunch that Francesca had picked a fight with Bryce, her salt-of-the-earth fiancé, because she was anxious about something else entirely, and that anxiety had morphed into obsessing over tiny details of her midnight wedding, six months from now. All she really had to do here was remind Francesca of what Francesca really needed at that moment.

No matter what you choose, you're marrying the man you love, the man of your dreams, the guy who sat beside you in the emergency vet's office at 3:00 a.m. last winter when that sweet boxer of yours had been injured. Just marry him. Everything else is icing. I love the idea of ceremony starting at the stroke of midnight—your first instinct when we sat down to plan out your wedding.

She clicked about ten different emojis, including a wedding gown, a top hat, two hearts, a man and a woman facing each other with lips pursed, and clicked send.

You are so right, Brooke! I knew I could count on you—even at 3:17 a.m.!

If only life were always this easy, Brooke thought, sending back a smiley face and then shutting off her laptop.

But she still couldn't sleep. All she could think about was that story Francesca had told her about her beloved dog getting hurt in the middle of the night when he went through the doggie door, into the yard, and found some preying animal out there, and she'd called her then-boyfriend, now-fiancé, sobbing and scared. He'd rushed over, gotten her into his car, gently wrapped the dog in a towel and rushed him over to the emergency vet, a half hour away, then handled everything, from talking to the vet to the medications to the bill. The kicker? Her boyfriend didn't like dogs and didn't want a dog, and hers had been a huge argument between them since they'd met a month prior, since he didn't want to come over to her place and hated how the dog's schedule determined hers. They'd been on the verge of breaking up.

But when Francesca was sobbing and scared, and the dog needed help? He was there. With everything he had. That night taught them both something about how they felt. Two months later: engaged.

That was what Brooke *really* wanted: someone she could call at 2:00 a.m., someone who'd rush over. Someone she could count on. Through her pregnancy and since the twins were born, she'd been on her own through it all, the scary moments, the joyous moments. She'd thought she was done with love, but the truth was that she wanted her person so badly, her heart hurt. But at the same time, she wasn't exactly in trust mode. Since her grandmother had died, Brooke had felt something of a crusty shell forming over her, inside her. Not hardened, exactly, but there.

She temporarily had Nick Garroway, who was so there for her, she almost couldn't process it. *There for me...until August.* Then poof, gone. Like Will Parker.

Tears stung her eyes, and she took a breath and focused on the faces of her twins. Everything she did, she did for them. She saw their dimples and their soft brown hair, those big blue-hazel eyes that the pediatrician said would probably turn her own pale brown shade in a couple of months.

A calm came over her and as she felt herself drifting off to sleep, she thought she heard a baby crying. *Nick's got it*, she thought, burrowing under the quilt as he'd told her to do. But instead of falling asleep in a warm cocoon, everything taken care of, her eyes popped open. Because she'd realized right then that letting Nick handle the 3:30 a.m. wake-up time while she went back to sleep—or tried to—meant that she did *trust* him.

There was basic trust, and then there was this deep sense of peace she felt in her bones about Nick Garroway. She had the crazy feeling he'd lay down his life for her and the twins.

But would he stay for her and the twins when he wasn't needed? No way. No matter what that man represented to her between now and August, she couldn't forget that he wasn't ever going to be hers—or be her babies' father.

There was no mention of the kiss the next morning. Nick wanted to bring it up in order to apologize again, but how awkward would that be? Brooke was moving around the house, avoiding whatever room he was in— and eye contact. Okay, fine, she needed some space from what had happened and so did he. He'd tried to sleep but couldn't, so he took a long, hot shower and got dressed, then checked out the *Gazette* online to see what was happening in town for kids and babies. Bingo: story time at the library for babies through eighteen months.

At exactly nine o'clock on the dot, he was about to head into the kitchen when he heard Brooke telling the twins a story about Grammy Aggie, and he was so touched that, for a moment, he held back and listened.

"Grammy Aggie was a magical nana who made everyone feel special," she was saying. "She had two kitty assistants, named Snowball and Smudge. One day Grammy Aggie's own granddaughter, a little girl named Brooke, was sad about not having parents, because a mean girl at school was making fun of her for it, and Grammy Aggie told Brooke that she did have parents, that they were in heaven and were her special guardian angels, just like your father is now."

Nick lowered his head at the mention of Will. He didn't hear the note of bitterness in her voice that had been there yesterday, and he was glad for that. If he did anything in his short time with the Timber family, he was grateful he could give all three of them a little piece of Will Parker back, the best part, the part that did care and had wished he'd acted differently. There were many moments of truth, and in that final one, these three had been loved by Parker.

"Ga ba ga!" one of the babies said. Nick could easily tell the twins apart physically, but he didn't have their babbles down yet.

"Ga ba ga!" Brooke said back and laughed, and one of the babies laughed, the sweetest sound on earth.

He figured it was safe to come in. The babies were in their swings, on the table.

She glanced up at him and then hid her face in a mug of coffee. "Morning," she mumbled.

"About that kiss," he said, then mentally whacked himself upside the head. Hadn't he just told himself it would be awkward to talk about it? They'd covered it night last—the kiss had been a mistake that wouldn't happen again. End of story.

Except things were awkward regardless right now and ignoring reality had never really worked out for Nick. It was his go-to, to just pretend certain issues didn't bother him when they were tearing his gut apart. He didn't want to do that with Brooke.

"Nothing to talk about," she said brightly, shutting her laptop. "Great news—I spent a good hour last night finalizing the Satler plans and sent it off before the twins even woke up this morning. Cross your fingers for me. Dream Weddings needs their triple business."

Well then. He'd tried. Perhaps he should just let it go.

"I'm sure they'll hire you, Brooke. Didn't one say you were 99 percent hired?"

She smiled. "Thanks to my manny." Her cheeks turned red. "Are you okay with being referred to as a manny? I could call you a nanny or a sitter."

"Manny, nanny, sitter. All good." He smiled, then glanced at the clock. "Ah, time to get to the library. It's baby hour. There's a story time for crawlers. For babies up to a year and a half."

"You want to go to that? I went once and wow, the noise. Between the shrieking and the crying and the crawler who pulled up on my knee and then spit up on me, I haven't been back."

Nick smiled. "Well, it sounds like my kind of event. I figured on that and then a stroll back here for tummy time, rest hour and then lunch."

She tilted her head and stared at him. "How do you know about tummy time?"

"It's my job to know." Plus he'd done a lot of research in those couple of hours after the kiss, when he hadn't been able to sleep. He'd gotten a crash course on three-month-old babies and read up on twins too.

She stared at him so hard, he would pay to know what she was thinking.

"Well, I'd love to come," she said. "Not being the sole responsible party for them at crowded baby events makes it lot more fun. And I'm all done with work for the day, until the meeting tonight with my new client and your dad."

Oh right. That. At least the question of whether or not he was going was taken out of the equation. He *had* to go for his new job. "I was trying to put that out of my head."

"Oh. Sorry. Is it really that bad?"

He nodded. "Well, at least not where my dad is concerned, so that's something. Maybe a happy occasion like a wedding will help my brother's mind-set. It's definitely helped my father."

She seemed about to ask a question about his family, so he rushed to mention he wanted to change the twins before they left, then dashed them upstairs.

Once back down, they each put a twin in the stroller, packed up the stroller bag and off they went.

Nosy Amy waved from her porch, where she was sitting on a white rocking chair and reading the *Gazette*, with a yellow mug on the little table next to her. As they crossed the street, she called out, "You look just like a family!"

Every muscle in Nick's body seized up, and he felt Brooke stiffen beside him.

He shot Amy a tight smile, noticing Brooke doing the same.

"Busybody!" Brooke whisper-muttered.

The woman continued to stare at them as they made their way toward Main Street.

"You just know she thinks we're involved," Brooke said. "She's probably spreading rumors all over town."

"We should make out in front of her," Nick said. "*Really* give her something to talk about."

Brooke grinned. "You're right. Why do I even let her get to me?"

"You're human. Can't be helped."

"It's really nice having someone on my team," she said. "I miss that more than anything."

"Your grandmother?" he asked. "I heard a little of the Grammy Aggie story you were telling the twins."

She glanced at him. "My gram and my friends who moved. I got used to being so alone and didn't realize how much I missed having people there for me. Even just people to diss Amy on my behalf."

"Oh, I'm happy to help there. Team Brooke, all the way."

She looked at him again, then kept her gaze straight ahead. "That promise you made really means something to you, doesn't it."

"Yes. It does."

She nodded slowly. It suddenly struck him that she thought *that* was what he was talking about, that that was why he was here, doing all this. It was and wasn't. The promise had brought him to her house, but Brooke had taken over in importance; it was *Brooke* who had him bending over backward, not a promise he'd made to the man who'd saved his life.

But there was no need to tell her that, and it was better that she didn't know. He wasn't sure *he* wanted to know. Still, somehow, when it came to Brooke, things were clear.

You look just like a family... Once upon a time, very briefly, he'd thought that about himself and another woman and a baby, but he'd quickly learned he'd been romanticizing, that he didn't share Elena's strong feelings so much as he was attracted to her and believed in the aid work she was doing at an Afghan orphanage. His heart had really only belonged to little Aisha, just a few months old. In the end he'd hurt Elena and destroyed his opportunity to keep tabs on the baby he'd found abandoned near their unit.

He'd screwed up so hard that, for a solid few weeks, he'd questioned every judgment he made and worried about the soldiers around him. Slowly he'd gotten himself back and tried not to think about Elena or Aisha, but he wasn't about to make the same mistake with Brooke and her twins. He was attracted, yes. He felt responsible for her and her children. But his heart had long been buried under rough scar tissue.

No more kisses in the middle of the night, he told himself. He glanced at her in her tank top and denim skirt and sandals and sparkly blue toenails. No matter how much he wanted Brooke Timber in his bed, being physically involved never came without emotional shackles. And unless he could imagine walking down Main Street with Brooke and her children as more than just the nanny—manny—he had to do something about his attraction to her.

Like ignore it. He wouldn't be part of her family or his own. That word had been blown to bits for him by the Garroways. But then Elena had envisioned exactly that—a family—of her, him and the baby girl who'd brought them together. He'd hurt Elena, and she'd been furious, and she'd shut him out of the baby's life. That was over a year ago and he was still surprised at how much it stung. In the end it was for the best, of course, but it still burned a hole in his gut.

He shut his eyes against the memories. As a soldier, he'd been trained to ignore everything but the mission. He'd simply take over as his own commander. Brooke Timber was off-limits and that was an order.

They turned onto Main Street and headed into the library, which easily snapped him out of the past. The children's room was crowded with parents and caregivers and lots of babies, both crawling and in strollers. Unfortunately story time meant sitting on the floor, and since he was a big guy, he chose spots in the back of the room. With the stroller parked, he and Brooke both took a twin and sat on the floor with a baby in their laps.

"Let me see those darling little Timber twins!" a middle-aged blonde woman sitting diagonally said as she scooted closer. "Aren't they adorable. What sweet cheeks! And look at those dimples!"

Nick was waiting for the lady to take a breath, but she kept going with her comments. At least she was being nice.

"You two are being good for Mommy and Daddy, aren't you!" the woman continued, tapping each baby on the nose.

For the second time in fifteen minutes, Nick froze. Daddy? Him? Nick thought he radiated "not a father" but then again, he *was* the manny.

"Actually, Natalie—" Brooke started to say, but Mikey started shrieking.

"Oh, you little cutie," Natalie cut in. "So temperamental. Well, better get back to my spot before someone takes it. Nice to see you!" After making the baby cry, she hurried off.

Nick scowled at her back, but story time was starting, so he kept his thoughts to himself.

Like that he'd been mistaken for Brooke's husband and the twins' father. He hoisted Mikey high in his arms and rubbed his back, and that ended the shrieks. The little guy wasn't exactly listening to the librarian with the melodic voice read a Curious George book or looking at the pictures she held up high, but at least he was quiet now.

As the hour ended and they left in a sea of toddlers and strollers, Brooke was quiet.

"Dollar for your thoughts," he said as they exited the library and stepped into the brilliant July sunshine.

"Worth that much? When we were kids, it was a penny."

"And no one ever got that penny, so I figured that was still the case."

She smiled. "I was just thinking."

"About?"

"About how much I liked Natalie Howaman mistaking us for a family."

"Because you don't like having a male nanny?"

"Because I like the idea of having a husband. A father for the twins. In that twenty seconds of her assumption, I did. And I *really* liked it. I thought I was done with men and dating and romance after Will. But I'm not. I *can't* be. That's giving up. And how can I give up when I have two very young, impressionable people to model life for?"

He stared at her, unsure what to say.

What he wanted to blurt out was, *I'm just the nanny, lady.* But he'd asked, hadn't he?

He knew his discomfort came from feeling responsible for what she'd said. About wanting a husband and father for her children. But that guy couldn't be him.

"I can understand that," he said. "You're a good mother, Brooke."

"That's the most important thing to me."

What was the most important thing to him? Making sure Brooke was okay and then hitting the road, buying the ranch he'd been dreaming of for a long time now.

Yes—that was it. He'd get Brooke settled, her real nanny would return and then he'd leave in peace. He always felt better when he knew, solidly, what he was doing.

"I'm surprised anyone could mistake me for a family man," he said. "Someone once told me I radiated loner." Not that that was a good thing. Elena had been right though. He'd bonded with her, to a point, over baby Aisha's well-being as she'd been nursed back to health, but that bond wasn't all that strong for him, not like it had been for Elena. He wasn't meant to be part of a family. Hadn't that been made clear to her? No, it hadn't.

She glanced at him. "What you radiate, in my now experienced opinion, is 'good with babies.' You said you took care of a baby overseas? In Afghanistan?"

He frowned. The topic was on his mind and she'd

just brought it up, so maybe that was a sign he should tell her. Talking about Elena and Aisha would bring it all back to the surface and remind him of what had happened when he wasn't forthright—even if it wasn't intentional. He absolutely *had* to be with Brooke.

"Yes," he said, that pretty, tiny face with round dark eyes and wispy black hair coming into his mind. "I helped care for a baby for several days during random time off when I was a soldier. I had to learn on the job, and for some reason, a lot of it came naturally."

"I'll push," he said, putting a hand on the stroller bar. He needed something to do.

She stepped to the side, tilting her head as she looked at him. "Whose baby was it?"

Aisha would be a toddler, talking, walking. "I came across an abandoned baby while on patrol outside our unit," he said, wheeling the stroller down the curb and then back up across the street. "She ended up being adopted by an aid worker, so she's fine." He shook his head. "But I wasn't fine—not for a long time."

Brooke stopped walking and put a hand on his arm. "What happened?"

"Let's keep walking," he said. "It helps to be doing something while I talk." *While I think about it.*

As they walked, slowly he told her everything. How he'd found the baby in a rough basket lined with a tattered blanket and a note handwritten in Dari. He'd made out the few words: *orphan, sick, help* and *needs a home*. The words had punched his gut. He could remember looking down into the basket, at the sweet, innocent baby, so helpless and alone and ill. Right then he was all the baby had. He'd left a note, in the basic Dari language he'd picked up, tacked to a nearby tree, that the baby would be at a local orphanage run by aid workers, since they had access to a doctor and nurse there.

The baby had been very sick and no one was sure if she'd pull through. One of the aid workers, Elena, a kind, young American woman from Indiana, named her Aisha, which was Arabic for alive and well, and promised to give her TLC while she was being evaluated and treated. He'd been aware that Elena had a crush on him; she didn't hide it, and he'd been so overwhelmed with emotion that he'd kissed her. And more. But he'd never really been thinking about Elena through any of it. And he regretted that more than anything.

Back then the relief he'd felt, that even if the baby didn't pull through that she'd be loved for her remaining time, had shaken him so much, he'd been oblivious to most else going on. When had he started caring? He'd had two days off and had gone back to see Aisha both days, holding her, rocking her, talking to her, asking her to pull through so that she could find a new family. And when the doctor had reported that Aisha had turned a corner, he'd picked Elena up and swung her around, setting her down with a kiss on the cheek.

Elena hadn't liked the cheek kiss. She could tell right away that something was different between them now that the baby was all right. She'd mistaken his deep concern for Aisha, the little one he'd found, with love for her—Elena.

What a disaster that had turned into. Elena had started talking about adopting Aisha together. She'd thrown the word *marriage* around. How had he gotten this so wrong? How could he not have seen any of this coming? Was he blind? Unable to see what was right in front of him? Maybe he was just selfish, self-absorbed, so used to keeping to himself that there was no room for anyone else in his head. But he'd had to come clean with her, and he had, as gently as he could. Elena had been devastated and had told him to leave.

He'd come back his next day off to be told that Elena was adopting Aisha herself and that he wasn't welcome, that he was a liar and had misled her. He hadn't meant to. Sometimes he'd jar awake at night, thinking about Aisha's big dark eyes, and Elena's anger, hating that he'd hurt her.

He didn't like thinking about it—the baby, the betrayal in Elena's eyes, his regret that he'd unintentionally made her think he had plans for the three of them as a family, even a makeshift one while they were overseas.

Nick knew his limitations.

"I'm glad that Aisha found a good home," Brooke said, stopping again and turning to look at him. "Although it sounds like it was rough going for you, at least that precious baby you rescued is all right now."

He nodded against the lump in his throat and pushed the stroller up the slight incline of the next curb. "That's true." He resumed walking and she did too.

"I hope you keep your thoughts on that," she added. "Instead of where you think you went wrong. You did so much right, so much good, Nick."

He shrugged. "I unintentionally misled someone. And then I got blindsided because of it. I hated being shut out of Aisha's life, not knowing if she was thriving, although I assume she was." He let out a breath and shook his head. "I thought I was pretty closed off before all that—when Elena slammed the orphanage door in my face and told me I wasn't welcome, I felt something else shutter inside me."

"Oh, Nick. I'm so sorry about all that."

He nodded because he'd run out of steam; he didn't want to talk about this anymore.

Because he was dangerously close to doing it all again. By kissing Brooke last night, he'd started down a path he had no plans to continue to go down; he was exiting on a different road in just a couple of weeks. He was buying a ranch, located hours from Wedlock Creek.

He couldn't imagine making Brooke think he had intentions other than to help her out, to be what she needed until her nanny returned. He had to be careful with how he acted, how he presented himself. And kissing her was exactly the way to mess everything up.

He had to be careful. He couldn't hurt Brooke. He wouldn't.

Chapter Six

As Brooke got ready for the dinner with her new client—and Nick's father and brother—she couldn't stop thinking about everything he'd told her. At least now she knew what she was dealing with.

She pulled a sleeveless floral sheath dress from her closet, and a pair of low-heeled sandals, aware of how nice it was to get ready without the twins in their carriers, on her bed. A few weeks ago, with no nanny or sitters available, she'd had to bring the twins with her to the Mayfair Hotel in Brewer for wedding-day prep for the Webber-Hayfield union, and she'd been on the phone with the very late florist when she realized she had two different shoes on. Between the stroller—albeit quiet stroller, thanks to the serious napping her twins had done that late afternoon—and her mismatched shoes and the spit-up on the lapel of her suit, she'd gotten more than a few raised eyebrows and zero referrals from the Webbers or the Hayfields.

She had a lot on her mind right now—Nick, the dinner at his family's home, not to mention hoping to secure his future stepmother as her client—and not having to worry about the twins right now was a relief. She could hear Mikey babbling in the nursery and occasionally Nick's voice as he talked to the twins. He was telling them they were going to get to meet his dad's dog, Fritz, and that he was probably the cutest dog they'd ever seen in their three months on earth.

She laughed, marveling at how Nick always managed to make her forget her stress—even when he was the cause of it.

She froze for a moment, wondering if being with her twins caused *him* stress, reminding him of Aisha and all he'd gone through. He'd walked into her life, picked up Mikey and taken the job as her nanny all to fulfill a promise, so if her babies did trigger memories, he certainly plowed through it. The soldier in him, she realized. But still, what did he do with all of those feelings?

He probably dismissed them. Ignored them. Fought them.

She sat on her bed and slipped her right foot into a flat brown hiking sandal before she realized it hardly matched the pretty silver one on her right foot. She shook her head and kicked off the brown one, then grabbed the other silver one. *Concentrate*, she told herself. *Stop thinking about Nick Garroway when he's not going to be here come August. Appreciate him while he's your hot manny, but stop wondering and speculating...and fantasizing.*

As if she could stop thinking about the way he'd kissed her, how she'd been backed against the wall, his hands roaming, the hard planes of his chest pressed to hers.

"Fritz has the floppiest ears you'll ever see," she heard Nick say.

"Ba ga!" Mikey yelled.

Then baby laughter.

"You little scamp! Does your chewy bunny like being thrown on the floor? I doubt it."

More baby laughter.

She sighed and strapped on the silver sandal. The reality of her life and the fantasy of Nick were one and the same. That was the problem. That was why she couldn't stop the crazy thoughts popping into her mind all day.

You look like a family...

Her family had always been just the three of them—she and the twins. She'd been alone in the delivery room. No husband, no significant other, no family. She'd been alone while pushing the stroller up and down Main Street these past three months, noticing all the families. Not just ones that included two partners, but generations of family. Grandparents, aunts, uncles, cousins. It wasn't her life, but what she'd give for her twins to have all that love and connection and a clan of their own.

"Five minutes to head out," came the loud, strong voice of her hot manny.

Nick Garroway wouldn't let her leave the house with mismatched shoes or baby spit-up on her lapel.

He wouldn't let her be late to a meeting. He was here for her, just like he'd said he'd be.

Like he'd promised to be.

She bit her lip. All those crazy thoughts she was having? She had to stop it. He'd promised a fallen soldier to make sure she was okay, and since she wasn't really okay, he'd stepped into her life and was taking over until her regular nanny returned. *That's all this is,* she reminded herself. *If you forget it for a second, you're an even bigger fool than you were with Will Parker.*

She took a deep breath and stood up. "Be there in a sec," she called back.

With no thoughts of Nick Garroway as her person, she told herself.

How she'd accomplish that when she was going to a family dinner of his was beyond her, but one thing at a time, right?

According to Nick, his dad and her prospective client were both thrilled about the idea of babies coming to their family dinner tonight. That gave Brooke a good feeling about Jeb Garroway. Anyone who'd welcome the wedding planner's twin babies to a dinner gathering had to be all right. By her anyway.

"What did he say when you told him your temporary job was as a nanny—and for the wedding planner?" she asked as they pulled into the driveway of his father's house.

Nick turned off the engine. "He said, 'You always do your own thing, that's for sure.'" I couldn't tell if he meant that in good way or a bad way."

Brooke got out and opened the back door to take out

Morgan's car seat. "I think most people admire those who do their own thing. Even when it doesn't serve them."

"I don't know about that," Nick said, unlatching Mikey's seat and carrying him in one hand while he grabbed the gift bag containing the bottle of champagne he'd stopped for. "Most people I know want their loved ones to toe the line. Do what's expected of them."

"Welcome!" came a male voice from the doorway as an adorable brown-and-white cocker spaniel came padding out, wagging its tail.

Brooke turned to see a man in his late fifties, tall like Nick, but with lighter hair and softer features, and a woman heading toward them.

"I'm Jeb Garroway, Nick's father. And this lovely woman is my fiancée, Cathy Wylie. The floppy-eared guy is Fritz."

"So nice to meet you," Brooke said. "And hello, very cute Fritz."

The dog sniffed her leg and padded back inside.

"Such a small world," Cathy said, smiling at them. "To have my fiancé's son working as the nanny for the wedding planner I made an appointment with. Something here has definitely been charted in the stars." Like Jeb, Cathy was in her late fifties. She had wavy blond hair to her shoulders and sparkling green eyes.

"I believe the correct word is *manny*," came another voice from the doorway.

Brooke glanced up. A guy who looked something like Nick stood there, holding a drink. He was tall and muscular and good-looking, but his half-wary, half-scowling expression took something away. The infamous brother, she presumed.

"Meet Brandon, my other son," Jeb said. "Jeb, this is Brooke Timber."

Brandon nodded at her, and she smiled back.

"And who are these darlings?" Cathy asked, peering into the car seats. "Let's get them inside and you can introduce us."

They headed in, with Brooke aware of the tension between Nick and his brother. Everyone seemed aware of it but was ignoring it for the time being.

They went into a big living room that had a gorgeous stone fireplace with two sofas set around it. Fritz curled up on a red dog bed by the fireplace. Brooke set the baby seats on the rug beside the huge wood coffee table, and Cathy rushed over to coo at them.

"This is Morgan and this is Mikey. They're three months old," Brooke said.

Cathy touched a hand to her chest. "They're precious."

"They are, indeed," Jeb said.

From the way Cathy slid her hand into Jeb's and squeezed, Brooke could tell that Jeb was thinking of his own two boys when they'd been babies. And that Cathy had had a hand in helping Jeb accept his older son for who he was, not who Jeb had wanted him to be. Or become.

Brooke smiled at Jeb and Cathy. "And luckily it's close to their bedtime, so they should conk out any minute. We'll have a nice, peaceful dinner and can talk all about the dream wedding you envision."

"Of course, if one or both get fussy, you've got your nanny right here to step in," Cathy said with a grin. "I love it. Former soldier turned baby whisperer."

Brandon rolled his eyes. "That's not a thing."

"Well, it is now," Jeb said with a piercing look at his younger son.

Brooke glanced at Nick, who was sitting as far away from his brother as possible while still being in the same room.

"A *temporary* thing, though," Brandon remarked. "Isn't that what you said, Nick?"

Nick nodded. "I'm at Brooke's service until her regular nanny returns at the start of August."

"So, then you'll come work at Garroway Paper, right?" Brandon asked, staring at Nick. "I'll have to train you, but we'll start you in sales and you'll pick it up fast. I'm sure you'll be regional manager by Christmas. Our guy right now is just about ready for a promotion. Then in a year, we can talk a VP title."

Nick cleared his throat. "We're here to talk dad and Cathy's wedding." He turned to Cathy. "Brooke said something about a wellness retreat?"

Brooke glanced at Brandon. The guy was frowning at being shut down, but at least he wasn't insisting on an answer.

"Sagebrush Sanctuary and Retreat," Cathy said. "It's just an hour from here but pure rural. The cabins blend right into the surrounding nature. It's so peaceful. The center offers yoga retreats, mindful-living seminars, everything to do with a calm mind and healthful body. I'd love to have the ceremony outside, in the gazebo, and the reception in one of the open-air structures."

"Sounds lovely," Brooke said. "I did some research on the place, so we can talk about options tonight."

Cathy smiled. "Great." She stood. "Let's head into the dining room. Dinner is ready."

Nick picked up both baby carriers and followed Cathy, with Brooke beside him. Jeb and Brandon were behind them.

"Have to say, I never thought I'd see Nick holding a baby, let alone two," Brandon quipped. "Wonders never cease, I suppose. Gives me hope that he'll take his rightful place with us at Garroway Paper."

Brooke turned just in time to see Brandon lay a hand on Nick's back, and she could see Nick stiffen.

"Ga ba da!" Mikey said, waving his arms. "Ba da!"

Nick seemed glad for Mikey's interruption as they entered the large dining room. "If none of you speak baby, that means 'pick me up right now!'"

"Oh, I speak baby," Jeb said. "You two were champion babblers."

Brandon laughed. "I never babbled."

"You most certainly did," Jeb said. "And I always knew what you were trying to say."

"Come on, you weren't exactly a hands-on father, even when we were talking in full sentences," Nick said, and then froze the moment the words were out of his mouth.

Brooke knew he regretted it, that it had just tumbled out before he could think, before he could stop himself.

Jeb stiffened too, his expression tightening. "No, I wasn't. But when my boys have children, I'll certainly be a hands-on grandfather."

"We can only move forward, not backward," Cathy said, nodding. "Nick, you can set the carriers down on the floor." She pointed to the left.

Nick closed his eyes for a second, then opened them, moving near a window. "Dad, I'm sorry. I didn't mean—"

"You'll say anything to defend betraying the family," Brandon snapped. "As if Dad working all the time had anything to do with you leaving."

Now the entire room was full of stiff, unsmiling people. Except for the babies, who were both wiggling and wanted to be out of their carriers.

Nick's expression was grim as he took out Mikey, and Brooke rushed over to take Morgan. They stood in front of the window, the filmy gauze curtains filtering the early evening light. Nick had told Brooke he'd changed and fed both boys before they'd left, so the babies should require just a little soothing and swaying, and they'd be ready to be put back in their carriers and down for the next few hours.

"Hush, little baby," Nick whisper-sang, rocking Mikey gently back and forth.

It amazed Brooke how Nick was able to compartmentalize. His focus was laser sharp on the baby in arms. Not the tension in the room. Or what he'd said.

"As I live and breathe," Brandon muttered, shaking his head. "All you need is the Mary Poppins umbrella."

Nick let out a ragged sigh. "I'd ask you what your problem is, Brandon, but I know what it is. Let's leave our issues out of tonight. This is about Dad and Cathy and their wedding."

So much for the laser-focus, Brooke thought, her stomach sinking.

"So big of you," Brandon said, but yanked out his chair and sat down.

Jeb sent each of his boys a sharp look and sat down, as well.

"Well, this guy is ready for bed," Nick said. "How about his twin?" he asked Brooke.

Brooke forced a smile. "Yup, he's ready."

They put the babies back in the carriers on the floor. Between the dim lighting, the candles on the table and the curtains filtering the still-strong sunshine at past six o'clock, this setting and hum of voices was ideal for baby sleep. Both little ones fought their eyes closing, but with a few rocks of the carriers, Mikey and Morgan were asleep.

"Ah, success," Nick said as he moved to the table and held out a chair for Brooke—the one directly across from his brother, so that he wouldn't have to sit there. Then he sat beside Brooke. Hey, she got it. She wouldn't want to face that scowl for the next hour either if it were directed at her.

"Brandon, will you help me bring everything out?" Cathy asked.

Brandon leaped up. "Sure." He followed Cathy into the kitchen, and there was some murmuring, which Brooke assumed was Cathy asking Brandon to chill out for the sake of their dad.

Moments later they returned with a huge tossed salad, an amazing-looking pasta dish and bruschetta.

"Help yourselves to whatever appeals," Cathy said, and they all stood and heaped their plates full. "Brooke, did you always want to be a wedding planner?" Cathy asked as they sat down, ready to eat.

Brooke nodded. "I think I got lucky—being a wedding planner was all I've wanted to do since I was very young. My grandmother started the business and I was her apprentice for as long as I can remember. Brides seemed like princesses to me, royalty for the day. I loved the idea of planning something so special. Wedding planner feels like an honor to me."

"I'm glad you see it that way," Cathy said. "Because *special* is the word for the wedding I envision."

Brooke smiled, heaping some pasta and salad on her plate. She had a feeling she and Cathy would get along just fine.

"That's the way I've always looked at family businesses," Brandon said, then took a bite of the pasta. "You apprentice young, learn the ropes and then suddenly you're running the enterprise. I'm impressed, Brooke."

She slid an uneasy glance at Nick, who was staring at his plate. "Well, as I said, I loved the world of weddings. It's what I wanted to do with my life. But what if I wanted to be a chef or an ambassador in the foreign service or a teacher? I think my grandmother would have wanted me to follow my passion."

Brandon sipped his wine. "She might have said so, but I'm sure it would have broken her heart to have you ignore the family business that put a roof over your head and food on the table."

"Oh, Brandon, give it a rest," Nick said. "We all get it. I did something different with my life and you didn't like it."

"No one liked it," Brandon snarled.

Nick slugged down his sparkling water. Brooke and Cathy made tight smiles at each other. And Jeb Garroway just looked uncomfortable.

"Why don't we talk privately after dinner," Nick said to his brother. "For now let's enjoy this delicious meal. The pasta is amazing, Cathy."

Cathy beamed. "Your dad made the pasta. I did the bruschetta and the salad."

"Wow, Dad," Nick said. "I didn't know you started cooking. That's great."

His dad smiled, the tension between the two of them thankfully forgotten. "And hopefully you'll come over often so I can try out my mad skills on you. I'm taking an Italian-cooking course at the community center."

Brooke grinned. Based on everything Nick had told her about his dad, it sure sounded like Cathy had had an amazingly positive influence on him.

Nick's shoulders visibly relaxed. His dad's acceptance of him and warm welcome meant the world to him, clearly.

But soon enough the pasta was gone and only crumbs of the bruschetta remained.

"Let's go into dad's office," Nick said to his brother.

Hopefully they'd talk and come out with their arms around each other, each accepting the other's differences.

Brooke, Cathy and Jeb watched the two Garroways head out of the dining room. A door closed.

"Well, fingers crossed," Jeb said. "I've talked to Brandon until I had no words left, and he was stubborn as ever about how Nick 'betrayed' us. I tried to tell him that we looked at that all wrong, that we should be proud of who he was, who he is, but he's just stuck on it."

Brooke heard voices coming from the room the brothers had gone into. Raised voices.

"Oh, so now you're Mr. Family Oriented?" Brandon's raised voice said. "Giving a crap about Dad? Please."

Uh oh. Brooke hadn't heard what Nick had said that had gotten that response.

"You have some damned nerve, Nick," Brandon continued, his voice booming. "First you disappear on us for ten years—eleven years—to do what you want, and now that you're back, what do you do? Get a job working for someone else. And as a *nanny*? Where is your shame?"

"My shame?" Nick repeated, his own voice not quite as loud but stone cold. "About being a nanny? Are you serious?"

"Oh, wait, I mean *manny*." Brandon laughed. "Do you want to guess how many people stopped me today on Main Street to tell me my brother, the soldier, is a manny? I told the first two that they were mistaken. By the fourth time I realized it had to be true. A manny," he repeated with a dry chuckle.

Brooke, Jeb and Cathy all glanced uncomfortably at one another, then looked away.

"They got along so well when they were kids," Jeb whispered, shaking his head. "I hate that this is how things are. Nick was right—I wasn't around much when they were young because I put work first. And when things turned ugly between them, I threw myself even more into work because I couldn't deal with it." He let out a breath and stared down at the table.

"Hey," Cathy said, putting an arm around him. "I think a family wedding will help bring them together. Bring you all together."

Brooke sure hoped so.

"We're done here," Nick said—through gritted teeth, if Brooke wasn't mistaken.

"Why the hell would you waste your time as a baby-sitter?" Brandon asked as a door opened and footsteps pounded toward the dining room. Nick entered the room, his expression furious, his brother trailing him. "Just tell me that. Tell us *all* that."

Nick ignored him and walked over to the baby seats on the floor, where Mikey was beginning to fuss a bit. Nick unlatched the harness and picked up the baby, cuddling him close against his chest. "I've got you," he said softly to Mikey, swaying him in his arms a bit.

Brooke glanced at Brandon, who looked half incredulous, half disgusted. It couldn't be fun to be that disgruntled, she thought, and she had a feeling Brandon Garroway was disgruntled all of the time.

"I worked hard on the tiramisu for dessert, so you two will sit here and enjoy it and be civil," Jeb said, pointing a finger at his sons.

Neither Garroway son responded.

"I'll help bring out dessert," Brooke said, following Cathy into the kitchen.

"A change of subject is definitely in order," Cathy whispered in the kitchen. "Let's talk wedding. That should shut up the guys."

Brooke laughed. She knew she liked Cathy.

They brought in the tiramisu, laughing over Jeb's account of failing miserably the first time, messing up the steps his cooking teacher had listed on the recipe. The dessert was definitely missing something—had he forgotten to soak the ladyfingers in coffee?—but was still scrumptious.

Jeb turned the conversation to Brooke, asking about the wedding-planning business and the craziest wedding she'd ever planned.

"The one where both the bride and groom got cold feet, right before the ceremony was to start," Brooke said, shaking her head as she remembered. "Big wedding, over 250 guests. But it turned out the best man, the groom's brother, had been madly in love with his lifelong best friend, the bride's sister, and he proposed right there, and the wedding turned into an engagement party. Both families were there, so it worked out."

"That is crazy," Jeb said, shaking his head.

"I had the big wedding the first time around," Cathy said. "Now my dream wedding is a small, intimate affair with a view of the mountains. Just close family and good friends. My two daughters—they're nineteen and twenty-one—will be my maids of honor, so that's it for the bridal party."

"And I'd like the two of you to be my best men," Jeb said, looking from Brandon to Nick.

Brooke slid a glance at the Garroway brothers. They both looked miserable under their tight smiles.

"Of course, Dad," Brandon said. "You can always count on *me*."

Nick smiled at his father. "Thank you for asking. It'd be my honor."

Brooke caught Nick's brother rolling his eyes.

Ooh boy, the wedding preparations were not going to be fun where these two were concerned.

For the next ten minutes, Brooke and Cathy talked

about the venue, food and flowers. Cathy was a vegan and didn't drink alcohol, and the wedding would not be typical. No problem. Brooke knew three vegan caterers whose food was amazing.

"There's one small thing, though," Cathy said. "Well, a big thing. My friend who owns the retreat center needs to up the date to *next* weekend. The whole weekend will be ours, but it's certainly short notice for you, Brooke."

"Next weekend?" Brandon sputtered. "What about our business trip to see the Midwest and Southern regional sales managers?"

"That's what right-hand employees are for," Jeb said. "Between our VPs, the trip will go fine without us. And besides, you could use a weekend away."

"I wouldn't call a 'wellness center' a vacation," Brandon muttered under his breath. "Do people chant there?"

Cathy laughed. "Only if they want. It's about nature and relaxing, Brandon. You'll love it there. I promise."

"I'll drive out to the center tomorrow, see if I can meet with the events manager, and then plan out the entire wedding, talk to my vendors and give you the details by tomorrow night. Sound good?"

"Perfect," Cathy said. "I leave my wedding in your capable hands."

Yes! Client secured!

Good news for Brooke, indeed. But how the two Garroway brothers would spend a weekend together—a dry weekend, at that—at a wellness center, without pushing each other off a mountain cliff, was something else entirely.

Chapter Seven

"What I want to know is, do any families actually get along all the time?" Nick asked as he carried both sleeping babies in their car seats into Brooke's house. "Where everyone respects everyone else's choices and everyone is just happy to be together? Does such a thing exist?"

She locked the door behind him and followed him up the stairs, with the cats trailing them. It was the first thing he'd said beyond the smallest of small talk on the way home from his dad's house about the weather and the light traffic and the lack of humidity.

She hadn't hit him with questions in the car, though she had a ton. She was dying to talk to him about the wedding, how he felt about standing up for his dad, what it meant to him, though she'd been able to tell he'd been deeply touched. She'd had the sense that Nick needed to be alone with his thoughts, so she'd kept the conversation to the mundane.

Snowball and Smudge disappeared into Nick's room. They liked to sleep on his bed, even though they'd never spent much time in the guest room. Baby whisperer and cat conqueror. Amazing.

In the nursery they each took a sleeping baby, very carefully transferring the twins to their cribs, and though Mikey stirred, neither woke up.

They tiptoed out and Brooke hoped Nick wouldn't go into his room and shut the door—shut her *out*. She wanted to talk, wanted to answer his questions. But she wasn't sure if he'd meant it rhetorically or not.

Her heart gave a little leap when he walked past his room and headed downstairs.

"Beer?" he asked, walking into the kitchen.

"I'd love one," she said, and he took two out of the fridge and went into the living room, sinking down on the sofa. She sat beside him, taking the bottle and twisting off the cap. "To be honest, I don't know how families are. It was always just me and my grandmother, since my parents died when I was so young. She was always supportive of me, and I was a pretty easy kid and teenager, I'd say. Didn't get in trouble, got good grades, dated nice boys."

"Wanted to follow in her footsteps in the family business," he added, taking a swig of his beer.

"I'm sure that it made it easy for both of us, the shared love of all things weddings. But paper is another story, I guess. Although I once watched a documentary about how paper is made, and I was riveted."

He burst out laughing. "Oh, wait, you're serious." He

gave her shoulder a playful squeeze and she wished he'd pull her into his arms. They were so close on the sofa, with only a few inches separating their arms and thighs. "That would earn you major points with the Garroways."

She took a sip of her beer to refocus from her wayward thoughts. "You know, now that I think about it, I had friends with all kinds of families—the TV kind and the big-problem kind. But no one I know really lived a charmed life. Stuff happens."

"That's very true," he said. "Though for a while there, I had it very good." He leaned his head back against the sofa. "I wish I hadn't let Brandon get to me tonight. I walked into that dinner with my back up, and because of that, I said stuff I shouldn't have to my dad when he's done a total 360. I have to stop being ready for combat."

She touched his arm, then quickly removed it. "Brandon's a tough one—I'll give you that. Your dad said you and your brother were very close when you were kids?"

"Very close," he said, with his arms crossed over his chest. "Especially when our mom first got sick, and our dad was always working, even when he was home, Brandon came to me a lot for his questions and when he had problems. I'd spend hours teaching myself math concepts he was struggling with so I could help with homework and to study for tests. For a couple of the hard tween years, he had issues with friends, and so I'd hang with him on weekends, take him fishing or to the movies and then Five Guys. We'd talk about everything and nothing. He had a lot of anxiety about our mom being sick and not wanting to bother her."

He stopped talking and looked up at the ceiling.

"I'm so sorry about your mother."

He nodded. "Me too. She was a wonderful person. It kills me to think I disappointed her, you know? Especially when she was so weak and tired from chemo. But she never said anything about my joining Garroway Paper. I always took that to mean she liked that I was going my own way."

"Did she say anything about that at all?"

"She just said what she always said, that I marched to my own drum, and would pat my hand. I thought that was her way of approving of me." His voice got heavy with emotion and he looked to the right, away from Brooke. "But she and Brandon were always very close, much closer than I was with her or my dad. When he said I broke her heart, I believed him. I cursed myself for being so selfish, for not making her final time more comfortable by knowing her eldest was joining the family business, that I was settled where I should be."

"But it wasn't where you should have been, Nick," Brooke said, this time daring to reach for his hand and holding on to it for a moment. "And it sounds like your mother knew that and respected it."

He gave something of a shrug and she let go of his hand. "Well, all that was a long time ago. I hate disappointing people, but I've done a lot of that during the past eleven years. So it's a good thing that I'm here for just a short time. If I let down you or those twins, I'd…"

He got up and walked over to the sliding glass doors to the patio, looking out at the night.

She walked up to him and risked putting her hands on his shoulders. He stiffened at the touch but he didn't move away. "You're a dream, Nick Garroway. You're heaven-sent. You couldn't possibly disappoint us."

He turned around, his blue eyes intense on her. "I won't intend to. But that's not what matters in the end."

"Nick, circumstances are circumstances. You can't control everything. Or anything, really."

"I think I hear one of the twins," he said, but she knew neither had made a peep. The conversation had gone places she hadn't expected, and it got to be too much for him. He headed for the stairs.

"I know exactly why you're here," she called after him.

He stopped in his tracks but didn't turn around.

"You made a promise to check on me, to see that I was all right. I wasn't, so you're here. How could you possibly disappoint me or the twins when your entire point is to take care of us until my regular nanny returns?"

Jeez. Obtuse much, Brooke? She knew damned well how. By *leaving*.

He did turn around then and looked at her. "Because things always get complicated. Don't they."

He went upstairs and this time she didn't expect him to come back down.

He was right. Things always did get complicated. Exhibit A was the fact that she was falling in love with him.

Last night, when Brooke had walked up behind him and put her hands on his shoulders, he'd almost turned and wrapped his own arms around her. He'd needed the hug after that dinner from hell. Well, not all of it had been hellish. It had felt so good to be there, sitting at the table with his family again. Not only invited to his dad's wedding but to be a *part* of it.

He'd been overwhelmed by it all, and then the conversation with Brooke had poked places inside him.

But he was glad he'd controlled himself and hadn't reached for her. She'd once smartly put a stop to something happening between them, and if she hadn't last night, adding sex, or even just kissing, to what was between them would bring those complications crashing down on his head.

He was glad she'd brought up the reason he was here—because of the promise. Giving into his attraction for her, knowing that he couldn't be what she needed or wanted in the long run, meant having to control himself for the short term. No matter how hard it was. He'd tossed and turned for so long last night, wanting to go next door and slip into bed beside her, forget everything but how good she'd feel in his arms.

But he'd known the next morning, he'd just have to add "last night" to the list of complications, so he'd stayed put.

And then an unexpected text from his brother around midnight had done a great job of taking his mind off Brooke.

Last night got out of hand. Sorry. Come by the office tomorrow at 5:00 p.m., if you can. We're having a small celebration for the company's fortieth year in business. It's a surprise—but I know Dad would love to see you there.
—B

This morning, Nick still couldn't decide if his brother was truly extending the ole olive branch or being manipulative. But an apology was something, especially for Brandon, and a celebration for forty years in business was a big deal. Of course Nick would go.

He forced himself to wait until 8:59 a.m. to go downstairs, not wanting to take time away from Brooke with her boys. She was in the kitchen, pouring a cup of coffee as the twins stared at the gently spinning mobiles attached to their swings.

"One for you too?" she asked him.

He nodded. "I'll need caffeine today. My brother asked me to go to a surprise fortieth celebration for Garroway Paper at the office today."

"That must mean you're going," she said. "Good first step for both of you."

"Both of us? Meaning?"

"Meaning you're both trying. He extended an invitation and you're accepting. That's how it works."

Nick nodded and already wanted to talk about something—anything—else. He added cream and sugar to his coffee, took a big gulp, and then turned his attention to the Timber twins. "How are my favorite babies, today?"

"Ba ga!" Mikey said.

"Ga!" Morgan added, tossing his stuffed donkey on the floor with a laugh.

"You little imp," Nick said, giving each boy a kiss on the head. "So, you two, how about a walk through town and then lunch in the park. You can visit your favorite squirrels."

"Sounds like a plan," Brooke said. "Especially because I have *a lot* of work to do. I'll be driving up to the wellness venue to get going on your dad and Cathy's wedding, and then I'll be making a thousand calls about the Satler triplets' wedding, because guess who hired me, after all?"

Without thinking, Nick took Brooke's hand and pulled her up for a celebratory hug, wrapping his arms tightly around her. She hugged him tightly too and he never wanted to let go. "Congratulations," he said against her hair, which smelled like flowers and sunscreen lotion.

"If you hadn't walked in when you did, I can't even imagine. No Satler wedding. No nanny. I'd be worrying right now about everything. Instead I feel like everything is possible."

"Good." He pulled back, instantly missing the feel of her against him. "Go work. I've got these little rug rats."

She grinned and gave each boy a kiss on the head, then left the room. He heard her footsteps go into the Dream Weddings office and the door shut.

He could still feel her in his arms.

He got out of the house in record time, needing air and space, and to get Brooke out of his head. In a ten minute walk down Main Street, pushing the stroller and minding his own business, he got four "so, you're the manny I heard about" and two eavesdropped "I'll bet they're involved." And since a group of smiling women with yoga mats were approaching and looked like they were about to pounce on him, he swerved the stroller left, down a side street that led to the three schools in town.

"That's where your mommy and your manny went to elementary school," he told Morgan and Mikey, stopping by the fenced playground. "Different times, since I'm five years older. I hope she didn't have mean Mrs.

Buckworth as a substitute." He'd lived for the yard in those days, waiting for the recess dismissal so he could rush out to the tire swings and slides, and leap across the monkey bars. "And this is where you'll go. Your very first day of school will be right here."

He glanced up at the one-story, winding building. Brooke had grown up in Wedlock Creek, and he was pretty sure her parents had too, since she lived in her grandmother's house. Generations of Timbers had put down roots in Wedlock Creek. Sometimes that seemed like a good thing, roots and family.

But his family tree felt all twisted, even with his father's warm welcome and the upcoming wedding this weekend.

Nick spent the next hour wheeling the stroller all over the three campuses, pointing out his middle school and high school. Then he headed back to Main Street and to the library to take out a few new picture books.

As he pointed out all the places he knew, buildings and shops and the movie theater where he'd seen favorite films with his family as a teen, no feelings of familial pride overtook him. No thoughts of roots and family bonds. He could barely stomach the idea of walking into Garroway Paper, because of what it represented to him—the big issue between him and his family.

As he passed Wedlock Creek Gifts, he stopped in for a wedding card, grateful the wedding section wasn't an entire aisle like the birthday section. He liked the fronts of some, but the inside messages were too hokey. A bunch poured it on way too thick. Then others didn't say enough. *Congratulations* wouldn't quite cut it.

"Which one, guys?" he asked the twins, who were looking at the bright cards.

"Ba!" Mikey said and laughed.

"Ga ba!" Morgan added, flinging his little stuffed monkey at the bottom row of cards.

As Nick picked up the monkey, his gaze landed on a card with a die-cut bride and groom underlaid with velum. His father would appreciate the papery aspects, for sure. Inside, the greeting read, "All my best wishes for a lifetime of happiness. You deserve it."

Huh. That was it. That was exactly how Nick felt about his father's second marriage.

"Thanks, Morgan," he said to the baby, giving his head a little rub. "You've got great taste."

Once outside, he sat down on the bench and grabbed a pen from the stroller bag, going with the moment to write something in the card while he was in the mindset. Otherwise he'd scrawl *congrats* underneath and sign his name, and he wanted to write what was in his head.

His heart. Which was still beating, after all.

He found himself filling the entire left side of the card. How glad he was to be back in his dad's life. How happy he was that the couple had found each other, and that he looked forward to sharing in their life together.

Before he could tell himself he'd gone overboard and had gotten all mushy, he sealed the envelope and slipped it in the stroller bag.

"Sometimes I surprise myself, guys," he told the twins as he stood and started wheeling toward Oak Lane.

When Nick came downstairs at 4:45 p.m., in a dark gray suit and shiny black shoes, Brooke did a double take and then couldn't stop staring. She knew why too. Yes, he looked very handsome. But it was much more than that.

He looked like a groom.

Granted, the suit wasn't a tux and Nick had forgone a tie, but Brooke had seen a zillion grooms in her years as a wedding planner, and her first thought at seeing Nick come down those stairs was *husband-to-be*. And a mighty good-looking one, at that.

"Wow," she said, putting Mikey into his swing, beside Morgan on the table. "You clean up well."

He smiled that dazzler that always also stopped her in her tracks. "I thought I'd blend in better in this thing than standing out in a T-shirt and jeans as 'the son who didn't join the family business.'"

"Looking forward to it at all?" she asked. "Or all dread?"

"I'm glad to be there for my dad. And to be part of something special to him. Forty years in business is a big deal. But yeah, there's the dread part. I have a feeling my brother is going to try to sell me on the company, lay on the guilt, that it's time, that I did my thing and now it's time to do the family thing."

"Why is it so important to him?" she asked. "That's what I can't figure out."

"Good question. I've thought about that a lot over the years. Maybe because he always saw it as his path, and since he once looked up to me as the older brother, he'd assumed it was my plan too and I blindsided him? I'm not sure. He really does look at it as a betrayal."

"I'll say it a million times, Nick. No one's life should be dictated by someone else's choices or dreams. Your brother was happy to step into his father's shoes and follow his footsteps. You weren't. Nothing about that makes your brother a better person than you or right."

"But I did break my mother's heart," he said. "I have to live with that. Choices we make affect other people. No way around that. No matter how right or wrong we are. People get hurt."

Didn't she know it. "I don't want to say something so trite like 'but that's life,' but Nick, it is. People do get hurt. Yes. I got hurt when Will Parker acted like our time together was nothing. And when my pregnancy meant absolutely less than nothing to him. But life goes on. Was I supposed to stay in bed, under the covers, for months, even though I wanted to?"

"Are you saying that's what I'm doing?" He stiffened, as though he hadn't meant to say that out loud.

He was *half* under the covers, half not—but because he had to be, not because he wanted to be. "I think you're trying. You're going to the party. You could have made an excuse. But you want to join in the celebration, mostly because it's important to your father and brother. That's big."

"How did we go from 'you clean up nice' to this conversation?" he asked.

"Neither of us are much for small talk. Way I see it, you might as well say what's really on your mind and what's really the issue. Or what's the point?"

He smiled. "I've always preferred to ignore and deflect."

"Sorry, house rules."

He laughed and the sound was like music and magic to her ears. She wanted to rush into his arms and hug him, tell him he was a good person, the best person she knew, and that everything would be okay. But honestly she had no idea if that were true. Which parts and how okay any of it would be.

Including her heart, which was at serious risk of getting broken again.

Chapter Eight

Garroway Paper was in a very dull five-story office building, in a small industrial park en route to the freeway out of Wedlock Creek. The company had the entire third floor, and the seventeen employees were in the large conference room. Nick glanced at the Garroway Paper logo on the wall above the long credenza. Once, he'd looked at that logo with pride. When he was a kid, he thought his father was like a king or the president of the United States for having his name on a company, and he had to admit that the logo still spoke to that little kid somewhere inside him. His family was important to him, so he wasn't all that surprised.

He shook a lot of hands as Brandon introduced him to sales reps, the controller, administrative assistants, vendors and the marketing manager—who'd immediately asked if she could do a social-media blast about a Garroway son returning home from a long military career. Brandon approved it with gusto before Nick could say a word. He shrugged it off, but he didn't like his military career being a bonus only when it looked good for the company. Whatever. He was long used to the machine.

With his brother chatting away to a vendor, Nick moved into a corner next to the buffet table and helped himself to something that looked like a very small quiche. He glanced around the room for his dad and found him surrounded by an animated group. His father sure looked happy. Jeb was in his element here. The smile, much like he'd had at the dinner where Nick had met Cathy, satisfied something inside Nick. His dad was happy here. Brandon was happy here. And Nick was happy for them. *I'm glad I came*, he thought.

"I can tell you feel like you're missing out," Brandon said, appearing on his left. His brother put an arm around his shoulder that suddenly felt like a clamp. "Your expression gives you away. You want a piece of this. And you can have it with a simple yes. There's even a private office waiting for you. Did you know that Dad kept it open for you all these years?"

Nick had gone from anger at Brandon's manipulative mumbo jumbo to the mini quiche in his stomach turning to sludge. His father had kept an office open for Nick? What?

"Come on, I'll show you," Brandon said, and Nick had no intention of following his brother out the door and to the office, but he had to get the hell out of this room, which was suddenly closing in on him. He could make one sharp right and disappear into the stairwell, gulp in some air. "Here it is," Brandon said, gesturing at an ajar office door, the neon-red Stairwell sign so close—yet so far.

At least his name wasn't on a placard on the door. Brandon stepped into the medium-sized room. Desk, chair, lamp, phone. Credenza. Small bookcase. Window facing the parking lot.

"Of course, if you prefer a view of the gardens out front, we can switch someone for you," Brandon said. "I'm thinking two weeks of intensive training by me and all of the department heads—of course, most departments are one-person operations, so we'll have to look at their schedules—and within a couple of months, you'll be regional manager. Like I said before, by Christmas I don't see why see why you couldn't be VP of operations. And sorry, older bro, but I'll always be President, so you'll have to settle for second in line to me. Seniority over age. You get it, right?"

Oh, he got it. This invitation was a ploy, just as Nick had suspected. Not about having him share in something special to his dad and to the company, but trying to force him into this office—where he didn't belong. Where he'd never belong.

"Brandon, I'm here today to celebrate the company's fortieth. That's all."

His brother scowled. "Right. I forgot. Being a nanny—a *manny*," he added, with extra scorn in his head shake, "is your chosen career path, now that you're a civilian."

"I told you, the nanny job is temporary."

Brandon's eyes lit up. "Ah, so it's just a summer

thing? So, when shall we expect you? How about the Tuesday after Labor Day? Fitting, don't you think?"

Long, hard sigh. "I'm not planning to join Garroway Paper, Brandon."

"What the hell are you planning?"

"I'm going to buy a ranch, a couple thousand acres. Cattle, sheep, chickens."

His brother stared at him. "What the ever-loving hell? Now you're a cowboy?"

"That's the goal," he said. "I've been thinking about it a long time. Remember when we'd visit Aunt Ginny on the ranch? It sparked something in me back then."

That small farm really had. The Garroways had driven the two hours out, and the minute Nick had gotten out of the car, breathed in that country air mingled with the scent of hay and horses, he'd felt the strangest sensation that he'd realized was akin to homecoming. It was the same feeling he got every time he came back stateside after a tour. Because he hadn't been welcome in his family home, Nick had stayed at guest ranches in Wyoming, researching the idea of having his own place one day. The more he read up, the more he visited, the more he talked to ranchers and cowboys, the more he knew it was the life he wanted.

Nick scowled. "Aunt Ginny was a crazy recluse who had two horses and four goats and operated a small goat-milk business, which she put her own labels on and sold in local stores. That's not ranching."

"It was to her," Nick pointed out. Aunt Ginny had passed away years ago. She was their mother's sister and had never married. She'd always said she wanted to live life her way, on her terms, on her own land, and have animals for company instead of people. Nick had always admired her. But to the family, she'd been crazy Aunt Ginny, even to Nick's mom, who often claimed not to understand her sister.

"Why start something when something already exists?" Brandon asked. "That's what I don't get. Garroway Paper is here and waiting for you. We need you, Nick."

Stab to the heart. Brandon had said that before, a few times, and it had always deflated him, whooshed the anger right out. And made him feel guilty as hell. *We need you.*

"Brandon, time to cut the cake!" a woman called out.

Nick glanced toward the voice. Saved.

"We'll continue this conversation," Brandon said, then walked back into the conference room.

Not if I can help it, Nick thought, the collar of his shirt tightening on him as he headed back too, staying near the door—the exit.

A huge five-layer cake that read Congrats, Garroway Paper: 40 Years! in red icing was brought to the long table. Jeb made the first slice of the cake to cheers and clapping, Brandon wolf whistling beside their dad.

As Nick clapped too, he caught his father's eye. The warm nod Jeb gave him touched something inside Nick, filled some hole that been there a long time. *Okay, I needed that*, he thought, feeling glad he'd come.

But the gleam in his brother's eye poked at his gut. As plates of cake made their way around the room, Nick slipped out and went down that stairwell and into the air, sucking in a long, hard breath.

What a day, Brooke thought, plunking down on the sofa, with one eye on the twins as they gnawed their little chew toys in their swings, and her mind going over details of the Garroway-Wylie wedding. Every detail was in place for this Saturday's big event. She'd spent the morning at the Sagebrush Sanctuary and Retreat and had managed to book the caterer, florist, jazz band and minister, while sipping a fruit-infused water, on a floor cushion in the gazebo where Jeb and Cathy would have their ceremony. Brooke had just followed up via text with the events manager, and everything on her list had been crossed off with a thrilling *done*.

She liked being so busy. Today her mind had been on her job and not her love life. Even if her job was a celebration of love itself. Oy.

Brooke loved that Cathy would wear the dress her mother had worn to travel to her honeymoon sixty years ago, and her daughters would each wear floaty satin sand-colored dresses they'd fallen in love with in a boutique last weekend, during a whirlwind shopping trip. The Garroway men would each wear a sand-colored suit that Jeb had arranged for at a fancy men's store, and go tieless in keeping with the outdoor, yoga-esque theme.

With all of that settled, she did a little work on the Satler wedding, organizing the emails each triplet had sent about what was a must for "their day" and what they could compromise on in the name of sisterhood. Shelley had insisted on each sister having her own cake, but Samantha had thought that would be weird at cake-cutting time, since none of the guests would want to miss the first cutting of the cake by each sister, and by the time they got to whoever went third, the guests would be bored and that poor sister would miss out.

Ah, the tiny and yet huge problems of a triple wedding.

Brooke had already booked the Wedlock Creek Chapel for the June wedding the triplets wanted, as well as the grand ballroom of the Wellington Hotel. She had set up tastings at seven caterers, all of whom offered a gluten-free menu, and had gotten live club dates for five of the bands on the list so that the triplets could see how they performed live. The sisters had been Pinteresting their wedding gowns and bridesmaid dresses for years now, well before they'd ever met their fiancés, so they were all now on special order. Each group of bridesmaids would wear a slightly different hue of pink. The entire wedding party, including the brides, would wear cowboy boots—stiletto-versions for the triplets.

Gram, you would have gotten such a kick out of this wedding, she thought with a smile.

After her work was done, Nick kept popping into her mind. She was dying to know how things were going at the party. She thought of him in that dark suit…and saw herself walking down an aisle to her waiting groom. To Nick Garroway.

Her breath hitched.

"Okay, boys. Time for a stroll. Maybe a trip to Java Jane's for a blast of caffeine for mama." She got Mikey and Morgan in their stroller and headed out, the sun still so bright at five thirty, the summer air warm and breezy and smelling like her neighbor's gorgeous rose garden.

In five minutes she was at the coffee shop, eyeing the slices of chocolate cheesecake and hoping the line would move quickly, when she felt a tap on her shoulder.

"Brooke Timber, right?" the woman asked, flashing very white teeth in a faux smile that didn't reach her eyes.

Interesting, Brooke thought. "That's me."

"I'm Allison Fielding of the newly opened Weddings by Allison. I heard you were my biggest competition."

Brooke laughed. "Well, I guess I should take that as a compliment, considering there are several wedding planners in Wedlock Creek. Welcome."

Allison didn't even bother with a smile. "I also heard you just signed the Satler triplets' wedding. Quite a coup."

"I'm enjoying planning the wedding. Lots of balls to keep in the air," Brooke said, something in the woman's tone making her wary.

"Yes. I know a wedding planner in Jackson who planned a twin wedding, and boy, did that turn into a disaster," Allison said. "The twins were at each other's throats, couldn't agree on anything, and my poor friend took the brunt of their anger and all the blame. She ended up having to move, poor thing. And you've got *triplets*."

Ah. Brooke knew this game. It was called I'm Trying To Psych You Out. But Allison Fielding clearly didn't know Brooke well.

"Well, I've got this," Brooke said, inching up in the line. "If I can singlehandedly raise twins and run a successful business, I can do anything. At least that's what I tell myself," she added so she wouldn't be completely fibbing.

Allison's gloating expression turned into a bit of a scowl before she caught herself. "Well, good luck. You'll need it."

"Actually, what I need is experience, passion and being good at what I do, and I've got all three covered, so I'll be just fine. But thanks."

Luckily Brooke had reached the counter, so she added a smile and turned back around to the barista.

The amazing thing was that, a week ago, this conversation would have derailed Brooke for the day, made her anxious and worried, and left her wondering if she *did* have what it took. But even before Nick Garroway, Wonder Manny, had come into her life, she'd gone after the Catlers' business and she'd made it work.

Yeah, fine, maybe they would have run screaming out of her office if he hadn't shown up just when he had. But she'd had them until that moment, and they'd known that she "got" them, knew what they wanted and would make the entire planning of the huge affair easier on all three. Even if they had gone racing out to save themselves from the hint of baby poop in the air, they would have come back. She believed that.

Because she was good at what she did. Her grandmother had taught her everything she knew. So take that, Ms. High-and-Mighty and—

"Hi, Brooke. Small iced coffee?" the barista asked.

"You know what? I'll take a large iced mocha. With whipped cream. And a slice of the chocolate cheesecake." She'd been dreaming of that frothy drink for months. And now that she'd landed a big account, why not celebrate a little?

I have my mojo back, she realized with a little thrill. *Hear that, Gram?* she thought, picturing Aggie Timber's lively, animated face and her signature chignon and colorful pantsuits. *I've got this. Dream Weddings is going to be more than fine.*

As she moved over to wait for her order, the word *celebration* echoed in her mind. She wondered how things were going for Nick at the Garroway Paper party. She hoped his brother wasn't being the equivalent of Allison Fielding, but she had a feeling he was.

Over the next bunch of days, Brooke couldn't help but notice that Nick had made himself scarce, which was difficult to do in a small house. He appeared like clockwork at 9:00 a.m., ready to take charge of the twins, and then reappeared at 1:00 p.m., with them changed, fed and ready for a trip to see their favorite squirrels. He'd text throughout the day.

Let me know if you need a break or some time to work. I'm here for you.

And her heart would clench. He was here for her but didn't want to be—that was what she was finally realizing. He was acting in good faith because of the promise, but he wanted to be anywhere but here.

The only place he'd rather be even less than here was anywhere his brother was. Ever since Nick had returned from Garroway Paper's fortieth-anniversary party, he'd been distant, both emotionally and otherwise. Except when it came to the twins. Even if he was faking it with them, he'd smile and come alive, with his voice animated and his hugs full of emotion. The cats seemed to cheer him up some too. She'd often find Nick sitting on the patio, deep in thought, with Snowball on his lap and Smudge wedged between his ankles.

And sometimes she'd think, *Well, maybe he does want to be here. Maybe it's just his family giving him agita and grief.* But he seemed to be avoiding her too.

Told you not to get all emotionally involved with him! she mentally yelled at herself. But today was Friday and they were leaving for the Sagebrush Sanctuary and Retreat tonight—and staying in the same suite. Which should feel no different than home, really. They'd have their own bedrooms and schedules. He'd probably avoid her there too.

Their group would stay until Sunday morning, and see the newlyweds off on their honeymoon for a week in London. The owner of Sagebrush, a very calm-sounding woman named Geraldine, had assured her that her daughter, who was working part-time at the center for the summer, would babysit the twins for all of the major activities—tonight's rehearsal dinner, wedding prep and the wedding itself late tomorrow afternoon. Everything was all set. On the home front, Cathy had hired a trusted dogsitter to take in Fritz for the weekend, and a neighbor's teenaged daughter would pop in three times a day to play with Snowball and Smudge and keep their food and water bowls clean and full.

Nick came downstairs with their suitcases and the twins' bag, and then he started packing up his Jeep. They settled Morgan and Mikey in their rear-facing car seats and Nick put the lullaby player on low for them.

"I was thinking today about how crazy things are," he said as they got inside and buckled up.

"Crazy?" she asked. Her feelings for him were crazy, but she had a gorgeous, sexy, six-foot-two-inch manny whose presence in her life was the first bit of absolute magic she'd experienced outside of the birth of her children. He made things less crazy in that regard.

"We're going to a wedding. My dad's. Your client's. At a yoga retreat. When I was driving from the Texas base to Wedlock Creek, I never could have imagined what was in store. Crazy."

"Ah, so good-crazy, really."

He smiled. "I guess so. Unexpected."

Oh yes. Very unexpected. Every bit of how life had unfolded since Nick Garroway's arrival in her life. "Definitely unexpected. Which is why we're headed to the right place to just relax a little. The country, nature, trees, winding paths, good energy and healthy foods. Sagebrush Sanctuary and Retreat is much more than a yoga retreat—it's a wellness center. The focus is on healing, whatever that word means to a particular person at that particular moment in his or her life."

"I don't think staring at trees or eating hummus is going to heal me," he said with something of a smile. "Cynical, I know, but I'm not one to stare off into the middle distance."

"We'll just see, then." She'd been to a couple of wellness centers with her grandmother, and if he thought looking at trees wouldn't help, he was about to find out how wrong he was. Nature, with very little else to distract, had a way of calming a person like nothing else could. You could think, listen to yourself and come up with answers when none had seemed forthcoming.

She could do with some tree-staring herself.

"What are the accommodations?" he asked. "Is it like a lodge? Or are there individual cabins?"

"Our yurt is a suite. That way we can both have easy

access to the twins when we're not at the rehearsal dinner or the wedding."

"Wait, a yurt? Like a tent-and-cabin one?"

"Yup. There are some traditional cabins and rooms in the main lodge, but they were all booked. The wedding party will be staying in the yurts, and most of the guests are just driving in for the wedding and leaving afterward, since it's over by ten."

"Brandon should love staying in a yurt," he said. He smiled at the thought, and so did Brooke.

If you don't ask, you don't get info that you're dying to know, she reminded herself. Sometimes a little prying was good. Nick had evaded her questions over the last couple of days, but maybe getting him to open up, even just a little now, would help with some of his tension.

She glanced at him. "Have you spoken to your brother since the party at Garroway Paper?"

All she knew of that day was that Nick "didn't want to talk about it," so she assumed Brandon had ratcheted up the pressure on getting Nick to work for the company. Or maybe his dad had too, but Brooke didn't get the feeling that Jeb was after Nick to work for the family business. Brooke had the feeling that his dad had come to some good conclusions about Nick going his own way.

And she also had a feeling that unexpectedly finding love—a second chance at happiness with another person—had a lot to do with that.

"He emailed me a bunch of documents the night of the party," Nick said. "Financials, company overview, five-year plan. He even included a speech he'd given at some conference about his favorite kind of paper. You should have heard the passion in his voice about brightness and opacity and coatings."

"Sounds like he really cares about paper too," Brooke said.

"Wish I did."

She looked at him, tilting her head. "Do you really?"

He nodded. "If I cared an eighth as much about paper as they did, I'd probably want to join the business. But I don't care about paper, Brooke. And that pits me against my family. It would be like if you didn't care about weddings."

"I think my grandmother would have been all right with me following my own passions though."

"After showing you the ropes? Working at her side since you were knee-high?"

She bit her lip. "Yeah, maybe she would have been a little disappointed that her company wouldn't go on. But I think she'd want me to be happy. She wouldn't want her happiness at my expense. That's not love."

He glanced at her. "Brandon doesn't look at it that way. It's not about happiness or giving up anything. It's about doing what's right. To him anyway."

"Do you think you two will be able to build a new relationship?"

"I don't know. I don't see how."

"It kills you, doesn't it," she said in almost a whisper.

"Yeah. It does. He's my kid brother, even if he's twenty-seven now. I was once everything to him. Now he sees me as a disappointment. I didn't realize how much that bothered me until I got here and started interacting with him."

"Maybe this weekend, two families coming together, a show of love, will help. And all the nature and yurts."

That got a smile out of him. "I hope so, Brooke. But I won't hold my breath."

I will, she thought. *If not for the two of you, then for the two of us.* But maybe that was just as hopeless. Nick could see how stubborn his brother was being, but he couldn't see how stubborn he himself was being. At his own expense. Denying himself love because of the past. Looking to run off to the Wyoming wilderness, hours away, to avoid everything.

She needed this weekend to work on him too.

She *would* hold her breath.

Chapter Nine

Nick liked the yurts. They were like round cabin-tents but looked more like cabins than tents. Certainly not military tents. Painted a robin's-egg blue with many large windows, and sparsely decorated with floor cushions and futons for beds, the yurts were cozy and welcoming. There were ten yurts in their part of the sanctuary, each with its own private bathroom, which Nick was glad to see.

Just across the path was a meditation center, a long, rectangular, open-air structure with billowy white sheer fabric draped and silver yoga mats on the polished bamboo floor. Nestled behind the meditation center, in a clearing in the woods, was a gazebo currently decorated for the Garroway-Wylie wedding ceremony. White roses—hundreds of them—were entwined across the top and sides of the gazebo, with a pale green runner stretching from the gazebo to one of the smaller yurts, which was where the wedding party would gather until it was time to walk down the aisle.

Their group had this part of the sanctuary to themselves. According to Brooke, there were four groupings for large gatherings and parties, each at enough of a distance to make everyone feel the place was theirs alone. A river flowed across the entire length of the sanctuary; Nick could see parts of it that weren't blocked by flowering bushes and leafy trees.

He had to admit, it was all very nice, and probably nothing at all like his father's first nuptials, which according to his mother had been a very traditional church wedding, followed by a reception at an Italian restaurant.

Nick glanced at the silver mats in the living room area of the suite he'd be sharing with Brooke and the twins. "Am I expected to meditate?"

Brooke smiled. "All you *have* to do is show up for the wedding. Nothing else."

"Huh. I like that. No pressure." The moment the word *pressure* had come out of his mouth, he realized he was wound up so tightly, he was surprised he didn't explode. But it was different from the pressure he'd felt when he'd arrived back in Wedlock Creek. Then, the buildup of his stomach acids and the tightening of his chest had been about something as simple, as ordinary, as stepping foot back in his hometown. And then there was the promise to the man who'd saved his life, to check on a woman named Brooke Timber.

Nick remembered when Will Parker had returned

from a leave and shown his tent mates the photo of the woman he'd met back home. Everyone had said she was gorgeous, and Will had put his phone away without lingering on Brooke's picture or staring at it for an hour like Nick would have done if she'd been his woman. If he'd met Brooke Timber, if he'd touched her, made love to her, and then had her photo on his phone, it would be his lifeline, his link to home—and that word would have mattered. The word *home* would have meant something other than heartache and pain and grief.

Brooke was special.

"No pressure," she repeated, but he barely heard her because he was caught on the word in his head. *Special. Special. Special.* "That's what a wellness retreat is about. Relaxing your way."

Nick sat down on the rattan love seat. A pitcher of fruit-infused water was on the coffee table. He poured two glasses and handed one to Brooke.

Yes, so Brooke was special. Special, period. And special to *him*.

She drank some. "Delicious."

He took a sip. It was crazy that they were talking water when he'd just come to the most amazing realization.

That Brooke had truly managed to work her way in past some of his defenses. Others were still up, as usual, fighting the good fight against anything that could do damage.

"Twins asleep?" he asked, needing some distraction from his thoughts. His crazy wayward thoughts. Okay, so she was special. What did that really mean? What was he going to do about it? If anything.

He could let up a little and see about giving the attraction between them a chance.

She nodded. "They seem to like their yurt crib." The mini futon lining the wooden crib was covered in a soft material, and the lullaby player they'd brought played a soft melody. Nick would have fallen asleep in that room if he weren't so wide awake. At being here with Brooke in this strange place. At being here with his family.

"So, here's the agenda for tonight," she said, sitting down beside him. He could smell the hint of perfume she always wore. He suddenly wanted *them* to be on the agenda. But at the same time, his feelings—ugh, he hated using that word—felt so…raw and new. It was probably best to let things happen naturally and not announce what she already knew: that he had a thing for her. He'd told her as much and then said in the same breath that he didn't want to and wouldn't do anything about it.

That had changed and yet hadn't…not completely.

One day at a time. One hour at a time. One moment at a time. Wasn't that the physical-rehabilitation center's motto?

"The rehearsal dinner will start at six thirty. The center's owner's daughter will babysit for us. She'll be here in a little over an hour."

He nodded. That was the second time he and Brooke were expected somewhere together, and the notion felt…right, as though they were a pair.

"Well, I'll go shower and change," he said, grateful for the getaway, for the chance to be alone with his all-over-the-place thoughts. "Then I'll bring the twins into my room, and you can get ready. I'll just need five minutes."

"Nice to be a man," she said with a grin.

"Brooke Timber, you could step out of the shower, put on your clothes and walk out the door and be as gorgeous as if you got all style-y with your hair and put on makeup. And that's a fact."

She held his gaze for a moment, as if touched by the compliment. "Well, I appreciate that you think so, but nah."

He smiled and went into his bedroom and sank down on the all-white bed, thinking of Brooke stepping naked and damp out of the shower.

What was going on in his brain? *Go with it, or don't go with it. Leave her alone, or don't leave her alone. Act on your feelings—or don't.*

He didn't know what was right. He didn't know where his own head was.

Another silver yoga mat was by the window, and the breezy July evening air was gently blowing the gauzy curtains. He lay down on the mat and fully stretched out, then closed his eyes, and his brain almost exploded. He bolted up.

So much for meditation. Then again, he was probably doing it wrong. He hadn't been doing much of anything; he'd just lain down and closed his eyes, and a bunch of images had shot at him: Elena slamming the door in his face; Aisha's round dark eyes embedded in his mind's eye; Will Parker yelling and diving on top of him; the torturer of a physical therapist who'd actually done wonders on his leg; and Nick's name on a magnetic placard on an office at Garroway Paper.

Over the past few months, Nick had had some night-mares about the first three. But it had been his name on that office door that had done him in this time and made him sit up, sweat breaking out on his forehead.

This was the guy he was going to present to Brooke as a possibility for the future she wanted? Really? And what? Now he was throwing around the word *future*? A minute ago he'd been wondering about giving their attraction a chance. Big jump from that to the future.

One thing at a time, one moment at a time, he re-minded himself.

He'd have to ask someone about meditating. Maybe there was supposed to be chanting or holding his fin-gers a certain way or sitting cross-legged.

He got up and sucked down half a glass of the fruit-infused water on his nightstand, then opened his suit-case on his bed. Brooke had given him a brief list of what to pack, since he had no idea what a yurt-yoga-wellness wedding would require, other than the suit he'd already bought for the wedding itself. The dress code for the weekend was "fancy beach-esque," and he'd had to ask Brooke what that meant. Apparently it meant a white linen shirt, sleeves rolled up, top two buttons undone and linen trousers with the cuffs rolled to the ankles. Loafers. No socks. He'd had to go buy all that, since he owned nothing made of linen, and he'd last had loafers in middle school.

He took a quick shower in the tiny, narrow private bathroom attached to his room, which helped get his head back on straight, and was drying off with the fluffy white towel and about to shave when he thought he heard one of the twins let out a cry. He stepped out of his room, into the main area, an ear peeled toward Brooke's bedroom right next door. She must have heard his shower shut off, because she turned hers on.

Waah-waah!

Yup, a crier. With the shower going, he couldn't tell which one it was. He waited a beat. More crying. He tied his towel more firmly above his hips, then went in, figuring he'd take out the crier so that Brooke could shower and get ready in peace. And just as he had Mikey in his arms, Brooke came out of her bathroom, barely wrapped in a white towel herself.

He stared at her.

She stared at him.

"I thought I heard one of them," she stammered, her gaze moving all over the place—up, down, anywhere but his eyes. He could barely handle looking at her straight on too. There was so little between them— two fluffy towels—and the possibility of sex, that he couldn't think straight.

Just walk out of her room, he told himself.

But he didn't.

He hoisted Mikey higher in his arms and walked over to Brooke, who was now looking him in the eyes. And he leaned forward and kissed her—a warm, hard, passionate kiss that summed up everything he felt at the moment, whether he'd meant to express that or not. More than desire. More than just caring about her. Much, much more than just fulfilling a promise.

She let out a small gasp and kissed him back, then turned and quickly shut herself in her bathroom.

He smiled and headed out of the room with Mikey.

"At least your mama and I are both on the same

page," he told the little guy. "The step forward and the step backward."

"Ga da," Mikey said, grabbing his still-damp chin.

"Ga da, is right." Nick let out a breath, gently swaying Mikey, wondering just what tonight was going to bring. After the dinner. When he and Brooke would return to their suite. If he touched her, if the "towels" came off, then he'd have to be ready to commit to Brooke and her twins. One guy had already hurt her in that department, and there was no way in hell Nick would do the same. That would be the opposite of the promise he'd made.

Will we or won't we? Should I or shouldn't I?

He had a feeling he'd only know in the moment. But if he *shouldn't*, then the "moment," which would entail taking another step backward, would do a lot of damage between them.

"Feelings are complicated, Mikey," he whispered to the baby, breathing in the baby-shampoo scent of him.

"Ba ga," was all Mikey would say on the matter.

"I'd like to make a toast to my dad and Cathy at the wedding tomorrow," Brandon said, and all eyes turned to him at the long wooden table set up in the meditation room for the rehearsal dinner. Tomorrow this structure would serve as the reception site and be full of six round tables.

The rehearsal dinner was just immediate family, a small group—Cathy and Jeb, the Garroway brothers, Cathy's two daughters, Lyndsey and Nina, and Brooke with her electronic notes and old-fashioned little planner.

Brandon glanced around the table. "I know the wedding came together very quickly, so this subject didn't come up—or maybe it didn't for other reasons—but I'd like a minute allotted for a toast to the happy couple."

Brooke groaned inwardly. The subject hadn't come up for those "other reasons," but not just the one that Brandon was likely referring to. Brooke had called both of Cathy's daughters to ask if they'd like to speak at the ceremony, whether to give a speech or read a poem or sing a song—anything they wanted—and both daughters had said they loved their mother to pieces but they were way too shy and reserved for that. Having spent the last half hour in their company, she would agree with that. Nineteen and twenty-one, both students in pastry school, they were very polite and doted on their mother, but both were on the quiet side.

On the drive here, she'd asked Nick if he wanted to say a few words at the ceremony, and he shook his head and said he'd put his well-wishes into a card—the entire left side filled out with how glad he was to be back in his father's life and how he wished all the happiness in the world to Jeb and Cathy. Brooke had been touched by that. Since three fourths of the bride's and groom's offspring had said no to speaking, Brooke had hoped to cross "speeches" off her list. Still, on the off chance Brandon wanted to give a toast, she'd planned to speak to him about it before the rehearsal dinner, so they could factor it in, but after that kiss…a lot had gone *whoosh* out of her head.

She mentally slapped a palm to her head. A wedding planner could not get sidetracked or distracted, especially by her own personal life, at the eleventh hour, and a rehearsal dinner was exactly that. She had to keep her focus on the details. Tomorrow all the deliveries would start arriving, and she'd be running around with her lists and her phone to her ear, making sure everything was perfect and as Cathy, her bride and client, wished. Luckily the events manager, a pretty young woman named Heather, was very attentive and take-charge.

That was what she had to do—focus on her job, not her lips and how much they craved more of Nick's. But *oh*, that kiss. There had been so much packed into it that, when she'd fled back into the bathroom, she'd had to sit down and catch her breath and go over everything that had been inside it. How could so much be inside one kiss? She'd felt his desire, but even more she felt how much she meant to him. That had been what had sent her scurrying for cover behind closed doors.

Because once again she'd been struck by the notion that he was in her life to fulfill that promise, not because he was falling in love with her. Maybe she'd just straight out ask him.

Nick, I can tell you care about me. But do you simply feel responsible for me, or do you love me?

Why couldn't she imagine him saying, "Brooke, I love you"?

Because he probably didn't know how he felt. He'd dealt with some emotional whoppers in his past. And everything was tangled up for him right now, his brother's pressure like the ole albatross around his neck, making everything else feel off balance too. Brooke had the feeling Nick was questioning himself. And she was sure that she and the twins factored in that questioning. *Do I? Don't I?* Then a flinging of hands in the air.

He very likely didn't know how he truly felt about her. He didn't know anything that was going on in that long-guarded heart of his. That, she'd bank on.

"If you could give me an estimate of how long you'd like for your toast, Brandon," Brooke said, "I'll factor it in for before the ceremony."

"Excellent," he said. "I've learned while speaking in public for Garroway Paper that a minute is a longer time than anyone realizes. I doubt I'll need more than forty-five seconds."

She glanced at Nick. He pulled at the collar of his shirt.

"I'd like to say a few words too," Nick said, surprising the heck out of her. "Twenty seconds," he added to Brooke.

She smiled and made some notations in her planner.

"Well, if the sons are speaking, we should speak too," Cathy's daughter Nina said, looking at her sister. The Wylie daughters had barely said ten words so far, but she was glad Nina had spoken up.

"We can read something, right?" Lyndsey asked. "It doesn't have to come off the top our heads?"

"Yes," Brooke assured her. "A short poem, a song or a short toast you write and read. Anything you want."

The sisters decided they would share the reading of a favorite love poem.

"I'm so happy!" Cathy said, leaning over to give each of her daughters a hug.

Jeb, meanwhile, sent nods of approval to both of his sons, and for the first time she'd known this group, everyone looked comfortable and happy.

"Perfect," Brooke said. And huh. Who would have

thought that Brandon Garroway would have been responsible for getting his brother and Cathy's daughters to stand up and give toasts at the wedding? She sent Brandon a smile and made note to talk to him privately later and thank him for teaching her a lesson. She'd figured that with three of the four "kids" not giving toasts, that one getting up to speak would call attention to the three who'd declined. But instead all four would be participating. And she knew that would make Jeb and Cathy happy. *Go, Brandon*, she thought.

As the waiter assigned to them cleared the table, their group moved over to the gazebo to go over where they'd stand for the ceremony and the basic setup.

The minister was due to meet them any minute, and Brooke could see her coming down the path with Heather, the events manager. Heather put her hands in prayer formation and said, "Namaste." Then Cathy made the introductions of the minister to the group.

"Namaste," Brandon repeated, more to himself, and Brooke glanced over to find him staring in absolute awe at Heather.

Brooke had to smile. Heather, a very pretty woman in her midtwenties, didn't immediately look like Brandon's type—not that Brooke had any idea what that was. He was so buttoned-up and black-and-white that she couldn't see him falling for a woman with two braids wrapped around the sides of her head like Princess Leia, with white flowers woven inside. She wore a long, flowy outfit in keeping with "beach-fancy" and seemed remarkably poised and at peace while being extremely efficient when it came to her job. Brandon still hadn't taken his eyes off her.

But then Heather was heading back to the main lodge, and the minister was talking about the ceremony and the vows and scheduling in the four new speakers.

"Guess I have homework tonight," Nick whispered. "To figure out what I'm going to say."

Brooke smiled—with relief. Maybe he'd be too busy working on his toast to bring up the kiss. Or do it again.

She honestly wasn't sure if she was glad about that or not.

Chapter Ten

In the yurt-suite's living room, Nick sat on the love seat, with a pad of paper on his lap that he was tapping a pen against. Four wadded-up paper balls were on the floor around him. Yeah, this wasn't going well. *Thanks, Brandon*, he thought, rolling his eyes, but he meant that *thanks* both sarcastically and not.

A wordsmith, Nick wasn't. He'd managed to eke out some heartfelt congratulations and best wishes in the wedding card he'd bought, but writing that was easy—no one was staring at him and hearing his words while he filled out the card. This was something else entirely.

Brooke glanced at the floor and his crumpled papers. "Need some help? I've only heard five thousand wedding toasts in the past several years."

What he would give to toss the pad and pick up

Brooke instead and sweep her into one of the bedrooms. The kiss they'd shared came roaring back to him, and his nerve endings were on red alert. How good she'd felt and smelled and tasted.

Except he couldn't do any of that and she was waiting for an answer to a simple question.

"Everything I start to write sounds so canned and clichéd, the usual stuff," he said, ripping off the page and crumpling it and sending it to join its fellow pathetic attempts. "I'm not trying to be Shakespeare, but I want to sound like I mean what I'm saying."

She sat down across from him, on one of the round floor cushions. "It's a small wedding—barely forty people. Family and friends and coworkers coming in tomorrow. These are the people who truly know your dad and Cathy, so you might as well speak from the heart."

"Give me a first line," he said, knowing he was cheating.

She grinned, but then her expression became more wistful as she stared out the window, clearly deep in thought. She turned back to him. "Okay, I've got your first line. 'My dad and I haven't always been close.'"

His stomach clenched. "I don't know…"

"Your reaction, Nick? It's called honesty. And that's what you're going for. Authenticity. Being here, among all this nature, somehow asks that. I think that's why you have so many crumpled pages."

"I don't want to say a bunch of canned lines, but I don't know how authentic I want to get either," Nick admitted. Opening up a can of honesty could let out who-knew-what.

"Well, humor me, then. 'My dad and I haven't always been close,'" she repeated. "What would your next line be?"

He didn't even hesitate before saying, "But I think we're on our way." His eyes widened as the lightbulb above his head dinged on.

She smiled. "My work here is done."

"My dad and I haven't always been close," he said slowly as he wrote it down. "But I think we're on our way. Nothing would make me happier—except maybe seeing how happy my father is because Cathy is in his life. The way the two of them interact makes me feel that anything is possible."

He glanced at Brooke to see if she liked the track he was on, and there were tears in her eyes. He stood up and walked over to her. "Hey, what's wrong?"

"You really mean that." She sniffled. "I know you do."

"Yeah, I do," he said, using the back of his thumb to wipe away the dusting of tears under her eyes.

"That's how I feel when I'm with you," she whispered. "Like anything is possible."

His first thought was absolutely nothing as a rush of what sounded like the roar of ocean waves filled his head. And then he heard himself say, "Me too."

And then he did pick her up and carry her into his bedroom, using a foot to swipe his overnight bag off the bed. He laid her down and kissed her as he stretched out on top of her. "Should we do this, Brooke?"

"We should," she whispered, putting her hands in his hair. "Damn the torpedoes, right?"

He pulled up a bit, propping himself on his elbows, and put her face in his hands. "No," he whispered back.

"Not right. I can't let myself touch you if I think I might hurt you. I made that promise to myself—and to you."

"So, the promise evolved?" she asked, the tears shimmering in her eyes again.

"Yes. A while ago." As he looked at her, he could feel his heart cracking open just enough to make him realize he felt more for her than he'd even realized. She'd gotten *way* deep inside where he thought he'd closed himself off.

"Forget the torpedoes," she said. "Let's just see what happens. That's all we can do."

He barely felt himself nodding, then reached for his wallet and pulled out a foil-wrapped packet. "This has been in here for over a year, but I'm glad I never chucked it." He set it down on the bedside table so that it would be at the ready.

She smiled. "So am I."

And then somehow she'd managed to flip him over so that she was on top of him. As she left a trail of kisses along his neck and collarbone, he closed his eyes, loath not to look at her, but the sensations were so overwhelming that he couldn't help it.

And then piece by piece, the beach-fancy wear came off and Nick Garroway lost all ability to think at all.

Brooke woke up just after midnight but kept her eyes closed in case everything that had happened earlier was a dream. She opened one eye and turned her head slightly to the right. Nope, not a dream. Nick Garroway was really beside her—naked, the quilt starting around his hips or so. For a moment she let herself fully appreciate his chest, so strong and muscled, his rippled arms a sight to behold. He had a small tattoo on his left bicep—purple mountains. From the patriotic song, she figured.

She watched his chest rise and fall, rise and fall, rise and fall, and instead of snuggling close beside him, reliving every delicious moment of their time together in this bed, her own chest tightened. He'd said the promise had evolved, that he wouldn't touch her if he couldn't do so without hurting her. But how could he make that promise? How could he know how he'd feel down the road, when he suddenly wouldn't be the manny but her *man*...and father figure—or even father—to her children.

Based on all he'd said, all he was going through, Nick was in flux. Adjusting to civilian life in this unlikely temporary job, killing two birds with one stone by easing into that new life and making good on the promise he'd made to the fallen soldier who'd saved his life. It was a very effective way to say goodbye to his military service in the most honorable way. She had a feeling that was why Nick had settled in so well, so easily. Because it felt right to him.

But he'd never planned on anything happening between the two of them. In fact he'd said, loud and clear, that it couldn't happen. Enter chemistry and attraction and their lives intermingling in this crazy way, with her planning his father's wedding, and yadda, yadda, yadda, they were in bed right now.

Granted, he was sleeping—soundly. So something must be all right for him.

Yeah, dumbbell, she chastised herself. *He just had*

sex. Of course he was sound asleep. Of course all was well for him. *Now.*

Just wait till his eyes opened. And the bright light of day had its way with him.

That was what she was afraid of. That he meant everything he said last night—and that he'd mean everything he felt in the morning.

Her chest tightened again. She needed air. She needed to go stare at some trees. She grabbed his yellow pad and scrawled a note, that it was—she glanced at the analog clock on the wall—12:04 a.m. and she was taking a walk along the river and would be back in a half hour.

Then she quickly dressed in yoga pants and a long T-shirt, threw her hair into a ponytail, slipped into her sneakers, and checked on the twins in her bedroom—fast asleep.

"I made you two a promise myself," she whispered to her boys. "That everything I'd do would be for you." *Falling for Nick in the hopes that he would join our family would be one of the best things I could do for you two*, she thought, running a light hand over Morgan's fine brown wispy curls and then Mikey's impossibly soft cheek. *But getting my heart smashed when he leaves instead will only make me an unfocused mess, and I need to be fully present for you two. I'm all you have.*

Oh God. She *was* all they had. For real. This was no newsflash, of course, but the reality of it blinked in neon above their cribs.

There would be no smashed heart. She simply couldn't allow it to happen. She had a business to run and children to raise, and letting herself be at the mercy of a broken heart went against every bit of the promise she'd made. She knew because she'd been there when Will had ghosted her: that state of turmoil, the checking of her email and phone for texts constantly, the anxiety. And when she wrote him that she was pregnant—with twins—and his response was to say sorry but no? She'd been a mess for months.

Then again, she'd been facing motherhood alone, with her beloved gram gone. She'd been so scared. Now she was firmly on her feet. She knew what she was capable of. She'd be fine. But not if she walked into the path of a steam engine in the form of a six-foot-two-inch former soldier who cooked and cleaned and changed diapers and hummed lullabies and told stories. And made love like every fantasy she'd ever had.

Air. Tree-staring. Pronto.

Brooke quietly left the yurt and glanced around—not a soul to be seen. It was so quiet. The sanctuary was such a distance from the nearest town that it would be unlikely that anyone would be lurking around, except a coyote. She'd watch out for those.

She headed down the path past the meditation center, past the beautiful gazebo and toward the river. Just the sound of the gentle whoosh helped steady her. *Breathe in, breathe out, Brooke.*

Someone was sitting on a big flat-topped rock by the riverbank, with an elbow on one knee, and tossing small rocks in the water. Who was that? She stepped a bit closer and saw the dark hair, the back of the white linen shirt and pants like his brother's, and she knew it was Brandon Garroway.

"Hi," she called out.

He bolted up and turned around, his expression going from hopeful excitement to disappointment. "Oh, hi, Brooke."

Interesting. Who did he think she was at first?

"*Oh, hi* sounds like you were hoping I'd be someone else." She recalled the way he'd looked at Heather, the sanctuary's events manager, earlier, and wondered if they'd made a midnight rendezvous that she hadn't shown up for. Brooke must be more of a romantic than she thought, because what was the likelihood of that?

"That obvious, huh?" he asked, his voice a bit mopey.

"*Were* you meeting someone?" she asked.

He sighed and returned to his spot on the rock. "In one of those crazy things that could only happen at a yoga wellness sanctuary in the middle of the Wyoming wilderness, I met someone."

Aha! She knew it. And yup, she was definitely a romantic. Could a wedding planner be otherwise?

"Heather?" she asked, joining him on the rock, her feet dangling.

He gaped at her. "How'd you know?"

"I couldn't help but notice the way you looked at her when she brought over the minister earlier."

He stared at the river, then glanced at Brooke. "I'm not surprised it showed on my face. I've never experienced anything like that before. I mean, I've looked at women and thought, 'Wow, she's very pretty,' but I've never looked at someone and thought, 'I'm going to marry this woman.'"

Now she gaped at him. "Seriously?"

"I guess this love-at-first-sight thing is real. I always thought it was nonsense. And I can't make heads or tails of it. I felt this instant connection, instant attraction, instant chemistry—before she even said a word. How is that possible? Is it just because I think she's beautiful?"

She smiled—gently. "I'm sure it's everything you just said—the instant connection. It's powerful but it's real. And it hit you."

"Hard," he said, nodding.

"So, you were supposed to meet here but she didn't turn up?"

"More like we did meet here, at eleven, when she was completely off duty from leading a bedtime meditation session, but the conversation took an unexpected turn and she ran off. She told me not to follow her. So I just stayed here, hoping she'd come back."

Oh boy. "What happened? If you don't mind my asking?"

He bit his lip. "No, I'm glad you're here. I could really use someone to talk to."

She hugged her knees to her chest, glad her own issues were far, far away at the moment.

Brandon ran a hand through his hair, hanging his head back for a moment. "I told her how I felt, that it was insane and made no sense, that I was a by-the-book, numbers-and-facts-oriented person and ran a company, but I saw her and knew I was going to marry her."

Brooke smiled. "You told her that?"

He nodded. "Sure did. She looked at me like I was nuts, so I said, 'I'm hoping that we can at least go on a date, so that no matter what happens, if you're not interested, not attracted, if you hate me within ten minutes, I'll know I tried.'"

Huh. Even Brooke would have gone for that. Not bad, Brandon. "I'll bet she said yes to that."

"She gave me the most dazzling smile, said she'd meet me at eleven at the flat-topped rock behind the meditation center, but that I 'should know this—things aren't always what they seem.'"

Brooke tilted her head. "What did that mean?"

"Oh, trust me, I paced around my yub-cabin—or whatever it's called—for two hours, wondering that very thing. Finally, at ten thirty, I had to get out of that weird circular hotel-room thing, and I waited here for her. She came, looking even more beautiful than before."

Brooke thought of Heather with her Princess Leia braids and flowy layers. She smiled, appreciating this side of Brandon. Who knew? People were complicated, never all this or all that. "So, what wasn't what it seemed?" Brooke asked.

He let out a deep breath and looked skyward before turning his gaze on the river. "Turns out she's three months pregnant. She told the father, and he accused her of trying to pin it on him because he had a motorboat. That was a month ago and he disappeared on her. She thinks he left the state."

Brooke sighed. "There's a little too much of that going around."

"What do you mean?"

"Same thing happened to me," Brooke explained. "With a soldier, home on leave. I thought we had something special, but turns out I was just temporarily special."

"A soldier? Wait—my brother? Nick's the father of the twins? No wonder he's the manny. Now it all makes sense. Sort of."

Brooke shook her head. "No, no, no. He's not their father." She told him the whole story, starting with almost losing the Satler triplets to Nick bursting in and explaining why he'd come, to having the best nanny that ever existed. She left out the more personal details.

"Wow," Brandon said. "I'm surprised he even bothered making good on that promise. He certainly didn't think he owed his family anything."

Oh Lord. "A soldier died saving Nick's life and asked for a favor. Of course he was going to make it happen."

"I guess…when you put it like that," Brandon agreed.

Brooke glanced away so she could roll her eyes as hard as she needed to.

"Think you two will get married?" Brandon asked.

She coughed on air. "Why would you say that?"

"Oh, come on. You think it's not obvious there's something between you two?"

She'd seen big-time emotion, clear as day, on Brandon's face earlier; it made sense that others would see *feeling* in her expression too. And maybe Nick's. He was more unreadable. "Well, whatever's between us is complicated. Let's just leave it at that."

"Complicated. That's the word of the day. I definitely wasn't expecting Heather to tell me she was pregnant. And do you want to know the craziest part of all?"

Brooke looked at him.

"That she's pregnant doesn't change how I feel about

her. She's the woman I'm going to marry. I just know it. Turns out the baby I saw far off in my future will come sooner than I figured—I was thinking a few years down the road, but hey, life happens."

"It sure does," Brooke agreed—in absolute wonder that she was having this conversation with Brandon Garroway. "So, why did she run off?"

He let out another breath. "I explained that her being pregnant didn't change a thing for me. And she said it might not today or in a few weeks, but when the reality hit, I'd be gone. I insisted that would never happen, to give me a chance to show her, and she shook her head and ran off and told me not to follow."

Brooke bit her lip. Hadn't she had this very conversation with herself, in bed, with Nick sleeping beside her? "She was probably overwhelmed. You must have seemed like Prince Charming falling from the sky, and her life likely doesn't feel like a fairy tale, you know?"

Which could apply to her and Nick. He was like her own Prince Charming and Mary Poppins rolled into one. Temporarily anyway.

"I think I do," he said. "So, do I storm the castle?"

Brooke laughed. "Nah. Not tonight. Talk to her tomorrow morning and let her know that you'd like to get to know her, for her to get to know you, and all you're asking for is a chance. That's pure honesty and that's all anyone wants."

His blue eyes lit up. "You're absolutely right. Thanks, Brooke. I can't tell you how much I appreciate you talking to me."

"Any time." She hopped down from the rock. "I'd better get back. Big day tomorrow."

He stood too and nodded. "Oh, you know what? You just gave me a good in with Nick about coming to work for Garroway Paper."

Oh God. How could she have possibly done that?

"Well, I keep thinking how everything I have to offer Heather will work in my favor—stability, a great job, all that. And the same goes for you and Nick. There's clearly something between you two. And if he's going to take on twins, he'll need a real job, steady hours. Not some cowboy's life. He'll surely come work for us now. I just need to put it to him that way."

"Brandon," she said, putting a hand on his arm. "Trust me when I tell you that you will send him running for the hills with that approach. Besides, we're not even a couple."

The moment the words came out of her mouth the truth of it all stung like hell. Her heart clenched and her stomach flopped over.

"Well, any man who comes home to fulfill a promise to the jerk who saved his life and ends up as a nanny to twins is someone who will always do the right thing. That's what I need to appeal to. I'll get him."

If there were a contest for Most Frustrating Wyomingite, Brandon Garroway would take first place hands down. "But you shouldn't," she said—way more emotionally than she meant. "Nick has made his feelings clear. He wants to be a rancher. He doesn't want to work for Garroway Paper. Why can't you let him be who he is?"

"You just don't understand, Brooke. I thought that, as someone who took over her own family business, you would. But you just don't." He shook his head.

Oh, Brandon, it's you *who doesn't understand.* And boy, was he going to be in for a rude awakening. Someone had managed to capture his heart, and that someone was going to turn him upside down. She smiled at the thought. Brandon Garroway needed to be turned upside and shaken like a snow globe. Of course, there was no guarantee he'd change his tune.

There were no guarantees in life at all.

"I'm going to save my brother from throwing away his legacy. And I'm going to save Heather too."

Brooke gaped at him. "Save her? She may not be looking to be rescued in the slightest. A partner is one thing. But a real partner. Not someone who's looking to run her life. Brandon, you really need to think about these things."

He stood there, biting his lip, looking so unsure suddenly that she wanted to invite him back to the yurt for a glass of wine and a piece of pie. But the sanctuary was alcohol-free, and white flour was strictly forbidden. Somehow she didn't think the welcome bag of roasted chickpeas and green-tea soda water would do the trick.

And besides, Nick was in their yurt, and the last thing he needed right now was for his brother to be making more demands. At some point Nick was going to implode from the guilt it brought up. And things would be said, things she wasn't sure she'd want to hear, no matter who it had to do with.

Brandon was still shaking his head. "Brooke, you do you, and I'll do me." He put his hands in prayer formation and added, "Namaste," with a bow. Then he hurried off toward his yurt, which was two yurts down from hers and Nick's.

She would have rolled her eyes, but she felt for the guy. She really did. Love, in all its glory, was about to teach him some very important life lessons.

A croaking frog woke Nick up; the green-brown amphibian that was sitting on the other side of the window screen was making a racket. He might have laughed; he wasn't used to being woken up by frogs, but the realization that Brooke wasn't beside him took the smile off his face.

He found her note and glanced at the time on his phone on the bedside table. She'd been gone for almost an hour. The front door opened and he heard light footsteps, then the door close and lock. She was back.

And returning to his bed?

He waited, listening, but she never came in. He heard the gentle click of her door instead.

Disappointment flooded him. Did she need space? Time to think? Was she unsure what was going through his mind? He'd made it clear he was leaving town when her nanny returned in August, so perhaps she was focused on that.

Just go talk to her. Stop speculating. Stop her from speculating. Talk openly and honestly.

But he felt rooted to the bed. Mostly because he wasn't sure what he felt, what he'd say if he walked in her room.

He'd promised not to hurt her. He wasn't even sure if he could hurt her, or if he'd be the one getting his heart handed back to him. She'd told him she was done with love, that she couldn't trust right now. But then she'd realized she wanted the whole shebang. Love and marriage. A good father for her children. A life partner.

But still, maybe this was all too much, too soon.

Let's just see what happens. It's all we can do.

That was what they'd agreed to. So what was happening? With him and with her?

The frog croaked a bunch of times, and Nick looked out the window. Was he really going to lie here and not make sure Brooke was okay? That was the basis of his promise, wasn't it? *So get the hell up and go see.*

He slipped out of bed and left his room, giving her door a gentle knock so he wouldn't wake up the twins.

No response.

Knock again. And again, if you have to. If the twins wake up, they're your responsibility overnight anyway.

He knocked again.

He heard her footsteps coming to the door, and then there she was, beautiful Brooke.

"Are you trying to wake up the li'l screechers?" she asked with a smile, but he could see she was conflicted about something. Him, most likely.

"I was hoping you'd come back to my room," he said. "You were gone a while. What were you doing out there?"

"Sitting by the river, on the most beautiful flat-topped rock."

So, the frog had woken her up and she hadn't been able to go back to sleep, and so she'd gone for a walk and did some of that tree-staring or river-watching she'd mentioned was good for the soul and the mind.

"You okay?" he asked, reaching out a hand to her chin.

"I don't know. I don't know what's going on here. You're pulled in different directions. I've got a busy life. And we…slept together."

"You want to know what's going to happen," he said. A statement, not a question. Because he sure as hell couldn't answer it.

"Yeah. I want to know. And I know I can't possibly."

"So come back to my room. I'd come in here, but I don't want to be inappropriate in front of the youngins. Just come lie with me, Brooke. A warm body beside you is a hundred times more potent than looking at a tree or skipping stones in a river."

She grinned. "Is that a fact?"

"Yes. So come on." He peered past her at the twins, who were fast asleep. He held out his hand and held his breath for a second—but she took it.

They settled back in bed, him spooning her, his chin atop her head, one outstretched arm holding her hand. She curved into him perfectly.

He wanted to look at her, but he had a feeling she needed the space amidst the closeness. He sure did.

"I'm glad you came and got me," she said, holding his hand tighter.

"Me too," he whispered, and kissed the side of her face—half hair, half cheek.

For a while he lay there and listened to her breathe, their chests rising and falling in sync, and then he must have drifted off to sleep, because the next time he heard the frog croak, the sun was shining.

Chapter Eleven

The next day was such a whirlwind for Brooke that she barely had time to think about the incredible man she'd shared a bed with last night. No matter what happened between them, she'd never forget that he came for her. He could have let it go when he had heard her return from her walk and then go into her own room. He could have pretended to be asleep. Instead he knocked softly on her door until she opened it.

And then wrapped those strong arms around her, making her feel wanted and cherished and cared for. And she'd fallen right asleep.

In the morning she'd been grateful for the need to jump in the shower and get ready for the craziness that a wedding day always meant for the planner. Her complicated relationship with her manny was *not* on her very long do-now list, which filled three pages. She'd crossed off the entire first page as deliveries had come in, with Heather, the events manager and unexpected holder of Brandon Garroway's heart, working beside her to make sure all was accounted for.

Now, as she and Heather were alone in the open-air meditation hall, which had already been decorated for the reception with white chiffon and pink flowers threaded across the wooden beams of the structure, they pulled out the centerpieces and placed them on the tables. Today Heather's light blond hair was in two loose braids down both sides of her shoulders, almost reaching her waist. She wore another flowy outfit in a metallic silver, with a tree-of-life necklace and some silver bangles complementing it.

Heather was staring so hard at the one centerpiece she'd just placed on Table Four that Brooke knew she was deep in thought—about her own life and where love fit in. Brooke knew, because she'd done that kind of staring at many a wedding setup when she was pregnant.

Should she pipe up? She wanted to let Heather know she had a friend if she needed to talk, if she was scared, which Brooke was sure she was. But she didn't want to betray Brandon's confidence, and honestly Brooke wouldn't have necessarily appreciated someone coming at her with "been there, done that" advice. Sometimes she was grateful for advice, and sometimes it only scared her more and made her feel even more alone.

"Beautiful, aren't they," Brooke said, admiring the white-and-red roses in their short square tin vases that she set on Table Two.

Heather turned to her and bit her lip, slowly pulling out the last centerpiece. "Very. Just lovely. So, um, Brandon mentioned this morning that you might be a good person for me to know." Heather looked so unsure and nervous that Brooke wanted to give her a hug. "I'm only having one baby. I hear you have twins."

Brooke put her hand on Heather's arm. "It's scary regardless. Feeling alone is probably what caused the most stress. But my twins are the most wonderful thing that's ever happened to me."

Heather's entire face lit up. "That's how I feel. Scared but every time I think about having this baby in six months, I get ridiculously happy. Then scared, then happy." She laughed. "Is that how it's gonna go?"

Brooke smiled. "It has for me." She pulled a card out of her tote bag and handed it to Heather. "My cell phone is on there. Call me anytime, day or night, middle of the night, whenever. I'm completely serious. I wished I had someone to call when those scary thoughts gripped me or just when I had a question or wanted to talk through my thoughts."

"I really appreciate that." Heather glanced around as if to make sure a certain someone wasn't lurking nearby, then turned back to Brooke. "What do you think of Brandon? Kind of intense, huh?"

Brooke laughed. "That's a good word to describe him."

"And incredibly hot," Heather added. "Those blue eyes, my God."

"I'm in love with his brother," Brooke blurted out, then felt her eyes widen and she clamped a hand over her mouth. "Did I just say that out loud?"

Heather grinned. "Sorry, but yes."

Brooke couldn't help her own grin. "My *point* was

that the Garroway brothers look a lot alike, and yes, they're both very handsome."

"Love at first sight," Heather said, shaking her head with a smile. "A load of bunk."

Brooke walked around the tables to ensure all the centerpieces were indeed centered. "Not for Brandon."

Heather laughed, and then her smile faded. She picked up one of the centerpieces and brought it to her nose, inhaling. "No one's ever said half the stuff he said yesterday and this morning. I'm honestly afraid to believe any of it."

"I know what you mean. If I have any advice, it's to go with your gut, even if your head or heart are pulling you in different directions. Gut instincts rarely lie."

"My gut instincts tell me to give Brandon a chance. That he's just crazy enough to be very, very sane."

Brooke pulled Heather into a hug; she couldn't stop herself. "I'm glad to hear it."

"I just want to do everything right," Heather said. "It's not just me now."

"I know exactly what you mean. And you will. Just trust yourself."

Heather squeezed Brooke's hand, her hazel eyes much less troubled than earlier, then glanced toward the main lodge. "I hear the sound of a truck pulling in. Probably the caterer. And right on time."

The next couple of hours went by too fast as Brooke made sure everything was all set. A few little fires to put out, a momentary catastrophe when Cathy's daughter Lyndsey thought she'd left her dress at home—she hadn't—and then finally Brooke glanced down at her planner and checked her online calendar and crossed off the final thing on her list. She was done.

Now she had to get herself showered and dressed and be the behind-the-scenes person, which thankfully was also Heather's role. Brooke had worked with plenty of events managers who were so type A and high stress and nightmares to deal with that she was grateful to have this sweet, hardworking, creative dynamo as her partner today. Plus they had something else big in common besides this wedding: falling for Garroway men.

Back at the yurt, she found Nick sitting on the love seat with Mikey in his arms, feeding him a bottle. Her little baby boy, so beautiful—everything to her, along with his brother—was being cared for by this man she loved.

Loved. Loved. Loved. There was no way around the word. She loved Nick Garroway.

As if he heard her mind echoing, he turned and noticed her. "Hey. Sitter will be here in a minute to take the twins for a walk, and then she'll entertain them until bedtime. She's on duty till midnight. But I doubt we'll need her that long."

Brooke nodded. "The wedding starts at five, and we have the reception hall for five hours, so by the time I'm done making sure things that need to be returned are taken care of, I should be back by eleven, eleven thirty at the latest."

"Well, why don't you shower first while I finish feeding Mikey—Morgan already ate—and then I will."

Or we can shower together and stash the baby monitor on the little bookcase holding all the candles. The minute she'd seen the spa bath and all those candles, she'd imagined her and Nick in bubble heaven, with the lights turned low and some soft music.

Except the sitter might come early, as she had yesterday.

She smiled at Nick, grateful that he could not read her thoughts, and headed into her bedroom. A hot shower did wonders on her mind and stiff muscles. Within twenty minutes her hair was dry and twisted back into an elegant wedding chignon. She wore a pale blue sheath dress, nude heels, some light makeup and simple jewelry she'd inherited from her grandmother, including her beloved pin that read Dream Weddings on her chest.

"All set," she said as she came out of the bedroom.

Nick stood up, staring at her. "Wow. I've seen you dolled up but you look absolutely beautiful."

She grinned. "Why thank you, sir. I'm supposed to blend in, so I always dress like a guest when I work a wedding."

The Garroway blue eyes were intense on her. "You're stunning. I can't look away. Sorry."

That did seem to be the case. Could she melt in a puddle any more than she was already? How was it possible for one man to make her feel so special, so beautiful, so everything?

I love you, she wanted to yell. She could climb up to the top of the yurt and scream it for all to hear.

But Nick was walking past her, into his bedroom, giving her one last lingering look that sent tingles up her spine and goose bumps along her arms. He was remembering last night—and now she was too. Not that she'd forgotten. But all this busy day she'd forced herself not to think about being in bed with him.

Now it was all she could think about. And after the wedding…

"Ba ga!" Morgan shouted from his swing on the coffee table.

"Ga ga ba!" Mikey added, flinging his chew toy at his mama.

Ah, thank you for distracting me, boys, she thought, smiling at her sons. She eyed the burp cloth on the coffee table, reminding herself to use it if she went near one of the little imps.

Not long after Nick came out of his room, so unbelievably gorgeous and sexy in his "beach-fancy" tan suit sans the tie, the sitter arrived. And then he held out his arm and she wrapped her hand around it, and off they went. Like a couple.

But are we? she wondered, thinking back to what she'd said to Brandon. *We're not a couple.* Maybe they were. Or getting there.

Or maybe she was headed for heartbreak hotel.

"My dad and I weren't always close," Nick began, trying to keep his focus on his toast at his father's wedding and not on the forty pairs of eyes staring at him. He noticed his dad sit up straight at his words. Jeb was probably worried about where Nick was going with this speech. "But I think we're on our way."

He took another glance at Jeb Garroway and could plainly see the emotion in the man's eyes. And his new bride, Cathy, sitting right beside him, had tears shimmering in her own eyes.

"Nothing would make me happier—except maybe seeing how happy my father is because Cathy is in his life. The way the two of them interact makes me feel that anything is possible." He raised his glass of sparkling water—Cathy didn't drink alcohol and had requested a dry wedding. "So a toast and a thank-you to my father for making me believe that."

Everyone clapped and cheered, and the happy couple kissed. Cathy's daughters were up next, so he took his seat at the head table, between Brandon and Brooke.

"Beautiful and perfect," Brooke whispered.

"Nice job, brother," Brandon agreed, displaying warmth and approval in his gaze. A rarity coming from the guy. Nick would take it.

He waited for Brandon to start in on family unity and legacy, but his brother turned his attention to his appetizer of vegan dumplings with an array of sauces instead. *Definite progress here*, Nick thought, as relief flooded him. Maybe he and Brandon really could repair their relationship, be brothers again. That would mean the world to Nick.

He forked a dumpling and dipped it into a sweet-and-sour sauce before popping it in his mouth. Delicious. "I like this wedding," he said to Brooke, realizing it had a lot to with her.

She grinned. "Thanks. Everything has gone off without a hitch. Ahh, so nice to sit back and relax for a few moments."

Jeb Garroway stood and tapped a fork against his glass. "I'd like to make a toast now."

The meditation hall quieted, not that it was all that loud before. All eyes turned to Nick's father.

"I loved listening to my sons' speeches," Jeb began. "To have both my sons with me today means everything to me. And I know Cathy feels that way about having her daughters here. We're starting a new life and you four are starting it with us. I know that someday soon the four of you will find partners to share your life with who will bring the joy and happiness that Cathy has brought to my life. Nothing else will ever be as important as love and family."

There were cheers and clapping, and a wolf whistle from Brandon. But then Nick noticed his brother's eyes had shifted over to a tree outside the meditation hall, where a young woman who worked for the sanctuary stood, watching. Heather, Nick thought her name was. She had a wistful expression on her face, and as Nick glanced at Brandon, who was staring at her, he realized his brother had it bad for the woman. He wasn't quite sure he'd ever seen that expression on Brandon's face.

"Something going on between those two?" Nick whispered into Brooke's ear, with a wag of his finger between Brandon and the tree just beyond the opening to the hall.

Brooke smiled. "Yup."

"Well, love is certainly in the air," he said, stiffening the moment the word *love* had tumbled out of his mouth. *Because we're at a wedding*, he wanted to rush to add. Amend. Correct.

"Is it?" she whispered, leaning closer, with a breathtaking smile and her beautiful driftwood-brown eyes now staring into his.

He froze like the ole deer in headlights, and because he was so obviously uncomfortable by the question, she glanced away, her cheeks slightly flushed, and picked up her drink. She took a long sip and then made small talk with Brandon about the dumplings.

Oh no. He'd screwed up. Hard and fast. It was a good thing he hadn't been eating one of those dumplings when asked the very simple question he'd brought up in the first place, because he would have choked and someone would have had to come over to give him the Heimlich.

Why did you have to bring up love if you can't handle talking about it? Idiot, he yelled at himself.

And there was no easy way to fix things between them right now without saying a bunch of stuff that would make it all worse and more awkward. He'd been there.

"Well, I'm going to see how the entrées are coming," Brooke said, rushing off her chair and out of the meditation tent toward the main lodge, where the facility kitchen was.

"Go after her," Brandon whispered. "Make things right."

Nick whirled around and faced his brother. "Eavesdropper."

"Hey, you guys are sitting two inches from me. You're just going to let her run off? Unless a lady tells you specifically not to follow, you follow and make it right. Say whatever you need to to fix things."

Nick scowled. "Whatever I need to? What if I don't know what the hell I want to say?"

"Well, that's your problem, isn't it," Brandon said. "Figure it out."

Luckily some friends of Cathy's came over to their table just then to compliment the brothers on their speeches, so Nick was saved from more talk with his brother about his love life. This was certainly a first.

In a way it was kind of nice. But Nick wasn't used to talking about his...feelings with anyone.

"Go," Brandon ordered as the group moved on.

"Yes, sir," Nick said, standing up and pushing in his chair. He turned to go, then looked at his brother. "Oh, and Brandon?"

"Yeah?" his brother asked, dipping another dumpling into a ginger sauce.

"Thanks," Nick said.

Brandon gave him something of a smile and a nod, which told Nick that that the guy was moved. For a second he could see fourteen-year-old Brandon in his brother's face, before their mother died, before, before, before, and it was like he had his kid brother back. It had been a long time since Nick had done anything that warmed the heart of Brandon Garroway. And now he'd done it twice in the last hour. It felt good.

And the only thing that could top this feeling was to find Brooke and make things right between them. Somehow.

Brooke was counting saffron-risotto-primavera entrées when she saw Nick enter the kitchen. She wanted to duck down and hide, but she was a grown-up. "Thirty-eight, thirty-nine," she said, nodding at the waitstaff. "Okay, guys, you can take these beauties out, and thank you."

As the three waiters filled up their huge trays, Nick stepped closer.

"Wow, that smells good," he said. "And *looks* good. I don't think I've ever had vegan food."

"Well, you have, without thinking about it. Potato chips are vegan."

"Ah. I do like chips," he said, making it clear how much easier it must be for him to talk food than feelings. He stared at her, then reached for her hand. "And I like *you*, Brooke." His face flushed in a way she'd never seen before. "I mean, of course I like you. Duh," he added, his voice getting very pitchy. "Oh God, I am making a colossal mess out of this."

Her heart clenched and her stomach twisted. All symptoms of a little something called heartache. She'd had that malady before. "Nick, let me put you out of your misery. I'm the one who said damn the torpedoes. *Que sera, sera*, I'd basically said, right? So no worries. I'm a big girl. I got caught up in the heat of the moment last night, and then all the romance at the wedding. Forget it, okay?" She forced a smile on her face that she hoped looked natural. *Yeah, sure it does.*

He stood there, staring at her, clearly wanting to say something but unable to articulate it.

He doesn't love you. That's the thing. He'd probably like to, but he doesn't. And Nick Garroway is not a liar.

Her eyes stung and she blinked back at it hard. "I need to check the tables, make sure the waiters are clearing appetizer plates properly," she said, and rushed out into the fresh, clean air, which she gulped down.

Do not cry, she told herself. *Your mascara will run and you'll look like a sad raccoon.*

But tears misted her eyes anyway.

How could this be over before it had even really started?

Chapter Twelve

That went well. *Not.* Nick kept looking for Brooke throughout the rest of the wedding, to talk to her—to try to anyway—but she'd made herself scarce. Every now and then he'd spot her in huddles with Sanctuary staff or Heather, whom he now noticed was dancing cheek to cheek with Brandon to a jazz standard.

He looked at the time on his phone. Just a few minutes to ten. The wedding was over, and the guests would be heading to their cars, save the few who'd booked yurts. Tomorrow he'd be back at Brooke's—

He hadn't really considered that. He was her manny till August, and he had to make things right between them. He had to be there for her, no matter what their status was. That promise he'd never go back on.

He caught Brooke giving final directions to two of

Heather's event staff about packing up the wedding gear, and then she headed over to the dance floor, where his father and Cathy were swaying, both looking very happy. She hugged each of them, and then he watched her leave the meditation hall, slip off her heels and head toward the river.

Right behind you, he thought. He let his father and Cathy know he was heading out, congratulated them again, wished them a great honeymoon if he didn't see them in the morning and then hurried after Brooke.

She was sitting on a flat-topped rock, throwing pebbles into the water.

"Can I sit here?" he asked, looking at the space beside her.

She started, clearly surprised to see him there, and gave a half shrug.

He took that as a yes and hopped up, glancing at the collection of pebbles she'd put beside her. "I've got *a lot* on my mind, Brooke. It feels like a jumble—that's the best way I can describe it. All I know for sure is that I want to be with you and the twins. I want to take care of the three of you."

She glanced at him, then back at the river, whooshing along the plants and rocks. "I know. But I'm looking for a husband, and a father for Mikey and Morgan. That's what I want. That's what I need. A life partner. Not a rescuer. Not a promise-fulfiller. Someone who's there because he wants to be. Every day."

A lump grew in his throat. A husband. A father. Was that him? Why did his head feel like it was stuffed with steel wool?

"I know what I want," she added. "You don't." She

stared at the water and her expression was so sad that he wanted to gather her in his arms and just hold her, tell her everything would be okay.

But of course he couldn't. He'd lost that ability, and it made him feel like hell.

Her expression changed—resolute, chin lifted. "And look, Nick, I can handle the twins from here on. My nanny is due back next week. I can take care of Morgan and Mikey, and do what I need to on the Satler wedding, on my own for a week. No problem there."

But…

Wait.

So, she was saying he wasn't her manny anymore? This was it? Didn't he just tell her he wanted to be with the Timber family, to take care of them? That was what he wanted.

And hadn't she just said what *she* wanted? A life partner. Not a rescuer.

Oh hell.

She hopped off the rock and picked up her heels. "I'm exhausted. Since this is your last night on duty, I wouldn't mind if you kept the twins with you in your room overnight. I could really use a solid night's sleep."

"Of course," he said, feeling his chest squeezing.

His final night with the twins. And Brooke—in the next room anyway. So, tomorrow morning they'd drive back to her house and he'd pack his duffel bag and leave?

That was exactly what he'd do. He'd go buy that ranch he'd been dreaming of for months.

That was his future. Him and the ranch, a couple of

horses, the cattle, sheep, and chickens, and a few rescue dogs.

Alone and without Brooke or her boys.

That was what he wanted?

Nick's entire life was in a green duffel bag and one garment bag containing his tan suit. How was that possible? This was everything he owned? He scowled at the realization that he didn't have much to his name, except a decent bank account.

It had taken him five seconds to pack, and he'd been hoping to prolong it. He and Brooke had barely spoken on the two-hour ride back to Wedlock Creek. He'd had so much to say and nothing at all. And now here was, standing in the guest room of Brooke's house, ready to go.

Dammit.

He slung the duffel over his shoulder and draped the garment bag over his arm. He'd said goodbye to the twins already. He'd actually said his goodbyes last night, in the yurt, and the fact that his eyes stung while doing so hadn't escaped him.

He loved those babies.

But he'd done what he'd come to do, he supposed, and then his relationship with Brooke had taken on a life of its own, and now it was time to go. She wasn't okay, because of him—and that was against the rules. But this was one time where he couldn't fix things. Not the way she needed them fixed.

When they'd gotten back this morning, she'd asked if he'd stay with the twins for a half hour while she did some grocery shopping, and he'd been grateful for the extra time with the boys. But then they'd gotten tired and he'd put them down for their naps, standing there over their cribs and staring at them. He'd gotten all…*verklempt* watching them sleep, their little bow mouths quirking. *This can't be it*, he'd thought, shaking his head. At the situation, at himself.

He'd been beside himself, so he'd given the house a final quick cleaning. He'd cleaned Snowball and Smudge's food and water bowls, changed the cat litter, his least favorite task, and scratched their backs the way they liked. He'd miss the independent fur balls. He'd also done the twins' laundry, and as he'd tossed a bunch of burp cloths in for a white wash, his heart seized. A tiny white square of cloth shouldn't have such an effect on a former soldier, but it did. And he hadn't been thinking about Elena or Aisha. He hadn't been thinking about his mother or the years he'd spent Thanksgiving and Christmas without family.

He'd only thought about Brooke and the twins.

He heard her key in the lock and came downstairs. She opened the door and her gaze landed on it, and he saw her suck in a breath at the sight of him—and his luggage.

She gave him a bit of a smile and walked in, holding up the grocery bag. "I bought three blocks of cheese, and I'll be having a roast-beef sandwich for lunch, with a bottle of my favorite Wyoming beer. A weekend is too long to go without cheese and alcohol."

He appreciated her trying to lighten things. "I hear ya. I wonder if my dad will be giving up his nightly bourbon, since Cathy doesn't drink. Name of love, I guess."

He froze again, and her cheeks flushed. What the

hell was wrong with him? Had he just done it again? He had. He really had.

He shook his head at himself. "I'm really, really bad at this. If it wasn't clear before, it is now."

She looked at him, her expression going from sad to forced neutral. "I guess we're all just who we are, right? Can't try to be something we're not."

He swallowed. He wished he could be. Because this sure as hell didn't feel like him.

"Need help putting anything away?" he asked, gesturing at the grocery bag.

"Nah. Thanks for everything." She turned her back to him and he knew she was crying.

Oh hell.

"The twins are napping," he said. "If you need anything, Brooke, you just call me. Text me. I'll be here in two seconds. Anytime, day or night."

She nodded, her back still turned to him.

"I guess this is goodbye," he said.

She turned around and lifted her chin. "I guess it is."

He took one last look at her, and Snowball and Smudge weaved in between his legs one last time, as though they *knew*. Then he hoisted his duffel and left before he imploded.

Nick didn't want to stay at his father's house without his permission—and wasn't about to text him on his honeymoon—and he wasn't quite ready to even ask Brandon about staying at his condo, so he got a room at the Wedlock Creek Inn. The bed-and-breakfast was just a minute's drive from Brooke's, at the far end of Main Street. If she did need him, he could be there in a flash.

He tossed the duffel onto the bed. The room was nice enough—*too* nice, since he missed the simplicity of the yurt in a really-missing-Brooke-and-the-twins way. He sat down and pulled out his phone, checking the notes he'd made on the ranches for sale. Going to check them out would distract him, give him something to do. A few were a couple of hours away, but he didn't like the idea of being that far away if Brooke needed him. An emergency. Anything. He should stay reasonably local, just in case.

There were two ranches for sale within twenty minutes, one just ten minutes out. He'd go see that one. He called the owner to set something up and got lucky—the guy was free in an hour. That would give him time to lie down and come to grips with what had happened, where he was, where he *wasn't*, and clear his head.

Ping. A text. He grabbed his phone, hoping it was Brooke, hoping she needed something heavy moved or a screen door fixed, but it was Brandon.

It was crazy how his chest squeezed at the sight of Brandon's name on his phone—probably same as it would have if it *had* been Brooke. Until very recently he hadn't had a text from his brother in twelve years. Now suddenly they had a relationship.

Lunch at 1:00 p.m.? Have a crazy update about Heather—the woman of my dreams—if you're interested.

Nick grinned. *Well, I'll be,* he drawled to himself, wishing he had a cowboy hat to take off like John Wayne would have in surprised respect. His brother wanted to talk about his love life—with Nick. Nick texted back.

Meet you at Burger Heaven?

See you then.

And perfect timing. He was meeting a Henry Fieldstone at the ranch for sale, at eleven o'clock, and would be back in town by twelve forty-five at the latest.

He unpacked his few things to remind him that this was home for the time being, and then did some research on the ranch he'd be checking out. Right size, but a lot closer than he'd ever intended to be to Wedlock Creek. Then again, with things so good between him and his family, maybe he should consider staying within thirty minutes.

He left the inn, grabbed an iced coffee from Java Jane's in the hopes that Brooke might be in there with the twins, just so he could see her again, but she wasn't, and then drove the half hour to the Three Dog Ranch.

He liked the name, and the owner even had a big iron sign above the gate, with the silhouette of three dogs. The half-mile drive from the road to the ranch house was lined with huge trees, and the moment the house came into view, the three dogs bounded up to the car, running alongside till he parked it. He gave the three happy-looking mutts a pat, then extended his hand to Henry, a man in his midsixties, wearing a Stetson, jeans and work boots. He had some hay stuck to the side of his jeans, and Nick thought he'd like to have that problem.

"Love that smell of this country air," Nick said.

"Me too. But I promised my wife we'd retire to Southern California, where it's always warm, so I'm looking to sell. I love this place, but it's time to go."

He understood that sentiment all too well. "Well, if I bought the place, I'd keep the name and the sign, since I'm planning on adopting a couple of dogs myself. I'll have to get three, of course."

Henry laughed and began showing him around. The white farmhouse was in nice condition; it had a big gray barn that had a huge weather vane atop it, and almost fifteen hundred acres. He'd had a lot more cattle than he did now, but he'd sold most in preparation for the big move. A creek ran a thousand feet behind the house, and a chicken coop, painted hot pink, was already beside the barn.

"Wife loves pink," Henry said. "The chickens were her pet project. The coop and chickens would stay."

He wondered if Brooke would like ranch life. He tried to imagine her chatting up a hen as they collected eggs together on an ordinary morning. What was he doing? Why was he even thinking about it? He'd never intended to get married. To anyone.

But he could see Brooke sitting on the porch with her notes and planning a wedding, along with the Timber twins running around the yard, playing with the dogs. There was a gorgeous screened-in porch on the back side of the house, facing a well-tended garden, with sliding glass doors to a patio. He could see it as the Dream Weddings office.

He swallowed. He could see it. He could see it all.

Brooke here. Children running around. A family, a life. Love. Commitment. Forever. The present and future in one.

But did he actually want it to happen? Why was he so damned stuck?

And besides, Brooke had a nice house, with her home office, and why would she want to move ten minutes out to the country, away from town and clients and her vendors?

Stop thinking about it.

An hour later he'd toured the property with Henry in his open Jeep, and listened as Henry told him the history of the place and the livestock he'd had, how the ranch had operated full swing. Nick drank it all in intently; he did want this life. Badly. He wanted to live here.

Then it was time to go. He shook Henry Fieldstone's hand again, thanked him for the tour and information, and said he was very interested and would be in touch. He gave the dogs a last pat, took another look around and felt himself relax at the thought of this being his home. He then got in his truck and headed back to town.

He wished he could talk to Brandon about the ranch, get his opinion from a financial perspective, since his brother was a businessman and money guy, but he had no doubt Brandon would be upset that he was really planning on becoming a rancher instead of a paper pusher—literally—at Garroway Paper.

Maybe he'd keep the conversation to the women in their lives instead. Not that talking about Brooke would be any less difficult.

* * *

Brooke should have been working on the Satler wedding, but she couldn't focus, not today. And with her heart barely hanging on, the last thing she wanted to do was to plan someone else's big day.

She pushed the stroller up the path in Wedlock Creek Park, turning onto the grass and heading for the stately oak tree, where the boys' favorite nature show, *The Lenny and Squiggy Race*, was always playing. She spread out a big blanket, parked the stroller and sat down beside it, waiting for the squirrels to make their appearance.

"I don't see Lenny and Squiggy, but I'll bet they're around here somewhere," she said.

"Ba da ga," Mikey said, shaking his stuffed lion in his hand with a big gummy smile.

"Ta ba," Morgan agreed, banging his fists on the little tray in front of his seat.

"Ah, there's one squirrel," she said, but it was too small and skinny to be either Lenny or Squiggy. Still, the furry gray creature darted from one branch to another, coming even closer as it surveyed the scene, then squeaked and started eating an acorn.

"Ba ba da!" Mikey said, mesmerized by the quick moving actions.

She'd never gotten to show Nick the park. Or the squirrels. She wondered what he was doing right now. Where he was staying. Maybe at his father's. Or his brother's. She couldn't quite see either.

What she would give to go home and find him in the kitchen, unloading the dishwasher or making spaghetti with his excellent meat sauce or folding the twins' one-sies. Or just to find him sitting on the sofa, doing absolutely nothing but being a great guy—just one who didn't love her.

She held back the sob that threatened. Be present for the twins, she reminded herself, her gaze on her children. You can't let a broken heart send you into a tailspin. They need you. You need you. The Satler sisters need you.

But she could use a good cry. She'd had one last night. Since Nick had kept the twins in his room at the yurt, she'd let herself cry long and hard over him, her hand stifling her sobs so he wouldn't hear and burst in and insist on holding her. Could you make someone feel better if you were the cause of their heartbreak?

She couldn't blame him anyway. She'd caused her own pain. She knew what she was getting into and she leaped right in anyway. She could hear her grandmother quoting, *Better to have loved and lost than never to have loved at all. No matter how bad it hurts.*

Brooke agreed. But it did hurt.

Nick took a bite of his maple-bacon barbecue burger. Ah, that was good. He could barely believe he was sitting in Burger Heaven with his brother. They used to come here a lot, years ago. Many years ago. The owners had changed a couple of times, but the burgers were still amazing, and the fries perfect.

He'd never forget taking Brandon here in the days after their mother was diagnosed. Brandon had been a wreck, feeling sure they were going to lose her. Nick had been a wreck too, but he'd wanted to be strong for his brother. Maybe he'd been too strong—outwardly. Maybe he'd made Brandon think he wasn't as affected as he was. But they'd come here and sat in the booth second from the door on the left, ordered two cheeseburgers with the works, and then both had just sat, staring at their plates, unable to touch their food, with Brandon sobbing. Nick had gone over to his side of the booth and put his arm around him, and the waitress had left him alone, except to bring a box of tissues, which Nick had appreciated. That waitress was still here too. He'd made a point of sitting in her section, unsure if she'd even remember them, but he wanted to be able to leave her a big tip.

"So, last night, after the wedding," Brandon said, "Heather and I met at the riverbank and sat there, talking for hours. We didn't leave until well after 2:00 a.m. And when I got back to my yodi or whatever that tent cabin is called, I lay in my bed, staring at the circular ceiling for hours, freaked out of my mind."

Nick smiled. "It's called a yurt. And if you and Heather are a couple, you should learn the lingo."

"We *are* a couple."

"Yurt. Yurt, yurt, yurt."

"Ha, ha," Brandon said, narrowing his eyes and taking a bite of his burger. But he grinned. "So, the thing I'm freaked out about is something you could probably help me with."

Nick couldn't be more surprised. "What's that?"

"How'd you learn how to be a manny?" Brandon asked. "You seemed to know what you were doing immediately, even that first or second day at the dinner at Dad's house. How'd you know how to even hold a baby or what to do when?"

That was when Brandon filled him in on Heather's pregnancy. *Wow*, Nick thought. Brandon really was full of surprises.

Nick smiled and thought of Aisha. It was crazy how those memories didn't poke and sting anymore. They simply felt like good memories. Right before he'd left Texas, he'd called the orphanage where Elena worked in Afghanistan and had asked how she was, how the adoption was going, and he'd been assured the two were doing great and that Elena was planning on bringing the baby home to Indiana by the end of summer.

"Turns out all you have to do is hold a baby once," Nick said, "and you kind of figure it out as you go." It was the truth. That was how he'd comforted Aisha in that first crazy hour he'd found her. And then he'd done some quick research on what a baby needed, based on her age, and he'd acted accordingly.

"Maybe I can practice with Brooke's twins," Brandon suggested. "Or twin. I'd like to stick with one."

Nick laughed. "I'm sure she'd loan you one for an hour or so in her house. It's like anything else new. You learn as you go. The key, though, is caring. That's half the battle, really."

Brandon took a sip of his beer. "Caring? What do you mean?"

"Well, when you care, really care, about something or someone, you want to get it right, you know?"

"I hope I get this thing with Heather right," Brandon said, frowning. "I know I can be a bit much. That's what my admin tells me sometimes anyway. It's why I haven't fired her for her insubordination. She calls me out when I need it."

Who knew there were so many sides to Brandon Garroway? Not Nick, that was for sure. He certainly hadn't known his brother appreciated pushback. There'd been a lot of that between them, particularly recently.

"I've been thinking about your refusal to come work for Garroway Paper," Brandon said.

Nick felt his appetite slip away. Good thing he'd eaten most of his burger already. "And?"

"I think what I need to do with the baby I'll be raising is start him or her in the business early. From the get-go. Bring the baby to work, even as an infant, talk about my day in the office and what I'm doing while I'm doing it. Kind of the way people talk to babies anyway. Isn't that how babies learn to speak?"

Nick could hear the tot's first word already: *paper.*

"Dad didn't do that," Brandon continued. "With either of us. But luckily I had it in my blood and veins anyway, so all's good. But for someone like you, who doesn't have that gene where family legacy is important, it needs to be instilled from birth. Every day."

...who doesn't have that gene where family legacy is important...

"I never said Garroway Paper wasn't important to me," Nick snapped, hating that his back was up.

"You didn't have to. The company *isn't* important to you. But I know now how to make sure it is important to my son or daughter."

Deep sigh.

Nick had been hoping that, with Brandon falling in love and putting someone else first, his brother might start to see the world and his piece of it differently. Nope.

"And what if this child you raise doesn't want to work at Garroway Paper, Brandon?"

"I can't see how that would happen if the baby grows up in the office, learning about paper from infancy. We'll spend all the major development periods in all the departments. Trust me, my child will have a love of paper and the family business."

Sure sounded like a lot to heap on a child who wasn't even born yet. "And if even after raising your kid at Garroway Paper, he or she wants to go a different path? Then what? Disowned? Out of the family? Out of the will? You go from love to indifference and disappointment just like that?"

Brandon looked away, chewing the inside of his mouth, and Nick could tell he'd finally gotten through that thick skull, even just a tiny crack. "Well, I'd be disappointed, yeah."

Nick let out a breath. His brother just didn't get it, and now Nick had gotten it through his own thick skull that he just had to let it go. The two of them were never going to see eye to eye on this. And that had to be okay. Because there was no other way for them to be brothers, to have a relationship.

"Can we agree to disagree on the subject?" Nick asked.

Brandon shrugged. "The company needs you. We'll be here when you get this ranching thing out of your system. Because that's how family is supposed to work.

I was mad at you for a long time, Nick. But I shouldn't have tried to kick you out of the family. That was wrong. When you're ready to join Garroway Paper, we'll be here for you."

Nick swallowed. The apology, if that was what it was, meant a lot to Nick. But he was never going to work at the company. Never. And he was tired of saying so. The good news was they'd reached their truce, a place where they could move on.

"Okay, then," Nick said, extending his hand.

Brandon shook it. "I never did get your advice about Heather. Here's my question. Would you propose right now or wait? She thinks we should wait till we know each other better, but I know what I need to know *now*. I want to marry her. I want to legally adopt the baby the moment he or she is born."

"Wow, you really love this woman," Nick said in total wonder.

"When you know, you know. And if I'm nuts and this blows up in my face, at least I tried. At least I went with my gut. Right?"

At least I tried. Nick hadn't tried very hard with Brooke, had he? Because his gut was sending him in the opposite direction. To the Three Dog Ranch. Alone.

"Follow your gut," Nick agreed. "Propose. It'll be up to her to accept or not. Worst'll happen is that you'll propose again in a couple of months."

Brandon beamed. "I already bought a ring. One carat. That'll show her I'm dead serious." He reached into his jacket pocket and pulled out a velvet ring box and opened it. The diamond was huge and twinkled. Wow. Good for Brandon.

"I hope she says yes," Nick said, wishing he had it in him to propose to Brooke.

But right now he couldn't imagine doing so. And he wasn't sure why.

Chapter Thirteen

As a wedding planner, Brooke thought she'd heard it all. She'd gotten her share of out-there requests. The groom who thought it would be "fun" if his four prior girlfriends were invited to the reception, only in order to watch the first dance and see what they had lost out on. The bride who'd met her groom at a fast-food restaurant and wanted to "pipe in the particular aroma of those yummy burgers and fries" during the ceremony. Brooke had talked both out of those. Then there was the mother of the bride who thought Brooke's role included babysitting all children at the wedding. No.

At this point she figured nothing anyone asked, for any reason, wedding or otherwise, could surprise her. Until she got a call yesterday from Brandon Garroway, asking if he could be a "mother's helper" for a couple of hours to learn the ropes of taking care of a baby. "I need to show Heather I'm serious," he'd said. "You can vouch for me that I basically took a class by training with you."

Between being heartbroken and busy with the Satler wedding, and managing without her excellent manny, Brooke had wanted to say that she just didn't have time to "train" a complete newbie in the art of baby care. But he'd been so danged earnest and she had to admit she'd been a bit moved by how hard he was trying.

He *was* trying. Other men with the last name *Garroway* weren't trying at all.

So now Brandon was in her living room, bent over the stroller, watching her every movement and taking notes. He'd brought a small notebook with him and had filled three pages already. When Brandon had first arrived, he'd asked why the babies were "just sitting there" and if that was normal. So she'd spent fifteen minutes on development and stages, and he'd stood there in wide-eyed wonder, scrawling away in his notebook.

"And that's how you unlatch the five-point harness," she said, doing exactly that. "Then you reach in, scoop up the baby, careful to protect the neck if an infant, like so, and voilà, you're holding a baby."

Brandon nodded. "Got it. Can you put Mikey back in and latch him up? I want to start from scratch."

She smiled, mentally shaking her head. "This is Morgan, but yes."

For the next hour, Brandon played house, and Brooke had to say that he really seemed to be enjoying himself. He'd watched how she fed Mikey and then carefully positioned Morgan for his bottle, careful to hold the bottle just so, and when Mikey let out a satisfying burp, Brandon looked like he'd won a spectacular prize. He'd played with both twins in their swings and then ran up to the nursery to choose storybooks to read them. And finally he practiced packing the stroller bag and then placing a baby in the stroller.

"Extra diapers, pack of wipes, burp cloths, change of pj's, sun hat, baby sunscreen—check," he said with an accomplished smile, recalling the necessities for a summer stroll out on Main Street.

"You really want this to work with Heather, huh?" Brooke asked. She was truly touched by his passion. She had no idea if it could be lasting, if once Brandon actually got to know Heather, lovely as she seemed, they'd have any real chemistry or get along or have anything in common, for that matter, but for now he was in the throes of a fantasy and she hoped it did work out. Stranger things had happened.

"Yes, I do. She's special. And the one. I've always heard I'd know it when I found her. And crazy as it is, since we just met a week ago, I *know*. I knew from the minute I laid eyes on her. Like you and Nick. You guys just knew."

There went her eyes again, stinging away. "Nick was my nanny. That's all. We were never a couple."

It had been a full week since they'd returned from Sagebrush Sanctuary and Retreat, and though she hadn't seen him since, Nick had texted every day with the same message. Just checking in.

And she'd text back.

Everything's fine. No need to ask. I'll let you know if the sky falls.

He'd send back a smiley-face emoji, but the next day he sent the same text. Just checking in.

A week without laying eyes on his face, hearing his voice. It was hell.

"Oh, please," Brandon said. "You so are a couple. He's being stubborn, right?"

"How'd you know?" she asked before she could stop herself. She shouldn't be talking about Nick behind his back—and not with Brandon. Nick would *not* like that.

"I know. Same way I know he belongs at Garroway Paper and not some ranch, chasing cows around a pasture. He's being stubborn about that and he's being stubborn about his real feelings for you. He can't face it. He can't face any of it."

Was it wrong that she was very interested in his brother's psychoanalysis? That very subject was all Brooke could think about last night and today. Why this and why that, and if only this and if only that.

"I know he'll come around to working for the company," Brandon said. "And trust me, the way he is with you? The way he looks at you? He's in love and has no idea."

She bit her lip, hoping against hope that Brandon was right. But she didn't want him to be right about Garroway Paper, since she knew that wasn't the case. Nick wanted to be a rancher. Not working in an office, even if it was the family business.

So, was it dopey to hope he was right about the second part—the part where she came in?

Brandon's phone rang and he glanced at it. "It's Cathy," he said with a smile. "They probably just got back from London." He clicked a button. "Hey, Cathy, how was the honeymoon?" He listened, his smile turning into a frown, then a grimace, and then his hands started shaking.

"Brandon, what is it?" Brooke asked, panic rising.

"My dad collapsed at the airport. He was rushed to Brewer General, twenty minutes away."

Oh no. "Did Cathy call Nick?" she asked.

He nodded but looked like he might faint. He was just standing there, trembling, still holding the phone in his hand.

She quickly put Morgan in the stroller, beside Mikey. "I'll drive. Let's go," she said, throwing open the door and rushing to her car. She got the boys in their car seats and hurried to the driver's side, but Brandon was standing by the car door, his complexion ashen. She ran around and opened the door and guided him in. "Hey, let's get over to the hospital," she said, giving his hand a squeeze before shutting the door and running back around to the driver's side.

As she drove, Brandon's cell rang and he answered it.

"We're on our way," he said, his voice cracking. "Did you hear anything? Is he okay?" He listened, biting his lip, and Brooke's heart broke for how nervous and scared he was. "Okay. Okay. See you soon."

"Was that Nick?" she asked. "They're doing tests?"

He nodded. "They don't know what's wrong yet. Cathy is beside herself."

"We'll be there in ten minutes," she assured him, driving as fast as she could without risking anyone's life or getting pulled over. Finally they arrived at the Emergency entrance, and against all odds someone was pulling out of a prime spot just as they were coming in. She grabbed the spot and got the twins into the stroller in record time, and they rushed in.

Nick stood at the sight of them. He looked as stricken as his brother, his face so pale, the blue eyes worried and scared.

Brandon flew into Cathy's arms for a hug. "Have you heard anything?" Brandon asked.

"An ER doctor came out to talk to us just a few minutes ago," Cathy said. "She said Jeb had a minor heart attack."

"What?" Brandon choked out. He stared from Cathy to Nick and back to Cathy.

Cathy took Brandon's hands. "He's going to be fine. It was minor. But it means he needs to take a couple of weeks off and take it very easy and change his diet. I've been after him about that, but trust me, he'll be eating the Cathy way from now on."

"He's going to be okay?" Brandon sank into a chair, staring from Cathy to Nick.

Nick nodded. "The doctor said Dad appears to be out of the woods and indications are that he should make a full recovery." Regardless, he looked so shaken and upset that Brooke wished she could pull him into an embrace, soothe him somehow. But of course she couldn't. "He'll take medication and, as Cathy said, completely relax for a couple of weeks. We can go see him in about ten minutes. A nurse will come get us."

Brandon sucked in a breath and let it out. "Okay. He's going to be fine. We've got a big meeting this week that

Dad was looking forward to, but I'll handle it. And I won't send him any details. No work, no news of work. He should just relax."

Cathy nodded. "We're on the same page, then. No talk of work or the office. Not a peep."

Brandon nodded. "I've got this, Dad," he whispered to no one in particular, then squeezed his eyes shut.

Nick stood up. "I won't leave you in the lurch, Brandon. You or Dad. And you too, Cathy. You're part of this family now. So I'll be joining Garroway Paper."

Brandon's eyes popped open and he gasped. "Really?"

Really? Brooke wanted to second but Nick looked as serious as a… She sighed, thinking he was operating on the same thoughts that had him becoming her manny. Doing what he thought was right. Regardless of what he wanted or needed. But that was Nick Garroway.

Nick nodded, standing ramrod straight, like a soldier. "Tomorrow's Monday. Good day to start."

Brandon stood up and extended his hand, then pulled Nick into a brief hug. "Means a lot, Nick. Thanks."

Nick nodded, and Brooke tried to read his expression. Somewhere between determined and grim.

Cathy patted Nick on the shoulder, and Brooke sent him a smile, but she couldn't keep it on her face.

Was Nick really going to work for Garroway Paper? He was going to show up tomorrow, at 9:00 a.m., in a suit and tie, with a briefcase, and become passionate about paper? Okay, his reasons for joining the family business had nothing to do with paper and everything to do with his dad, who was lying on a hospital cot. And about his brother, who needed him.

Finally a nurse came in and said they could go see the patient, two at a time. Nick sent Brandon and Cathy, and he and Brooke sat back down, Brooke giving the stroller a gentle push as Mikey started to fuss a bit.

"You're joining Garroway Paper temporarily until your dad is back on his feet?" she asked.

"I'm not looking at it that way," he said, his blue eyes full of emotions she couldn't pinpoint. Regret and re-solve, maybe. Worry. Sadness. "I'm needed there. My dad needs me. My brother needs me. That's all that mat-ters. We could have lost my father. Just like that—gone. Like my mother. I want to do what's right."

Oh, Nick, she thought. But she couldn't say anything, so she just reached out for his hand and held it.

On Monday Nick put on the tan suit and showed up for work at Garroway Paper an hour early, at 8:00 a.m. He'd barely slept last night, his mind a jumble—the com-pany, his dad's health, the fear in his brother's eyes, even though Jeb was okay. And Brooke. Seeing her last night at the hospital with the twins had seemed so nat-ural, as though of course she'd been there, because she was family.

He hadn't blinked an eye at her being there. Until he'd realized why. And then his skin had gotten all itchy. The word *family* was loaded for him—maybe that was why. He'd tossed and turned, trying to figure it all out, and then he'd given up and read over some Garroway Paper information he'd asked Brandon to email him. The reports might as well have been in French or Swa-hili for all he could make sense of them. And they were boring as hell too.

He was sure he'd find his niche in the company. He'd try a few departments and see where he might be able to do some good. There had to be one. He wasn't a business guy. Or a finance guy. Or a salesman. He was all right at strategy though, making a plan and leading troops through dangerous territory. There might be some kind of equivalence at Garroway Paper, sort of.

There was one car in the parking lot when he arrived. Brandon's. He parked beside him and headed in, sucking in a deep breath as he pulled open the glass door.

Here goes nothing. And everything.

He found Brandon in his corner office, his head burrowed over a stack of memos.

"Nick Garroway, reporting for duty," he said.

Brandon looked up, looking weary. "I've been here since six o'clock. Couldn't sleep."

"Me either."

"I called Cathy a little while ago," Brandon said. "Dad was demanding a cappuccino with three sugars, a cheese Danish and today's *Wall Street Journal*. She had the nurse bring him a clementine, a hard-boiled egg, a slice of whole-grain toast and bottled water, and gave him a gratitude journal to record his thoughts."

Nick smiled. "Thank heavens for Cathy."

"Right?" Brandon said with a nod.

"Well, I'm ready to start my day, my new role, at Garroway Paper," Nick said. "I'll buy a briefcase at lunch. No idea what you business types put in those, but I'm sure I'll find out fast."

Brandon stared at Nick for a moment, then stood and reached into his desk drawer. He pulled out a magnetic door placard and held it up. It read Nicholas Garroway.

"I can't remember the last time anyone called me Nicholas," Nick said, the sight of that thing making his stomach clench. He'd have to get over it. He was here now. He worked here. This was his future.

"Mom called you Nicholas," Brandon said.

Nick almost gasped. He hadn't expected Brandon to say that, let alone remember.

"She loved that name and liked using it," Brandon said. "You want to know what she said the night before she died?"

Nick felt his legs get wobbly and he sat down. So did Brandon.

He wasn't sure he did want to know.

Brandon was looking at the floor, then out the window. Finally he turned to face Nick. "She said, 'Nicholas always follows his heart. That's the way to happiness. The only way.'"

Now Nick did gasp. "She said that?"

Brandon's eyes filled with tears, and he nodded. "It was one of the last things she said. Other than 'I love you and your brother more than anything in the world. And your father, of course. The love of my life.' That was the last thing she said to me."

Tears stung Nick's eyes too. He hadn't been at the house that night; the tension between him and his brother and father was so high, and of course Nick hadn't expected to lose his mother that night. No one had. "But you said—"

"I was a stupid fourteen-year-old who hated you for being about to deploy. Stuff flew out of my mouth, anything I could think of to make you feel like the hell I felt."

Nick sucked in a breath. "I did already."

"I'm sorry," Brandon said, wiping at his eyes. "I'm so sorry. For being a terrible brother. And a terrible person. But when I thought I might lose dad, all I could think was, I have Nick back, I have Nick back, I have Nick back. And all those old feelings came back too, you know? I mean from before, when we were close."

Nick could barely find his voice. "We're close now."

Brandon took a breath. "I want to be the person Heather deserves. That her baby deserves. So this?" he said, holding up the placard. He stood and opened the window, then chucked the name sign right out of it. Right below the window was a gated area with bushes blocking the heating systems, so Nick had no doubt Nicholas Garroway was lying in those bushes somewhere.

His brother had just thrown his name sign out the window.

Nick stared at him. *"What?"*

"You *don't* belong here, Nick. I finally get it. You've been saying that your whole life, but I didn't want to hear it. I didn't care. I only saw you through my eyes, not as you were. Are. You were meant to be a soldier. Now you're meant to be a rancher. And you're meant to be with Brooke and the twins. You have to follow your heart, like Mom said you did. Do it now."

You're meant to be with Brooke and the twins. He'd put his feelings for the Timber family in a square box called Responsible For. They'd been on his checklist and he understood checklists. Why had he been able to walk away from Garroway Paper when it came to "responsibility" but not Brooke and her twins? He'd immediately become her nanny. He'd felt solely responsible for her and the twins' well-being. So why hadn't that sense of commitment extended to the family business? And if it was a sense of commitment, why couldn't he actually *commit* to Brooke? None of this made any sense.

He'd never been able to answer these questions, and they'd kept him up at night all week.

"One thing at a time," Nick said. "I'm on overload as it is."

"Go buy your ranch," his brother said. "I'll even help you name those chickens you want. And propose to Brooke already. Wedlock Creek Jewelers has really nice diamond rings."

He swallowed, keeping his gaze out the window instead of on his brother, who was eyeing him with the look of a guy who thought he knew the deal.

Nick *did* belong with Brooke and the Timber twins. That was never in doubt. From a taking-care-of-them standpoint. But could he be with her the way she wanted and needed? A husband, a father?

How could Brandon have this all figured out when Nick was so far behind?

Something occurred to him just then. Wouldn't marrying Brooke be the *ultimate* in taking responsibility for her and the babies? When he looked at it that way, he felt instantly more comfortable.

"Where's the jewelry shop?" Nick asked.

Brandon grinned. "Two doors down from Java Jane's. Next to the florist. Might as well pick up a bouquet too."

"Wait, did you propose to Heather?" Nick asked.

Brandon grinned. "Sure did. She said no. For now.

She told me to ask her again in a month. And a month after that."

"That sounds like a plan," Nick said. He had a feeling that, despite how short a time Heather had known his brother, she knew exactly how to deal with him. He wouldn't be surprised if Heather turned him down a month from now, but said yes when they were together three months. She'd probably insist on waiting a year to actually marry.

Marry. He mentally shook his head, but the word didn't dislodge as it usually did when he tried to relate it to himself. It stayed there, hanging out in his brain. Marry. Marriage. Husband and wife.

He could take care of Brooke and the twins. And have them with him all of the time. That was what he wanted. But something was missing, something he couldn't put his finger on.

Maybe he should stop thinking so much and just *do*, act.

And now that he didn't have to work this morning, that was his new plan.

Chapter Fourteen

On Monday night, at around six o'clock, Brooke couldn't take the suspense. She had to know how Nick's first day at Garroway Paper had gone.

She sat at the kitchen table, sipped her iced tea and pulled out her phone, dying to call him, but she opted for a text. She was about to hit Send when the doorbell rang.

Nick.

"I was sending you a text," she said.

His expression immediately changed. "Everything okay?" he asked, peering past her. "House is quiet. Twins are all right?"

"There's a whole area of existence beyond whether I'm okay or not," she said, feeling a frown edge her lips.

"I care about you, Brooke. You know that."

"I do know that," she said, holding back the sigh and opening the door wider for him to step in.

"So, what you were texting me about?" he asked as he followed her into the living room. He stopped to pet Snowball and Smudge, who were sitting on the back of the sofa.

"I was dying to hear how your first day at Garroway Paper went."

"My brother had a name placard made for me. He must have had it for years. And this morning, not ten minutes into my arrival, he opened his office window and tossed it out. Literally threw the thing out the window."

Brooke's mouth dropped open. "Really?"

Nick laughed. "Brandon is one complicated guy. Deeper than I realized. He's been doing some heavy thinking, and between Dad's health and falling madly in love, and all that's happened since I've been back in town, he's started to see things differently."

"Wow. I'm really glad to hear it."

"And I have too, Brooke."

She tilted her head. "What do you mean? You're not going to stay on with the company, are you?"

He shook his head. "No. But what I am going to do depends on your answer to a question."

Curiosity bloomed inside her. "What question?"

He got down on one knee, and she gasped. He pulled a velvet box out of his pocket and opened the top, revealing a beautiful diamond ring that twinkled at her. God, it was gorgeous. Square and surrounded by tiny diamonds on a gold band. "Will you marry me, Brooke?

Spending my life taking care of you and those babies I love as if they're my own will make me very happy."

Oh. Her heart sunk, and her stomach flopped—in a bad way. "I thought you said you also started to see things differently."

He stood up, staring at her, confusion in his eyes. "I have. That's why I'm here. Proposing. But you don't exactly look happy."

"Nick, it's a beautiful ring. And believe me, as a woman who's madly in love with you, I want to scream yes at the top of my lungs. But unless you can say you want to marry me because you're in love with me, and that's why you want to be my husband, my answer is no. I told you I'm not looking to be rescued. I'm looking to be *loved*."

"But—" He stopped speaking, as though realizing he had no argument.

Because either he loved her or he didn't.

"Brooke, I—"

"Do you love me, Nick?" she asked.

He stared at her. Unwavering. "I care so much about you and the twins. I want to be with you three. I want us to be a family."

"Me too," she said. "But you didn't answer my question. And we both know why not. So I think you should go."

Her eyes stung. She wanted him gone so she could run upstairs and fling herself on her bed and just cry it out.

She turned away, sending up a prayer that he'd say, "Of course I love you. I love you so much." But instead she heard the door close gently behind him as he left.

And then she did run upstairs and cry.

* * *

"Can't you sneak me in a chocolate milkshake? Something besides this god-awful green tea," Jeb asked Nick, grimacing at the steaming mug Cathy had brought in a few minutes ago. He'd been released from the hospital yesterday and was convalescing on his favorite recliner in his living room, with Fritz in his dog bed near Jeb's feet.

Nick laughed. "Sorry, I want you heart-healthy too."

Jeb patted Nick's hand. "I'm glad to hear that. I wasn't always fair to you—or there for you—but you stuck by me. What you said at the wedding, what you wrote in our wedding card, I'll tell you, you brought tears to my eyes."

"I love you, Dad. It's that simple."

I love you. It's that simple.

He sat up straight, the words echoing in his head, on his tongue.

I love you.

It was as though a Mack Truck had swerved into the living room and had run right over Nick, shaking loose something in his very thick skull.

He loved Brooke. It really was that simple.

His father was staring at him. "So, who's getting married first. You and Brooke, or Brandon and Heather?"

Nick laughed. "Anyone's guess."

"Ah, so it is true. I told Cathy I didn't think there was anything going on between you and the wedding planner, but Cathy told me she knew love when she saw it, and she said she saw it plain as day on your face. Isn't that something? A newcomer to the family knows you better than I do. I hope we can change that."

Nick gave his dad's hand a gentle squeeze. "We will, Dad."

"I have some big news," Jeb said. "I've told your brother on the phone, right before you arrived, since it affects him directly." Nick's curiosity was piqued. "Cathy and I have decided to get out of dodge. We're buying the Sagebrush Sanctuary and Retreat from her friend and moving there. We'll be doing a little restructuring, as suits us, as we learn the business better. I'll be Chief Financial Officer, and Cathy will run the yoga and meditation program. Heather promises to find a replacement for herself and train him or her before she moves to Wedlock Creek."

Wow. "That all sounds great," Nick said, blown away. And not. It made perfect sense, actually. "How'd Brandon take it?"

"You know, I was surprised at how well he did take the news. He said he's come to some big realizations lately. And he knows he was born to take over Garroway Paper and run it now that I'm moving on. He also said that if the baby he and Heather are expecting grows up to be bored by paper, that'll be fine too. 'Everyone has to follow their heart,' he said."

Nick felt his own heart grow two sizes bigger. "Wonders never cease, do they?" he asked with a smile.

"No, and what a good thing that is," Jeb said. "Life is one big surprise. Sometimes in a good way, sometimes in a bad way, and sometimes in a bad way that delivers you where you need to be after all."

Nick nodded. That sure was right.

Jeb took a sip of his tea. "I'm slowly—key word being *slowly*—getting used to this stuff." He set down the mug and resettled under the blanket, on the recliner, with his eyes starting to drift closed, and Nick was almost glad to be able to sneak away a bit earlier than he'd intended.

He had a proposal to get right.

"Ga ba!" Mikey said, flinging his chew toy at Brooke for the thousandth time in his young life. His gummy grin was too irresistible, so Brooke gave him a raspberry on his onesie-clad tummy.

"Ba ba da?" Mikey said, tilting his head.

Brooke stared at the adorable baby, marveling that it sounded as though he were asking something. Huh.

I know what you're asking. You want to know where Nick is. You miss him. Like I do.

I could have been wearing that ring. I could be planning my own wedding. My dream wedding. Not that it would be her dream wedding if it wasn't her dream situation. *Still, I could have settled for what I could have instead of what I really want.*

Her grandmother would turn over. *Don't settle when it's less than you deserve, or then "just okay" will become the new normal,* Aggie Timber had said more than once. *And "just okay" is not all that okay.*

The doorbell rang, and Brooke had a feeling it was nosy Amy from across the street, who'd darted over a couple of hours ago, while walking her dog, to mention that she hadn't seen "that handsome manny" in a while and ask if he still worked for Brooke.

Brooke had said something about hearing one of

the twins and had dashed inside. God, what she would give to move away from these nosy gossips. She could move to the country and build a farmhouse-wedding chic office, maybe a yurt like at the Sagebrush Sanctuary and Retreat.

She smiled at the thought. Maybe she should think about buying a bigger house out of town, where you got much more for your money, a place where her twins could have some real land to play on and she could adopt the dog she'd always wanted, not that Smudge and Snowball might approve. She'd stay within fifteen minutes of town and her farmhouse-chic she-shed office would appeal to a range of clients. The Satlers would love it. She had no doubt.

This is what it's about, boys, she thought, her gaze on her sons. No time for a broken heart. No time for crushed hopes and dreams. Onward and upward, forward thoughts. The future.

But then she pictured Nick in his white linen shirt, with his blue eyes all intense on her, and she missed him so much, her legs wobbled. She sank down on a chair, feeling her heart aching.

Who was she kidding? Her heart was killing her. It would be a long while before she'd get over Nick Garroway.

The doorbell rang again. Oh blast. *That woman does not give up.* She wiped away her tears and stalked to the door, prepared to tell Amy that yes, her nanny had moved on, and to give her a piece of her mind about minding her own beeswax.

But it was Nick. Standing there in her doorway, looking so gorgeous, she could barely breathe.

"You asked me a question yesterday and I didn't answer," Nick said. "You know why?"

Oh God. She really didn't think she could handle this a second time. The first was bad enough. "I know why."

He shook his head. "Nope. You thought you did. But the reason was that, sort of like my dad, I had some kind of blockage right here," he said, putting his hand over his heart. "You cleared it up so fast, I couldn't handle it. Know why?"

She bit her lip, not quite sure where he was going with this. "Why?"

"Because I *do* love you. So much, Brooke. I want to marry you because I'm deeply, hopelessly, completely in love with you. And those little imps listening behind you in their swings have known it the whole time. From day one."

She laughed. "I agree. They always knew."

"Yeah, they did. All that 'ba ga, da ba' stuff. Code for 'he loves her. He's going to be our daddy one day.'"

She flung her arms around him and he picked her up off the ground and held her. "I love you too. So much." She kissed him, never wanting this moment to end.

"If we get married at the Wedlock Creek Chapel, will we have another set of twins?" he asked, setting her down, but keeping his arms around her.

"Maybe triplets," she said with a grin. "Or quadruplets. Want to risk it?"

His eyes widened. "You made me believe in magic, so honestly? No. I'm good with two right now. Maybe a couple years from now, we'll renew our vows there and really see what happens."

Brooke's heart had runneth over to the point that

she could barely form words. She took a deep breath
to get some air in her lungs. "I like it. You know what
wedding I'd like to plan for myself? An elopement. To
somewhere crazy-fun, like Las Vegas."

"So, no planning," he said.

"Right. Just you and me and a quickie-wedding chapel."

"And the wedding night. Can't forget that."

"You know what else I was thinking? About moving to the country. Having a farmhouse-chic she-shed
of an office that will make my clients drool when they
drive out for meetings. Kind of fits with your whole
plan to buy a ranch."

"I was going to give up the ranch idea to move in
here, but I've found the perfect place, and it's still available. It's called the Three Dog Ranch, so we'll have to
adopt three dogs to live there. House rules. Think these
two can deal?" he asked, nodding at the cats.

Smudge and Snowball wrapped around his legs, rubbing their faces against his calves.

"They've always wanted to be indoor cats *and* barn
cats," she said. She bit her lip. "You know what? I feel
like my grandmother is looking down at me and smiling."

"I feel that way about my mom now too," he said,
wrapping her in another hug. "Turns out her motto was
Follow Your Heart. It's a good one."

"I agree. Always follow your heart."

"Ga ba!" Morgan shouted.

"Ba ga da!" Mikey added.

Nick pulled her close and kissed her. "Think those
Timber twins would like to become the Garroway twins?"

Tears poked at her eyes. "I think they'd love that."

"I promise to be a father worthy of them," he said.

She touched his cheek, loving him so much, she was surprised she didn't burst into a million pieces. "That's a good new promise."

He held her close and leaned his head on top of hers. "I can't wait to start forever with you and our boys."

"Me too," she whispered. With their boys and her manny-for-life.

* * * * *